ALL THE SKILLS

ALL
THE
SKILLS

— BOOK 1 —

HONOUR RAE

Podium

To my mom, who reads all my books.
And to Murphy and Lyra, who bring mischief and joy to my life.

Cover design by Miblart

ISBN: 978-1-0394-7021-7

Published in 2024 by Podium Publishing
www.podiumaudio.com

Podium

ALL THE SKILLS

PART 1
MASTER OF SKILLS

CHAPTER 1

Arthur sprinted across the scourge-deadened fields. The soil was gray and life-less, and the black remains of weeds disintegrated under his boots.

Though he ran flat out, he breathed as little as possible, inhaling with quick gasps of air only when his burning lungs couldn't take it anymore.

It wasn't a good idea to breathe in scourge-dust. That's how rot got into the lungs.

A shallow ditch bordered the field at the other end, the water fetid with green scum on top. But even scum was still alive, which made it the opposite of the scourge.

Timing his running steps just right, Arthur jumped the ditch. When he landed on the other side, it was on scraggy yellowed grass.

This next patch of land had been reclaimed from the scourge last season. It wasn't alive enough yet to grow crops, but any dust kicked up here wasn't actively toxic.

Putting his hands on his thighs, Arthur bent and breathed in deep whoops of air. Like most kids in his borderland village, he was small and skinny from too little nutritious food and too much time spent laid up in bed, fighting off one scourge infection or another.

Now, straightening, he looked across the reclaimed field to the empty dirt road beyond. He grinned. His shortcut had worked. He wasn't too late.

Arthur stepped forward quickly, clutching a stitch at his side and limping just a little. The farther away from the scourge-land he got, the thicker the vegetation underfoot. At the very edge, where the field met the road, stood a cluster of scraggly hedges.

He ducked in among them, laid low, and peered out.

He didn't have to wait long.

He felt the clop-clop-clop of shod hooves on the soil before he saw the carriage arrive. It was pulled by four gleaming pure white horses. Or, they had probably been pure white before the trip.

Now their legs up to their underbellies were coated in sickly gray. Arthur's village did their duty to reclaim the scourge-tainted land, but they couldn't do anything for the dust blown in from the dead kingdoms. Hopefully, the drivers and footmen had enough sense to wash down the beasts of scourge-dust every night. Any dust that got into a wound, even a tiny cut, would cause it to fester.

His attention went from the horses to the magnificent carriage they pulled. Nearly as wide as the road itself, it gleamed with fresh red paint. Golden filigree and ornamentation stood out from every edge, making it one of the finest things Arthur remembered seeing. Certainly the most colorful that had ever passed through his borderland village.

Best of all, it was guarded by five men in the baron's colors of brown and rust red.

Not that Arthur had any warm and fuzzy feelings for the sight of the baron's men. These weren't the normal thugs and bully boys the baron employed to enforce his orders. They were carded men. Taller and broader than any man in the village, without a trace of pockmark or scar. They reaped the benefits of a spell card in their heart.

Come on, Arthur thought. *No one is watching you. Loosen up. Do some magic. Any magic!*

Just a little spell . . . please.

The men remained consummate professionals. Silent and foreboding, they even marched in lockstep. Their eyes scanned ahead of the dusty, empty road with occasional sweeps out to the dark and dead horizon to the west. None so much as glanced at the underbrush.

Arthur's shoulders slumped as the last man passed by.

The chance to see real magic in action had been a long shot, but the disappointment still tasted bitter. All his life, he'd heard of the deeds of carded men. Some could shoot fireballs from their fingertips, turn a regular sword into a magical masterpiece, or have the strength to pick up a horse one-handed: all depending on the power and strength of their spell cards. He craved those stories like a man dying of thirst craved water. It was enough to put aside his distaste for the fact that the baron's men were spies.

Looking on forlornly, he was determined to watch until they were out of sight. He knew he'd have to run back to the village and still be lucky not to be missed. There was a new dragon soil shipment, and all hands were needed—

The air exploded above him.

A hurricane of wind kicked up out of nowhere. Branches and twigs from the brush rained down on Arthur, blending with the guards' sudden shouts. Half shielding his eyes, Arthur glanced up to see the red underbelly of a dragon not fifty feet overhead.

He froze.

The beast was smaller than the stories said they were—a mere three times the size of the monstrous carriage instead of a mountain.

From where Arthur lay, it was plenty big. Each leathery snap of its wings drove more wind downward, throwing dust and debris into the eyes of everyone on the ground.

Despite that, Arthur's mouth hung open. A dragon rider? Here, at the border? He couldn't imagine for what reason . . .

One thing was for sure: this was even better than seeing a magic spell!

Only . . . there was no saddle around the base of the beast's neck. It seemed to be riderless. Did dragons leave their hives alone?

When the dragon looked down at the chaos it had caused, its yellow slit-pupil eyes were angry.

The men guarding the carriage seemed to be as confused as Arthur. Several in the front tried to get the panicking horses under control. The two in the back swung around to face the beast. One held a massive sword Arthur was certain had not been there a moment before.

"What is the meaning of this?" the sword wielder demanded. "Explain yourself."

The dragon's voice came out in a growl, chewed up in daggerlike teeth. "You protect Baron Kane's assets?"

Dragons could talk?! The stories never said that.

The sword man scowled. He didn't look surprised that the dragon was able to speak. "That is no business of yours, worm! Return to your hive. That is an order!"

"Ah, but I come to fulfill a promise to your arrogant lordling."

The man's feet spread. The sword he held in both hands flashed bright blue at the edges. "You dare—"

"I do, and gladly."

And with that, the dragon spit a gobbet of fire directly on the carriage. It landed at the yoke that connected the horses to the carriage. Wood splintered. The beasts screamed and bolted down the road, leaving the carriage behind.

The men reacted at once. One of the drivers slammed a flat hand on the side of the carriage. Wood erupted into sharp, thorny spikes all around it like an angry hedgehog. His partner gestured upward, and the spikes detached and threw themselves up toward the dragon.

Meanwhile, the two men to each side raised their palms. Green acid arced toward the dragon.

The second turned cupped hands flowing with water over the still-burning yoke.

There was a snap and a chemical smell as lightning erupted from the great sword, forking toward the dragon.

The lightning was the only spell to hit. It struck the dragon's side, leaving a scorch mark the size of Arthur's head. A massive wound to Arthur . . . but not much to the dragon.

The red dragon roared a laugh and breathed out a series of small purple flames as tiny and delicate looking as the tops of candles. Wherever these landed, they *undid* what they touched. The tiny flames ate into the oncoming acid stream and turned it orange before it exploded into vapor. The rest of the thorns burned to ashes well before they reached the dragon.

This only consumed a small portion of the cloud of candle-like flames. The rest continued to fall, as ethereal as snow, but what they landed on was *changed*.

The wood of the carriage disintegrated in patches, as did whatever clothing the flames happened to fall on . . . and the same with flesh.

Arthur was lucky the carriage had already passed him by. The cloud of tiny flames fell with precision, blanketing the carriage, and the men started to scream as their own magic spells failed them. It seemed none of them had shield cards.

Arthur covered his ears but didn't dare shut his eyes in case he needed to bolt. The dragon was terrifying, but Baron Kane's men were the enemy. He wasn't exactly rooting for them.

The moment the men were suitably distracted with their clothes catching on fire, the dragon dropped to the ground.

It landed with a too-light thud for an animal its size. The claws came down, and in the next few moments, the dragon showed that teeth and claws were every bit as effective as magical fire.

The swordsman got in one more lightning strike. This left a sizable hole in one wing and earned him a crushing overhead strike with a tail.

Finally, all the men were dead, and the dragon turned to the carriage.

The odd flames were still merrily disintegrating whatever they touched. Half closing its eyes, the dragon breathed in, and all the flames were extinguished.

The action must have caused it to catch Arthur's scent. The dragon's great head snapped to the side to stare down its nose right at the stand of bushes where Arthur was hiding.

Every muscle in Arthur's body locked. At that moment, he knew exactly what a mouse must feel under the gaze of a cat.

The dragon's lips lifted over its teeth in an oddly humanlike sneer. "What's this? A coward hiding? You think you'll live long enough to bleat news back to your master?"

"I . . . I . . ." Arthur licked dry lips. Half of him was still frozen in terror. The other half was gibbering in fear. The only thing he could think was that he didn't want to die burning alive, should the dragon set the shrubs alight.

Arthur had seen enough death in his twelve years to know there were very bad ways to go. Better to be snapped in half with those teeth. At least it would be quick.

Somehow he coordinated his limbs enough to crawl out from under the shrubs.

His legs shook too much to stand, so he sat up on his knees. "I . . . I'm not . . ."

What he wanted to say was, "I'm not one of Baron Kane's men, and I sure as scourge-shit won't be once I grow up!"

But all he could do was stutter and try not to piss himself.

The dragon let out a sulfur-scented snort. "Oh? A cub? Did I just kill your father?"

Pride reconnected his tongue back to his brain. "My father ain't a baron's man! He hates him. I do too!"

"A borderland serf with a spine? Interesting."

The dragon seemed amused. It turned, discounting Arthur as a threat . . . which was fair, because he wasn't one.

The once-beautiful carriage was a wreck of its former self. Great holes and gaps showed through the wood. The paint and filigree Arthur had admired so much was cracked and ruined, as if it had been left out in the sun for years without cover.

Arthur tried not to look at the dead bodies. Death was a fact of life in his village, but there was a difference between seeing someone decline due to an illness and seeing them viciously murdered.

"I won't tell anyone what I saw," he said and backed up a step, glancing over his shoulder down the road. It was empty. It wasn't like trade ever came to his town. There was no one to come help, but maybe if he ran . . .

The dragon didn't bother glancing back toward him. "If you try to escape, you die."

Arthur swallowed and put his foot back down.

The dragon stood on its hind legs and sank clawed hands into either end of the carriage. Muscles rippled under red scales. With a crack of wood and a twist, the carriage split down the middle.

The inside must have once been luxurious. The fabric padding inside was dyed in bright pastel colors Arthur had only seen in rainbows. The feathers that exploded from ripped seams must have been actual goose down.

It was also entirely empty.

Arthur hadn't considered it before, but surely there should have been screaming or something from inside once the dragon attacked. Why had a team of men been sent to accompany an empty carriage?

His silent question was answered a moment later. The dragon reached into the middle of the wreckage and plucked out a single wooden box.

Like the rest of the carriage, the box was decorated in intricate designs. The wood was beautiful and thin—proven when the dragon crushed it between its fingers like a nut.

Something slipped out of the shards and fell to the ground.

The dragon nodded down. "Pick that up, cub."

Obeying that order meant getting right up underneath the dragon. Arthur understandably hesitated but knew if he didn't, the dragon would surely kill him anyway.

With jerky steps, he walked forward. The dragon watched him with unblinking eyes.

He saw that the wooden box contained . . . another box. This one was slim and metallic. Likely too small for the dragon to grasp within its claws.

He glanced up at the dragon for permission and then picked up the metallic box.

The box was heavier than it looked, bracketed on two sides by a clasped lock.

"Open it," the dragon said.

Swallowing, Arthur did.

The clasp was simple, but his fingers shook so badly he fumbled it twice before he finally got the lid open.

When he saw what rested inside, he nearly dropped the box.

It was a spell card.

CHAPTER 2

The spell card was encased yet again within a thin sheet of glass with a lock surrounded by complex runes.

It was . . . beautiful.

Larger than a man's spread hand, the card was thick, as if he were looking at a piece of metal and not paper. Jade green, it was edged in glowing purple jewels with golden threads running along the length. If the card weren't magic, he would have thought it had been painted on by a hair-fine brush.

What truly caught his eye were the stamped pictures within the card—pictures that shifted and moved before his eyes. An anvil and hammer, an ax, a sewing needle and thread, a fishing line and hook, a simple figure of a man in mid-stride, a book . . . and more. One replaced the other in a pattern he couldn't quite determine.

There were words etched on the top of the card and a glittering paragraph below the shifting pictures. Arthur's father never had time to teach him more than a few words of reading, but he thought he recognized the word "skill" as well as a few numbers.

The dragon spoke, making Arthur start in surprise.

"You said your father hates the nobles?"

Tearing his eyes from the card, Arthur croaked out, "He does."

Everyone in the village had reason to hate the nobles. The baron, especially.

The dragon cocked its head. Though its scaly lips didn't move, Arthur could have sworn that it smiled at him. "A card of this magnitude in a serf's hands? That could be . . . fun."

Arthur said nothing, though his fingers tightened on the glass casing. He never would have imagined he'd see a card, much less hold one. Even if it was the last thing he did . . . Well, it wouldn't be worth it, but what a way to go.

The dragon rumbled, sounding too much like a growl for Arthur's peace of mind.

"Give this card to him," it said. "Or whoever is the headman of your village. Whoever can cause the baron the most mischief." It leaned down until its chin was nearly level to the ground, eye to eye with Arthur. "But if this card finds its way back into Baron Kane's hands, I will know. And cub . . . I have your scent. I *will* find you and any blood kin."

"I . . . I . . ." Arthur babbled.

The dragon didn't seem to care to hear his answer. It raised its head. "But first, I have a few more chores to attend to."

Appearing in a grand mood, it turned its attention to the men it had killed.

Arthur followed its gaze. There was now a misty glow above every man's chest—or the remains of a chest in some cases. It was as if there was an inner light trying to peek out.

The dragon waved a clawed hand over each corpse. A new spell card rose from their bodies.

The new cards were as big as the one in the glass case. Four were cream-colored, like a fancy piece of paper. The one from the swordsman was a metallic steel blue. All lacked the intricate designs on the borders. The icons were flat and painted on. They didn't move.

With a wave, the dragon brought the cards, one by one, to float in front of its face so it could view them.

"Basic cards," it muttered but gathered them into his palm. Then it brought its palm to its chest. When it lowered the clawed hand again, the cards were gone.

The dragon had just added the cards of the men it had killed to its heart deck.

That done, the dragon turned its attention back to the corpse of the swordsman. After pawing at it for a moment, the dragon returned to Arthur with a thin chain hanging off the tip of his claw. At the end of the chain hung a delicate key.

"A runic key to unlock the card. Take it," he said cheerfully. "Remember: If you speak of me or let the card fall into the baron's hands, I will find you and roast your family. Now go."

It was a good thing Arthur knew every footpath, every animal trail on the way home. After touching the runic key to the lock, the glass and key melted down into harmless water, which dribbled through his fingers, leaving only the card behind. It was as heavy as a piece of sheeted metal, impossible to bend.

Arthur didn't wait, couldn't afford to be surprised. He sprinted from the dragon, half blind with shock and amazement.

A dragon. The creature he'd always been taught that preserved human lives, whose very fertilizer brought entire fields back from scourge-death. Something he never even considered could talk. Now he had just seen one raze a carriage, kill five men, and steal their cards.

He cast a fearful glance over his shoulder. The dragon was nowhere in sight. Only a thin tracing of smoke marked where the remains of the carriage lay.

With the entire village occupied with the current shipment of dragon soil, it might be hours or days until the scene was discovered.

He had to ensure no one connected him with the carriage. More than that, he had to protect the card he'd been gifted. It was literally worth more than his life.

He had to get this to his father.

His heart racing, Arthur used every trick of bush-craft he could think of to ensure he didn't leave tracks behind. Luck was with him, because the gray dirt of the scourge-field was too hard-packed to leave an easy mark on the ground.

Soon he'd recrossed the bad patch and was on live land again. Scraggly yellow-green grass helped hide his tracks further.

Arthur made a looping path to the small cottage he and his father shared.

The moment he set his eyes on the cottage, he knew his father wasn't in. No smoke came from the chimney, meaning no one had fed the fire in hours. That made sense. His father would likely be in the village square directing the workers and helping out himself.

Before he went to the door, Arthur stopped, as he always did, at his mother's and sister's graves.

Both had been killed three winters before last when a scourge-mutated cough raged through the village.

Before Arthur had gotten the bright idea to follow the baron's carriage, he'd managed to steal a few handfuls of dragon soil from the incoming delivery carts and stick them in his pocket. He withdrew the soil now, rich and dark and full of life.

Once dragon soil was shoveled out of a hive, it would be left to bake in the sun for a year and a day, mixed with regular dirt and organic leavings from trash pits. The result was a crumbly, rich soil that was so potent a few cartfuls could revive an entire scourge-ridden field.

Arthur carefully sprinkled the soil around the two gravestones. In a few days, they would be surrounded by a riot of flowers.

Then he knelt in between the graves. It was a good place to think.

His father would be busy for the rest of the day. Possibly the night, too. Arthur couldn't risk giving him the card in sight of other adults and gossipy kids.

He had to hide the card.

But where? Surely not in the house. The baron's men sometimes searched all the villagers' homes for valuables. A few of the men always followed the dragon carts.

In the woods? His father had shown him some trees that had hollow places inside. They hid knives there "just in case," though Arthur didn't know exactly when "just in case" was meant to be. The only danger came from the baron's men, and no villager dared stand up to them. They were too poor to attract outlaws.

Arthur's best friend, Ernie, told him the baron had carded men with abilities to sniff out treasure. No, he couldn't hide the card in the woods.

Arthur held the card between his hands. His fingers were grubby and left prints on its fine face. Hastily, he tried to rub them away with a corner of his shirt, but his shirt wasn't much better.

"Where can I keep this safe?" he asked the graves in front of him.

He swore he felt a breeze touch his cheek. He glanced up, but the bare winter branches overhead weren't moving.

Then the answer came. In reality, he'd always known, but he'd wanted to explore other options first.

Once a card was placed inside someone's heart, it could only be removed by the caster or by death. Some great heroes had entire decks of cards encased in their hearts. One new power for every occasion. The red dragon now had the powers of acid, water, and the lightning sword from the dead men. Those seemed like small magics compared to the fireball and purple unmaking candle flames, but . . . perhaps it had been enough not to want this card too.

Arthur gazed back down at the card. Yes, he would keep it with him, tucked safely in his heart. Then when his father was done tilling the dragon soil in the new field, he'd give it to him.

But . . . Arthur was twelve years old. Was his heart big enough to hold a card?

Only one way to find out.

CHAPTER 3

Holding his breath, Arthur pushed the card to his chest. He had doubts this would work. A man's heart was supposed to be the size of a fist. This card was longer than his hand from the heel of his palm to his fingertips.

It didn't matter because the card stopped dead at his shirt. Even magic cards couldn't pass through fabric.

Arthur yanked down his collar, wincing as a few bad seams popped. He tried again.

This time the card seemed to sink straight through his skin. There was no blood, only a sensation of growing pressure. It seemed like it should have hurt . . . only it didn't.

Closing his eyes, Arthur shoved the card the rest of the way. Straight into his heart.

The card vanished under his skin.

Suddenly, in his mind's eye, he saw the card, blazing bright. His mind was flooded with information.

You have activated your heart deck dashboard.
Master of Skills (Legendary) has been added to your heart deck.
As Master of Skills is a utility-based card, it has automatically been
slotted into your Spirit slot.

Master of Skills
Legendary
Utility
*This card grants the wielder the ability to immediately gain proficiency in
any skill. Skills are automatically organized into categories and broken
down into assigned values.*

The wielder of this card learns skills at a base 25% accelerated rate.
Newly learned skills automatically start at base level 3.
Previous experience and/or learning a skill taught by a master may increase
the initial starting level and further accelerate proficiency.
This is a utility-only card. Seek additional cards in this set to include
combative, magical, body, and special abilities.

Congratulations! You have accessed your heart deck dashboard.
Total cards: 1
Total completed sets: 0
Paired cards: 0
Linked cards: 0
Mind: 0
Body: 0
Spirit: 1

Arthur sat down hard. He was certain he'd never heard half of those words before, and yet while reading them with his mind's eye, he knew them intimately.

Though he still wasn't certain what Body, Mind, and Spirit slots were for.

It didn't matter. Dad was going to love this card.

He looked down at his hands in wonder, curious if he could see any change. But all he saw were his own hands, dirty with dragon soil. He wiped them on his pants.

Now that the card was hidden in his heart, he realized he would have to move quickly. It would be suspicious if he was not seen helping the village tonight. When dragon soil was delivered, everyone not on their deathbed was expected to pitch in. Sometimes the baron's men dragged the ailing out of their homes to work the fields.

Standing from the graves, Arthur bade his mother and sister goodbye. He ducked into the cottage long enough to grab a few small apples from a kitchen basket. Then he headed out.

The men and women of Borderland Village #49 worked hard, as a rule. However, on dragon soil delivery days, that went extra.

Dragon soil had to be tilled into scourge-ridden fields, and it had to be done before the soil lost its life-giving strength.

It also had to be done carefully. Working scourge-ridden land was dangerous. Any cut, no matter how minor, could go bad. Most everyone had some pock-marks and deep scars from a rotted infection. The majority of the adults were missing fingers or toes.

So for this occasion, the baron's men handed out thick leather gloves to all adults. The gloves would be counted by the time they left to ensure no one stole from their noble lord.

Meanwhile, children and younger teens were sent as runners back and forth on different tasks. They retrieved cold water from the stream, fetched tools for the adults in the field, and helped ladle out boiled oats from the steaming kitchen kettles. Whatever it took to keep the workers going.

If the sun was setting and the work was not done, then torches would be lit to keep people tilling through the night.

Everyone was so busy that Arthur slipped into the chaos without notice. Though his friend Ernie gave him an odd look.

Before Ernie could do more than open his mouth, he was handed a pail of water and a dipping spoon to take to the field hands. Arthur moved to join his friend, but old Martha caught him by the elbow.

"Not you, Arthur. You have a bucket of carrots to chop with your name on it."

He gave the old woman a disgusted look. "Chopping carrots? What for?"

"For the stew, brat. The baron's men want everyone to work until they drop tonight. That means we serve dinner. Hurry up, now."

She pushed him to the kitchen tent and added a swat to his backside when he wasn't fast enough.

Grumbling, Arthur headed over there. Kitchen duty was women's work . . . though he wouldn't complain about being close to the cooking fires. The early spring air had already taken on a night chill. Arthur couldn't handle the cold as well as he used to before the flu swept through the village.

Except . . . he felt the sting of the chilly air, but it didn't seem to instantly sink into his bones the way it usually did. It was as if he wore an invisible sweater that kept him just a bit warmer.

Was it the card?

He glanced down to his chest, half expecting to see a glow to show off his guilt to the world.

There was nothing. He looked normal. He just felt a little warmer than usual.

It was said that carded men and women grew taller, stronger, and faster than normal folk. Maybe just having the card for a few hours would kick-start a growth spurt?

That pleasant thought was cut short when he entered the kitchen tent. To his dismay, Old Martha hadn't been exaggerating. There was indeed a full bucket of carrots set out just for him.

Arthur groaned, though quietly, so the kitchen women didn't hear. Last dragon soil delivery he'd been set to peeling a bucket of potatoes, and he'd made the mistake of complaining. That had only gotten him two more buckets to join the first.

By the time he was done, Arthur hadn't been able to look at a potato without a shudder.

One of the kitchen workers was a woman named Yuma. She had lost both feet to a scourge infection before Arthur had been born, so she couldn't work in the fields. Spotting Arthur from her customary place sat on a stool by a fire, she waved a wooden spoon threateningly.

"Mind you peel those carrots before you chop them. And don't you dare throw the peels to the pigs afterward."

"Why not?" he grumped. "Some of the sows gave birth last week. Peels will do 'em good."

"The peels go into the broth to thicken it up. It's going to be a cold night tonight, and the workers will need all the thickening they can get."

Arthur opened his mouth to shoot back that half the bucket ought to go in the pig sty anyway—many of the carrots were rubbery, and even the best of them had the beginning of rot spots on them.

But Yuma had turned away, and Arthur thought better of giving her lip. It would only earn him more work.

He set to the task, using the peeler to try to cut the dark spots from the rest, though he didn't know why he bothered. It was all going in the same pot anyway.

He was on his third carrot when something odd happened.

Words popped up in front of his face. Just like when he had hidden the card in his chest. He understood what the words said even though he was certain he hadn't read any of these in his life.

New skill gained: Basic Meal Preparation. (Cooking Class)
Due to your card's bonus traits, you automatically start this skill
at level 3.

With a jolt of fear, Arthur looked around to see who else saw the alert. Not everyone in the village could read, but they'd certainly notice this.

The message moved smoothly along with his field of vision.

Sitting on her stool with a bucket of onions in front of her, Yuma scowled in Arthur's direction.

"Stop daydreaming. The sooner those go in the pot, the sooner we all get to eat."

She said nothing about the words floating in the air only a few feet from Arthur's nose. None of the other kids working in the tent mentioned it either.

He was the only one who could see them.

Letting out a long breath, Arthur nodded and bent back to his work. As he did, he dismissed the message with a mental flick so automatic that he didn't have to think much about it.

He grabbed up a fourth carrot and frowned. Something about his grip didn't feel right.

Now that he was paying more attention, he saw his fingers were much too close to the scraping tool. One slip and he'd skin himself rather than the carrot.

He adjusted his grip until it felt right, switching the angle of the peeler so he was shoving away rather than peeling toward himself. There. That felt right.

He peeled that carrot and the ones after it faster than he had before. He was also able to shave down the brown bits with much more ease.

Done with the bucket, he received another message.

New skill level: Basic Meal Preparation (Cooking Class)
Level 4

"Now cut the carrots," said Yuma, who never wasted an opportunity to tell someone what to do when they were in her tent. Arthur's father called it "micromanaging." "Use that knife on the table, and be sure you replace it afterward. I'll be counting all the knives come night's end."

Arthur rolled his eyes. As if anyone would take one of the kitchen tent knives. They were village property and dangerously dull anyway. He hated this part the most whenever he helped in the kitchen.

Now he approached the task with a sense of anticipation.

He placed the entire bucket of peeled carrots on the table and started chopping.

He was a few carrots in when he received another message.

New skill gained: Knife Work (Cooking Class)
Due to your card's bonus traits, you automatically start this skill
at level 3.

A grin spread across Arthur's face. He quickly pulled a new carrot.

Again . . . the way he usually chopped carrots felt off, like he was doing it wrong. He adjusted his grip, curling in the first joint of his fingers to keep the tips out of the way of the dull knife.

The motion of the knife, too, felt subtly wrong. He'd always used a basic up and down chopping motion. Like one would with an ax to a stubborn block of wood. Now, he felt like he needed to sort of roll the knife in his hand as he pressed down.

The old carrot, as rubbery as it was, yielded to the knife. He was left with a perfectly edged chunk. Not ragged like the others.

Huh.

Arthur repeated the process, slowly gaining speed as he grew confident.

"That's a fine-looking pile, Arthur."

He glanced up in surprise to see Yuma had stumped over on her peg legs. She was looking at the pile in satisfaction. The carrot chunks were all in a neat golden pile. And except for the first few carrots, they were mostly uniform in size and consistency.

"Yes, very nicely done," Yuma murmured to herself.

Arthur had never heard so much as an approving grunt from the woman. He was pleased . . . but also a little wary. There was every chance that properly done work would be rewarded with more work. That was a lesson the adults drove into the village children—to prepare them for the time that they, too, would be under the baron's eye.

Nobles would work a man to death just because they could, and not give a sniff for the wife and children he left behind.

Yuma cast a glance at him and then snorted as if she'd read his mind.

"Well, there's not much more to do here. Toss the carrots into that pot, and the skins into the broth over there. Then get out to the field. We'll be working to sunup, more likely than not."

Arthur nodded and did as he was told, scooting out of the tent as quickly as possible.

Once free of Yuma's gaze, he let himself grin in wonder.

Chopping carrots was a small thing, but suddenly he was excited to see what other skills this card would grant him.

That thought came with a prickle of shame. This wasn't his card to use and explore. He was going to give it to his father.

Would Arthur keep the skills he gained? Or would they be lost the moment the card left his heart deck?

"Arthur!" called a voice.

He looked up to see one of the men on the edge of the field waving him over.

The time for daydreaming was over. Now he had work to do.

CHAPTER 4

Even when the promised stew was done, Arthur only got to snatch bites on the go, between ladling out more into bowls for the working adults.

The setting sun did not earn the field workers a break. Instead the baron's men, who mostly lounged near the dragon soil carts, handed out torches to be staked into the fields and lit.

That allowed just enough light to see by.

Eventually, as some of the weaker adults pleaded exhaustion, the elderly were pressed into service to replace them.

Before, on dragon soil nights, Arthur had always been on the verge of dropping from exhaustion a few hours after midnight. When he'd been little, he'd been allowed to nap under the carts with the rest of the children. Now he was expected to endure until he dropped. It had happened before.

This time, however, he felt as if there was a wellspring of energy he could draw from. He certainly wasn't fresh, and he wasn't stupid enough to show enthusiasm in front of the baron's men, but he could grimly keep going.

The last of the dragon soil was scraped out of the final cart as dawn broke.

A ragged cheer went up from the adults. Yuma and the tent workers provided thick, hearty oatmeal for breakfast. It pepped everyone up enough to till the last of the soil in.

What had once been a gray, deadened patch of land was now rich brown. Soon, greenery blown in from seeds on the wind would take root. The village would allow it to stay fallow for a few seasons. Then it would be ready for planting.

Another small bit of land was reclaimed for the kingdom.

Arthur's father found him just as Arthur was finishing his last bite of oatmeal. His father was dirty—they both were—and the lines that etched his face seemed more pronounced than usual. But his eyes were sparkling.

"I saw you working through the night." He clapped his son on the shoulder. "Good job."

Arthur beamed back at his father. "I guess I'm growing up."

The air was so cold in the dawn chill that their breath steamed as they walked down the trail back to their house. Yet Arthur felt perfectly comfortable. Normally, he would be shivering in his ratty clothing.

It had to be the magic of the card, warming him from the inside out.

Carded people were stronger and healthier than unfortunate uncarded folk.

He was going to miss that benefit once he gave the card to his father . . . but cards were usually passed down through the family, weren't they? And he and his dad only had each other. So he would get it back eventually. That made him feel better.

"Home sweet home," his father said.

Arthur looked up, realizing he'd been staring at his scuffed boots as they walked.

Their cottage had come into view. Not a wisp of smoke came out from the chimney. The fire had completely died, leaving the building stone cold.

It seemed the moment he crossed the threshold, the last of his energy drained out of him. Arthur stumbled to his cot-bed, which was set in the far corner.

Now that he and his dad were alone, protected by the walls of the house, he ought to tell him about the dragon, the carriage, and most importantly, the card. Arthur hadn't had time to think much about it. There had been so much work to do.

But he was so very tired, and for once he wasn't going to bed shivering. It wouldn't hurt to keep the card for a few more hours, just to feel the sensation of going to sleep and waking up warm.

Arthur was jerked out of a deep sleep by a fist pounding on the door. It was so strong that it shook the adjoining walls and rattled the simple plates and bowls they used for crockery.

"What in the world?" his father demanded, voice thick with sleep.

Arthur saw him rise out of his own bed, which was nearer to the front door. Like Arthur, he had fallen asleep in his clothing, pausing only to kick off his boots.

His father had not reached the door before the rusty hinges gave. It fell open, and three burly men wearing the baron's colors of rust red and brown stormed in.

One grabbed his father and shoved him against the closest wall.

A smaller, reedy man demanded, "Where is it, Calvan? Where did you hide it?"

"Hide what?" his father demanded. "What's going on?"

Meanwhile, the third man had walked around his father and started to rifle through the shelves, pulling some of the plates and bowls down and smashing them to the floor.

Arthur yelled a protest. "Those were my mother's plates!"

They had been some of the few objects she had brought from their old house, when they'd been banished to this village.

Arthur's memories of the house they used to live in were dim and vague. Everything had seemed overly large and grand, he was sure, because he had been so small. Most of the time he was half convinced he'd made it up in his mind. Just a little story of better times to make himself feel better.

But the one thing he was certain of was that his mother had loved those plates and the beautiful, idyllic scenes of nature that had been etched on each one.

Throwing his ratty blanket to the side, he rushed to stop the man, but his father managed to reach out and snag him by the collar, stopping him.

"Arthur, stay by me. What is the meaning of this?" he demanded to the intruders.

The reedy one, who looked to be the leader, sneered at him. "Theft from the baron. A carriage was attacked, the contents stolen."

Arthur stared, feeling like all his joints had been locked into place by shock and looming terror. He should have guessed this would happen. He should have told his father.

"Theft? When? The entire village was tasked to reclaim the field yesterday," his father snarled. "Sounds like our lord baron has a brigand problem."

In answer, the man slapped him—open-faced and contemptuous. Then he turned to the others.

"Search the house."

The two other men moved to continue where the first had left off, pulling absolutely everything off the shelf and throwing them to the floor. When they were done, they tore through Arthur and his father's meager pile of clothing, upended the baskets of roots, and flipped the straw mattresses. Then for good measure, they took knives and cut open the sacks that held the straw in, pouring out the contents of their bedding all over the floor.

His father remained silent but stared at the process with hard eyes. Arthur shrank back to press against the wall.

Finally, the men returned to the leader, shaking their heads.

The head man turned back to his father. "I'm going to ask you once, Calvan. My man, Dino, here is a Treasure Seeker. He can sniff out the magic from a card from ten miles away. You know what that means?"

Calvan's eyes widened at the realization of what they were looking for—and what had been stolen from the baron—but his voice remained level as he answered: "I do."

"If we find a card on your property, we will kill you and your boy. But if you give it up now, it'll only be your life."

Calvan met the other man's gaze square on. "I know the terms of my sentence. I don't have possession of a card. All the villagers can vouch for me."

The man simply stared, letting the moment lengthen as if silently asking for Arthur's father to reconsider.

Rising fear made Arthur fidget. Should he say something? Would they kill both of them if he confessed now? It wasn't like anyone would believe he had the power to destroy a carriage . . .

No, they'd think he had help from his father, or other men of the village.

He'd heard of Treasure Seekers. They were men with spell cards that gave them the ability to find rare and valuable objects. The variety, type, and restrictions of the treasures were as varied as cards.

Some of them could only find objects above or below a certain value. Or a certain type of object—metallic, magical, or mineral.

Some extraordinary cards could identify specific items the caster searched for. Those were rare and almost invaluable and usually worked over short distances.

His father had once told Arthur that for all the baron's power over their lives, he was a minor lord in the grand scheme of the kingdom. Would he be powerful enough to have a high-powered Treasure Seeker on this staff?

Maybe.

Arthur would have confessed at that moment . . . if the man's threat hadn't included his father dying.

The silence dragged on. Calvan didn't so much as break a sweat as he stared back at the reedy man.

"We don't have what you're looking for."

The head man snorted. "So be it. Dino?"

The biggest of the two goons grunted and kicked away chips of pottery and loose straw with the side of his foot to create a clear area. Then he sat down with his legs crossed and his hands resting on his knees. He let out a long breath and held his palms upward. A soft blue glow emanated between them.

Arthur held his breath and resisted the urge to raise his hand to cover his chest where the card lay.

Could a Treasure Seeker see into his heart?

Dino's eyes fluttered closed. He was silent for a moment, which felt like an age, until he spoke in a slow intonation.

"There is a cache thirty yards to the north in the woods."

The headman smirked in triumph.

They roughly marched Arthur and Calvan, barefoot, out the door.

Dino the Treasure Seeker followed and pointed to one of the large oak trees, and Arthur tried not to look relieved.

This was one of the hollow tree caches.

Unerringly, Dino walked to the dark hole in the bark and reached in. He swore and yanked his hand out.

"Be careful," Calvan said. "Things bite out here in the borderlands."

That earned him another slap.

The second goon walked over, literally grabbed a handful of bark, his fingers sinking into it as if it were a soft sponge, and ripped it away.

He had to have some kind of a body-strengthening card.

The man tore pieces of the trunk in chunks around the blackened hollow. Inside were three simple knives and a few silver coins.

One of the knives still had a spot of blood on it from Dino.

The headman growled, and for a moment Arthur was afraid his father was going to get hit again. But the man simply reached over and pocketed the coins.

Then he looked at the two of them.

"March," he said.

CHAPTER 5

Arthur and his father were forced to walk back to the village, still without their shoes. However, they weren't the only ones. Up and down the lanes, people were being shoved out of their homes by teams of the baron's men.

Some were in nothing but their underclothing. Arthur and Calvan were lucky that they had fallen asleep while wearing their work shirts and trousers.

Aside from being undignified, it was also cold. A thick fog had rolled in over the late hours, making the air damp and chilly.

They were herded into the middle of the square. No comforts such as food, water, or even a place to sit were offered.

The baron's guards set up positions at every corner to watch for escape attempts. Meanwhile, the rest of the baron's men continued their house-to-house search.

But the guards could not contain the gossip.

"I heard they found a carriage overturned . . ."

"Burned out . . ."

"All dead . . ."

"Four men, all carded."

"I heard it was ten men!"

"Must be bandits. Surely the baron will see . . ."

"We were doing his dragon-damned work . . ."

"We've been telling the baron about the bandit problem for years."

"Pah. He won't do nothing . . ."

Arthur edged away from his father, who stood in the center of the storm of gossip. Borderland Village #49 was not allowed to have elected leaders, but the adults often saw him as their spokesman.

No doubt that was the reason why they had been visited by the Treasure Seeker first.

Feeling sick with a combination of anger and guilt, Arthur found a knot of kids and joined them.

Ernie, his best friend by virtue of being the only other boy his age, brightened. "Art! You know why the baron's got his garter belt in a twist?"

Arthur grimaced and glanced over his shoulder. Thankfully, the guard's attention was on the adults rather than the kids.

Arthur lowered his voice. "Remember that fancy carriage that rolled in with the dragon soil shipment yesterday? It got attacked just out of town."

Ernie made a face. "It couldn't have been anyone here. We were all busy in the field. Maybe bandits, you think?"

"That's what my dad said." He wanted to add more about the missing card, but Ernie had the biggest mouth in the village. He'd blurt it out for sure, and Arthur wasn't certain if it was supposed to be known information.

He felt a tug on the hem of his shirt and looked down to see one of the little girls. "What's gonna happen to us?" She glanced at the guards anxiously, sucking on dirty fingers.

Ernie answered before Arthur could. "They'll waste time here, trying to shake news of where the bandits who did this are hiding. Then they'll go back to their fancy houses and leave us good folk alone."

That felt too optimistic to Arthur, but he nodded anyway.

They waited, and the damp cold crept in. Some of the quicker mothers had insisted on grabbing blankets for the children as they were pushed out of their house, so those who had a little warmth to share huddled together.

Arthur's guilt along with the fact he didn't feel particularly uncomfortable allowed him to decline a piece of blanket.

Ernie tried to follow his example but was soon dancing from foot to foot to keep warm on the cold cobblestones. He finally gave up and ducked in with the rest of the kids.

The stones were certainly cold under Arthur's bare feet, but it was as if the cold couldn't sink in. He felt the cold, but not deep down inside.

No, most of his discomfort came from gnawing guilt.

If he had any honor, he would go up to the guards and confess everything he'd seen. But even if he fibbed and said the red dragon had taken the card with it, the baron's men would likely take out their anger on the whole town. They'd do it just because they could.

But it wasn't my fault, insisted a stubborn thought. *It was the dragon.*

Why did the baron's men think that a band of dirty, starving bandits could take out five carded men? Then destroy the carriage with magic to boot?

Because they were idiots and it was easier to blame the borderland town. All of the adults were convicted criminals and not to be trusted.

Arthur sighed. No. There wasn't a point in telling the guards they were barking up the wrong tree. Plus he hadn't forgotten the red dragon had promised to kill him and his family if the card somehow fell into the baron's hands.

So Arthur kept his mouth shut and hoped the guards would mistake any guilt on his face for fear.

The townsfolk were made to stand in the courtyard without food or water for hours as the baron's men went from house to house. This would have been uncomfortable at the best of times, but coming straight from an entire night of tilling dragon soil in the dead field, it was miserable.

Sitting huddled together with the rest of the kids, Ernie was the first to perk up. He poked a hand out from under a blanket and pointed. "Someone's coming."

Through a gap between two ramshackle buildings, Arthur caught a glimpse of the road. Two foaming horses pulled a carriage at a fast clip.

This carriage was highly decorated, though much smaller than the one the dragon had destroyed. And unlike the last one, someone sat inside.

The carriage was driven to the town's square, scattering townsfolk. It jerked to a halt, and the footman jumped down to open the door.

A murmur swept through the crowd as Baron Kane stepped out.

Arthur didn't know the man's first name, only the insults the adults called him by, all spoken under their breath.

He cut a fine figure in rich clothing of rust red and rich soil brown. His dark beard was trimmed short, his skin free of the scars and pockmarks that were so common in the village.

And he looked at all of them as if they were worms.

Every man in uniform, including the Treasure Seeker, immediately gathered around him to make their reports.

Whatever they said made the baron's face cloud with anger.

His gaze swept around and landed on Arthur's father.

"Search him."

Though two burly men gripped Calvan's arms to pull him forward, he went willingly. His back was straight with his chin lifted proudly.

"I heard you lost a card, Mace."

The baron looked at Calvan coldly. "You have one chance to give it up and spare your people." He paused. "And whatever is left of your family."

In answer, Calvan spat to the side. "I can't give up what I don't have. We were tilling your fields. Your men likely deserted and stole the card. You still underpaying them, Mace?"

The baron's eyes narrowed.

Calvan smirked. He leaned in as if to impart a secret, but his words were loud enough for all to hear. "Every man and woman here is already under a suspended death sentence from the crown, but the kingdom needs us to reclaim the dead fields. You can't kill us to search our corpses for the card. Who would till scourge-ground for you? How would your *quaint* barony expand?"

"There are always more criminals to be found, as you well know."

Calvan didn't flinch. He continued to stare at the baron with half his mouth quirked, as if he found the other man amusing and more than a little pathetic.

The baron was the one to break the stare-off. "Nevertheless, you're right. I don't need to waste good manpower by searching corpses." He turned and gestured to the carriage. Out stepped an old woman. She was tiny, wrapped in so many shawls that Arthur couldn't see her shape. Her eyes peered out from within, fierce and glittering.

One of the baron's men extended a hand to help her step down.

"Scan him," the baron said. "Make sure all can see."

She nodded and pressed one twisted hand to Calvan's chest.

Calvan gasped as if the air had been punched out of him. At the same time, a list popped into view in the air. It was similar to the one Arthur had seen when he'd pressed his card into his heart.

Heart Deck: Calvan Rowantree
Total completed sets: 0
Paired cards: 0
Linked cards: 0
Mind: 0
Body: 0
Spirit: 0
Total cards: 0

All the card slots were empty.

Calvan sucked in an unsteady breath. He looked pained, though his words were defiant. "I told you, Mace."

The baron backhanded his father, then turned away to glare at the rest of the crowd. When he spoke, his voice was high-pitched at the end, as if it were close to breaking.

"Search them all!"

The old woman was a card seeker. If they searched Arthur, they'd find the card.

Arthur backed up a step to place himself within the group of other kids.

One by one, the adults were pulled forward. The old woman placed a hand on their chests.

Information popped into existence in the air, but theirs was different from his father's. A simple message:

Heart Deck Not Active.

Arthur realized for the first time how much taller his father was from the rest of the townsfolk. His shoulders were broad, and while he had a few pockmarks on his chin and cheeks, they were recent.

Once the men and women were done, the baron pointed at the older teens.

Arthur had to concentrate on breathing normally. If he went faint, would they believe it was a lack of food or water? No, they might search him anyway.

The only good thing about his stomach-churning anxiety was that he felt too sick to feel hungry. He was in no danger of throwing up.

The search took a long time. Eventually, the fog burned off and was replaced by a cold wind. It only made the townsfolk more miserable.

Finally, the latest to be searched, a fifteen-year-old girl named Poesy, returned with:

Heart Deck Not Active.

The baron seemed to have had enough. His voice boomed out.

"The card is here in the village! Who has it?"

He was met by a sullen silence.

Someone in the back of the crowd yelled, "The bandits took it, didn't they?"

"Then you know who the bandits are! Who is hiding them? Tell me!"

Again, he was met by silence.

The baron turned to his guards. "Search the village again. Every house, every corner."

"Mace," Calvan said, "some of these women are young mothers with babies to feed—"

That was a mistake. The baron swung back to him, his sculpted face ugly with rage.

"Then they have more incentive to speak than anyone else. No," he snapped at his men. "Never mind searching these hovels, we'll ask the peasants directly."

With that, the men were pulled out of the crowd one by one and shoved into one of the nearby houses with two guards in attendance. By the time they returned, many had black eyes and split lips.

Arthur felt so guilty he could barely stand himself.

Finally, as the bottom of the sun touched the horizon, more riders wearing the baron's colors rode in. They dismounted and spoke to the baron directly.

Arthur was too far away to hear what was said, but rumor swept through the crowd in whispers: a bandit village had been found in the dead lands.

The baron called his men back, and without a glance toward the town he had been harassing all day, they all rode out.

CHAPTER 6

Arthur and his father trudged back to their cottage to find it in shambles.

It was obvious their small home had been searched multiple times throughout the day. Everything that had been inside the building not nailed down had been tossed out the front door. The two windows with the thick, warped glass had been broken out for good measure.

As they got closer, an acidic smell told Arthur that the blankets had been pissed on.

He stood there, looking at the shattered remains of his bed, the food they'd set out for storage which was now ground into the dirt, and the shards of what used to be his mother's favorite plates. He was so angry that tears fell silently down his cheeks.

His reaction was nothing next to his father's.

Calvan let out a bellow of rage and pain. He grabbed broken splinters of what had been their table and flung them into the forest. Kicking the wet blankets, he stormed into the house. From the open doorway—the door now hung off its hinges—Arthur saw him beat on the walls as if he were trying to knock new holes into them.

Seeing his father so out of control snapped him out of his own despair.

He had never seen his father like this. Never under the weight of all the little cruelties that came with every visit from the baron's men. Not even when Arthur's mother and little sister died.

Fear took root in his heart. Arthur stepped back, nervously, to the tree line. Not that he was afraid his father would turn his fists on him. It was just that his dad was the only one he had left.

If he were to learn that Arthur was the cause of all this . . .

I've got to keep the card a secret for a little bit longer. At least until I'm sure the baron's men have left, he thought. *Then I'll dump it in the forest. I'll bury it in a hole so deep, not even the Treasure Seekers can find it.*

Finally, his father seemed to tire himself out. The noise of pounding stopped, and even from outside, Arthur could hear him taking ragged, controlled breaths.

"Arthur," he said in a too-calm voice. "Go get wood for the fire."

With a quick nod, Arthur scampered into the woods. The sun was less than an hour from setting. Daylight grew thin through the winter-bare branches. Arthur ranged out farther than he normally did, both because he wanted to give his father space and because he realized he could see better in the dimming light than he ever had before.

Another benefit of the card. Regret twinged at his heart, but it was far outweighed by the guilt on his conscience.

The townspeople had suffered because of him. All their possessions, their food was destroyed . . .

Wait, was that fair?

He stopped in place, frowning. It was easy to blame himself for this mess, like rolling a rock down a steep hill, where the bottom was self-loathing.

But what if Arthur had never followed the carriage? The dragon would have still attacked and then flown away with the card. The baron would have blamed the townsfolk, just because they were the closest nearby, and he could.

This wasn't his fault. Not really.

It didn't make him feel any better.

He returned home with his arms full of dropped dead-fall branches, which made good kindling. There was also a small shed out back where they stored seasoned wood. Thankfully, the baron's men had ignored it.

Going to the shed, Arthur picked out several pieces of the split and seasoned logs—oak, which would take a while to catch fire but would burn hot and long. These few pieces would see them through the night.

When he returned to the cottage, it was to find that his father had scavenged several unbroken items from the pile. Nothing special: a stone pitcher they used to store fresh drinking water, a few unbent utensils, and slab of polished wood they used as a cutting board but would now be their plate tonight.

The roots and smoked meat had been thrown into the dirt, but the animals hadn't yet had time to take it.

With his father organizing the food, Arthur bent to the woodstove, which seemed untouched, and started the fire.

It was a task he had done hundreds, maybe thousands of times before. Taking out a blade so tiny and inconsequential that not even the baron's guards had looked twice at it, Arthur used the sharpest edge to shave bits off the sticks of kindling until he had made a nest of thin wood and sawdust.

Then he took a flint rock his father had laid out and started knocking sparks into the nest.

Within three strikes, a spark large enough to catch hold fell into the kindling. Arthur blew gently on it, feeding it more out of the nest until he had a viable flame. Only then did he place the first oak log just above the burgeoning flame, balanced on the two inner edges of the woodstove. That way it didn't crush the delicate nest and let air into feed the fire.

If he hadn't gathered so much kindling, he would have used poplar to help it catch. However, the oak was well dried. All it would need was time.

New skill gained: Fire Making (General Class)
Due to your previous experience and your card's bonus traits,
you automatically start this skill at level 7.

Arthur blinked. It seemed all those times waking up to a cold house and patiently feeding a fire while trying not to shiver had paid off with extra levels.

As before, the message came along with more knowledge.

His eyes went to the flue, and he realized he hadn't checked it. It was still dampened, and the fire was in danger of eating all the air inside, snuffing itself out.

He quickly adjusted it. Hot air rose up the pipe and sucked up wisps of smoke before they could drift through the house and choke them. The flames instantly leaped, and the outer edges of the dense oak started to catch.

Without the knowledge from the card, Arthur might have caught the error . . . but not before they were coughing on smoke.

"Dinner's ready," his father said, breaking Arthur out of his wonder.

He turned to see his father had made up a single plate of sliced apples and cheese. Usually, apples were saved for dessert on special occasions—they were carefully hoarded for the sweetness.

But the thin red skins were bruised from the rough handling today. They'd go bad soon if they weren't eaten.

His father looked down at the cutting board they were using as a single plate and grimaced. "What little dinner there is."

"Did they get to the smokehouse?" Arthur asked. While they kept some strips of meat in the cottage, the majority was in a separate lean-to on the other side of the far wall. He hadn't had time to check it.

Calvan nodded. "They took everything."

Arthur winced. When he grabbed the slice of apple, he made sure to eat it slowly. No doubt the entire village would be hunting food for tomorrow, which would make game harder to find.

They ate in silence while the sun set. Soon, the only light in the cottage came from the open door of the wood-burning stove. The candles had been destroyed.

Gradually, his father relaxed. Arthur kept shooting glances at the door he'd propped up against the door frame until the hinges could be fixed. It wouldn't keep out a stiff breeze, much less the baron's men.

"Dad?" he asked. "What will happen if the bandits don't have that card? Will the baron's men come again?"

To his surprise, his father chuckled. "The baron will be down on his knees and praying to all the gods that those bandits have that card."

But they didn't have it, Arthur knew. He swallowed. "Why?"

"Because some cards are worth more money than a noble's entire holdings. Most use high cards as a type of currency."

"They use them like money?"

"There's no point in lugging around boxes of coins when you can trade a card instead. Some high lady's entire dowry can be a Rare card." His grin was a little sideways. "I don't doubt the baron lost a good one. Maybe even a Rare one. Did you see how desperate he looked?"

Arthur thought back on it. He hadn't noticed before, but now that he reexamined his memories of today, he realized something he had missed. "He looked scared."

"He is. He may not have the money to pay back the worth of that card, depending on its rarity."

Arthur didn't know much about cards, but he would bet that "Legendary" level was rare.

Speaking of rare, his father hardly ever talked of cards, even when Arthur begged to know. And none of the other adults had a clue.

"How do you know a card is rare?" he asked, half certain his father would brush off the question.

Calvan leaned back against the wall since the two chairs they had were currently outside in broken pieces. Then, to his surprise, he answered. "It says on the card. There are five categories: Common, Uncommon, Rare, Legendary, and Mythic."

Legendary was second from the top.

Yes. His card was likely worth a lot of money.

His father continued, voice bitter. "I hope the baron never finds it and whoever has the card has run away . . . and keeps running."

He couldn't take it anymore. "Dad, how do you know so much about magic?"

His father looked away. "I've lived a long time. Picked up things."

Except when the Treasure Seeker had touched his father's chest, his card dashboard looked different from everyone else's.

Arthur wasn't stupid. His father had once had a card.

It wasn't even a surprise. Arthur's vague memories of a life before his family had been forced to relocate to Borderland Village #49—it had been a life of ease surrounded by smiling people. A time when Arthur had never known hunger or cold.

That had been a long time ago. His sister had been born in this village. And she had died here.

Guilt swamped him once more. It was too much. He thought he could say nothing, take the card and bury it in the dead woods . . . but even if his father ended up angry at him, he had to know.

A small part of Arthur hoped and feared that Calvan would ask for the card, himself. Surely he would know what to do with it.

"Dad . . ."

Instantly, he felt his father's attention on him. Something in the tone of his voice must have alerted him that this was serious.

Arthur swallowed and continued. "You know that carriage? The one that got destroyed? I followed it out of the village."

His father gripped his wrist hard, his fingers strong and callused. Arthur stopped, and his father released his grip. The message was clear: Be silent.

Rising, his father rose to the door, leaned it back from the broken opening, and looked out as if he was afraid someone was listening from the other side.

Replacing the door, he looked at Arthur and jerked his chin toward the back of the cottage. It was two rooms in total. One room for living, eating, and sleeping. The other small, closet-sized room was for cold storage of root vegetables. Arthur had to step down into it as it was partially dug into the soil to keep cool in the summer months.

His father crouched down in the storage room and gestured for Arthur to do the same. If someone was listening by the doors or windows, they would be hard-pressed to hear them speaking down here. The soil built up around the storage room provided them extra security.

With all that, his father still spoke in a low tone. "You saw the bandits attacking the carriage?"

"It wasn't bandits. It was a dragon." The story spilled out of him. "It didn't have a rider. It even spoke, Dad! It killed the baron's men and destroyed the carriage with magic. I don't know how they could have thought it was bandits."

Again, his father gripped his wrist but not nearly so tight. "Arthur, you will never speak of this again. Do you understand me? Even if the baron's men come back, even if they threaten the whole village or me. You give them nothing."

There was a light in the back of his father's eyes he didn't like. Arthur still nodded.

"Did you see what happened to the card?"

He couldn't bring himself to say it—barely had words to even explain it. He simply touched his chest.

His father stared at him for long seconds that seemed to stretch into infinity. Then he chuckled, low. He shook his head. "They didn't search the children . . ."

"Dad . . ."

Still chuckling, his father released his wrist, leaning back, now wiping at the sides of his eyes. "My boy. My bright boy. You fooled them all, and no one had any idea."

"I didn't mean for it to happen," he blurted. "I didn't ask for the card. I wanted to give it to you—"

That stopped his father short. "Do you know what you're offering? No." He shook his head. "You have no idea. No, Arthur. Even if I was inclined to take a spell card from my own child, I would be the first person in this village the baron will search if he comes back. You saw it today."

"You're saying I should keep it?"

Despite himself, a little hope leaked into his voice.

His father gave him a sad, wistful smile. "Yes. You proved you're the man for that card today by keeping smart and not saying anything."

A man. Arthur felt his chest swell a little with pride.

That odd light had returned to his father's eye. "Remember, the baron and his men are the enemy. If you ever find yourself wavering, remember it will hurt the baron more than you will ever know to keep that card away from him."

"Really?"

"Really. Imagine what will happen when he can't repay the value of that card. Every time you are tempted to say something, remember that."

"But . . ." Arthur didn't know a lot about the world outside his village, but he listened to the adults talk and complain. A vague memory of the time before his family had moved here worried him. "But won't he tax the people to make up for the loss?" He wasn't sure what taxes were, exactly, other than the adults thought they were bad.

Calvan shook his head. "We're in the borderlands. Every single adult in the village is condemned here until death. There is nothing more he can take."

Arthur frowned. It wasn't something he hadn't heard before, but seeing the baron's brutality today brought it home.

It occurred to him that he was six years off from being an adult himself. It always seemed so far away, but if he were only a couple of years older, or better grown, he would have been searched by the Treasure Seeker.

"My boy is carded," Calvan murmured, breaking into his thoughts. He seemed lost in his own memories for a moment before he refocused on Arthur. "Do you know what this means?"

"I didn't get any magic spells, if that's what you're talking about," he muttered, looking down. So much had happened since the dragon had attacked the carriage, he hadn't had time to process it.

Every spell card he'd heard of were flashy, interesting spells like Fire Lance, Water Arrow, or Air Blade.

Arthur . . . he could now chop vegetables better.

"It doesn't matter," his father said. "Any carded child will grow up stronger, taller, healthier. You don't have to worry about the scourge. You won't ever be sick again—unless you cross paths with a plague carded. All cards provide this, even the minor ones." He paused. "Do you want to show me your card?"

That was an odd thing to ask. As if Arthur would say no.

"Is it safe?" Arthur asked anxiously. "Will the Treasure Seekers know?"

"Likely safe enough tonight since the baron and his men are off on a wild goose chase in the bandit village."

His father seemed amused. Arthur just hoped that those bandits gave the baron's men a lot of trouble. They'd always been described as hard-bitten men by the other villagers . . . whatever that was supposed to mean. At the very least, they wouldn't take kindly to noble visitors who demanded they turn over a card they didn't have.

He looked down at his chest. From the stories, he knew it was possible to show someone a copy of the card without removing it first, but he had no idea how.

Calvan seemed to read his thoughts.

"You never let it leave your heart unless you are at the point of trade or switching it out for another. Even then, you never let your deck reach zero, or you lose all your health benefits. Do you understand?"

Arthur nodded, though he doubted he would ever have the fortune to add a second card to his heart deck. It was the luck of a lifetime to get one.

"Access your deck menu. There should be an option to view the card," his father coached.

Arthur looked inward with what he was starting to think of as his inner eye to view the deck menu. Sure enough, he found the option. An image of the card popped into his mental space.

He spent a few moments mentally gazing at it, and although he didn't realize it, there was a slight smile on his face. The affectionate expression of a parent looking down at a child or a favorite pet while it slept.

His father cleared his throat.

Arthur jerked in surprise and said, "Got it."

"Good. Now focus on projecting the card—make it visible, but actively think about keeping the image small. The size of your hand at most. We don't want an image of the card glowing over the roof."

"That can happen?"

"Oh, I've seen it happen," his father said. "I could tell you stories."

Arthur waited a moment, but none of the stories came. They never did when they were tales of before they came to the village.

So, he nodded and did as his father had instructed. To his surprise, an image of the card popped into view in front of him, a thin cone of pale blue light connecting from the card back to his heart. At the tip of the cone sat the ghostly image of the card, all of the colors washed out.

His father nodded. "Good work." He shuffled around to view the card from Arthur's angle. "When you get better at this, you will be able to project the card so people can read it without having to look over your shoulder. But for now, this will do . . ." He trailed off as he read the card.

One of his hands landed on Arthur's shoulder and squeezed, hard. "It's . . . Legendary."

"That's good, right?" Arthur asked. He wasn't looking at the card—he knew the contents as if they were printed on his heart. Instead, he watched his father's reaction and how his face drained of blood.

"Yes, Arthur. It's good," he said weakly. "It's extraordinary. Actually, it's Legendary."

His little joke fell flat as his father leaned back, looking like he was winded. "Dismiss the card."

With a twist of his mind, the ghostly image faded back into his heart. Arthur turned to him. "What's wrong?"

Calvan frowned and shook his head. Whatever his thoughts were, he kept them to himself.

"Nothing, Arthur. Nothing's wrong. For once . . . I feel things are about to go right."

CHAPTER 7

Arthur's body may now be magically boosted from having a card, but the last two days had been exhausting. He slept in late on the cold floor with a ratty, torn blanket thrown over him. It was one of the few cloth items that hadn't been soiled.

He was barely aware of his father rummaging around in the early predawn hours.

Arthur must have fallen asleep again, because the next thing he knew, his father was shaking his shoulder gently. "Time to get up."

Cracking open his eyes, Arthur looked around and was surprised to see the table was back inside the cottage, though the legs looked in bad repair. One of the kitchen chairs had been mended using the remains of two others. A dented pot sat on the woodstove. From the smell bubbling up within it, his father had put in oats to boil.

Arthur's stomach rumbled loud enough to be heard.

Smiling, his father said, "Get up. We have a big day ahead of us."

Instantly, his mood sank. Yes, repairing what the baron's men had destroyed would make for a busy day.

A cynical part of him wondered if the work was worth it. Sure as anything, once they fixed everything up and somehow scrounged up replacements, the baron's men would think of another excuse to come again. This last time had been one of the worst, but not unique.

But . . . they hadn't returned so far. Plus, the alternative was to sit around in a nest of broken things.

Swallowing a sigh, Arthur got up.

His father was a man who took his duties seriously, but he seemed unusually energetic this morning. As Arthur spooned a ladle's worth of oats into the bowl, his father placed what wasn't hopelessly beyond broken recognition on the shelves.

"Take two ladlefuls' worth," his father said, barely glancing over his shoulder.

Arthur hesitated even as his stomach clenched in greedy anticipation. "Are you sure?"

One was usually all he was allowed for breakfast. Rations were thin in the village. Most everyone ate just enough to take the edge off their growling hunger, and no more.

"I already ate one of the bruised apples," Calvan replied.

Arthur might have questioned it further—he'd caught his father lying about how much food he had eaten before—but he was just too hungry. The second ladle's worth was enough to nearly empty the pot. He quickly dumped it in his bowl and started eating.

The oats were satisfyingly hot, though undercooked. His father had never picked up the knack for cooking like his mother had. But food was food.

Arthur ate quickly, scraping out the last bits with the side of his finger. When there wasn't so much as a taste left, he went to dunk the bowl in the rain barrel outside to wash it.

When he returned it was to see that his father had collected several papers together in a stack.

"I guess we have to wash out the blankets now?" Arthur asked, wrinkling his nose at the thought. They'd have to bundle up all the piss-soaked blankets that were still outside and then trudge them down to the river, wade in the icy water to weigh the blankets down with rocks, and let the current take the worst of the filth away.

On top of all that work, the blankets probably wouldn't be dry for days.

"I'm going to take care of that," Calvan said. "It's well past time you got started on your letters."

"Letters?"

"Your mother did start teaching you to read, didn't she?"

Arthur nodded but didn't add that those few lessons had stopped after she died. For a long time afterward, both had edged around the memories of his mother and sister. Her favorite plates were put high up on the shelf, never to be used and only occasionally looked at. His sister's baby toys were given to needy families in the village except for a stuffed bear, which had joined the plates on the shelf. That bear's head was now missing from its body. One of the baron's men had looked inside to see if anything valuable had been hidden in the straw stuffing.

Calvan pointed to the chair. When Arthur reluctantly sat, he said, "Tell me what you know of the alphabet."

Arthur paused for a moment and then slowly began to repeat the letters, dropping into a singsong cadence. He was pleased he could repeat them all without being corrected. And he didn't even need the card to do it. The alphabet had come from his own memories.

His father eyed him closely until he reached the end. "Did you get a notification?"

"About what? My letters?" He nodded his head. "I got one yesterday while chopping carrots. It took a few of 'em, though."

"Repetition to build a foundation." His father nodded. "Go through the alphabet again, without singing this time."

Arthur sighed. "Why?"

"Do you think that carded mages with a fireball or ice-spike spells can conjure and throw instantly?"

"Uh . . ." The answer was *yes*, but he knew that wouldn't be wise. "I don't know?"

"They don't. I knew one boy with a card for instant freeze who could only conjure cold air between his fingers for months until he got the knack." His father smiled, but it was gone again in the next instant. "Noble sons and daughters practice until their card's magic becomes second nature. You need to learn how to do the same."

Arthur fidgeted for a moment, still unsure. "But I can't make ice or fire or . . . anything. I just learn stuff! What's the point? Will it even stay with me if the card is gone?"

"What do you mean?"

He blurted out the worry that had been plaguing him, despite his father's assurances last night. "The dragon gave it to me to give it to you!"

"Arthur, we talked about this—"

"I know the baron's men would search you first, but we've never seen Treasure Seekers before. They might not come again. You could do more with the card than I could. It's not right!" His hand bunched a fistful of his shirt over his heart. It hurt to say, because deep down inside . . . he didn't want to give it up.

His father watched him for a moment, eyes narrowed and lips pressed together. Then he nodded to himself and bent to put himself level with his son.

"Arthur, listen to me. How much do you remember of our old home? I know you were very young at the time . . . Do you have any memories of before?"

"A little. But you and . . ." He swallowed. "You and Mom didn't ever want to talk about it."

"Because it's painful. I think you have guessed by now that I was a carded man. I had three spell cards of my own." He grimaced and touched his chest, right over his heart. "I was forced to give them up when my land was taken from me."

"Your land?"

"Arthur," he said, looking shocked that he didn't know. "I was a noble. A duke."

Arthur rocked back so hard that his father caught the edge of his chair to set him back on balance. He barely noticed, eyes wide and staring at his father.

"You were like . . . the baron?" he whispered.

"I was nothing like him." Calvan's expression clouded over. "Nothing."

"But . . ." It was a knowledge Arthur felt he had half known, once, but had pushed down out of sheer survival. His mind boggled.

His father had been a duke. That was even more important than a baron.

He could have been a duke's son.

What would that have been like? Would he have grown up as cruel as the baron?

No. His mind rejected that immediately. No, he wouldn't, because his father wasn't a cruel man.

Still . . . this village was all he knew. He could hardly conceive of a life outside of it except for the fantasy of riches. Of eating whatever he wanted, whenever he wanted. Of being able to go out and play with his friends, or hunt deer on top of his own stallion . . .

Would he have had the pick of his own cards?

"What happened?" Arthur asked.

"It doesn't matter," his father said, sharply in a way that told Arthur he'd better not push. "The important thing was, when I came here, I was forced to take a vow that I would hold no more cards. They've taken everything from me, but I still have my honor and the oaths I made. I will stand by them."

Arthur didn't point out that the baron broke his oaths all the time. He didn't know much about the outside world, but he knew that nobles weren't supposed to steal from and abuse their serfs for no reason.

His father's eyes softened. "Had you grown up as you ought to have, you would have been given cards at about this age."

"But the dragon told me to give it to you," he insisted. "It said it would kill me if the card fell back into the baron's hands."

"Then that had better not happen," Calvan said lightly. Seeing his son wasn't reassured, he leaned forward. "You don't know much about dragons. Yes, they can talk, but they are beasts who don't know the intricacies of human society. That is why they bond their cards with their riders. If the one you saw was without a rider to guide it, it was little more than an animal. A talking animal, but still. Chances are, it flew off afterward and forgot."

Arthur was certain his father was wrong. No regular animal would act out of revenge, and he was certain that was what had driven the dragon.

"In any case," his father continued, "we will work on your ABCs, and you will tell me when you receive a notification. So, repeat them."

Arthur did, this time making an effort not to sing them. It was easier this time since they were fresher in his mind.

The message did not come the second time around but on the third. As he finished his litany, it felt as if something clicked into place.

New skill gained: Basic Reading (Scholarship Class)
Due to your card's bonus traits, you automatically start this skill
at level 3.

Apparently, he hadn't known the ABCs well enough to gain bonus levels. Oh well.

"I got it," he said. "Basic reading."

"Excellent. Now repeat your ABCs backward."

Arthur blinked but then shrugged and started with the last letter. To his surprise, they came to him one by one, each clear and shining in his mind.

Then his father took him outside and had him scratch them out on a patch of dirt using a stick.

Arthur figured he would gain a level. Instead, he received an entirely new skill:

New skill gained: Basic Writing (Scholarship Class)
Due to your card's bonus traits, you automatically start this skill
at level 3.

When he told his father of this, he had Arthur return to the cottage. There, he handed him the papers he had been sorting earlier.

"They're nothing exciting, I'm afraid. Just kingdom notifications. I kept them around in case we needed paper to wipe ourselves. Read through them as best you can and take this." He shoved a charred stick into his hand. "Underline the words you can't puzzle out yourself. When I come back, we'll work on them together."

CHAPTER 8

By the time Arthur finished with the flyers an hour later, his **Basic Reading** skill had increased up to level seven which raised it as high as **Fire Making**, something he had practiced almost every day since he was old enough to set a fire.

He could sound out most of the words easily enough, though some of the bigger ones tripped him up.

As promised, they were dry notices: One was a chart with the expected dragon soil yields the village was to receive and the dates they were to arrive. Arthur thought those came randomly. At least, the adults acted surprised and like the carts were interrupting other business.

Though that might be a way to annoy the baron.

The most unsettling flyer was the reminder that all men and women who reached the age of eighteen years old had three days from their birthday to report to the baron's guard station for relocation.

The guard station was a bit of a joke. It was never manned, except when dragon soil shipments arrived or other nobles toured the village. So anyone wishing to report in had to do so at one of the non-borderland towns, easily a week's walk away.

By kingdom law, children did not pay for the crimes of their parents. So at eighteen years old, or what the kingdom called the age of majority, a new adult was allowed to apply to leave the borderland village—and their family—forever.

Of course, because the baron was a jackass, he made it as difficult as possible for a grown borderland child to start a new life.

Some managed it. Most, however, chose to stay out of loyalty, to take care of sick parents and siblings who were struggling to put food on the table. Or to finally marry a childhood sweetheart, now that they were old enough.

Those who stayed three days past their eighteenth birthday were added to the border village rolls. They were expected to stay.

"Brenna Dunberry was the last one to leave, wasn't she?" Arthur asked after his father had returned and helped explain a few words he'd had trouble with.

"She was, may the dragons help her," he muttered.

Arthur frowned. Brenna's leaving had caused a stir in the village because usually when someone left, it was a boy.

Also, by all reports, both parents had been counting on her to stay and raise grandchildren to help with the workload around the house.

"What do you think happened to her? The baron is supposed to help her go to another town to settle, right?"

"He's to provide her *transport* to a village or a town on his barony," his father corrected. He had been trying to get Arthur to speak all proper ever since he learned about the card.

"Transport to his barony," Arthur said obediently.

"And, yes. Though I'm afraid the girl won't have an easy time of it. Dirty and scarred from tilling dragon soil, with no education, no trades or dowry . . ." His father let out a great sigh, eyes slightly unfocused as if he were lost in thought. "But it's a better future than staying here."

Arthur swallowed hard.

His eighteenth birthday was still a long way off . . . but he wasn't sure what he would do.

He was grateful his father didn't ask.

His father collected the paperwork and tapped it into a pile. "I believe the Roy family has some books," he said. "I'll see what they want to trade in exchange for borrowing."

New guilt made Arthur squirm. "You don't have to do that."

His father just gave him a tight smile and nodded to the woodstove.

"Cut those vegetables for dinner and mind your skills."

Over the next few days, Arthur almost regretted telling his father about the card.

He was used to working hard. Their village was small, and people became ill and died regularly. No traders ever stopped by. Their clothing and other luxury items such as thread and planks of precut wood were provided on a donation basis by the baron when the ration carts arrived.

As convicted families sent to the borders for their crimes, they were allowed no real trade jobs.

So everything not provided by the baron had to be made by hand and bartered or traded for with other village families: lye soap, woven baskets, fruits and vegetables from hidden gardens . . . anything and everything had a price.

Children were pressed into service from the time they could stand—even if it was small chores like taking out feed to the chickens or scouring the nearby woods for twigs to add to the cookfires.

Arthur was used to hard work, but in the past, there had always been down-time. Hours, even half days where he could sneak away and be with his friends.

Ever since he told his father about the card, he had been kept close to home doing chore after chore in a deliberate, methodical process. Yesterday after reading and writing, he was set to helping his father mend furniture. He'd gotten a new skill for that right away.

Today, he was tasked with chopping wood. It was something he had done often in the past. He wasn't too surprised when, on the third log, he received a message:

New skill gained: Wood Chopping (General Class)
Due to your previous experience and your card's bonus traits, you automatically start this skill at level 5.

With a small smile, Arthur brushed the message away and picked out a new log. He set it in place, took up the ax . . . and hesitated.

There was nothing different about the log that he could see, but he had the vague sense of a flaw in the wood. If he brought his ax down just right of center . . .

Arthur swung the ax and missed his mark by two inches. Enough to split the wood a quarter of the way down the log.

He backed up and aimed again. This time he hit the mark straight on. With a louder crack than usual, the log split into three chunks—two neat thirds, and one ragged, thanks to his first bad hit.

New skill level: Wood Chopping (General Class)
Level 6

That was another thing he had noticed—what his father liked to call "part of a pattern"—was that when he followed these hunches the card was more likely to reward him with a skill level. Those led to more of a likelihood of hunches.

Last night while he had been sent to get more roots for supper, one of the hunches had led him to a beetroot that looked touched by the scourge. That happened sometimes, despite all their precautions.

Luckily, Arthur was able to throw it out before the scourge spread to the whole bucket. Eating scourge-touched food would have been a disaster.

On top of that, he had received another skill-up for his cooking, raising its level higher than his **Fire Making**.

As Arthur lined up another log to cut, he glanced at his internal chart.

General Skills:
Fire Making - 7
Furniture Repair - 3

Tidying - 3
Wood Chopping - 6

Cooking Class:
Basic Meal Preparation - 9
Knife Work - 5

Scholarship Class:
Basic Reading - 7
Basic Writing - 5

He inwardly grimaced at the **Tidying** skill he'd picked up while making his bed every morning. Not that it was bad, but along with the cooking classes . . . well, he could imagine what Ernie would have said: All he needed was breadmaking and he might make somebody a good housewife.

Better not say that around Yuma or any of the other women. Not if he didn't want a swat with a spoon.

Before he knew it, he'd finished chopping today's logs. Arthur carefully set them in the shed for seasoning—bark side down.

He headed back into the cottage to see his father sitting at their repaired table. His father was bent with a needle and thread, carefully stitching Arthur's sister's old stuffed bear back together.

Instantly, he felt a pang for thinking of such things as women's work.

"Do you want me to help?"

His father didn't glance up from his work. "I don't suppose you have a skill for sewing?"

"No."

"Well, I may not have skills, but I have experience." He carefully inserted the needle under the bear's chin, making the stitch so tiny it would be impossible to see without tipping the toy's head upward.

Arthur went to the kettle and poured some fresh water into a pot to set on the woodstove. They'd be eating potatoes again tonight, more likely than not.

"Hey, Dad, if I go out and, I don't know, start lifting buckets full of rocks, do you think I'll get a skill for strength?"

That might offset the **Tidying** skill . . .

His father rose out of his chair to check out the window hole. They still hadn't replaced the glass and likely wouldn't for a long time. Then he turned and shook his head.

"No, each card has a specific power. Yours seems to be limited to skills only. If you wanted something for strength, you would have to add a body-modification type to your deck."

He slumped. "That means no magic, either?"

"I'm afraid not. You don't have access to mana, do you?"

Arthur frowned and shook his head. He'd been over his internal card deck countless times over the last few days. There was no mention of mana anywhere.

Sitting back down at the table, his father took up the bear and the thread. "Most cards are part of a set—you can think of them as brother and sister cards. Generally, they come in a set of five."

His eyes widened. "There are four others like mine?"

"Not quite like yours. Each card in the world is unique, even if the differences between them are slight. For example, one generalized water mage may be able to work with only salt water, others a certain volume or water temperature." He shook his head and returned to the subject. "If I had to guess, other cards within your set would be body enhancement, combat, magic, and of course, the Special card."

"Mine's a Legendary rank, so if someone else has one in my set, they're probably nobles?"

"High nobles," his father confirmed. "Nothing like our local pissant Baron Kane. The world out there is much bigger than you know."

Arthur frowned in thought. "What's a Special card?"

Calvan's lips twitched in a smile as if he had been expecting that question. "You've seen a regular deck of cards? Think of the high cards: Aces, Kings, Queens, and Jacks. Well, the Special Card would fit into the joker category. It's the card that is slightly outside the norm and usually has the power to upset the rest."

"It's the strongest?"

"Not necessarily. It's a wild card, so they usually have some of the minor abilities of each other card in the set. A Special Card in your set will likely have some skill bonus—not as large as yours, and with some hefty restrictions. Someone with only a Special won't be able to compete alone against anyone else in their own set. The real power of the Special card comes when it's added to the rest of the set. The Special card is the only one which can add powers to other cards, but only within their own set." He smiled at Arthur as if imparting a secret.

"Have you ever seen someone who had a whole set?" Arthur asked, awed.

His father shook his head. "No, it's vanishingly rare nowadays. Even pairs and so on are risky. It's too much power in one person's hands. The crown has encouraged nobles to split sets for generations."

"Oh." Arthur tried not to feel a little disappointment at that . . . and the knowledge that there was another card out there like his, but which would give him magic or strength.

At the same time, he had been beyond lucky to get *any* card at all. Even if all it did was help him chop potatoes a little better.

Speaking of potatoes, the water was starting to boil.

Arthur went to the potato bucket, dunked 'em in the wash water, and set to chopping. With his Cooking Class **Knife Work** skills, he found it almost easy to cut the lumpy potatoes into equal-sized squarish cubes.

When he was done, he picked them up using the side of his knife to help him scoop and put them in the water to boil.

New skill level: Knife Work (Cooking Class)
Level 6
New skill level: Basic Meal Preparation (Cooking Class)
Level 10

For reaching level 10, your skill has been upgraded from Basic to Apprentice.

Arthur blinked. He was still looking at the boiling water, and it occurred to him that the potatoes might taste a bit better with some salt.

Salt was, of course, expensive. So he took only a pinch and added it to the boiling water. Still, it was better than nothing.

Grinning, he turned to tell his dad of the apprentice upgrade.

There was a knock at the door.

Arthur's heart froze. He turned, half expecting the baron's men to come piling in with the Treasure Seeker in tow.

But the knock was soft and tentative.

"Stay there," his father said and rose to check the door.

It wasn't as if the cottage was large. Arthur was easily able to see as his father open the door.

Old Mable stood on the other side, one gnarled hand wringing the other in anxiety.

"Calvan," she said. "We need you to *attend*."

His father let out a long breath.

What Mable meant was that his father was meant to attend someone's death. To officially witness it.

Because living and working in a borderland village was a punishment and no one was allowed to escape, deaths had to be carefully recorded. Calvan was the closest they had to a leader, and he knew how to fill out the needed paperwork.

"Who is it?" Calvan asked.

"Amanda Youngblood and her son."

Arthur's breath felt like it froze in his chest.

"Ernie?"

CHAPTER 9

Arthur! Arthur, wait—" his father called, but Arthur was already out the door and pelting down the road.

It can't be real. It can't be him, he thought desperately, trying to remember if there was another Youngblood family by that name. Someone, anyone other than his friend. Sometimes, if the crime against the crown were serious enough, an entire extended family could be sent to the border towns.

But Mable had said Amanda's son. Amanda Youngblood had only one living child left.

No, Arthur thought. Ernie couldn't be dying. He'd just seen him, what, three days ago?

But scourge-born sicknesses took people that fast.

The flu that had taken the life of his mother and sister had burned through the entire village like wildfire. It seemed like everyone had caught it at once.

Distantly, he heard his father shout again. Arthur was already well down the lane that led to the village.

Arthur had raced his father before—short sprints up and down the dirt road. They were rare occasions when his father was in a good mood and wasn't exhausted from working the fields or just trying to survive.

Always before, Calvan's longer legs won out. Arthur was small for his age, never quite hitting those growth spurts his mother used to promise were right around the corner.

Now, before he realized it, he had well outdistanced his father.

He wasn't even out of breath.

Despite his worry for his friend and the blunt edge of pending grief, Arthur wondered if it was possible to get a running skill.

. . . He should have told Ernie the news about the missing card the other day—not that Arthur had it, he wasn't stupid—but that the baron had lost it.

The baron had ended up announcing it to the village anyway, and Ernie loved to gossip. It would have made him so happy to know something before everyone else . . .

Ernie and his mother lived close to the village square in a ramshackle hut that was smaller even than Arthur's cottage. Like Arthur, he'd once had a larger family, too. One sibling had died from the same flu that had killed Arthur's mother and sister. Another brother died later on from a bad cut gone scourge-rotten. Ernie's father died out in the fields. One day, he simply clutched his chest and fell down dead.

People said it occasionally happened to uncarded men.

Anyway, for a while now, it had just been Ernie and his mother in their house.

As Arthur ran up, puffing but not entirely out of breath, he saw several adults standing outside Ernie's house. All wore grave expressions.

Arthur tried to barrel past them, but a man named Sam caught him around the shoulders and pulled him short.

"Where do you think you're going, Arthur? Where is your father?"

"Behind me. Where's Ernie? Is he . . ." Arthur couldn't finish.

"He and his mother are very sick," Sam said kindly. "Yuma is in there with her healing herbs. The men are to stay out and not get in her way."

That wasn't the reason. Every able-bodied person got well clear of a house filled with a scourge-sickness. Yuma, with her stumpy legs, didn't bother.

But I won't get sick! Arthur nearly blurted. He pinched his lips, horrified with himself. Stupid. Stupid. Only carded people didn't need to worry about getting sick.

Sam looked on with sympathy, misreading Arthur's expression for him trying not to cry. "We'll talk to your father about it once he gets here—oh, here he is now."

Arthur turned to see his father jogging up the same lane. Mable, who'd followed, was much farther back.

Calvan looked annoyed but didn't say anything specifically to Arthur as he came up. Instead, he looked to Sam. "How bad is it?"

"Bad," Sam said flatly. "We think it's not catching, but there wasn't much food in the house. I saw what they had left before I got out—it's scourge-infected."

Calvan let out a long sigh and rubbed a hand down his face.

"Yuma's making her medicine inside," Arthur said quickly, looking hard at his father. "I can . . . I can help."

It was a desperate hope. If healing was a skill, if he could learn from Yuma . . . then maybe the card would offer some wisdom to help Ernie and his mother.

His father hesitated, likely thinking the same thing. "You're sure it's not in the air, Sam?"

"Yuma didn't seem worried about that."

Calvan nodded. "Okay, Arthur. Go in and give her a hand, but mind you don't get in her way."

Arthur nodded, and Sam stepped aside for him to open the door. Neither one of the men followed him.

The inside of the house had an unpleasant smell of sewage, like a privy bucket had overflowed. It was one room with a cookfire on one end and a bed on the other. Ernie once told Arthur a story of the edge of the blankets falling into the coals and the family waking to a bed half on fire. Being Ernie, he said it with a laugh, like it was the biggest joke in the world.

Now every blanket in the house—even one with old char spots on it—was piled up on the single bed. Two shapes lay listless and unmoving.

Yuma sat on a chair, squished between the bed and the table, frantically grinding herbs with a mortar and pestle. She looked up as Arthur came in.

"What do you think you're doing, boy?"

"I came to help." Edging up, he looked at the shapeless lumps, but they were so well covered he couldn't see either of their faces. Neither stirred at the sound of him coming in.

"Ernie is your friend, right?" Yuma sighed. "Come on in. They're sleeping right now."

Arthur noticed she didn't make a point of keeping her voice down. Clearly, she wasn't worried about waking them.

"I can help," Arthur said. "You know I can chop stuff and . . . and I can fetch whatever you need."

"What you can do is grind these herbs. It takes some strength, and I'm afraid I don't have much in me." She pushed the mortar and pestle over. "Grind it down hard. It needs to be a powder. I'll work on mincing the ginger root."

Arthur eagerly bent to start grinding. The stuff inside the mortar looked like flakes of bark. "What is this?"

"White willow root bark. Don't make that face! It's very expensive and good to ease the fever. The ginger and peppermint I'll add will help the stomach, too. It's going to make a dreadful tea, but if they drink it and manage to keep the fluids down . . . well, maybe."

But she seemed doubtful.

Arthur swallowed. "Sam said they ate scourge-touched food? If they were hungry, they coulda come to us . . ."

"Chances were, they didn't know. It can take people like that, if you're not paying attention to where you're planting your crops. Amanda has been scatterbrained ever since her husband died, and the boy doesn't know how to cook," Yuma said.

Will they be all right? Arthur wanted to know, but he was afraid of the answer if he asked. The still forms under the blankets were an answer itself.

He could imagine Amanda not only planting in a bad spot but not noticing the vegetables were bad. People had called her a dim bulb before, though not within her hearing.

The villagers weren't allowed to have their own gardens or take from the field harvests. All their food came from the baron as payment.

Of course, they had their own gardens anyway—just not out in the open. And they stole whatever they could from the fields, ripe or not. Just to spite the baron.

Though it was hard to find safe places to plant. Most found a spot on the edge of the recently reclaimed fields, where the baron's men were less likely to look. However, there might be patches that weren't healed of the scourge and would still leak poison into the plants.

Though Arthur had seen scourge-tainted vegetables before. How could Ernie or Amanda ever think they were good to eat?

Because they were hungry and exhausted and Amanda never paid attention at the best of times. Ernie didn't like to do what he called "women's chores," so he wouldn't have paid attention.

Arthur sighed. Maybe women's chores weren't so bad if not learning them got you sick.

Suddenly, he received an alert.

New skill level: Apprentice Meal Preparation (Cooking Class)
Level 11

"It's not a meal, it's medicine!" he snarled.

Yuma looked up. "What was that?"

He shook his head. "Nothing."

"Hmm. Keep grinding."

He did, redoubling his efforts until it was a fine powder.

When Yuma asked, he checked the kettle, which hung on a hook over the fire. It was boiling, so Yuma had him pour it into two mugs.

They mixed the herbs—the willow bark, dried peppermint leaves Yuma had already powdered, and the finely minced ginger. Then Yuma directed him to stir them into the cups until the powders were dissolved as much as possible.

Finally, he got the skill notification he was looking for.

New skill gained:
Herbal Medicine Preparation (Healing Class)
Due to learning the basics of this skill from another, your starting level
has been increased.

Because your teacher is not a master in this class, the possible experience
gained has been reduced. You automatically start this skill at level 5.

He had finally gained the skill, but no great revelations came to Arthur, other
than they should let the tea cool. From the way Ernie and Amanda had not
stirred, they'd have to tip it down their throats.

Now he could hear raspy breathing from the bed. He wasn't sure who it was
coming from, but it sounded terrible.

The mug he was staring at became blurry. Angrily, Arthur blinked back the
beginnings of tears.

He'd had the card for days now. If he had worked harder on his skills, or
focused on useful ones instead of woodcutting or mending furniture, he might
have gotten more levels. Somehow.

And done what?

Herbs were rare. He couldn't just go around grinding things from people's
gardens to practice his skill. He didn't know he'd need it until now!

And the fact was, he'd never heard of anyone who ate scourge-food live to
tell the tale.

Arthur continued stirring the tea so he didn't cry.

Finally, Yuma declared it done.

"Help me sit them up. Ernie first."

When Arthur pulled back the covers, he found his friend waxy, pale, and
shivering. A terrible smell came up from him, and he didn't stir as Arthur sat him
up. He was limp as a fresh corpse.

The blanket that fell away from his arm exposed veins that stood out dark
against his pallid skin.

Yuma pursed her lips but said nothing.

Tipping back Ernie's head, they slowly, very slowly, poured the tea in.

Ernie swallowed reflexively. Arthur knew the tea must have tasted awful, but
Ernie made no reaction. His eyes didn't even flutter.

They tucked him back in and did the same for Amanda. She was the one with
the raspy breathing, and when they pulled back the blankets, she looked even
worse. The veins had spread up her neck to her face.

In the end, Arthur got another skill: **Basic Nursecraft** at level 3, with the
added wisdom of maybe moving the two to lay on their sides to help them breathe.

But there was no cure. He only had the most basic knowledge and no tools.
Worse, the scourge had gotten a head start.

His friend was dying.

The best that could be said was that with the infection already inside them,
they were oblivious to any pain. Not like when people died of a scourge-infected
cut and were awake and aware as the infection traveled up their body.

Arthur's father came in to witness the last breaths and record the time and reason for kingdom officials.

Amanda died around sunset. Arthur made another infusion of tea—this one without the willow bark because Yuma had to keep the last scraps for the village.

The tea didn't help.

He didn't cry as Ernie's rattling breaths finally stopped. Just stared at the boy who had been his friend and felt so angry. So angry at the baron, who never gave them enough food . . . for condemning them there at all.

Ernie hadn't done anything wrong. Neither had Amanda. Her husband had been caught stealing horses, and the whole family had been condemned. They hadn't been allowed to leave when he died.

And Arthur was angry at himself, too. For being too weak and too stupid to help.

He and his father walked back to the cottage in silence. His father slung an arm over his shoulder.

"Are you okay?"

Arthur shook his head. "Dad? I want to read some more. I want to . . . I need to do something. I need to grow stronger."

The arm tightened briefly before his father dropped it. "You will," he said. "I can *promise* you that."

CHAPTER 10

To Arthur, the next few days passed in a blur.

His newly forged determination to learn as many skills as he could, to not let another tragedy happen again on his watch, was still there. But it was cloaked by a fog of grief so choking that he had trouble rising from his bed to go about his day.

Though he went about his chores, he did so in a listless haze. Without putting effort into what he was doing, none of his skills progressed.

It was a vicious cycle, where he felt like he was betraying the memory of his friend by not advancing . . . and yet couldn't find the inner willpower to break free, work, and progress.

He was used to death in the village. Before he had lost his mother and sister, all the other boys and girls his age had been chipped away, one by one.

But Ernie was different. They'd been instant best friends since Arthur had come to the village as a little kid.

Now he was gone, too.

He wanted to snap out of it, to somehow rebuild his life. But as with fixing up the cottage . . . he was afraid that if he did, the baron or the scourge would come and take it all away.

It didn't help that his father was hardly in the cottage.

Arthur was used to him being out and about: Calvan was an important man who often took it upon himself to help out whenever he could. But even lost in grief, Arthur knew he could have used his father's guidance.

What was more important, the village or his son?

That kernel of anger grew hotter, like a lump of banked coal in his heart given new tinder. On the evening of the fourth day, Arthur rose from his cot and found himself stalking around the house, clenching and unclenching his fists.

He hated it here. Hated the village, hated the scourge and the baron and . . . and everything!

Irritated with himself and the world, he went out to chop wood. It felt good just to work until he sweated and feel the bite of the ax in the logs.

Because he was doing it without care and focus, his skill didn't progress. That was important to discover, but he found himself irritated . . . and thinking of Ernie.

There were no funerals in the village. People didn't have time, and deaths were too common.

Soon another family would move into Amanda and Ernie's house, if it hadn't happened already. Arthur hadn't gone into the village yet to find out.

Though, according to the charts he had learned to read, there would be a new dragon soil shipment soon. He would have to visit the village then.

His thoughts halted in surprise when he heard the clop-clop-clop of hooves on the lane behind the cottage.

The baron's men, he thought with a jolt of fear.

There had been no word of what had happened when the baron's men searched the bandit camp. His father had said the villagers guessed they'd found what they were looking for . . . though Arthur and Calvan knew differently.

Chances were the baron had widened his search to other border villages. But he could return at any time. It was doubtful he would let it go.

With dread, Arthur put down the ax and walked around the house. The back lane stretched to the east—away from the deadlands and toward the middle of the kingdom. It was common for the baron's men to come up from that direction.

But it wasn't uniformed and armed men.

It was his father, accompanying a stranger who was riding on an old donkey.

This was unusual for a few reasons. There were no strangers in the village. Not unless they were newly assigned there, fresh from being convicted for their crimes. Those people were never allowed to bring livestock.

This man didn't have the look of a borderland villager. Though he was short, there was extra flesh on his bones. No scars or pockmarks to be seen. Though he was unshaved, and his hair was long and gray, he didn't have that pinched look to suggest he'd been sick recently.

The donkey, too, looked well-fed and relaxed.

Calvan saw Arthur and waved him over. "Arthur, glad to see you're up. Red's going to need someone to help brush down his donkey."

The man, Red, though there was nothing red left in his salt-and-pepper hair, guffawed. "That's Arthur? Why, he's sprouted up like a weed. He has to be what, nine, ten years old?"

"I'm twelve," Arthur muttered but came over to do as he was told anyway.

Red dismounted and handed over the donkey's reins. "Brush is in the left saddle pack." Then, with a long look Arthur's way, he and Calvan walked to the cottage.

Occasionally the children of villagers were made to take care of the horses that carted in dragon soil, so Arthur had some knowledge of what to do. Keeping a firm hold on the reins, he clucked his tongue and started toward the side of the cottage.

A horse would follow immediately. The donkey hesitated for a long moment, turning its shaggy head to look toward where its master had gone.

"Come on," Arthur muttered. "I got a patch of juicy grass around the corner. Hasn't been scourge-touched for generations, I think."

That seemed to be what the donkey was waiting for. It reluctantly followed him.

Arthur led the donkey past his mother's and sister's gravestones. Flowers had already sprouted from the dragon soil offering he'd given it the other day. Arthur hadn't noticed until now, and for a few moments, he forgot about his grief.

The donkey reached for the flowers as if to eat them.

Pulling the donkey's head up, he took a firmer hold on the reins and moved it well out of reach of the graves. Then he tied the reins to a low branch of a tree.

The donkey bent its head again to crop at the grass nearby. Arthur went around to pull up even more grass, setting a pile in front of the animal to keep it occupied.

He rummaged in the saddlebag for the brush and found it right away.

The donkey nipped at him half-heartedly, almost as if to tell him to hurry up. With a chuckle, Arthur pushed its head away, took off the saddle and blanket to stow to the side, and started brushing the animal down.

Odd. There was not a trace of scourge-dust on the beast. Just regular road dirt and a little redder than Arthur was used to seeing.

Wherever this donkey and his rider had been, it wasn't close to scourge-lands.

Arthur had just swiped his brush for the last time when he received a notification.

New skill gained:
Basic Equine Care (Animal Husbandry Class)
Due to your previous experience and your card's bonus traits, you automatically start this skill at level 4.

Smiling softly, Arthur patted the donkey and scratched up its neck to its big ears. The donkey leaned into him.

It was a small thing, but he felt the weight of his grief lift just a little.

When he returned to the cottage, it was to find that his father and the stranger had taken the only two chairs.

His father had a broad grin on his face which was so unlike him that it took Arthur aback.

Before he could recover, Calvan gestured to the woodstove and the table, which was loaded down with several sacks. "Red has brought some food to pay for his visit here." He slapped the man on the shoulder. "Why don't you see what you can do with those ingredients?"

"It ain't much. Just some supplies I picked up here and there on the road," Red said.

With a silent nod, Arthur went to the table, surprised to see more bundles out of view behind the bags. His eyes widened. There were several large fish wrapped in wax paper, at least five different pouches of dried herbs—most of which he didn't have names for, but all smelled delicious—huge potatoes nearly the size of two man's fists pressed together, freshly picked greens, and one strange fruit that was a bright, sunshiny yellow.

He glanced up to see the two men watching him.

"Your father says you know how to cook?" Red asked.

There was a particular weight to his words, but Arthur simply nodded.

"I can. How much of this can I use?"

Red barked out a laugh. "All of it, of course. Men got to eat, don't they?"

Maybe so, but this was more food than Arthur was used to seeing for three days' worth of meals.

His stomach growled. He hadn't managed to eat much since Ernie—

Arthur shoved that thought away before the grief could drag him back down.

He reached for the potatoes and focused his mind on his card skill. Then he got to work.

The first thing to do was to figure out the herbs. He could tell which was garlic and which was salt, but the rest were a mystery. One of the green herbs smelled like it might be good with the fish. The fish, too, he couldn't recognize, but the meat was red and fatty.

He was used to filleting the bony trout that managed to survive the streams. This large fish was easy in comparison. His knife cut through it like butter.

After laying three large fillets aside and wrapping the fourth to be smoked or eaten for later, Arthur turned his attention back to the herbs. He bruised the green herb and rubbed it all over the fillets, tucking some of the broken leaves here and there.

He rewrapped them in parchment and put them in a dry pot with the last of the herbs to slow cook over the woodstove.

Then he worked to bring the potatoes to a boil in a large pot—adding extra salt to the water to account for the large tubers.

He turned his attention to the greens. They were nothing like the wilted things he was used to. Though they must have been picked hours ago, they were still so crisp, droplets of water leaked out the ends when he cut into them.

Lastly, he turned his attention to the odd fruit. Was it supposed to be a dessert?

"That's a lemon," his father said. He and Red had been quietly talking while Arthur worked, though he'd felt their gazes on him every once in a while. "It's very sour. Best to use it to dress the greens."

Arthur nodded and used his knife to cut into it. The skin was exceptionally thick, the flesh exceptionally juicy. He tasted the tip of his finger, and Red laughed again at the face he pulled.

Hard-won experience with occasional wisdom from his card had carried him so far. But he was at a loss as to what "dress the greens" meant. Sometimes his father spoke fancy like that—words from another life.

Deciding that none of the odd lemon should be wasted, even though it was sour as all get-out, Arthur cut it into thirds. That way each person could decide what to do with theirs. Arthur planned to ditch his part, soon as someone wasn't looking.

The fish was done, and he took it off the heat to steam out for a few minutes. By that time, the potatoes were ready, too. He mashed them quickly and added more salt and some of the garlic.

New skill level: Apprentice Meal Preparation (Cooking Class)
Level 12
+
Level 13

Arthur flinched in surprise, then had to bite his bottom lip to keep back a grin. Two levels out of one meal!

Not a surprise considering the quality of ingredients and all the methods he'd had to use.

A new burst of wisdom came to him, and he took one of the lemon slices, squeezing it over the fish. There. Done.

He grabbed some of the plates that had been recently scavenged from the broken ones and served the food out.

Red's bushy eyebrows lifted as he saw the dish. They went even higher when he bit into the fish.

"Well now, this is nearly as good as one of those fancy restaurants in Calla."

Arthur nodded, cheeks bulging. He'd dug in the moment he was able.

"He's always been a talented boy," Calvan said for him.

"And you can read and write, too."

"Yes, sir," Arthur said thickly, through more potatoes. "Both."

"Hmm."

Red and Calvan exchanged a look. Arthur wondered what it was about but was more interested in clearing his plate.

"And how did Bella treat you?"

"Who? Oh," he realized. "The donkey. Fine. She tried to nip me but didn't manage it."

"But she let you brush her down?" He seemed skeptical when Arthur nodded.

Abruptly, Red pushed his chair back and put the plate to the side. "Pardon me."

With that, he went to the door.

Arthur glanced to his father, who shook his head, eyes to the door.

A few moments later, Red returned with the saddlebag in hand. Now he was smiling.

"I'm sorry, Calvan. I have to admit that I laid a trap for your son: There was a pouch of money plain within sight of the donkey's brush. But I just counted. Every one of the coins is still there."

"I wouldn't have stolen!" Arthur said, indignant, a few crumbs flying. The truth was, he hadn't even seen the pouch, nor would he have known what to do with the money. It wasn't like traders came to town.

For the first time in a long time, his father looked relaxed. He nodded. "He's an honest boy, too. Takes after his dad that way."

"I hope not." Red snorted. "But I take your point. Fine, Calvan. He's undersized but clearly a hard worker. Yes, he can join my crew."

The last delicious bite of fish seemed to lodge halfway in Arthur's throat.

CHAPTER 11

Arthur coughed his throat clear and then stared at his father in disbelief. "What do you mean?" His voice grew higher pitched. "You're sending me away?"

Red guffawed again. "You can't seriously tell me you want to stay here."

"Red, it's all he knows." Calvan turned to Arthur. "In other villages, it's normal to apprentice children your age to masters."

"But we're not in another village. We can't leave. It's against the law. If the baron finds out . . ." Arthur didn't know much, but he knew that. His father was in charge of the record-keeping and would be held accountable if someone went missing. There were no funerals, but bodies were strictly accounted for—his dad said the baron got compensation from the crown, whatever that meant.

Calvan glanced at Red. "Do you mind giving me a minute?"

"Take your time." Red got up heavily from the chair. "But I need to be back on the road an hour before sunset. I'm not staying in this scourge-haunted place."

Calvan nodded sharply, and with another long look toward Arthur, Red escorted himself out.

Arthur didn't see the point. The cottage walls were so thin that Red would be able to easily hear their conversation unless they kept it to whispers.

"Arthur, listen to me." His father rose from his chair and placed heavy hands on Arthur's shoulders. Arthur tried to wiggle away, but his father held him firm and made the boy look at him. "You don't know what it is to live outside this village. I don't think you realize that it's a death trap."

"My best friend just died!" Arthur snapped back. "I know! But Dad . . ." He lowered his voice. "You don't need to worry about me getting sick."

With a glance at the broken-out windows, his father lowered his voice too. "No, now I need to worry about them finding you with a card. Eventually, the baron will return. Maybe he'll have his Treasure Seeker or a Lie Detector look at the children . . . or maybe in a few weeks, or a few months, people will realize you're shooting up in height. That you're growing taller and stronger and never seem to get sick."

"I can stay here in the cottage and only come out when the dragon soil's delivered. Please, don't send me away . . ."

"Why do you want to stay?" His father's expression hardened. "For me? Arthur, I don't want you here."

Arthur leaned back. It felt like he had been slapped.

Dropping his hands, Calvan rubbed at his face. "That came out wrong, but it is the truth. You deserve far more than can be offered here. You deserve a life. And to expand your skills."

"I . . ." An offer to give up the card was on the tip of his tongue. Maybe they could sell it to Red for extra supplies. That would take care of many of their problems—at least until the baron's men came to destroy it again, or outright rob them.

His hand clutched convulsively at his chest. The words didn't come.

He didn't know quite when it happened, but somewhere over the last few days, the card had settled into his heart.

Learning new skills had been the first bright spot, the first purely good thing in . . . he couldn't remember.

Yes, he couldn't save Ernie, but there was the promise in the future of saving someone else.

Not if he gave up his card, though.

His father seemed to sense the direction of his thoughts. His expression softened.

"I would have kicked you out on your rear when you turned eighteen, any-way. And as I said, it's not unusual for a twelve-year-old boy to go off and learn a trade."

"But . . ." This conversation was getting away from him. Now that the shock was wearing off, he found he didn't despise the idea of leaving the village. He just wished his father could come, too. It felt too childish to say, "I don't want to leave home." Instead, he latched on to one of the few objections he had left. "We aren't allowed to leave until we're grown up—until we're adults, I mean. The baron's men will know that I'm gone. They'll want to account for a body—"

He stopped as a horrific thought occurred to him. His eyes snapped to his father, a question in there.

Calvan's answer was a grimace.

"You're gonna say that Ernie's body is . . . mine?" It was spoken in a hushed whisper.

Arthur was horrified, though he had to admit that had Ernie been alive, he would have said it was a good trick. He and Arthur used to love talking about how they would like to pull pranks on the baron's men.

New grief flashed over him. He scrubbed at his face with the side of his arm to keep the tears back.

"I will report Amanda and Ernie's defection from the village in a few weeks. It will take that long for the baron's men to go through the rolls for dragon soil duty," Calvan said it so calmly it was clear he had been planning this. "It's not too unusual for a pretty woman Amanda's age to run off with a bandit husband."

That felt wrong to the memory of Amanda. She had been a little stupid, but never unfaithful to the memory of Ernie's father.

Arthur had to admit that Ernie would have liked the thought of living with dangerous bandits, though.

"And everyone else will just say the same?" Arthur demanded.

"I have some pull in the village. You wouldn't be the first child that we hustled out."

"Who else?" Arthur asked.

His father gave him a stern look. "For the safety of their families, we don't speak of it. In any case, I still have some connections back to my old life. Though they can be dubious." He glanced outside, almost as if he expected Red to be listening right below the window hole.

"What does Red do?" Arthur asked. It occurred to him that he should have asked this before but had been taken too much by surprise.

"He runs a caravan moving trade goods from one part of the kingdom to another. I suspect not everything he moves is legal, though he doesn't trade anything particularly despicable."

Arthur had no idea what that was meant to mean, or why his father acted like it was supposed to be reassuring.

"It will be hard work," his father continued. "And Arthur . . ." Again, he glanced toward the window and lowered his voice to a bare whisper. "You must *not* tell anyone of your card. A Legendary card is more valuable than you can imagine. As soon as you can, add a second card to your deck."

Arthur stared at his father as if he had grown a second head. He had needed almost unfathomable luck to get one card. He couldn't imagine two. "A second card?" he repeated dumbly.

"You will be growing up soon and fast. Some of that can be put to your age, but those who know the signs of a carded child will wonder. Get your hands on a low-ranked card—any card. Save up your money or steal one if you have to."

"Steal?!"

Stealing wasn't something he was unfamiliar with. All the villagers stole from the baron's harvests any time they could. It was a matter of survival.

But to steal from someone else . . . well, that was a matter of survival, too, wasn't it? Arthur wanted to live. That wasn't what shocked him.

What did shock him was that the only surefire way to steal a card from some-one else was when they died. He had seen the red dragon harvest the cards from those guards. Their decks had been for the taking.

He looked at his father beseechingly, silently pleading for him to take it back, to suggest something else . . . to confirm he wasn't saying what Arthur thought he had said.

Calvan's hard gaze didn't look away from him for a moment. "It's hard in a different way than it is in this village. I think you'll do well. You have the tools." His gaze flicked to Arthur's heart and then back again.

Because of the card, Arthur realized.

His father wanted him to leave when he was a full-grown man. But now that he had the card, he could leave earlier.

"Dad, what did you do?" he blurted. "Why did we get sent here?"

He had asked that question before when he was little and didn't know any better. His father had never answered. But now, at the end, he deserved to know.

His father heaved a sigh.

"Politics, mostly. It wasn't one thing. I got on the wrong side of the king. My duchy was taken from me and given to one of the king's loyal men, instead. Twenty generations of rule, from one first-born child to the next in an unbroken line . . . gone." He gave a mirthless chuckle. "My cards were taken from me, and I was given the choice of a swift execution of me and my family there, or a linger-ing death while serving the kingdom out in the borderlands. You're the reason why I'm glad I didn't choose the swift option."

Arthur swallowed. "But . . . you'll be okay, right? When I'm gone?" It was the first time he admitted he was going. Because he was.

His father could be a hard man when he wanted to be, and Arthur did not doubt that he would truss up his son and throw him on the back of the donkey if he had to.

More than that, though . . . Arthur wanted to go. He didn't want to leave his father, but he was the only reason to stay. There was nothing for him in the vil-lage. His mother and sister were long dead, his best friend was gone. He'd almost blabbed about not getting sick in front of Sam, and soon he would get too good at these skills. He would finally hit that growth spurt.

People would start questioning, especially if another sickness came around and he was the only one not ill.

The villagers were all united in hate against the baron . . . but starvation was hard to endure, and the baron rewarded those who snitched on others.

Everyone hated the snitches afterward, but Arthur would still be dead, and the card would be in the baron's hands.

Arthur could take the card away from the baron. Keep him searching forever.

That . . . that was satisfying.

"Arthur," Calvan said heavily. "I will be happy knowing you are as far away from here as possible."

"I'll come back," Arthur said. "I'll be a great man. You'll see."

He fell into his father's warm embrace. Calvan wasn't a man who hugged often, but he was strong and warm and smelled like the cookfire of home.

I will come back, Arthur promised. *I'm a duke's son, and I'll find a way to get you so far away that the baron will never find you again. Then he'll have to till the dragon soil himself.*

When it was time to go, Red showed Arthur how to blanket and saddle Bella the donkey. That earned him another skill level in **Equine Animal Care**.

However, there was only room for one on the donkey's back. Arthur was to walk beside his new master, as befitted an apprentice.

He looked back once to see if his dad was watching from the cottage. The door was closed, but he thought he caught movement behind the hole where the windows used to be.

The small cottage, with the thin tracing of smoke coming out of the chimney, was his last sight of the place he called home.

PART 2
THE SECOND CARD

CHAPTER 12

The first time Arthur was smacked across the face took him completely by surprise.

It was his second night away from his father's cottage, and the first traveling with the trader's caravan. He and Red had met up with the rest of the group earlier that day.

Red ran what he called a small caravan. Three giant canvas-covered carts hauled by four oxen apiece. There was a host of smaller carts, too, leading the group and trailing after. These were usually pulled by donkeys or small, broken-down horses.

Each cart had its own team of men to accompany it. These teams, Red explained, all paid a certain amount to Red to travel along with him. In return, Red knew the best waypoints and cut-through trails to get where they needed to go. He paid camping fees and introduced sellers of goods to interested buyers in different towns. Red's personal cart was filled with supplies to support the rest of the caravan—everything from food to extra bedding. All came as part of the fee.

There was also safety in numbers while traveling on the kingdom's backroads.

Arthur had nodded along and kept his mouth shut. Partially because he was more homesick than he thought was possible. It was like there was a gaping hole in his heart, and he was half afraid if he opened his mouth, he'd just start bawling like an infant.

The other reason he kept quiet was that he was intimidated. Every one of the men who followed the carts was big and brawny and obviously carded. They made Red look puny in comparison.

For the first few hours, Arthur followed along on foot behind Red, who had hooked his donkey to help haul his personal supply wagon. Red rode in the driver's seat and didn't offer Arthur a seat alongside him.

Finally, Arthur got up the courage to speak.

"Red? You're not carded?" It was one of the first things he'd said all day.

Red looked down at him and pursed his lips. "That's a mighty personal thing you're asking there, *Ernest*."

Arthur tried not to flinch at the name. Along the way, Red had explained that it would be for the best—especially while they were close to the border villages—that he go by a new name.

The former Rowantree Duchy was on the other side of the kingdom. The surname may not be well-known over here, but it was best not bandied about.

So, Arthur had chosen Ernest Youngblood as an honor to his friend, Ernie.

Yes, Ernie and Amanda would eventually be marked as deserters, but he didn't think they'd be so well-known that people would be out looking for them.

"But as it happens," Red continued, "no. My beliefs forbid it. No tattoos, no piercings, and no gods damned cards." He spat to the side.

"Why?" Arthur asked.

"To alter the body that was given naturally to you . . . well, it ain't right."

Arthur might have looked skeptical because Red smiled grimly at him.

"When you get a bit older, you might be tempted to seek out a card for yourself. I'd advise you to think twice about it. Too many people lean in on their cards to the detriment of everything else. Take me for example: I am the caravan leader, and these carded men . . . well, they pay good coin to ride with me on this piece of road. You remember that."

Soon, Arthur was told to run messages back and forth, up and down the line of moving carts. Most of them were instructions for the lead cart to turn right or left at different junctures, and general announcements of where they would be camping during the night.

Arthur was at a constant jog. If not for the extra stamina his card provided, he would have dropped long ago.

The work beat back his homesickness, and he grew powerfully curious about the other carts. The biggest, in particular, was heaped so high the tops threatened to brush against low branches. It was covered in tight tarps and had an interesting, complex smell.

Having just delivered a message from Red to this cart's leader—Red's second-in-command, whom he just called "Second"—Arthur paused at the back of the cart to peek under the tarp.

He had barely gotten one corner lifted before he felt a blow to the side of his head. It was so strong that it staggered him back a few steps.

Reeling, Arthur's first reaction was to ball his fists and set his stance so he didn't fall, so he could jump back at his attacker, and—

His vision cleared. He stared up (and up and up) at Second.

Second was a bear of a man with dirty black hair that fell to his shoulder, a matching goatee, and a perpetual smirk on his face. That smirk was full in place as he looked down at Arthur.

"You trying to steal from me, you little pissant?"

Arthur loosened his fists. What was wrong with him? Had he seriously been about to attack a man twice his size? "I wasn't stealing!"

"Yes, because I caught you. Go back to your master, pissant."

A couple of the other men chuckled.

Red-faced, Arthur returned to the back of the caravan. He didn't start rubbing his stinging ear until he was well out of sight, not wanting to give Second the satisfaction.

When he got there, Red looked at him. "What's wrong?"

"Second smacked me! And he called me a pissant."

"Your fault for getting in his way. He's a mean son of a bitch. Most of them are."

And that was that.

They might be criminals in the borderland village, but no one hauled off and smacked kids around for something like looking under a tarp of a cart.

Arthur seethed, but he was used to injustice from the baron's men. So, he seethed quietly.

By evening, he was dismayed to find that his new nickname had stuck.

Red identified a safe spot to pull off the road and camp as the sun was going down. Then he and Arthur got to work hauling out a truly gigantic stewpot from his cart, pouring in water from a nearby stream, and starting a stew.

Red was a dab hand at cooking for a large number of people. Once he started unloading the cart, Arthur found himself boggling. He had more herbs than Arthur thought existed, dried, chopped, in glass jars and in bags. There were different colors of potatoes, too: blue, yellow, and red, along with the dirty browns he was used to seeing.

Red also had meat. Real beef, which was smoked to jerky. But Arthur had only had beef as a treat a few times in his life.

Arthur bit off a chunk of jerky. Unfortunately, it was within view of one of Second's friends—a spidery-looking man everyone called Hivey.

"Stop stealing food and get to cookin', Pissant!"

This time, Arthur was smacked right across the face.

That didn't feel so unjust as the last time. He would have gotten whacked with a spoon had Yuma caught him doing the same back at the village.

But Arthur still seethed.

Again, Red stayed silent on the subject and simply directed Arthur to grab the powdered soup stock from the cart.

With the stock and the added vegetables they chopped, the soup was done just after the sun had finished setting.

No one complimented Arthur or Red on the stew, even though it was delicious. Mostly, the other men sat around the campfire laughing uproariously at jokes that went over Arthur's head.

Red sold skins of wine for an extra cost, and occasionally someone would yell at the Pissant to sell him one. Arthur would then put down his own bowl of soup and do the transaction, giving the coins to Red, who silently pocketed them.

The only good thing about the meal was that Arthur was allowed seconds and thirds. There was plenty to go around, and Arthur rarely felt so full.

After, he was tasked with doing the dishes, which added another level to his **Tidying** skill.

"Get back to your bedroll," Red said after the last of the dishes were stowed back in the cart. "You look half done-in."

He was indeed tired, and the men looked intent on staying up late, laughing and drinking around the campfire.

After excusing himself, Arthur headed back to where he'd stashed his bedroll, by where Red had tied up the donkeys.

Halfway there, he paused and looked back over his shoulder.

All of the men, including Second and his friends, were still around the campfire. A fire that would destroy their night vision.

No one was watching him.

Arthur stepped off the trail and into the thicker vegetation.

Underbrush crackled at every step. It wasn't the long-dead crackle he was used to in the scourge-lands. This was just dry brush . . . and there was so much of it. It was odd not to have to worry about scourge-dust at all.

He was making too much noise.

Pausing, Arthur took off his boots and held them in one hand, feeling his way carefully forward barefooted.

He had traveled fairly quietly for a few dozen feet when he received a new message.

New skill gained: Basic Stealth (Rogue/Thief Class)
Due to your previous experience and your card's bonus traits, you automatically start this skill at level 4.

He must have gotten extra experience from all that time sneaking around the village with Ernie.

Arthur ruthlessly pushed away the memory before it could overwhelm him and cause him to make a mistake.

Eventually, he was sidelong to Second's cart.

He waited a long moment, triple-checking to make sure no one was around. Then he stepped out of the brush and back onto the trail.

The tarp was tied down tight, so it took him a few moments to find a spot loose enough to lift.

There were leaves underneath. Big, long leaves with a tapered end. There were spots of green left, but most had wilted to muddy brown.

When he took a pinch, it crumbled between his fingers.

Arthur sniffed it, getting an intense smokey-spicy scent that was familiar . . . though he couldn't place it.

He was about to bring it to his tongue to taste when a fuzzy memory rose to his mind. It was old. He couldn't have been more than a toddler.

He and his father were sitting in a rich red room, and his father was stuffing crumbles into his pipe just like this, before he smoked it.

Tobacco, Arthur realized. Second was trading in tobacco leaf.

Immediately, he was disgusted. Was that all? The tarp wasn't there to hide something illegal, just to keep all the product safe.

He'd taken offense just for the excuse to hit Arthur and call him mean names.

Annoyed, Arthur went to the nearest knot that tied the tarp down. He loosened it and then reached in, shifting an armful of the stuff off balance. Just a little.

If no one caught that this corner was loose, that armful had a good chance of falling out the back when the cart lurched into motion tomorrow. It would serve him right.

Arthur quickly returned to the thicker brush and made his way back. He took a long way around, concentrating on being as quiet as possible. For his efforts, he got another level.

New skill level: Basic Stealth (Rogue/Thief Class)
Level 5

That wasn't the only skill with its own class, but it was the only one that had two of them.

"What are classes?" he whispered to himself.

The card didn't answer back.

He wished he could ask someone. Too bad the only friendly face in the caravan was Red, and he didn't like cards.

Still, Arthur smiled to himself. Unlike the **Tidying** skill, he could see some real value to **Stealth**. He resolved to practice it as much as he could.

CHAPTER 13

Arthur's trick worked, though with unexpected consequences. As soon as Second's cart started moving, a small mound of the loose leaf slipped free, fell out of the cart, and landed on the dirt road.

Before it could be run over by another cart, one of Second's men hustled over. He waved over the mound and muttered, "*Let what was broken be remade whole.*"

Instantly, the leaves lifted upward and replaced themselves in the cart, the tarp covering it once more.

The man, now red-faced and panting, wiped at his forehead where he'd broken out in a sweat. That little effort seemed to have cost him a lot. He looked over his shoulder toward Second's direction, as if to make sure the man hadn't seen.

"Dumbass," Red muttered. His second-in-command hadn't been watching, but he had.

"He has . . . uh . . ." Arthur searched a moment for the word. Most of what he knew about cards came from stories. "A Telekinesis card?"

What was a man with the power to move stuff with his mind doing in a trading caravan?

"Hardly." Red rolled his eyes. "From what I've heard, it's some sort of minor trap card."

"How is that a trap?" Arthur asked. "He just fixed something."

"Trap powers activate only when some precondition has been met. Don't ask me the details, you know I'm not carded. But when something breaks or goes wrong in a minor way, he can undo it . . . if he gets there fast enough. Damn fool nearly exhausts himself when a little elbow grease will serve just fine." Red waved a hand in disgust, not bothering to keep his voice down. "He could have just reached down and picked up what had fallen much easier, but nooo."

"Hey, Red," Second called from his cart. "Stop telling the Pissant all our trade secrets."

"It's no secret your teamster's an idiot," Red called back. "And his gimmick is on cooldown till sunset. Better hope you don't break a wheel today."

Second shot a glare toward his boss, but then aimed an even darker one at the man with the trap card.

Turning, Red winked at Arthur. "Between you and me, there's nothing I like better than winding up the carded. They're all jealous over each other's piddly little powers, and all think that they would be able to do it better if they had the card instead."

Arthur looked down. He had been thinking at that moment what he would have done with a trap card.

"Hmm," Red said, seeing. "I keep telling ya, cards aren't what the hero's stories make them out to be. Most of the time, they just make things easier, not better. Mark my words, if he keeps using his trap on minor, stupid shit, he's going to wake up with a knife in his heart, and someone will steal the card from him."

Arthur's eyes widened. "You think?"

"It's happened before. Stay away from cards," Red warned.

Then the cart in front of them moved, and it was their turn to urge the donkeys to pull their cart into motion.

The first time Arthur encountered other cards came just two days later when the traders' caravan rolled into what most of the men sneeringly called "a podunk stick-shot town" but was easily five times the size of Arthur's old village.

He boggled, eyes wide, as he took in the main street, which was bordered by buildings each two stories high. The street underfoot was inlaid with flat stones to make it easier on wagon wheels. Everywhere he looked were people. All of them strangers, most well-clothed, and hardly a sunken cheek to be seen.

Best of all, some of them were carded. One man casually walked down the lane with a log the size of half a tree on one shoulder. A nearby woman, who, when she shouted at her kids to behave, made the nearby hanging sheets wave. A girl a few years older than Arthur carrying a recently hunted line of pheasants spoke back and forth to her hunting dog as if she were having a one-sided conversation. A young man stood at the edge of a puddle when it hadn't rained for days, raising and lowering the level of the water with his hand.

Yes, Arthur spotted a couple of underfed beggars tucked in the shadows between buildings. But none of them had scourge pockmarks or missing fingers and limbs from infections gone wrong.

The traders' arrival caused a general hubbub in the town. People called out greetings, asking what was being sold.

A few of the carters called back with their general wares.

"We will be eating dinner at the inn on the other end of town," Red said from his driver's seat on the cart. As usual, Arthur had walked alongside it. "You won't be expected to help cook. Most of the men will be buying rooms tonight, too. You are to sleep in the stables and guard the donkeys."

Arthur wrinkled his nose, but he knew better than to complain. He wasn't sure he wanted to share a room with Red, anyway. The man snored louder than anyone in the caravan.

As soon as they pulled up to the inn, they were greeted by one of the local baron's officials. Thankfully, they were no longer in Baron Kane's lands, though Arthur watched the man cautiously.

All that happened was an exchange of coins for the right to set up stalls and trade goods in the town. The baron's man did a cursory inspection of the carts for illegal items—though Arthur saw money exchanged a couple of times for the official to look the other way—and that was that.

He wasn't used to interactions with the higher-ups being so . . . friendly.

As Red was in charge of supplying the other carts, he had nothing to sell. So Arthur was given a free afternoon. And, to his surprise, five copper pennies to spend.

He had never been allowed his own money before, but instantly had about a hundred ideas of what he wanted to spend them on. Most of them were exotic types of treats.

The caravan had passed a bakery halfway through the town. Arthur quickly walked in that direction, swiveling his head this way and that to take in as many of the sights as he could.

A gleam of pure white against a darkened window backdrop caught his eye. He stopped and stared.

The General Store he was passing had a display set up against the window. Sitting pride in place, safely locked in a clear case and tethered by a thick chain, was a spell card.

Arthur practically plastered himself against the glass to read it.

Minor Materials Strengthening
Common
Utility/Boon
The wielder of this card is granted the ability to strengthen material objects. The user must be in physical contact with the object. This temporary boon ends within three heartbeats of loss of contact. This ability will not work with water-based, incorporeal, or enchanted objects.

The card was simple in design. It looked like a fancy sheet of paper with golden filigree bordering the sides. The words were in stark, bold print, and nothing about it moved. It seemed barely alive.

To the side, the shopkeeper had placed a handwritten note.

Excellent for soldiers who wish to strengthen the durability of their weapons or farmers who wish to extend the life of their tools.
10 gold pieces.

Arthur wasn't sure how many pennies made up a gold piece, but he suspected it was much more than the five he had.

With a sigh, he stepped away from the window and walked on.

There was a second window display on the other side of the door, and another white-paper-looking card.

Basic Object Duplication
Common
Illusion

Create a temporary replica copy of a single, non-living object. Initial levels create Light-based illusions only. Additional levels add sound and substance to the illusion. The detail and length of time are based on mana costs.

Again, there was a handwritten note from the shopkeeper placed to the side of the card. It simply said:

Inquire within for the price.

Arthur hesitated. He needed a card. Any card. Even if it was something Common and possibly useless.

He had been wolfing down at least three, sometimes four, bowls of soup. Soon that food would translate into growth, if it wasn't already. He didn't feel like he was getting taller, but he couldn't exactly look at himself from the outside.

Red had said the carded men were jealous of each other's powers. But they wouldn't care if the "Pissant" had the power to make the illusion of a rock next to another rock. They wouldn't ever guess that he had two cards.

"I guess it won't hurt to ask . . ." he said to himself, turned, and walked in the door.

The General Store had all manner of items for sale. Most of it was clothing, though the shelves were stuffed with boxes and sacks of basic foodstuff.

A balding man stood on the other side of a long counter. He frowned upon seeing Arthur.

"Yes? Can I help you?"

He gestured to the window. "The note said to ask for the card's price?"

The shopkeeper snorted. "More than you can afford, sonny boy."

"I have five pennies," he tried.

"Are you joking?"

The illusion card was probably worth a lot more than ten gold, then. Well, he hadn't been very excited about it anyway.

"Do you have any other cards I can look at?" Arthur asked.

"This isn't a fancy city card shop, it's a General Store. If you want my advice, earn some more pennies and buy yourself a decent shirt."

Arthur looked down at himself. His clothes looked fine to his eye, but when he glanced at the finely hung, new clothing . . . well, yes. His shirt did look ragged. And there were a lot of stains.

They didn't often do the washing back home, and he hadn't had the opportunity since leaving.

The shopkeeper was glaring at him, so Arthur took his pennies and hurriedly walked out.

He did find the bakery and discovered that one penny would buy him a sweet roll covered with delicate white icing.

Arthur bought three and munched on them as he walked down the street.

He had hours before Red told him he'd need to be back to the inn for dinner, and nothing to do. If he had been back home, he would have set out to find Ernie . . . but that wasn't an option anymore.

Another wave of grief and homesickness hit him, though it wasn't as intense as it had been before. He didn't even feel like crying.

Finishing up his last sweet roll, he wiped his sticky fingers clean on his pants. Then he noticed a group of kids a little older than himself standing around in a circle just down a side street.

Arthur wandered up to see a circle marked out in chalk and a boy and a girl knelt on either side with marbles in their hands. Three dice sat on one end.

One boy who stood as referee threw the dice. The total came up to twelve. The boy groaned, and the girl laughed and flicked a blue marble to the circle. It knocked a blue one from the innermost circle and to an outer one.

Several people grumbled, and coins changed hands.

"Hey." The referee noticed Arthur watching. "Who're you?"

Instantly, Arthur felt all eyes on him. But he was used to that. People in the village were always looking at him, on account of his father being an important man. Arthur shrugged. "I'm Ernest. I came with the caravan." He hooked a thumb back toward the direction of the inn.

"You ain't a spy for the baron's man?" the ref challenged. Standing, he balled a fist. "You'd better tell the truth. I got a card that smells lies."

Well, that was a lie, considering Arthur had just told him a fake name and the ref hadn't blinked. He shrugged again. "No, I ain't a snitch for the baron."

He must have put enough venom in his words for the nobles, because several kids relaxed. The ref, though, squinted at him.

"Well, you can't just watch. If you're here, you're betting."

Arthur hesitated. "I don't know how the game's played."

Several of the kids started explaining the rules at once. It was a little disjointed, but Arthur got the impression he was betting on the players: whether one would roll higher than the other, and then be able to knock the opponent's marbles from the circle. The payout, if any, depended on the outcome.

"I got a penny," Arthur said. "I'll bet on the girl."

"Her name's Sanda," the ref said but took Arthur's penny anyway.

The first round came as a push—Sanda won the dice roll but didn't manage to knock any of the boy's marbles out.

Arthur got his penny back and bet it on the boy, whose name was Mic.

Mic lost the dice roll, and Arthur lost his penny.

But he did gain something more valuable.

New skill gained: Game Proficiency: Circles and Squares
(Gambler Class)
Due to your card's bonus traits, you automatically start this skill
at level 3.

He supposed that Circles and Squares was the name of this game. And with his level 3 proficiency, he understood that the girl was easily beating the boy.

Her expression was confident while his was strained. The other gamblers kept placing their bets on the boy, sure that his luck would turn. Yes, the roll of the dice was a toss-up, but every time Mic got a chance to shoot his marble, he either missed or picked badly.

Arthur used his last penny to bet on the girl. She scowled at him, and he got the impression her earlier misstep that caused the push had been on purpose because she didn't like a stranger betting. But this time when she won the dice roll, she shot her marble true.

Arthur got his penny and another one. With a grin, he placed his bet again. This time with both pennies.

Arthur did well for himself. While he didn't bet correctly every round, most of his "losses" ended up in a push.

By the time he was up to five pennies and had gained two more levels in the game, he was aware of resentful looks from the others.

He was a stranger and taking their money. Maybe he shouldn't hang around.

"My master's expecting me to help for supper," he explained as he stood from the circle. Most of the other gamblers had been crouched around at various points, carefully watching the marbles for any sign of cheating.

"You should stay," the ref said. He had become too friendly over the last couple of rounds. "I'm sure your master can do without for a few more minutes."

Arthur shrugged. "That's a good way to earn me a slap." Then he turned and walked off, hands in his pockets.

A couple of the boys called after him. Arthur ignored them, ducking into the shadows of the next building.

Instead of heading in the direction of the inn, he turned right and quickly stepped into the next gap between buildings he saw. Then he concentrated on blending in with the shadows, on being stealthy.

Maybe it was his imagination, but he thought he felt as if he merged into the shadows. Just a little.

He counted twenty breaths before he saw two of the largest-looking boys from the gambling group walking down the street. They were headed toward the inn.

Arthur let out a breath. Red wouldn't miss him for more than an hour yet. He planned to spend it working on his **Stealth** skill.

CHAPTER 14

Arthur picked his way from building to building, slinking along to the dark and out-of-the-way places. Luck was with him in that the sun was sinking and elongating shadows.

He didn't spot the other kids from the gambling ring but used his wariness as an excuse to try to make his way to the inn, unseen. It was like a game.

He was nearly there when he was rewarded with a message from his card.

New skill level: Basic Stealth (Rogue/Thief Class)
Level 6

With that came the wisdom of how to step with a rolling motion so he might better obscure his footsteps.

He was grinning as he finally stepped out of the shadows to the road, walking right up to the inn. There was no sign he'd been followed. He had gotten away cleanly.

At three full stories, it was the tallest building in town. Possibly the widest, too, because an equally long stable house was attached to the property.

He assumed that most visitors to the town were traders going from one part of the kingdom to the other. So, it made sense that the inn got a lot of business.

The lobby was more like a saloon where visitors and locals alike sat around tables to drink.

Red sat at one of these with a fan of playing cards in his hand. Unfortunately, he was playing against Second and several of his friends.

Arthur quietly walked up and stood just to the side where he could view Red's playing cards. They were the normal kind, of course. Not the magical. He didn't know much about card games but watched as the men made bets against one another, exchanged cards, and added coins to a growing pile in the middle.

Two hands in, Second snarled, throwing down his hand of cards. "Your pissant apprentice is bad luck, Red."

Arthur flinched, but Red didn't blink.

"Poker is less about luck than it is skill."

Skill? Arthur's ears pricked at that.

Second glared at him, but Red hadn't told Arthur to go away, so Arthur stayed where he was, carefully watching the next couple of rounds. Slowly, he got a sense of how the game was played, though he didn't gain an official skill for it.

He guessed he needed to play to grasp a full understanding.

His chance came when Second lost the pot again. He rose from the table with a snarl. "I'm getting a drink."

"Can I play?" Arthur asked the moment the man had stepped from the table.

Several unfriendly gazes slid his way. No one said anything.

Arthur reached into his pocket and pulled out his hard-earned pennies. "I have coins."

Red frowned at him. "You were supposed to spend those in town."

"There wasn't anything I wanted to buy," Arthur lied.

"Eh, deal the pissant in," one of the men said. "At least until Second comes back."

"Fine," another agreed. "But I'm not going to go easy on him."

Red nodded, and Arthur quickly took his place at Second's seat.

The buy-in was one penny, so he flicked one into the pot along with everyone else.

He had very little clue of what he was doing. His first hand was a pair of eights. Not great, but it was something.

Arthur decided to bluff, only exchanging one card when the dealer asked.

His next card was a two of clubs. Useless to him.

He ended up losing that hand, and two of his pennies, to one of Second's friends. But to his delight, he got the skill he was looking for.

New skill gained: Game Proficiency: Poker – Five Card Draw
(Gambler Class)
Due to your card's bonus traits, you automatically start this skill
at level 3.

It had taken him a few rounds earlier with the dice game to gain a skill. It seemed that careful observation at first quickened the process.

He had no time to try out his new skill. Second had come back from the bar with a fresh mug of beer. He scowled at finding Arthur in his place.

"You keeping the seat warm for me, Pissant?" He grabbed the back of the chair with his free hand.

Arthur hastily rose before he could be dumped out.

"He was just filling up the table," Red said calmly. He looked to Arthur. "Ernest, the staff will be serving supper soon. Why don't you make yourself useful in the kitchens? They may discount us for the extra pair of hands."

Reluctantly, Arthur put down his cards. He wasn't too upset, because Red plucked the penny he'd just used as a new buy-in and flicked it back to him.

No one objected. Arthur got the impression they just wanted him gone. No one wanted to play cards with a little kid.

He made his way through the back door and to the kitchens. There, he introduced himself to the head cook.

She looked harried and also not interested in help. "Go get us a couple of fresh buckets from the well out back, then get out of our way."

That task was done easily enough. Arthur marveled a little about how little people expected from him. Since traveling with the caravan, he hadn't worked nearly as hard as he did when it was time to till in dragon soil.

Since no one wanted him underfoot, he figured he would check out the stables now and see what kind of a bed he was in for.

To his surprise, all the carts had been wheeled into a large, clear area of the stables. That way they were guaranteed to be out of the weather if it began to rain.

The donkeys, oxen, and the caravan's few horses had been bedded down in their own boxes for the night. There were large piles of fresh straw that would easily serve as a bed.

Satisfied, Arthur turned to head toward the entrance. Then he stopped.

Three large boys stood behind him about twenty feet back, blocking the exit to the stables. It was the referee from the dice game and two of his friends.

The referee sneered. "We were wondering where you went off to, you little sneak."

Arthur stiffened. "What are you talking about?"

"You're a cheater, and we want our money back!" one of the other boys growled.

The ref nodded. All three boys advanced menacingly. "That's right. You came in, pretending like you didn't know anything about the game. Then you walked away richer for it. Did you and Sanda have a deal?"

This was bad. Arthur curled his hands into a fist. "I don't know who Sanda is—wait, the girl? I never met her before. It was just luck!"

And his skills.

"Luck, nothing," the ref said. "We want our money back."

Arthur backed up, but he didn't have far to go. They'd boxed him in good, and he cursed himself as an idiot for not taking their threat seriously. "I don't have your money," he lied. In actuality, he had several pennies left.

"Then I guess we'll have to beat it out of you," one of the boys sneered. He looked like he was going to do it even if Arthur had given him the coins.

Arthur backed up another step. His shoulder hit something soft and crackly that smelled of a rich, spicy smoke scent. Great. Second's cart.

"He's lying about the money," the ref said. "My card says so."

"No, *you're* lying!" Arthur snapped. Not the best comeback, but he doubted any of these boys were carded. They were larger than him, but only because they were a few years older.

As one, the boys lunged for him. Arthur tried to duck away and rush through a gap between the ref and the leftmost boy. He wished he had some skill for escape or swordplay or something. But he had nothing. Only his wits, which had failed him tonight. And his speed, which wasn't much.

To his surprise, he nearly managed to plow through the gap between them . . . until one of the boys grabbed him by the collar and hauled him back.

Arthur swung. His fist glanced off the boy's shoulder, and it felt like hitting a brick wall.

One of the boys grabbed his flailing arm. The other snagged the second.

While he was pinned, the ref swung his fist and hit Arthur hard in the stomach.

Arthur's breath blew out. He doubled over, and for a horrible moment, he thought he was going to throw up right there.

"Get his money!" Ref yelled.

Grabby hands started searching his shirt and pants pocket.

"What's going on here?"

The three attackers stopped dead at the booming voice. They turned.

Second stood at the open doorway, looming large and dangerous.

Arthur opened his mouth to yell for help. He didn't much like the man, but he was Red's apprentice. That had to mean something, right?

But in the next moment, Second's entire form blurred forward. In one eye-blink, he was at the stable's entrance. The next he stood right in front of them all.

He grabbed the boy on Arthur's right and hauled him away with a surge of strength that sent the boy tumbling.

The other two yelped and dropped their grip on Arthur to run. Not fast enough.

Second aimed a kick at the ref's backside as he passed. The boy actually flew forward a few feet at the blow, hit the ground on all fours, and then scrambled to run away with one hand over his butt and limping.

Arthur sagged back, realizing at the last moment that he was leaning against Second's tobacco.

He managed to straighten just as Second turned to him. "You causing trouble, Pissant?"

"No." With one hand wrapped around his aching stomach, he reached the other into his pocket. He still had the coins. "I just played dice with them. They thought I was cheating. I *wasn't*," he snapped.

"So that's what you were doing today? You good at dice?"

Arthur was taken aback by the question. "Yeah. Kind of. I walked off with more than I came with."

Second's eyes narrowed. Thoughts were churning behind his eyes, but Arthur couldn't guess what they were.

Well, he supposed he should say something to the man for saving him from a robbery and possibly a beating. "Thank you," he bit out.

Second snorted. "You owe me one, Pissant. Remember that, when I come calling." With that, he walked back to the stable's entrance, then paused and looked over his shoulder. "Supper will be up in a couple of minutes. Clean yourself off and get in."

Arthur nodded, a little thrown. He hastened to a clean bucket of water to do as he was told.

As he did, he wondered what had brought Second into the stable in the first place. Surely it wasn't to come to tell Arthur that supper was almost ready.

No. He'd come to check on his cart, Arthur realized. The man was protective of his tobacco.

Too protective.

And the other day, one of the men who worked for Second had activated his trap card just to keep a mound of leaves from falling out.

Arthur turned from the bucket to take a long look at the cart.

Why was the tobacco piled up that high? Shouldn't it be in bags or crates to protect the leaves? The tarp kept them from drying out to the point where they might go moldy. It seemed like an awfully stupid way to transport tobacco.

Unless . . . that wasn't the point.

The tobacco smelled potent. People smoked it all the time to feel good. Maybe it had other qualities, too. Maybe qualities that would block a Treasure Seeker.

Of course. Second wasn't hauling a mound of tobacco at all. He was hauling something under it.

A surge of excitement washed away the lingering pain from the gut punch.

There were only a few things he could think of worth that kind of treatment.

Tonight, Arthur intended to discover what Second was hiding.

CHAPTER 15

The food served in the inn was excellent. Freshly baked bread, still warm from the oven, sliced roast beef slathered with thick gravy, and some kind of steamed vegetable Red had called broccoli. It had an intense, earthy green flavor he found he liked a lot.

The meal was so good he wished he had spent more time in the kitchens to learn how to cook. This was a meal that would have definitely earned him another level.

Though the mug of ale that Red had ordered for him was watered down, Arthur found himself blinking tiredly anyway.

Red told him to get to sleep, and Arthur stumbled off to the stables, glad he didn't have to stay up and wash the dishes for once. He wished they could stay in inns every night.

Was this what his father meant when he said Arthur didn't know about the wider world?

There was nothing more he wanted to do than to stagger into his bedroll set in the straw and fall asleep. But if he did, he would miss his chance.

With a groan, he instead fished through Red's saddlebags until he found a stiff boar-hair brush. Then he went to Red's donkeys and gave them all a thorough brush-down.

They had already been cared for by the stable staff, but it had been cursory at best, and Arthur needed to move to stay awake.

By the time he was done, some of the ale had worked its way out of his system. He was feeling more alert, and the donkeys looked positively gleaming.

Finally, after checking their hooves for stones, he was rewarded with another notice from his card.

New skill level: Basic Equine Care (Animal Husbandry)
Level 9

He had been steadily gaining levels toward this skill and now had a very respectable nine. Soon, he would move the skill up to apprentice.

What would happen then? And would the skill help him if he ever tried riding one of the donkeys?

He figured it might not help, but . . . it might not hurt, either.

That was a matter for another day.

Lights still blazed through the inn's windows. No doubt the men were all up, drinking and playing cards.

Arthur stayed up too, walking in slow loops around the interior of the large stables. He kept an eye on the doors in case the kids from the dice game came back.

There was no sign of them. Likely, they'd leave him alone as long as he didn't come to them looking for trouble. It was only a matter of pennies, and it was probably pride that had caused them to come after him more than anything.

Finally, one of the workers from the inn came out to extinguish the oil lamps that burned at the entrance to the inn, and the one that lit the pathway to the stables. That was their way to indicate they would take no more customers tonight.

Soon, the lights from inside the inn went out, one by one.

Ideally, Arthur would have liked to make sure that Second or any of his men were asleep in their rooms, but it was very late now. This was as good of a chance as he was going to get.

He tiptoed to the cart and examined the tarp. The knots tying it down were well-made—likely reinforced after some of the leaves had "accidentally" fallen out before—and were now almost ridiculously convoluted loops.

It would have been far easier to cut them away and lift the tarp, but that would have given him away for sure.

So, with his tongue poking out of the corner of his mouth, Arthur worked at one of the knots. It was so tight that the tips of his fingers were sore by the time he unknotted one.

That had taken forever. Too bad he didn't have a skill for knot-work . . . or could he?

Arthur bit his lip, considering. Then he walked across the stables to a little side nook where the stable hands stored supplies. There was all manner of tools and odds and ends, as well as pieces of extra rope.

He grabbed a small length and proceeded to start knotting it, then untying it again.

He knew three basic knots: the regular loop, the slipknot, and the knot he used to tie the laces of his boots. He had always done them unthinkingly since he'd first learned to lace up his boots as a small boy. No doubt that was why he hadn't gotten a skill yet. To earn a skill, he had to be deliberate.

So, as he worked, he focused hard on every twist and loop. Then he would undo his work and start again.

It only took him about five repetitions to gain a skill.

New skill gained: Basic Knot Tying (Sailor Class)
Due to your card's bonus traits, you automatically start this skill
at level 3.

Sailor class?

Arthur had never seen so much as a large lake, much less the ocean. Oh well, he'd gotten the skill anyway.

One day, he was going to have to figure out what these classes meant.

Returning to the cart, he started working on the next knot down the line. This time was much faster with the aid of his skill. By the time he had unknotted that section of tarp from the cart, he had gained another skill level.

He carefully lifted the loose corner of the tarp and carefully considered his next move. If he was right, the smelly tobacco was a cover for something else. He couldn't sort through the pile without the risk of an avalanche of leaves falling on his head.

First, he had to make sure his guess was right. If this was a cover for something, it would make sense that the treasure was in the middle.

He grabbed a push-broom from the tool nook. Flipping it, he carefully poked the handle into the mass. It took some prodding, but eventually, the end of the handle struck something hard sitting in the middle of the pile at the very bottom. Something that, when he tapped against it, felt wooden.

The giant mound of tobacco was covering a wooden box.

He moved the handle back and forth, up and down, trying to feel out the dimensions.

It was slim, which was good for him.

Gnawing at his lower lip, Arthur started pushing the box very slowly across the bed of the cart to the other side. He worked carefully so as not to unbalance the leaves. Eventually, he went to the other side of the cart to unknot that corner of the tarp and push away some of the leaves to keep them from piling up in front of the box.

Finally, after nearly an hour of continuous, careful pushing, the box emerged.

It was smooth, polished wood, so dark it was almost jet black. Utterly beautiful.

Something that could contain jewels, money . . . or something even better: cards. It was also locked. Of course.

Arthur rubbed his forehead, feeling like an idiot. Why had he expected this to be easy?

However, unlike the lock that had protected his card, this one didn't look magical . . . unless there were some hidden runes that killed someone who tried to break in. Arthur had heard stories.

He considered for a moment and then shrugged, deciding he had come this far. He might as well continue.

There were some farrier and construction materials scattered among the disorganized nook, including a pile of very thin nails.

Arthur wasn't a hundred percent sure how to pick a lock, but he would at least give it a try. He just made sure to be very careful not to scratch the polished metal lock.

He poked a nail in and moved it around, listening carefully for some sort of give. One of the mechanisms gave a click when he pressed upward with one nail. Holding it there, he added a second, hoping to engage. Most small lock keys had two main teeth, didn't they?

He didn't have luck for a long time. In fact, he was halfway nodding over his work, on the verge of dozing off while sitting up, when he heard a second click.

Arthur froze in place, unsure if he had dreamed the sound or not.

New skill gained: Lock-Picking (Rogue/Thief Class)
Due to your card's bonus traits, you automatically start this skill
at level 3.

"I'm not a thief," he said as he carefully shifted to use his pinky finger to see if the lid for the box he had stolen would open. To his shock, it did.

All his brave ideals about not being a thief were blown out the window when he saw what lay within.

He hadn't dared to hope. But of course, the box could only hold one thing: cards.

There were five magic cards in the box. All of them were as common as dirt—that same papery white color with the golden etching on the borders.

But to his amazement, it was a complete set. The twining golden filigree on the sides was the same, and there was an indefinable something about them that made them feel like different parts of a whole. The cards he had seen for sale at the General Store had not had it.

With trembling fingers, he picked one up. While his senses told him it should feel like a thick piece of paper, it was as hard as metal and faintly warm, as if it held its own life.

Soil Affinity
Common
Elemental Affinity

The card grants the wielder a basic affinity with soil. As affinity levels are gained, the user may gain additional empathy and knowledge of the living skin of the earth. Affinity does not extend to rock or rock-based substrates.

What was the difference between soil and rock? Arthur shook his head and skimmed on. The others were in the same class.

Minor Earth Illusion
Common
Illusion

This card grants the wielder the ability to create minor, short-term illusions out of earth-based substances. All illusions are Light-based. As levels and proficiency are gained, these illusions may take on tangible qualities.

Minor Earth Strike
Common
Spell

Cast a spell to fire a ball of earth at an opponent. The wielder must be in physical contact with the earth to cast. Two-second cooldown.

Minor Earth Golem Summon
Common
Summon

Summon a minor earth golem. The wielder must maintain physical contact with the earth to continue casting. Golem increases in size and strength with additional levels. Twenty-four-hour cooldown.

Minor Earth Card Cohesion
Common
Special

Anyone who has two or more cards in the set may combine them into complementary powers. This card also reduces the overall mana and stamina cost for all activations with the set by 50%.

He understood a little of what his father had meant by the Special card. It had no power on its own, but when combined with others in the set, it became valuable.

Arthur traced his fingers over the cards. He wanted to shove them all in his heart deck and activate them. They weren't much individually, but certainly more than what he could currently do with magic, which was zero. And with the whole set . . .

He could defend himself. He could go anywhere and get a job on any farm. He could go back home and help till the dragon soil into fields faster and better than anyone else.

But no. Cards weren't allowed back in the border village. Plus, he would never make it back there. Second would kill him. Literally kill him.

I could take them and run away, he thought. He had maybe four hours of darkness left. He could take Bella the donkey or maybe one of the old horses, and run.

He could steal from people who had trusted him to guard their things. Who, while they had slapped him around, hadn't been overly cruel. Red had never hit him and hadn't had an unkind word. Second had saved his bacon just today, and Arthur owed him for that.

Arthur would be betraying all of their trust.

Scrubbing at his face, Arthur gritted his teeth. He wanted these cards. They would solve his problems . . . and yet pile on so many more.

Even if he stole them, played innocent, and stayed, he had no idea how often Second checked the box's contents. What were the chances he wouldn't check the box after the cart had been out of sight all night? If Arthur were in his place, he would have a latch under the cart or something to reach up and—

Arthur tore himself from the box and crawled underneath the cart.

Sure enough, there was a latch leading to a drop-hinged door right in the middle. That was probably how Second had stuffed the box up there in the first place.

Arthur cursed himself as an idiot for spending so much time with the tarp and poking the box out of the leaves. He would have to use this drop-latched door to make sure the box was properly positioned. Or else Second would know.

He closed his eyes and groaned, head flopping back against the ground.

He wanted those cards with a fierce intensity that scared him a little. But it would be foolish in every conceivable way to take them. Most importantly, that wasn't the man he wanted to be.

"I'm going to get a second card," he muttered to himself. "More, if I can help it. But not like this."

Feeling glum, though knowing he was doing the right thing, he returned to the box. He made absolutely sure everything looked pristine before he closed the lid. It automatically relocked.

Then he crawled back under the cart and used his lock-picking nails to work on the latch. This was a lot easier seeing as he didn't have to worry about scratching anything. By brute force poking the nails in, he got the latch to open.

Leaves started spilling out. He quickly shoved the box up and in, reclosing it.

The next hour was spent cleaning up after himself. Arthur shoved all the leaves that had fallen out back under the tarp, kicked straw around the crumbles left over, and then retied the tarps. The knots weren't exact, but he thought they would pass muster with a quick check.

Then he looked down at his hands. Handling the tobacco leaf had left a greasy film on his fingers, which had turned black.

Maybe Second was smarter than Arthur had thought. He'd picked a plant that would leave evidence of tampering behind.

Well, Arthur had buckets of water and stiff brushes all around to take care of that. It took some effort, but there was little he could do about the blackness under his fingernails. Hopefully, people would think it was dirt.

Finally, he dragged himself to his bedroll and closed his eyes. Dawn was due soon.

The next morning, he was woken up by the roar of a dragon.

CHAPTER 16

For a startled moment, Arthur wasn't in his bedroll on top of a thick mat of straw. He was back at his home village, hiding under scraggly bushes as the red dragon roared and killed the soldiers underneath it.

A second dragon's roar shocked him out of sleep.

It was real. It wasn't a dream.

He's found me, was Arthur's first, panicked thought. The red dragon had told him to give the card to his father. It didn't matter that his father refused to take it. The dragon would only see him as a greedy, disobedient child . . .

Heart pounding, Arthur untangled himself from his blanket and stood. He was torn between running to the door, to explain to the red dragon what had happened . . . and fleeing.

The animals in the stables shifted around nervously. They didn't like the sound of the predator outside, but the walls gave them the illusion of safety. It was early, too. Predawn light had just started filtering through the cracks between the planks.

Why weren't people screaming? Surely others must have been woken by the roar?

That curiosity was enough to cut through his fear. Arthur edged to the open entrance and looked out.

There was a dragon in the sky. Not the red, but a silver beast with a blue underbelly. It was making wide circles around the town, roaring at intervals as if to announce its presence. A silhouette of a rider sat on its back, swinging their arm back and forth in an exaggerated wave.

Arthur's fear melted away. He looked up in awe. A dragon and its rider were visiting the town.

All around, doors opened from houses and apartments as the townsfolk were alerted to their new visitor. Most looked tired but interested. Some seemed downright relieved.

The baron's man, the overseer, strode to a wide spot in front of the inn. As the largest building in town, it was the most distinctive. In contrast to the sleepy townsfolk, most of whom were still in the clothes they'd slept in, he was dressed in finely pressed pants and a fancy jacket. The buttons of his station gleamed in the early morning sun.

Turning, the man gestured for two boy assistants to come out from the crowd. They did, both carrying green flags. The boys went to either end of the courtyard and waved the flags.

Up high, the dragon gave a short bark of acknowledgment and completed a sharp turn.

As it came closer, Arthur saw it was smaller than the red dragon had been. It was thinner overall, with delicate proportions, including longer wings that looked almost translucent in the sun. The muzzle was sharp and pointed downward at the end, like an old man who had a crooked nose.

It landed with easy grace. Its eyes were as blue as the sky. It looked around with alert interest and started sniffing deeply, swinging its head toward a nearby group of townsfolk. They drew back quickly.

The baron's overseer came trotting up to the dragon, desperate to be the first to greet and bow at the rider. He called up something to him, but it was too far away for Arthur to hear.

Whatever he said, the rider ignored it. Instead, he straightened in the dragon saddle and stood up tall to balance effortlessly on the beast.

He was every inch a large, carded man. His dark skin was smooth and free of all marks. His eyes glowed the same color as his dragon's—an eerie blue that stood out from his face.

"Good people!" the rider called in a booming, practiced voice that easily reached down the street. "I am Sir Rider Chancy and this is Doshi. Our hive has received a request to settle the matter of a crime. What has happened here?"

Immediately, several townsfolk cried out with strident voices.

"My home's been broken into!"

"My jewelry stolen—"

"The schoolhouse has been ransacked!"

Chancy turned to indicate a squat white one-story building at the other end of the square. "Is that the schoolhouse?"

He waited for several affirmative answers before he leaped from the dragon's back and landed easily on the ground.

The growing crowd of townsfolk parted for the rider as he strode toward the school.

Arthur was enthralled. Forgetting all fear, he jogged to see what would happen next. Though more people were filtering into the square as word spread, they gave wide room for the dragon. Arthur squeezed in through the gaps. The dragon wasn't doing anything scary anyway. Just sniffing hopefully at people like an overly friendly dog.

He got close enough to see the rider point to one of the broken-out windows of the school. "When did this happen?"

"Three nights ago," the overseer told him, and added something else, but the dragon was sniffing so loud, so close, that Arthur missed the rest.

He turned to see the dragon examining a nearby girl up and down. The girl stood stock still, pale in fright. She sagged when the dragon moved on.

What is it looking for? Food? Arthur wondered.

His father had told him that dragons were like beasts. The red dragon had spoken and mostly acted like a person, but this one was more like a friendly dog.

"Doshi!" Chancy called.

Immediately, the silver dragon's head popped up, and it trotted over to its rider—as fast as a beast half the size of a house could trot. People quickly made way.

"Oh, this will be fun," said a familiar voice to Arthur's side.

He looked up to see that Red had joined him. The man had his arms crossed and was chewing a bit of wheat in his mouth.

"What do you mean?" Arthur asked.

"I've seen these two work before. The Harvest Moon Hive usually sends this pair out to resolve small-town complaints. Watch."

Both the dragon and rider faced each other. The man's face was blank in concentration, the dragon's eyes half closed.

Suddenly, the entire town square was transformed.

It was still early morning, yet the pinprick of a hundred thousand stars now dotted the sky. Everything but the people had a strange, ghostly double outline. Like they were there . . . and yet not.

Some of the townsfolk murmured and were shushed by their neighbors. Arthur looked up at Red to see the man's attention fixed on the schoolhouse. Arthur did the same.

The windows looked . . . strange. Both broken and unbroken at the same time. An outline of the fake overlaid on top of the real. It hurt his eyes to focus too closely.

"Go later into the night," Chancy told his dragon.

The stars above wheeled a quarter turn, like Arthur was seeing the night pass by in seconds.

Then the dragon spoke for the first time. "Yes, I see them."

The stars stopped. Around the corner of the schoolhouse in the not-quite night came the translucent image of four boys. They were laughing and joking, though no sound came from their open mouths.

With a jolt, Arthur recognized them all as boys from the dice game. Though out of the group, only the referee had been the one to rough him up.

And it was the ref who, laughing silently, picked up a stone to fling it through the schoolhouse. The others quickly joined in.

Arthur flinched as the glass broke, even though there was no noise. Glass was expensive and precious back in his old village. To just ruin it for a laugh was . . . unthinkable. To do it when they were lucky enough to have a schoolhouse at all for teaching? Criminal.

When the windows were shattered, one of the boys got the bright idea to kick the door in.

Arthur wasn't the only one annoyed, judging by the angry buzz of the crowd.

Chancy turned away from his dragon, and the strange scene faded away. "Are these children known to you all?"

"Yes, Sir Rider."

"Then fetch them."

Arthur turned to Red. "What kind of card can do that?" *And how did he get ahold of it?* he added silently.

Red shrugged. "Dragons and riders link cards, you know."

Arthur shook his head. He had no idea.

Red snorted. "I've seen this pair's song and dance before—rumor has it, they've got no cards good for scourgling eruptions, so the hive sends 'em out to put on a nice face for the common folk."

Arthur did not care a bit about politics. He wanted to know how the cards worked. "Linked powers? Does that mean the dragons have a Special card? Like part of a set?"

Red shrugged again. Right. He was the wrong person to ask.

At that point, several of the boys were brought forward. One was the ref, who looked sullen and defiant.

The baron's overseer pounced at once, demanding their ages and family names. He seemed disappointed when they were all under eighteen.

"If you were of age, I'd send your worthless hides to the border!" he snapped. The blood drained from the boys' faces. "As it is, maybe a public caning and repayment for the damage to the schoolhouse will have to do. Until then, you will sit in the cells and think about what you did—"

Abruptly, the silver dragon thrust its long muzzle forward, sniffing so hard that several nearby ladies' skirts flapped in the wind. It seemed fixated on the ref. In fact, it nearly knocked the boy over in his enthusiasm.

"Chancy, we must not let this one go!"

"Easy now, Doshi."

The rider gently pushed the beast's head away and looked down at the ref. "What's your name, son?"

"B-Bertum. Everyone calls me Bert." He stared from the dragon to the rider to a frightened-looking couple who had to be his parents.

"Well, Bert. How about instead of a caning and you working off the damage here, you come work for the hive instead?"

Bert's eyes grew wide. "Really?"

"Really. In fact, I'm certain the hive can replace those windows you broke right away if you agree to stay the summer. Is that a fair deal?" The last question was directed toward the overseer.

The man nodded. "Yes, yes. If you can handle him. And I'd better not get any word of you discrediting our town," the overseer said sternly to Bert.

Bert frantically shook his head that he wouldn't. The boys beside him looked shocked and stared at the rider pleadingly, but he ignored them. It seemed only Bert was to be given this chance.

Arthur, meanwhile, watched with a growing burning in his chest. It was envy so deep he could not put it into words.

Not that he wanted to see Bert get caned. Okay, not a lot. But he'd done a crime that would have had him sent to the border had he been a couple of years older. Instead, he was getting his sins paid for and, from the sounds of it, going with a dragon rider.

It wasn't fair. Arthur and his mother hadn't had the chance to go to a hive when his father got in trouble with the king. Not that they'd have left his father, especially since his mother had been pregnant at the time, but still! It wasn't fair.

One of the townsfolk gathered the courage to step forward. "Begging your pardon, sir dragon rider, but there's the matter of our burglarized home."

"And my jewelry!" a woman added. "It was stolen right out of my shop."

Chancy leveled a stern gaze down at Bert. "Did you have anything to do with these crimes? We'll see the truth soon."

"No, sir!" Again, Bert shook his head. "I didn't, and neither did my boys. It had to be someone else."

Chancy stared at him for a long moment, as if weighing his words.

"Well, then let's find out who was responsible. Shall we?"

With that, he nodded to the man who'd had his house broken into. The man started leading him down the street. With a cheer, the townsfolk followed. The unlucky boys who had not been noticed by the dragon were pulled away, presumably to the cells.

Arthur started to follow the crowd. He was stopped when Red put a hand on his shoulder.

"Why do you stink of tobacco? And what's this?" He plucked something out of Arthur's hair. To his horror, it was a bit of crumbled leaf.

Arthur froze, his mouth working, trying to verbalize an excuse that his brain had yet to provide.

Being a short man, Red wasn't that much taller than Arthur. Yet at that moment, he seemed to loom over him. "This is from Second's cart, isn't it? If I go through your pack right now, what will I find?"

"Nothing!" he said. "I just looked, I swear. And I put it all back. *I swear!*" he repeated. "I didn't take any of the—"

"Stop." He held up a hand. Then he sighed and looked around to see if anyone was nearby to listen. "I don't want to know what Second's carrying under there. It's safer for me. Safer for you, too."

Bert had said he had a Lie Detector card. Arthur had been mostly sure he had been lying at the time, but what if one of the local officials had something like that? Or stronger?

Red waited for a beat for Arthur to process that thought. Then in a lower voice he said, "I'm the caravan leader, but Second's a carded man. If he finds out what you did, I can't stop him from dealing with you in a way he sees fit. You understand me?"

Arthur felt the blood drain from his face. He felt faint. "Yes. I only looked, though."

"I don't think he'll care. Do you?"

Arthur shook his head.

Red sighed. "There's a stream just this side of town. Go wash. While you do, I'll be searching your packs. You swear you don't have anything you shouldn't have?"

"I swear."

"Go on, then. Wash like your life depends on it."

Released, Arthur sprinted away.

The stream was more like a river, and it was ice cold. Arthur plunged in anyway, clothes and all. He came up sputtering.

It was a sheltered bend with a rocky bank and large green trees providing shade. The whole place was pretty and lush in a way he wasn't used to seeing yet.

The water was calmer in this bend of the river, too. In the gentle current, he saw a dirty film come up from around him.

He swore he felt a twinge from his **Tidying** skill. There was no need to wash much in the border village, but he wondered if one reason why the adults disliked him was because he was a dirtball kid.

Arthur ducked under again, rinsing out his hair. Then he shucked off his shirt, pants, and shoes.

He set the boots on a nearby rock to dry and started working to get the worst of the stains out of the rest. The worst came away in blooms of dirty water, but he kept scrubbing to loosen the ingrained stuff.

He would have rather seen the dragon and rider using more magic than doing his laundry, but he was well aware he'd gotten off lucky. He'd gotten so used to the pungent tobacco scent that he hadn't realized it was on him. And if Second had noticed the bit of leaf in his hair . . . well, he might have killed Arthur just to make sure he carried none of his cards in his heart deck.

Again, he was lucky Red didn't know enough about cards to check there.

Stupid, stupid, stupid! he berated himself.

How many times was he going to avoid disaster by luck until it caught up with him?

He scrubbed his shirt harder, annoyed with himself.

There was no warning. There was no noise or any sign he wasn't alone in the river at all.

Arthur turned, shirt in hand to lay it on the rock to dry.

Doshi the dragon stood on the riverbank.

"Hello, boy. Why did you run from me?"

CHAPTER 17

Arthur stared.

His first impression had only been partially correct. What stood on the rocky bank was a ghostly illusion of Doshi the dragon, transparent to the point where he could see trees behind it. It was the same type of semitransparent outline he had seen in the village square—all colors washed and dim.

"Wh-what?" he stammered, and then his mind caught up with what the dragon had asked. "I wasn't running from you. My master ordered me to wash." He gestured to himself and then remembered he was standing naked, hip deep in water.

Thankfully, the dragon didn't seem offended by his unclothed state. It stood patiently, looking down its long, crooked muzzle with a calm but curious gaze.

"Yes, the magic plant confounded me. Once I realized the power I sensed in the town came from you, I thought you had rubbed it on yourself to obscure your scent. But why would that be?"

The dragon seemed to be speaking more to itself than to Arthur, so Arthur didn't answer. Carefully watching to make sure the dragon didn't react badly, Arthur took the opportunity to place the sopping clothing on the rock. It was still early in the day, but the morning light would hopefully warm and dry it soon.

"How are you doing this?" he asked, gesturing to the ghostly image.

Doshi lowered his head as if to get a closer look at him. "My card is of time-illusion, of course. It's useful when I wish to be in two places at once. Still, my card doesn't have nearly the power of yours."

Reflexively, Arthur opened his mouth to deny he had a card. Before he could, the dragon continued. "It is rare to catch a scent of a Legendary-rank card. Even rarer to find it in the heart of one so young."

"Please don't tell," Arthur said. "My master doesn't know."

"Very well."

The easy acceptance surprised him. Arthur blinked, then was instantly on guard again. He fully expected the next question to be how he had gotten such a card, but to his surprise, the dragon only settled down on the bank, feet tucked under itself like a cat. He seemed much less bouncy and energetic than before. Maybe it took concentration to cast an illusion? Or maybe Doshi was just pleased he'd found what he was looking for?

Doshi seemed to be a very different creature from the red dragon, which had been so menacing. It carried an air of contentedness around itself as if it was willing to wait at the bank all day. Nothing felt dangerous about it.

Arthur chewed the inside of his cheek, then mentally shrugged. The dragon didn't seem offended by his bathing, and he needed to rid himself of all tobacco scent before Second caught him. He bent for a bit of coarse sand and used it to scrub his hands and arms.

Doshi watched without comment.

"You can smell cards?" Arthur ventured. "Is that why you asked for Bert? He really did have a card?"

"A low-ranked Common. I'm certain *some* hatchling will be happy with him."

Arthur gaped. "You want him to be a dragon rider?" The thought of that boy riding a beast like Doshi made his envy flare up anew.

"If he wants to be, and if a hatchling will have him," Doshi said with equanimity. "Would *you* like to be a dragon rider?"

Arthur had never considered that. He had been out of the village for such a short amount of time, and the idea of riding a dragon had been so out of the realm of possibility that Doshi might as well have asked if he wanted to walk on the moon. "I don't know. Could I?"

Doshi rumbled a laugh. "Anyone carrying a card may be a dragon rider if a hatchling with a compatible card is born."

"I don't understand," Arthur said, and elaborated when Doshi cocked its head. "This isn't my town. I didn't have a schoolhouse. I don't know much about dragons, but I heard you link your cards with your riders?"

"Compatible cards, yes."

"But how do dragons get cards in the first place?" Arthur asked. "Does the hive hand them out?"

Doshi laughed again. It was gentle and patient. "We are magical creatures, and so born with cards. How do you think new cards come into the world?"

Arthur had never considered it, but he supposed it made sense. Dragon soil—their fertilizer—was life force itself. So potent that it had to be aged over a year before it could be safely tilled into scourge-dead land.

Doshi continued. "Chancy has a Rare-ranked card of Far-Seeing. When I sensed it as a hatchling in the creche, I knew my Rare-ranked card of time-illusion would match perfectly. I was right: we make a wonderful team and accomplish great feats."

Far-Seeing plus Time-Illusion . . . "You use him to look back through time, and then you make an illusion of it to show up now," he realized. What he had seen in the town hadn't been one card, but two working as if they had one power. "But how does that work? Are the cards part of the same set?"

"No, they do not need to be. Not when you have a dragon."

Arthur's mind spun with the possibilities. What would go with a Master of Skills card? "Then I could—?"

"Not right away," Doshi said with regret. "It took Chancy five years of waiting for a dragon with a Rare, compatible card to hatch. There are dozens of Common-ranked hatchlings in the Harvest Moon Hive waiting for boys and girls right now. There are a handful of Uncommon eggs with a line of boys and girls waiting for *them*. As for Rares like me . . . a few are hatched annually from every hive—we have one close to breaking shell now. When it does, the entire hive will celebrate with a festival. It's great fun." He paused. "Legendary hatchlings are rarer still. It's been three years since a Legendary egg was laid in our hive. And then, the hatchling's card must be compatible with yours."

"Oh." Visions of himself, so powerful that he was untouchable, on the back of a dragon, faded from his mind.

It was a disappointment but also had been a short-lived dream. Besides, he didn't know much about dragon riders other than they fought scourglings. He wasn't sure that was something he wanted to do.

His skin was starting to smart from all the rough scrubbing. Arthur held his nose and ducked underwater again. When he came up, he had more questions.

"Can all dragons tell I have a card?"

"Oh, no. It is a private magic—one that does not use a card. Silvers, like myself, see a particular way to the truth of the world. It's why we're mostly illusionists." It stretched its neck forward, so close that if it had been solid and real, Arthur would have been able to reach out and touch it. "To me, the strength of your magic is like a pleasant beam of sunlight. If you wish to keep your secrets, stay away from the silvers . . . and some of the whites."

So cards were like catnip to the silvers. That was why Doshi had projected itself to the bank. Well, that was fine with him. This was only the second dragon he had seen, anyway.

Arthur swam back over to the rock and tested the clothes. Still wet, but warmer.

He spent the next little while thinking about what Doshi said and looking under rocks for crawdads. The dragon was content to keep him silent company at the bank.

Finally, however, Doshi rose to its feet. Though it was an illusion of a dragon, it stretched out its wings as if it were flesh and blood. "I must go. Chancy says we are to carry the wicked men who steal from their neighbors to a transport dragon. From there, they will go to the border."

With a mingled pang of homesickness and regret, Arthur wondered if they would end up in his border village. He wanted to ask, but he knew the value of keeping secrets.

"There are transport dragons?"

"The purples mostly, the poor simple creatures."

"Wow." He shook his head. "I didn't know there was so much to dragons. My father said you were just talking animals." He didn't realize what he had said might be rude until it was out.

Doshi, however, took it with calm grace. "We do talk. But we find that children, especially carded children, are the only ones who talk back."

"Thank you," Arthur said, "for talking to me."

Somehow, though the dragon's lips didn't move, he got the impression of a smile.

Then Doshi's form started to drift away into the breeze. Within moments, it was gone completely.

Arthur stared at the spot the dragon had been, then shook his head.

Did that just happen? It felt like a dream.

Dream or not, the water was beginning to grow cold. He dunked himself fully one last time to make sure he was as clean as one good swim could make him. Then he headed for his clothing.

His shirt and pants were close enough to dry so that they didn't stick too badly to his skin.

By the time Arthur made his way back to the town, Doshi and Chancy were gone, as were Bert and two of the men arrested for breaking into houses.

Red and the rest of the men were packing up the caravan and readying to go.

Arthur stole a few quick looks at Second. The man was talking with some of his men, not looking unusually upset. Most importantly, he paid no attention to Arthur.

He might have gotten away with his snooping.

Red caught him a few moments later and told him to yoke up the donkeys. After that was done, they were on the road.

Arthur glanced back once toward the town. Then he glanced toward the sky. Far, far up was a lone flying figure. It might have been a bird, but privately he thought it could be a dragon in flight.

CHAPTER 18

Over the next few weeks, Arthur settled into a routine. Rising from a bedroll with the fading dawn stars overhead became normal. The pain when he thought of the village slowly lost its jagged edge.

Once or twice he caught himself using the word "home" when referencing Red's cart.

Meanwhile, the caravan traveled steadily east and continued to stop at one town after another. Some were smaller than the first Arthur had seen. Some were marginally larger. None had an extraordinary encounter with dragons.

He found himself looking up at the sky, unable to get Doshi's question out of his head: Did he want to be a dragon rider?

He wasn't sure. What he *wanted* to know was what kind of dragon would choose him? What card would link with his own?

Something where he would learn skills even faster? Was it worth becoming a dragon rider for that? And would that help or hurt his goal of helping his father and the rest of the village? What if it was a card that could give him combat abilities? Or magic? There were too many unknowns.

Skill-wise, he seemed to be doing pretty well—especially his **Meal Preparation** skills. Second hadn't complained about the stew in days, which was a new record.

In addition, he had picked up a flurry of new skills over the last few days. One of which was Cartography. He had earned it a few days ago when Red had rolled out a map of the kingdom.

At first, Arthur wasn't sure what he had been looking at. No one used maps in the border village, where everyone knew every turn, practically every bush.

Red had guessed this and started pointing out features, including the wavy line that represented the road they were currently on.

Once that clicked, Arthur received the Cartography skill. It was as if something snapped into place and Arthur understood.

The kingdom was one general mass separated into dozens of different colored sections that represented duchies. These duchies were further separated into individual baronies, but this map wasn't detailed enough to show those.

Outside the main borders of the kingdom were the gray-colored scourge-lands. Most of the dead lands sat to the west, though there were thick patches of it surrounding the kingdom in all directions.

"Where is my village?" Arthur had asked eagerly.

Red silently pointed a gnarled finger not far from the road they were on. All this traveling, and they hadn't even moved a knuckle length on the map.

Most of Arthur's entire life had been lived on a black dot marked #49.

Homesick ache made him look away. His attention turned back to the kingdom at large.

The outline of the kingdom was a sort of blobby circle sitting off center in the middle of the continent. The core of the blob was thick with markings for cities. Yet Red kept the caravan on a road close to the border.

"Are we going to ever travel inward? Wouldn't there be better trading in the cities?" he asked.

Red shook his head. "I'll let you in on a secret: this area here between the border and the settled land is the best part of the kingdom."

"Why?"

He'd heard the other men in the caravan grumbling about all the "stick-shot" towns being stingy and how no one wanted to pay a fair price. Considering they all had enough to stay at the fanciest inns and drink their profits, Arthur wasn't sure how much was just bellyaching.

"Of course, we want to stay away from the dead lands. But the settled inner cities have their own problems." Red pointed to little triangles scattered all through the map. "These are scourge-eruptions. Tell me what you see about them."

"Uh . . ." He took a moment, then frowned. "There's hardly any near the border. There's a couple here and here." He pointed. One was scarily close to their current location. "But most are near the cities . . ." He whistled under his breath. The marked cities were a jumble of information—name, dutchy, and border lines. Now that he was looking, he recognized that there were quite a few triangles for eruptions, too. "Does the scourge like cities?"

"They eat life," Red corrected. "And you'll find more life bunched together in the cities than you will out here. Even if I were a carded man, I wouldn't live in one of those charnel houses for a whole Mythic set. Now, what do you think when I tell you that this map has only the last five years of eruptions?"

Arthur took that in. He had never thought much about scourgling eruptions. They never erupted near already dead land. There was nothing for them to feed on. "That it's a lot. Have you seen an eruption?"

"Yes. Luckily, we have these." Red pointed to a funny little marking on the map.

Arthur glanced at the legend and saw that it was to indicate a dragon hive. Whoever had drawn this map had made it look like a bee hive.

He started counting the hives and found there were twelve in total, arranged in a ring around the middle of the kingdom.

Unfortunately, none were remotely near their road. They would have to travel far inward to ever see one.

Well, maybe it was for the best. He couldn't avoid more silvers if he went to their home. But once he got another card . . . maybe.

One good thing about moving from town to town was the different things to learn. On his off time each night, he made sure to explore the darkened streets while trying to remain unseen.

He had gotten his **Stealth** up to level 9 but seemed to be stuck there. It was as if the skill was waiting for something before it moved from Basic to Apprentice, though he wasn't sure what it could be.

Frustrated, Arthur turned to other skills. He soon learned the inns in different towns had different card games. He watched the men play enough that he earned a **Card Counting** skill. Occasionally (usually when the men were in their cups) they allowed him to play.

One night, Arthur lost almost his entire supply of pennies but earned up to a level five in **Blackjack**. He considered that a fair trade.

At the very next town, he won several pennies by joining another kids' dice game of Circles and Squares. This time, once the other kids started looking at him sidelong, he made sure to lose several times in a row. He still left richer than when he'd arrived, and no one followed him back to the inn to beat him up.

Slowly but surely, he was getting a handle on this new life.

When his breakthrough came, it wasn't in Stealth.

The traders had such a profitable day at their newest stop that they decided to stay an extra day. That was fine by Arthur. This town was the largest he had seen so far, with much more to explore. Also, as long as the men were staying at the inn, his duties were minimal.

He still had three pennies burning a hole in his pocket from his salary and eight more he had squirreled away from previous stops.

Ten pennies were equal to a copper, and that was enough to buy himself a new simple shirt.

But when he stopped in the local Mercantile, a shirt wasn't what caught his eye.

It was a deck of playing cards.

Not a new deck—those went from five whole coppers all the way up to silvers if the faces were fancy enough. No, it was used but well-kept with no creasing on the edges or wear on the back to give the card underneath away.

Arthur walked out of the store with it for the princely price of nine pennies, talked down from a copper. He had the feeling he might have gained a haggling skill if he kept going . . . or the shopkeeper might have just thrown him out on his ear. He hadn't been willing to miss out on the prize.

He remembered the ref, Bert, from the first town. How he had organized the dice game. He'd gotten a small cut from the pot.

If Arthur could manage something like that as he moved from town to town, he might earn himself a nice source of income. Maybe enough to buy himself a low-ranked spell card.

Ah, but he would have to know what he was doing with the playing cards, first. No one would trust a dealer who fumbled his cards. Arthur found a good sitting rock on the edge of town and carefully started to shuffle his deck. It was not as easy as people made it look. Cards flew everywhere. He winced every time, hating to accidentally bend one.

If he worked slow enough, he picked up the knack. Soon, the cards were fanning together more or less reliably.

New skill gained: Card Shuffling (Gambler Class)
Due to your card's bonus traits, you automatically start this skill
at level 3.

That was standard. The message that came next surprised him.

New Class!
You have learned five synergistic skills.
You may combine these five skills into the basic Gambler Class:
Card Shuffling (Level 3)
Card Counting (Level 3)
Blackjack (Level 5)
Poker – Five Card Draw (Level 3)
Circles and Squares (Level 5)
This class will be the average of all added skill levels. Newly learned
compatible skills may be added to the Gambler Class. However, adding
a lower skill level contributes to the overall average, possibly lowering
the overall skill level.
Gambler Class (Basic: Level 4) 3.8 average with initial rounded bonus.
When equipped, card wielder will learn all Gambler Class levels at a
1.25 times rate in addition to existing skill bonuses.
+3 to Luck
+5 to non-class skills associated with an arithmetic foundation
Do you wish to combine these skills now?

Arthur gaped, then quickly shut his mouth, realizing he was gaping to midair.

He reread the alert. As far as he could tell, the only downside was that if he learned a new card game and added it to the class, he might lower the average of all his class skills.

That was no burden. He could always wait to level up the skill before adding it to the rest. All it took was patience.

What was the gain to luck? Did he have a luck skill?

No, he had raked everything about his card over and over. There was no mention of luck. There hadn't been any mention of classes, either.

It didn't matter. He was doing this.

Arthur nodded to himself. The moment he made his decision, the message disappeared.

In his mind's eye, a new card-shaped object swam up. It was more basic than even a Common-ranked card: Simple cardstock with bold letters.

Gambler Class
(Basic: Level 4)
Skills:
Card Shuffling (Level 3)
Card Counting (Level 3)
Blackjack (Level 5)
Poker – Five Card Draw (Level 3)
Circles and Squares (Level 5)
Do you wish to equip Gambler Class now?

Again, there could be only one answer.
Yes.
In his mind's eye, the Gambler Class card slotted into a new space.

Equipped Classes
Tier 1:
01/03
Tier 2:
0/2
Tier 3:
0/1
Non-Equipped Classes: 0

"Wow," he whispered.

His Gambler Class wasn't a real card. It was a figment of his Master of Skills. He instinctively felt that if he were to lose or give away his Master of Skills card, his classes would disappear as well.

Arthur heard a burst of laughter nearby. A group of teenagers walked down the street. They were joking, and several pushed each other playfully, but one had the shifty-eyed look of someone searching for a good time.

Playing cards in hand, Arthur stood. He was a Gambler, and if he was lucky, these teens might be interested in a friendly game of poker.

CHAPTER 19

While convincing people to part with their money, Arthur soon learned he needed to work on what the traders liked to call their "sales pitch." He and the rest of the caravan were a welcome oddity when they rolled into town but weren't necessarily trusted.

Unless Arthur spoke quickly, most assumed he was just setting them up to be cheated out of their money on a scam of a card game. That wasn't the case at all. Arthur wanted to *win* their money. Big difference.

However, his age helped out. If he were a full-grown man or even an older teenager, he would have been met with even more suspicion. But Arthur was twelve years old. Though the card in his heart was doing wonders, he still looked small and underfed. Harmless.

It was much easier to join a friendly game than to start one himself. Arthur found that once he had a seat at the card table, the little card tricks he'd learned over the past few weeks helped him gain favor.

He now knew three ways to shuffle—each flashier than the last. And once he pushed that skill to Apprentice, he never lost a card. His **Blackjack** and **Card Counting** skills weren't far behind.

Soon, he could count his little stash of coins in coppers instead of pennies. He had eight coppers in total and would have had more if he hadn't been forced to buy new shirts, pants, and boots for himself.

He was still small but growing. His old clothing no longer fit.

If he wasn't careful, people would notice he was growing quickly. Maybe too quickly for a boy hitting a normal growth spurt. He had to get his hands on a second card.

His newly gained coins were nowhere near enough to buy a card, however. From what Arthur heard, the bigger cities near the kingdom center had entire stores dedicated to cards. And if the rumors were to be believed, the Common cards went for a cheap price. Still more than what Arthur currently had—but a price measured in silver coins, not gold.

Still, things were looking up. Red was turning into a grumpy old uncle he never thought he'd had, and as long as he stayed out of Second's way, his life in the caravan was comfortable. It was a life Arthur never expected to have, but he found he was settling in quite nicely.

That ended the day of the eruption.

It was a day that started like any other. Red had pulled the entire caravan off to a little-known campsite the previous evening. They were still at least two days away from the next town on the schedule. Most of the men had done well selling their goods at the last town and were still in a celebratory mood. That meant Arthur had stayed up late selling them bottles of wine and doing the dishes.

He yawned contentedly as he brushed down the donkeys and yoked them up to the cart. Bella took the opportunity to nuzzle his hand.

Donkeys were finicky creatures, but Bella had taken a shine to Arthur ever since he finally passed Apprentice in **Equine Animal Care**.

Now Arthur felt a sort of invisible, nebulous connection between himself, the donkeys, and the horses. The oxen weren't included—he supposed it was because they were hitched to different carts, and he didn't work with them very much. Or maybe they weren't equines and so weren't included in his skill. He wasn't sure.

Idly, Arthur wondered if he should skip the card games in the next town and see if he could help out more at the stables. It might be useful to gain another animal-type skill. He'd rather get another class in that direction than, say, Thieving.

"We'll be moving the caravan soon, Ernie—oh." Red came up short, having called out to the boy before fully seeing what he was up to. "You've got the donkeys yoked? Excellent. We're going to have to move fast to make the next campsite before sunset tonight." He frowned at the men who were still packing away their carts and walked off before Arthur had time to respond.

Arthur turned to Bella. "Is he always like that?"

Bella's lips rose from her teeth, and she brayed in donkey agreement.

The caravan started moving before long, though at a slower pace than Red wanted. The day was both warm and pleasant. It was the sort of summer day that made Arthur wish there was a stream nearby to swim in.

The road took them over sharp-cut ridges that overlooked a small, lush valley.

Arthur paused a moment to gaze down. He hadn't yet gotten used to how things looked so green away from the border. Sometimes, back in his village, he would have to search for something that looked alive. Here, his eyes were full of the color green in more shades than he thought existed.

"Arthur!" Red barked.

Arthur flinched, thinking the man was calling him out for dawdling. Then his mind caught up, and he realized the man had used his real name.

Red gestured toward the line of carts rolling ahead of them. "Go to the lead wagon and tell them to stop. Now!" he barked before Arthur could question why.

Arthur took off like an arrow shot, racing past plodding oxen-pulled carts. Second was leading the caravan today. His huge, overstuffed cart blocked any view of the road ahead.

Running up to the driver's seat, Arthur puffed out, "Red says to stop."

Second glanced down at him, annoyed. Then, with a sharp whistle to the men and beasts, he pulled back hard on the reins. His oxen came to a stop. Behind them, the other carts did the same.

Hivey, Second's friend, glared down at Arthur. "What's wrong, Pissant? Someone break a wheel?"

"I don't know. He just asked—"

"Shut up," Second snapped. He looked grim. "Do you hear that?"

Arthur swiveled around, ears alert. The only thing noticeable was the harsh call of crows in the trees.

"The crows," Hivey confirmed.

Glancing up, Arthur saw dark shapes flitting from tree to tree. "Don't they get like that when there's food around?"

It was a mistake to offer his opinion, and he received a slap upside the head.

"Get back to your master, Pissant," Second said.

Rubbing the back of his skull, Arthur did. The people in the carts he passed were also looking up toward the trees. All seemed unhappy.

When he got to Red's cart, he found him checking all the tie-downs as if to make sure all was secure. He glanced up as Arthur approached.

"Check the donkeys. Make sure they're ready to run at a moment's notice."

Arthur did as he was told but called back over his shoulder, "What's going on? Is it the crows?"

Red shrugged. "Might be the crows found a good meal somewhere, or maybe some hunter stirred up one of their nests. But they're usually the first to know when there's a scourgling eruption nearby."

That stopped Arthur cold. "What? Now?" He looked around, half expecting the vegetation around him to start boiling with the dreaded creatures.

"We'll know if the donkeys start going crazy, too. They'll want to run away, and we're going to let them."

Swallowing, Arthur checked the donkeys' gear. He had recently oiled the leather reins and cleaned the rings that secured the ropes to the yoke. Everything was still in order.

However, the crows continued cawing. There were more and more of them— harsh croaking that was soon joined by other, shrill noises as more birds in the forest took up the call. Soon enough, every winged thing with a throat was trilling.

The donkeys began shifting from foot to foot. Bella lifted her head, flattened her ears, and let out a coughing bray.

Red came from around the back of the cart, took a look at the donkeys, and then met Arthur's eyes.

"Get in the driver's seat." His voice was forcefully calm. "When they bolt, they won't stop for nothing."

Arthur scrambled up. He hadn't been allowed in the driver's seat before. Red followed after. It was a tight fit, even though Red wasn't a big man.

Up and down the line of carts, the hooved animals grew more agitated. Oxen stamped their feet, snorted, and bellowed. One of the horses tried to stand up on its hind legs as if to buck.

Arthur's mouth went dry. He turned to Red to ask a question. Even though he was sitting right by the man, he still had to yell to be heard over the noise. "Do you know where the scourglings will come up?"

"Could be anywhere, though I think this one will be farther away. When I was a little older than you, one erupted practically under my feet. You shoulda seen the animals then." He grinned, almost feral.

At that moment, something deep inside Arthur quivered. He thought it came from his heart.

And off in the low valley, seen through a gap in the trees, the ground cracked open.

CHAPTER 20

With a scream of braying donkeys, the cart lurched forward so hard that Arthur nearly lost his seat anyway. Red grabbed him by the collar and hauled him back into place.

Every other animal hooked to a cart was rushing blindly forward. Meanwhile, the birds in the trees all shrieked as if the world was ending.

The cart bounced over stones and ruts in the road with enough force to put his teeth on edge. It would be a miracle if they didn't break a wheel.

Red kept a tight hold on the reins, trying to guide the screaming donkeys as much as they would allow.

Turning, Arthur looked back toward the direction of the eruption. He could only catch flashes of it down in the valley, visible through thick brush and trees. Loose gray soil was pushing itself out of the fissure.

As more and more built up, the new soil sprouting from the top to replace the old, a steeply sided cone formed. It was just as Arthur had always imagined a volcano to look. That might be why people called it a scourge-eruption.

But dirt wasn't the only thing coming from the top of the cone.

From this distance, the tumbling balls could be easily mistaken for clods of dirt or boulders. However, as they rolled out they uncurled and sprouted legs. From there, they charged into the world with eerie whistling shrieks.

Some unfurled wings instead of legs and took to the air.

Scourglings.

They seemed to come in a variety of shapes and sizes. From creatures so small he could only see them when they moved in groups, to larger, plodding forms the size of one of the cart oxen.

Wherever they touched the ground, the vegetation wilted back.

Scourglings were the opposite of life. Given enough time, their presence killed every patch of land they touched, down to the nutrients in the soil that allowed roots to take hold.

The cart jolted again. Arthur looked ahead to see they were rounding a bend. This would take them to the other side of the ridge, putting it between themselves and the valley.

Would it be far enough to get away from the scourglings?

He glanced at Red. The man was serious and grim-faced, but he didn't look frightened. Arthur decided that was a hopeful sign.

"Hold on," Red advised again.

They had just about reached the top of the ridge. In the next second, every cart practically careened down the slope.

Shouts came from ahead as the men applied handbrakes to the carts. They drew back on the reins to try to pull the panicked animals under some control. Gradually, it started to work.

Now that they were separated by vegetation and the land, the scourglings' terrible whistling shrieks became quieter. But not gone completely. Straight up through the trees, Arthur caught flashes of flying scourglings flapping by on leathery wings. They were like twisted, halfway versions between dragons and vultures. Long-necked with cruel sharp-pointed heads and four grasping limbs tipped with claws. Thankfully, none hunted below the trees. Instead, they went for the calling birds, who quickly went silent . . . or were silenced.

The road widened at the bottom of the hill as the land turned into a natural meadow, clear of trees.

Second was finally able to pull his animals to a stop at the edge of the tree line before they went into open meadow. Though, judging by the animals' heaving sides, stopping was more due to their exhaustion than Second's skill. Red's donkeys were not doing much better.

Once all were stopped and the handbrakes applied, every man jumped down to check on the animals and carts.

Arthur headed for Bella, who was trembling from head to hoof. Her eyes were wide and rolling. Arthur did his best to soothe her, reaching for the power of his Animal Husbandry skill.

She and the rest of the donkeys slowly calmed.

Suddenly there was an almighty ripping sound, like two giant hands had taken a piece of the sky and torn it apart.

Arthur startled in surprise and looked up.

There, hundreds of feet up, hung a ragged black line in the sky. With stomach-dropping fear, he thought that the scourglings must have done this. He had no idea that they could ruin the blue sky along with the land.

Then something came out of the line. It was a dragon colored a green so deep, it would have looked black except for the iridescent flashes when the sun-light caught its scales.

The dragon crawled out of the tear as though struggling from a narrow crack in a rock wall. Then its wings caught air, and it flapped to the side.

Another dragon, a similar shade, if a bit lighter, quickly followed the first but took position on the opposite side of the tear.

As one, the dragons took hold of the rip in the sky as if it were a physical thing and pulled it apart. It widened to a black crescent, like a burnt version of the moon. The dragons flapped in place, holding it open.

Through this newly enlarged rip poured out more dragons. Just a handful at first, which came in all sizes, from three times the length of the monstrous red to the size of Bella the donkey. Then a dozen, and then more and more. A rainbow of colors shading from snowy white to spring green, flamboyant pink, deep blue, and purple—most of them a glittering combination of two colors, with occa-sional three-tone triads.

Then a second rip in the sky tore itself open. Another pair of iridescent green dragons widened it, and more dragons poured in.

Red came to stand by Arthur.

"Those would be the hives," he said in satisfaction.

Arthur closed his mouth with a snap. His jaw had been hanging open.

Sure enough, the first of the dragons set upon the flying scourglings. One red-and-orange dragon dived down with claws that lengthened to curved, gleam-ing swords. It easily sliced a scourgling out of the air. The remaining body fell in chunks.

The sword-claw dragon folded its wings and dived down to the falling remains. As it did, it half rolled on its side. The rider, who was securely strapped on, reached out and grabbed the scourgling's torso, ripping something glowing from it before tossing it away.

The sword-claw dragon righted itself and flew on.

"What was that?" Arthur asked. "Did he take a card from the scourgling?"

Red ignored the question. "I think we should be safe enough here. We have some distance from the eruption, and the hives will be on the hunt now."

Ashamed that he had been staring and not working, Arthur glanced toward the rest of the caravan. The men were still scrambling around, but they weren't busy battening everything down. Some were grabbing for cudgels or long dag-gers. They wore grim, anticipatory expressions.

One man brought two clenched fists together. When he pulled them apart, his arms up to his elbows were covered in glittering purple lines of magic shaped like gauntlets. Within a few seconds, the lines had crawled up each arm, building an outline of armor around his torso up to his neck. Lastly, the man put a rough leather helmet on his head.

He must have a card power that armored his arms and chest . . . though it looked a little silly with his legs unprotected.

Second came striding up to Red. "You staying behind?"

"Yes, and if you had any sense, you would too," Red replied. "I tell you every time, it's not worth it, and every time you don't listen and come back less a man or two."

Second shrugged. "We all take our chances. I come back richer while you miss out."

Red scowled and shook his head. "I suppose you'll be taking your whole team?"

"Not all of them. Axel lost everything but his trap card on a bad hand of poker the other night. He doesn't have anything worth fighting with. That leaves me down a man, so I'm taking the Pissant."

Arthur went from being shocked that anyone would bet spell cards in poker to just flat-out shocked. *"Me?"*

Red growled, half standing from his seat. "That's scourge-shit. He's just a boy."

"He's old enough to hold a knife and watch our backs. Besides." Second smiled over at Arthur. It wasn't a nice smile. "He owes me one."

Red swung around on Arthur, a question in his expression. When Arthur only stared back with wide, guilty eyes, he grimaced and looked at Second. "He's too young. He doesn't have a card to protect himself."

"Maybe he'll get one today. What do you say, kid?"

He'd just called him kid. Not Pissant.

Arthur knew this was Second's way of buttering him up, but he still felt marginally warmer toward the man.

"He doesn't need a damn magic card," Red snapped.

Arthur looked from one man to the other. Red was supposed to be the leader of the caravan, but Second was nearly two feet taller than him and twice as wide. And he had just walked up and demanded Arthur, Red's apprentice, like acquiescence was expected.

Red might talk tough and he might own the business on paper, but Second was the one with the power. He had the cards to back up any demand.

"What do you need me to do?" Arthur asked carefully.

Red's expression sagged as if he had already lost the fight.

Judging by his widening smile, Second thought so, too.

"Like I said, I need an extra pair of eyes to watch our backs." He pointed a thumb toward the direction they'd come from. Toward the eruption. "Scourglings drop card shards, and dragons . . . well, they have a nasty habit of dropping out of the sky, too. That means there's whole cards to be had. You want in?"

"Of course he doesn't," Red grumbled, but it was half-hearted.

Arthur took in a breath. He needed a second card. He would be a fool not to take this chance.

"Second's right. I owe him," he said stoutly, then looked at Second. "If I go with you, we're square?"

"Yeah, kid. We'd be even."

Red tried one final time. "Whatever this is about, whatever you owe him, it can wait. It's not worth your life."

"I want to go," Arthur said, and hated the way Red's shoulders fell.

"Some idiots have to learn for themselves," he said. "No card is worth your life."

"I'll be careful."

With a shake of his head, Red turned away. "Do what you want. I can't stop you if you truly want to go."

The dismissal hurt.

"Red—" Arthur started.

Second cut in. "We don't have time for this. Come on."

He turned and walked away.

Arthur hesitated, pained, but then followed after Second.

As he did, he made sure his Gambler Class was still equipped. It granted him three points of luck, and he had the feeling he was going to need all of them today.

CHAPTER 21

"Y ou know how to use this?"

Before Arthur could answer, Second pushed the handle of a simple dagger into his hands. It was cheap and not well maintained, with rust spots on the spine of the blade. At least the edges looked sharp enough.

"I can use it," Arthur said with more confidence than he currently felt. His only **Knife Work** skill came from meal preparation.

He now bitterly regretted learning different ways to shuffle cards instead of different ways to use a knife.

"Good. You'll get the opportunity soon." Second turned and waved toward his cart.

One of his men, Hivey, broke off from a conversation with Axel and jogged over with a gleaming machete in one hand and a heavy mace in the other.

"Here you go." He handed the mace to Second.

"You made it stronger?"

"Yeah, it won't break even if you spent all afternoon bashing it against a rock."

The man must have a material-reinforcement card, like the one he'd seen in the general store.

Arthur held out his dagger. "Can you do mine?"

Hivey barely spared him a glance. "Gotta save my mana."

And that was that.

Second didn't seem to care either. Silently, he turned to stride toward the line of trees. Hivey followed, and after a moment's hesitation, so did Arthur.

They weren't the only ones leaving the caravan. Men in pairs and small groups were heading toward the tree line, leaving only a few people behind to guard the carts and animals. Every group was spread out, none coming close to one another.

Above their heads, dragons were still battling occasional flying scourglings. The sky was much clearer than it had been a few minutes before. Judging by the whistling cries and distant booms, the main bulk of the battle had moved to the other side of the ridge, toward the small valley.

Arthur followed behind the two men, letting them break a trail through the foliage. It seemed they were ignoring the road completely, though he saw several men heading there.

Soon, Second located a deer trail, which cut through the worst of it. Second glanced over his shoulder at Arthur.

"If you come across any scourglings, you stab them and try not to get scratched or bit. That's how you get scourge-sickness. Anything that gets bit, you lose."

"So watch your dick," Hivey said with a high-pitched laugh.

Arthur shuddered. He'd seen his fair share of scourge-sicknesses and knew how fast they rotted a body. "Will that happen, even if you're carded?"

Second snapped around. "You're not carded, are you?"

He realized his mistake at once. "'Course not. I thought you said we could get cards out here."

Second looked at him for a moment as if weighing the answer. Arthur just stared back with what he hoped were wide, guileless eyes.

Finally, Second gave a slow nod. "Don't get greedy. We might get enough card shards to make a card or get lucky enough to come across a whole one. But I get the first pick of the loot. Hivey's second, and if anything's left over, you get some. You understand?"

Arthur made a show of reluctance, going so far as to sneak a look behind himself as if he were considering going back. If he weren't carded, it wouldn't be an act. "I don't want to lose my . . . uh, I don't want to lose *anything*," he said, and Hivey snickered like a child who had just heard a dirty word.

"Then act smart, be quick, and keep a look out. Hivey and I don't have to worry about scourge-sickness. We'll take the hit if we need to," Second said, but the quick, unsure look Hivey sent him wasn't reassuring. It was good to know Arthur had some protection because of his card, though.

He nodded as if he was relieved anyway. Satisfied, Second turned back.

New skill gained: Acting (Thief/Performer)
Due to your card's bonus traits, you automatically start this skill
at level 3.

Really? He hadn't received a skill for lying but he got one for acting? Arthur didn't like to think of himself as a big liar, but he had sold Red and the rest of the men a few fibs during his weeks here.

Maybe it was the stakes that counted. All the fibs he had told to Red and the others had been small. Now he was in a dangerous place with men he didn't trust. Arthur had to sell any lie for all he was worth.

They continued, pushing through the vegetation back toward the direction of the valley. Second led them in a direction that wound around the low spar of the ridge.

The distant racket of whistles, roars, and crackling magic grew louder. The sheer quality of it grew thicker. Arthur assumed this was because dragons continued to pour out of the gaps in the sky. They had joined the fray, and he wasn't sure there would be anything left soon.

That was both a relief and a disappointment. He didn't want to get killed by a scourgling, but he did want a shot at a card. Or a card shard.

"What are card shards?" he asked.

Second ignored him completely. He'd snatched Hivey's machete out of his hand and started slashing at the thick underbrush.

It was Hivey who answered. "Shards are tiny parts of cards. You put enough of them together, like a jigsaw puzzle. Then you get a card out of it. See?"

Arthur didn't. "So you have to find the right shards out of the hundreds of scourglings—"

"No, no. Except for the corner and end pieces, most of them look the same. And they're blank—scourglings start with card shards, but if any of them live long enough, or eat enough, then they might develop a full card." He smiled as if he found the next thought funny. "And if they eat somebody with a card, then they add that to their own."

"They can use magic cards?" Arthur asked, feeling sick.

"We'll be out of here before any of them grow strong enough to cast spells," Second grunted, and with a final slash, the thick vegetation parted in front of him.

Handing the machete back to Hivey, he pushed on.

They moved for a few more cart lengths. Suddenly, Second stopped so quick that Arthur nearly ran into his wide back. Stepping around, he looked to see what had caught the man's attention.

Ahead, the underbrush opened thanks to a huge, ancient tree with graceful branches. The light was low under the tree, but it was still visibly wilting before their eyes—leaves drying out, brown and curling up inward.

Arthur concentrated. It was hard to tell over the background of battle beyond, but he thought he heard something scrabbling. Wood fibers parted, and the grand old tree shivered.

Slowly, the three of them walked around. Something had dug a hole at the base of the tree, and the weeds all around it had blackened.

"A digger," Hivey whispered. "Shouldn't be too hard."

"But what's it doing?" Arthur asked. "Eating the tree?" The scourgling—because that's all it could be with the land gone dead like that—seemed to be digging right to the root ball. That didn't make sense. If it wanted tasty wood, why not scrape off the tough outer bark and start on the inner flesh? Even Arthur had occasionally chewed pine needles on hungry days.

"They go for the life force," Hivey said. "The base of the tree, near the roots, is where—"

"Shut up," Second snapped.

It was too late.

Either the scourgling had heard them or sensed them some other way. The frantic scrabbling from inside the hole stopped. A moment later, two beady eyes peered out, cast in red light like burned coals.

With the high whistle of air escaping a teakettle, the thing launched itself at them.

Or at least, it started to.

Second blurred in that same too-fast-to-see motion he'd used that time he'd saved Arthur in the stables.

One moment, he stood in front of Arthur. The next, he was bringing his mace down on the charging scourgling.

The mace landed solidly on the head, crushing the skull in an instant.

Arthur had barely begun to step back in surprise, and the scourgling was already dead.

It had been about the size of a house cat, completely bald. Its skin was a mottled gray that looked faintly rotten. Though it had the round shape of a beaver, there hadn't been a tail. The big front teeth—or what was left of them—were like two jagged daggers.

Hivey cheered.

With a grunt, Second placed one foot on the forequarters of the thing as if worried it would get back up, splattered brains and all. He didn't need to worry. A moment later, a visible green light emanated from the creature's chest.

Second bent and gestured at it as if wafting up a loop of smoke.

A tiny triangular shard of white obediently floated up. To Arthur's eye, it looked like cardstock.

Second snatched it out of the air and brought it close to his eyes to examine it. "Common piece. Figures." Then he stuffed it in his pants pocket. "Let's go. I bet this one was one of the first to erupt and got the jump on the others out here, but there will be more."

They walked on. The noise grew louder and louder—a constant resounding chaos that all melted together until Arthur couldn't pick out one tone. He wanted to put his hands over his ears but didn't want to look like a weakling in front of the men.

Finally, the forest broke into a clearing. They were on the edge of the ridge, the land pointed sharply down. From there, they had a view of the valley.

Arthur gaped. What had been a cone of dirt maybe the size of the largest building in his old village had grown. Now the base of it took over a good quarter of the valley. Its peak stretched up nearly as tall as the ridge they stood on. More soil and scourglings fountained out of the top.

It was a true volcano.

The sky all around it was thick with dragons: flying, roaring, battling in midair. It was a free-for-all between scourglings and dragons, the air thick with magic.

Flames of all colors, lightning bolts, ice bolts, weather anomalies that spun wind to suck scourglings into miniature tornadoes, and hundreds of other techniques that either flashed by too quickly to identify, or Arthur had no name for.

Those were only the battles in the air. The valley beyond the cone was decimated. Everything that had been green was now black and dead. From this angle, Arthur saw it had once been farmland. The homes that dotted the fields were on fire or just gone.

And the earth was a crawling morass of scourglings.

Scourglings were being pummeled from above and below by earthen spikes, crushed by giant golems made of tree limbs, drowned by mobile puddles of water, and melted by green clouds of acid.

Yet many survived to range out and eat anything still alive. More erupted out of the volcano in a never-ending stream.

Arthur's legs shook. "I'm not going down there."

"Of course we're not, idiot," Second snapped. "We're staying near the outer edge. Whatever scourglings crawl out from the valley, we kill and harvest."

Well. That didn't sound too bad. Especially since Second had killed one in a single hit.

Second continued, "Any dragons or riders fall, we go for them first."

Arthur started to nod. He was grateful for the brave dragons and their riders for protecting them against the scourge. Of course they would help.

Then he noticed the grim looks on Second's and Hivey's faces.

"To help them, right?" he asked, half afraid of the answer.

Second slapped him upside the head. "What do you think? You go for their cards, idiot."

"But we can't! They're out there fighting for us. We can't just—"

"If they've fallen, they're already dead," Hivey said.

Second took one step toward him, looming dangerously. "If that happens, you do what you're told. I don't want to hear you sniveling—"

There was no warning. Then again, it was hard to hear anything over the fighting.

A scourgling the size and shape of a naked gray wolf leaped out from the underbrush. It landed with its teeth clamped on Hivey.

CHAPTER 22

Hivey let out a high-pitched scream, which almost blended in with the whistling scourglings.

Arthur acted on pure instinct. Had he been thinking, he would have expected to freeze. He should have run.

Instead, he whipped forward and brought his dagger down on the hindquarters of the beast. The blade sank deep and stayed there, hitting bone.

He'd reacted quickly, but not as quick as Second. In a blur, he had brought his mace around to hit the thing. His strike was off center and didn't crush the skull, but it did knock the beast away.

Whistling in distress, the scourge-wolf tried to get up, but the leg Arthur stabbed crumpled under it. It reached around to bite at the dagger still stuck in its hindquarters.

That gave Second enough time to bring the mace down one more time. That was all it took.

Hivey had collapsed, moaning. His shoulder was a mass of bloody, shredded flesh.

Arthur's **Nursecraft** skills kicked in. He knelt by the other man. The first thing to do was assess the damage. "Keep pressure on it." Grabbing the man's hand, he brought it to hold his shoulder. "Are you hurt anywhere else?"

"Idiot!" Second barked. For once, it wasn't aimed at Arthur. "I told you to keep your damn eyes open."

Shoving Arthur away, he looked Hivey up and down. "Well? You going to let it fester?"

Hivey blinked as if coming out of a daze. Then he shifted to lift his good arm. Pure water started forming in the cup of his hand. He brought it over and, wincing, tipped it over his shoulder.

So, Hivey had at least two cards. One for strengthening weapons, one for conjuring water. Arthur made a mental note to remember that.

Second backed off enough for Arthur to help the man clean the wound. The scourge-wolf's teeth had been like knives. The shoulder was bleeding, but the blood wasn't spurting.

The man had gone pale, though if it was from pain or shock, Arthur didn't know.

"That's a neat trick," he said, nodding to the water forming anew in Hivey's hand.

"Minor wellspring," Hivey said. "Useful. I'm never thirsty, even in— Ah!" He winced as a small movement shifted his wound. "Even in the desert."

Meanwhile, Second had returned to the corpse of the scourge-wolf and harvested it. "Two shards," he said, and gave one to Hivey. The smaller one, Arthur noticed.

Hivey took it with his good hand and painfully tucked it into his pocket. "I think I'm tapping out, boss."

"Are you serious? We've just begun. I've only got two shards. That's nothing!"

Arthur couldn't believe what he was hearing. "He's bleeding real bad. I think this'll need stitches." He didn't add that he thought Hivey might lose the arm, carded or not.

Hivey nodded. "Yeah . . . I'm out."

It was as if a thunderstorm passed over Second's face. "Fine. If you're quitting, you can find your way back to the trail yourself. Come on, kid."

Arthur stared. "We can't just leave him here."

"Are you reneging on our deal?" The words were simple, the tone silky and dangerous.

Swallowing, Arthur looked back to Hivey. The man was all but pleading for help with his eyes. A few minutes ago, he hadn't wanted to waste mana on making Arthur's dagger stronger. Now he wanted his help.

"Give me five minutes. We can fix him up, bind the wound. You can walk, right, Hivey?" Arthur could hear the desperation in his voice, silently begging for forgiveness. He barely waited for the man to start to nod before Arthur rose and retrieved his dagger from the scourge-wolf's corpse.

The beast was even uglier now that he had time to get a good look at it. The mottled markings on its bare skin gave it the appearance of being infected with mange. The teeth were so large they jutted up, down, and out from the jaw in all directions. No wonder Hivey was so chewed up.

Pulling the dagger free, he returned and asked Hivey to wash the worst of the gunk off it. Then he cut the remains of the man's sleeve off. With that, he tied it awkwardly around the shoulder. He hoped it wasn't too tight.

Finally, he helped the man to his feet. Hivey leaned all his weight against him, nearly making Arthur's legs buckle.

"Maybe a walking stick?" Arthur asked through gritted teeth.

"Yeah," Hivey agreed, making no move to shift his weight.

Arthur looked to Second, but the man had turned away in impatience and disgust.

He convinced Hivey to lean against the trunk of a tree while Arthur fetched a stick long and strong enough to help him. It was a crooked, gnarled thing, but it was better than nothing.

Using it, Hivey was able to stagger a few steps before he stopped, panting.

New skill level:
Basic Nursecraft (Healing Class)
Level 4

"All right. Let's go," Second said. "We've wasted enough time."

Hivey seemed to agree. He made a few careful, stumbling steps back the way they'd come. He didn't look back, and he hadn't thanked Arthur for his help.

He can make it, Arthur told himself. But it was with a sick feeling that he turned and followed Second to the downhill slope path again.

He didn't like this. First, he had hurt Red's good opinion of him. Now he was leaving a bleeding man to stumble his way back to the caravan.

No question that Arthur owed Second a favor, but he was starting to think the man's price was too high.

They hadn't gone more than twenty feet down the hill before they were set upon by a group of small scourglings. These were half the size of the digger before and were shaped like bunnies. Demon bunnies with raking claws and a mouthful of needle teeth.

Thankfully, the group—warren?—was charging up at them at a steep angle. That gave Second plenty of time to ready his mace and Arthur to jump onto an outcropping of stone.

Second swept his mace like a scythe, clearing out several scourge-bunnies at a time. It only took him three sweeps to kill all of them. But not before one got close enough to tear a pants leg to ribbons.

Afterward, Second glared at Arthur. "Are you ever going to help, or are you just going to stand there?"

"I'm keeping a look out," Arthur said from the safety of his higher rock. "You told Red that was my job."

"That was then. Now we're down a man. Either you help or you don't get paid."

Second grunted and started harvesting the scourge-bunnies. Each one produced a shard. He had to have close to ten.

"I don't have a card," Arthur reminded him. "Do you have enough shards to make me one? Maybe if you put them together—"

Second whipped around to face him, nostrils flaring. "You don't get paid before the work's done, Pissant."

He was back to being called Pissant. Arthur had known the man was just being nice to get him to join him, but confirming it grated on his nerves.

"Why should I lift a finger to help you?" he snapped back. "If I get hurt, you'll just leave me out here to die like you did Hivey."

Second took a threatening step toward him. "Because if you're dead weight, I'll break your kneecaps and leave you out here for the scourglings."

Arthur resisted the urge to step back in alarm. Second was a mean son of a bitch, but he wasn't an idiot. Maybe he could be negotiated with.

"I want to help—I want to get shards and cards of my own," he improvised when Second's face darkened. "I *really* do. But I can't fight scourglings with this." He held up the dagger, which looked small and pathetic. "And I won't do it if it costs me a limb."

Second stared at him for a silent moment. Arthur could practically see the thoughts churning behind his eyes. He had his attention.

So, he took a risk.

"I know you have more than one card," Arthur said, adding hurriedly, "Hivey has two and he's a nobody, when you practically lead the caravan. Just give me one. A Common-rank I can defend with. I'll work hard to get you more cards, and either you can let me keep it or exchange it for something else."

Again, Second was silent for a moment. "Do you know how a man steals cards from another's heart?"

"They . . . they have to kill them, right? If they're not given willingly?"

"Smart boy." Another step and Second was within easy arm's length of Arthur. Not that it mattered with Second's speed-boost power.

Then Second pulled down the collar of his shirt and reached to his chest. He pinched his fingers and pulled out a card.

From the simple matte-white look of it, Arthur knew it was a Common card even before Second flipped it around so he could read it.

Sharp as Nails
Body Enhancement
Common
This card grants the wielder the ability to lengthen fingers and toenails to sharp knife points using mana. Higher mana costs will result in sharper nails. Advanced levels allow the user more control over this body enhancement.

Arthur had no idea Second was carrying that around in his heart. He'd never seen him use it. Just the quick speed attacks.

It made him wonder what else the man had been carrying around. More importantly, Arthur wondered what he could do with it. His very hands and feet would become weapons. While that wouldn't do much to a scourge-wolf, he could at least give scourge-bunnies a sharp kick.

Second met his eyes and smiled. He must have seen Arthur's desire for the card.

"If you fail me, I'll cut out your heart and take my card back. You get me?"

"I do."

Arthur took the card. It buzzed warmly in his hand as if it were saying hello.

A desperate dragon shrieked high above.

There was so much noise that one more sound should have gotten lost. However, the shriek had been like a woman's scream, and it caught his attention.

He looked up, fully expecting to see a dragon in mid-battle with a scourgling.

Instead, he saw two large dragons—a brassy orange and a sky blue—attacking a smaller, delicate pink dragon.

The attackers didn't use magical spells. No fire, ice, wind, lightning, or anything else that had run so thick around the eruption. They were simply ripping at the pink dragon with claws and teeth, ignoring its piteous shrieks and thrashing.

And then, with an even worse soul-wrenching cry, something toppled flailing from the pink's back.

It was the rider.

The pink screamed again and tried to dive for its rider. The other two held it back and went for the neck.

Blood spurted. Suddenly, the brassy orange and sky blue were fighting each other for the remains—each reaching for the card now glowing in the pink's chest.

Arthur was horrified.

The dragons should be fighting the scourglings, not each other. That had been . . . that had been a murder. Cold-blooded murder. And for what? A card?

Abruptly, Second snatched the Sharp as Nails card from Arthur's hand.

"Hey—" Arthur objected, but Second just pushed it back into his own heart.

"Change of plans," Second said. "We're getting that rider before anyone else can harvest him. You don't need a card for that."

Arthur shook his head, still reeling from the awful thing he'd just witnessed, and his change of fortune. He should have stuck the card in his heart the second he had his hands on it.

He wouldn't make that mistake again.

Second wasn't waiting for him to get his head together. Grabbing Arthur by the back of the neck, he practically propelled him down the trail.

"Did you see where he landed? Over this way, right?"

He didn't reply. It was everything he could do to keep his feet. Second wasn't using his card to blur his speed, but he was still a powerful man with a longer stride.

They reached a flat area, still above the valley, but only just.

Arthur glanced up to see the dragons still fighting. The pink was nothing but a scrap of meat between them.

Around, other dragons wheeled and fought actual battles with scourglings. If anyone had seen what happened, they didn't do anything.

That felt like a betrayal.

Second growled under his breath, looking around. "I can't see him. Can you? Never mind, we'll have to split up."

"What?" Tearing his gaze from the sky, Arthur looked around. They were still above the valley, but closer than he would have liked. He half expected scourglings to leap out and get him at any moment.

"I'll go this way." He pointed to the left. "You go over there. Let out a shout the second you find him. You understand me?"

"I . . . yes," he said, still shocked but knowing Second wouldn't take it well if he disagreed. The man was practically humming with frantic greed.

With a blur, Second was gone.

And Arthur was all alone with treacherous dragons above him and scourglings all around him.

CHAPTER 23

Arthur held his dagger out in front of him as he walked—part threat, but mostly as a talisman.

He looked around, alert for any sign of scourglings. Or the fallen dragon rider.

Inside, his heart seethed.

They were close to the valley. So close that when he got glimpses down below through the tree breaks, he could pick out individual scourglings rampaging. The air had taken on an acidic burnt flavor. It was the tang of dead land. To Arthur, it tasted like home.

The only thing he had going for him was the fact that he was carded. But Second didn't know that. He had just left Arthur alone to find the dragon rider or die.

Or maybe to find the dragon rider *and* die.

He should have listened to Red. Should have told Second to stuff the favor he thought Arthur owed him where the sun didn't shine. Arthur had never asked him for help with Bert and his boys. In hindsight, he would have rather taken a beating than face down scourglings.

But that sense of rage and injustice wasn't enough to make him turn back. That dragon rider might be alive and need help. And . . . well, the fact of it was, Arthur wanted to collect card shards of his own.

His newfound determination carried him through the next patch of vegetation, right up until the bushes next to him started to crackle and shake.

Whipping around, Arthur held his dagger in a ready position. His face was stern and cold. Inside his thoughts, however, he blubbered, *Oh, no, no, no I'm not ready . . . just go away . . .*

Several men walked out of the bushes. They all wore boiled leather shirts and rawhide coverings over their pants and carried mean-looking swords.

They seemed as surprised to see Arthur as he was to see them.

"Hey, kid, what are you doing out here?" one asked.

Arthur jutted out his jaw. "Hunting scourglings. What're you doing out here?"

"Scourge-shit. You're looking for that dragon rider, same as everyone else." The man leveled the point of his sword at him. "You find him yet?"

Arthur gulped, eyes locked to the point. "I saw him land that way," he invented, pointing to the right, which was not at all in the right direction. "But he's on a rock spar. I . . . I was trying to find a way around."

New skill level: Acting (Thief/Performer Class)
Level 5

The man didn't lower his sword. "That's what I thought." Then he jerked his chin. "You walk ahead of us. You'll be the scourgling bait."

Arthur made a show of nodding and stepped to do as he was told. The moment he got more than an arm's length from these guys, he planned on running. He couldn't say why exactly, since they all were bigger than him, but he didn't think they were carded. They didn't have the magic to stop him.

Carded or not, they were full grown and stronger. As Arthur passed, one snatched his dagger from his hand.

"I'll be taking this," he said. "As prepayment."

"Payment for what?" Arthur snapped. The moment he'd said it, he knew he had just made a mistake. The mask he had put on to show he was meek and harmless had slipped. Well, he was probably harmless to these taller, stronger men. But he wasn't meek.

The man's face crinkled in rage, and then he punched Arthur, hard in the face. It wasn't anything like the dismissive slaps that Second and the others used. This was a real punch.

Arthur fell to the ground, cradling his head. The skin and bone around his right eye was a blaze of pain, and though his instincts screamed to get up and fight, the world around him was swooping and unstable.

One of the men picked him up by the collar and settled him on his feet. It was everything he could to stay upright.

"March!"

Someone shoved him, and Arthur staggered, nearly falling again before he righted himself.

He strode forward blindly for the first dozen or so yards. Then his head started to clear. They had pushed him toward the direction where he thought the dragon rider must have fallen.

Second would be around here, too. If he saw Arthur's predicament, would he save him?

Maybe. Maybe not. If he did, he would claim Arthur earned him another favor. He wasn't sure if he could bear that.

He wanted a second card with a burning fervor. Even Second's fingernail-sharpening card gave him the possibility of protecting himself.

Instead, what did he have? A Gambler Class, **Animal Husbandry** skill . . . Ugh, **Tidying** . . .

Wait. He had **Stealth**.

It was stuck on Basic level 9. He still didn't know what it would take to break into Apprentice, but his ability to blend into the shadows wasn't too bad.

With that in mind, Arthur subtly angled his walk toward the denser part of the forest. He kept his gait a little awkward, as if he were still reeling from the blow. That wasn't too much of an exaggeration. Already, he could feel his eye swelling.

The men followed without much comment. They knew if there were scour-glings ahead, Arthur would be the first to go.

There was a big, wide tree not far ahead with a nest of other saplings near what would have been the sunny side of the trunk. They grew so thickly together that the area was shadowed.

That was the best chance he could get.

Fiercely concentrating on his skill, he stepped around the tree and into the small grove.

Something changed. His footsteps felt fluid, as if he was sliding between the thick saplings. Barely a branch rustled.

Something told Arthur to kneel down low, stay out of their direct line of sight. One hand slid to his chest, pressing over his heart.

The men knew he was pulling something the moment he stepped around that tree. But they had been more than a dozen feet behind, and it took them a few moments to catch up.

They came around, glancing back and forth.

"Where'd he go?"

"You see footprints?"

"Here." The leader, the one who had punched him, stalked directly for the tiny grove. He frowned at the thick bunch of undisturbed saplings. His eyes focused up around Arthur's chest height.

Arthur held his breath, mentally holding on to that skill with both hands. The hand over his chest curled into a claw, willing the skill to work.

New skill level:
Basic Stealth (Rogue/Thief Class)
Level 10
For reaching level 10, your skill has been upgraded from Basic to Apprentice.

After a moment, the man turned away.

"Let's keep going. If he finds the rider's body first, we'll—"

He was interrupted by a whistling shriek from ahead in the brush. It was followed by another, and another.

The men instantly clustered together, their weapons drawn.

Something crashed through the brush to their right, and the whistling took on a fevered pitch.

A scourgling broke through the trees at full gallop. It was roughly shaped like a boar—one of those monster creatures half the size of a donkey. Only in place of a pig's snout, it had a sharply pointed muzzle utterly filled with teeth.

It was followed by two more, equally as large.

The men made a brave show of swinging their swords. Even the dagger they'd stolen from Arthur came into play. None of it helped. They were overwhelmed.

In his mind, Arthur was dragged back to the moment where he had hidden under the bushes back at his border village. Too terrified to move, he had watched the red dragon kill the baron's men.

This time, he didn't intend to be caught once the scourglings were done. Holding on to the **Stealth** skill like a lifeline, he slowly backed farther and farther into the grove of saplings. He kept each movement smooth and slow to create as little noise as possible.

That was difficult, especially when the scourglings started to eat the bodies of the men. It turned out Arthur had been wrong: one was carded, though the card obviously hadn't been combat oriented.

The scourgling pulled it out of the man's heart and gulped it down. It briefly flared blue as if it had gained a new power, then continued eating the organ meat.

Arthur reached the other end of the grove. He backed up and then slowly rose.

Then he jogged away.

He wasn't sure of the direction that he ran. Somewhere along the line, he had gotten completely turned around. The whistles of feasting scourglings were easy to pick out, so he decided to head away from that.

Screw Second and the favor Arthur owed him. He was done.

Which was, of course, the moment he found the dragon rider.

A scrap of cloth caught his eye. Mostly because it was garishly pink and stood out on the green-and-brown forest floor.

The man hadn't had the fiercest-looking dragon, but he had been proud enough of it to wear its colors into battle.

Swallowing, Arthur stepped forward. There were broken branches above that the rider had snapped on the way down.

He was dead. Obviously so with a visible bloody crack in the skull where his head had hit a rock. Though judging by the broken branches above and scattered around, he had probably been gone before he hit the ground.

Arthur had seen a lot of people die. He'd just seen three men eaten a few minutes ago. This sight tightened his throat.

A throb of, what? Greed? Obligation? He wasn't sure, but it made him step forward.

The man had been large and burly, and it took some effort to roll him on his back. When he did, Arthur saw there was a glow emanating from his chest.

No one else had found the body yet. He still had the card.

Arthur had seen card harvesting done a few times, though hadn't ever tried it himself. Kneeling over the rider, he waved his hand in a beckoning gesture over the glow.

Something tugged at his fingers, as if invisible spider strands had stuck to his hand. When he lifted it, not one but two cards lifted from the man's chest.

Which, of course, was the moment he heard Second's voice right behind him.

"I thought I'd told you to call for me if you found him."

Arthur had zero time. Something twinged from his Gambler Class, pulling his attention to the leftmost card.

His only hope was that his body would block his actions from Second's sight.

In one flick of his fingers earned from his **Card Shuffling** skill, he snapped the left card under his palm while he grabbed the other. He half turned, pressing the first card into his heart.

Images of the card flashed before his eyes. He ignored them, extending his hand with the other card held out to Second.

"Bad idea to start shouting," Arthur said. "I saw other teams looking for the rider, too. But I got the card. Here."

The other man was striding up to Arthur, a dark scowl on his face.

He snatched the card from Arthur and looked it over. The card was golden in color, as if someone had dripped sunlight onto the back to guild a twisting mass of woven vines. Some sort of plant-based card?

"Uncommon rank," Second sneered. "That's all?"

It was an effort to not look at the blinking presence of the other card in the corner of his awareness. His new card wanted his attention, but Arthur had to live past the next few moments first.

"Uncommon's not bad, right?" he asked brightly, adding, "It's better than the one you offered me. It's got to be worth something, right?"

Second grunted and pushed the card to his chest, where it slid into his heart. Then his gaze fixed on Arthur. "Is that all you found on him?"

"Yeah?" He looked the man right in the eyes, trying not to sweat.

"Then why aren't you angling to keep it for yourself?"

"W-what?" But he had the sinking feeling Second was right. If it were the only card on the rider, Arthur would have argued at least a little to keep it or trade it with another one of Second's.

No wonder he hadn't gotten another **Acting** skill level.

Second's face darkened as if he just had his suspicions confirmed. He held out his hand. "Give it."

"I . . . I just did. There wasn't another card, Second. I swear. I didn't call out for you because other people are looking for the rider. I ran into a group of them. They got eaten by scourglings and I just got away." He was babbling. He could hear himself do it but couldn't stop.

Arthur backed up a step, and his heel hit the rider. His arms pinwheeled as he fell back over the body.

Second advanced on him. "I told you what would happen if you crossed me, Pissant."

"I didn't, Second. I didn't!"

"Guess there's one way to find out."

He gestured to one of the branches above. With a creak of wood, the branch twisted as if called to his hand. Arthur flashed to the back of the Uncommon card—how the decoration had looked like vines. Second must be trying it out.

His father had told him it took time and practice to adjust to a new card, but other than a look of fierce concentration, Second wasn't having difficulty.

Arthur turned to run.

The branch shot out. The tip sharpened to a spear point.

Sharp pain bit at the side of his throat, just under his chin. Then the world went white.

Trap Card conditions met.
Return to Start: Activated.

CHAPTER 24

The bright light faded. Arthur found himself lying face down in the middle of a forested clearing.

Jerking to his feet, he stared around with wide eyes. He was in a different area than he'd been a moment before. Second was nowhere to be seen. Neither was the body of the dead dragon rider.

The clearing looked familiar, but it took him a few seconds to figure out why. This was the campsite the caravan had used last night. The one they had taken off from in the morning. Now that it was clear of carts, burden animals, and people, it looked completely different.

Too bad it wasn't far enough from the eruption. Scourgling whistles sifted through the forest in all directions.

Cautiously, he touched a stinging spot on the side of his throat. His fingers came back red with blood. It was only a deep scratch and could have been so much worse. What had the card done?

He turned his attention inward to the card that had been nudging at his mind for attention.

It was a deep metallic blue, shining like the finest polished steel. The glowing outline of a boy pulsed, faded to black, and then reappeared slightly off center in the card. That new outline pulsed and reappeared in another spot.

As with the Master of Skills card, as he read the card, the description imprinted itself on his mind.

Return to Start
Rare
Trap
When the wielder of this card is attacked with another card's power, they will be instantly be transported to a previously keyed-in location point at no

mana cost and with no restriction due to distance. If a location has not been
designated, the wielder will be transported to the physical point they last
started that day—either one second after the stroke of midnight or at the
moment they last woke, whichever point is later.
This trap card has a once-per-sunset usage restriction.

After that was another message. The one that had attempted to get Arthur's
attention.

Would you like to key in your location start point now?

Slowly shaking his head, Arthur dismissed the message.

A Rare-ranked card. He suspected once the shock wore off, he would feel
smug about that.

The answer as to why this card had not saved the rider was plain to see:
The card activated when its wielder was attacked with another card's power.
The orange and blue dragons had attacked the pink with teeth and claws
only.

It had been a brutal attack and showed they knew enough about this card
to keep their prey from getting away. Since dragons linked their cards with their
rider, the pink dragon likely had something similar in its deck.

They had planned out how to kill the pair of them.

Arthur gulped and rested his hand over his heart. He wouldn't make the same
mistake. He'd make sure no one ever learned the conditions of this, or any other
Trap card.

A scourgling whistle cut through the forest. Dropping his hand, Arthur
turned toward it. Suddenly, he felt very exposed. His dagger was gone, and his
new Trap card wouldn't work until after the next sunset.

He was also more than a half day's journey from the caravan.

He vaguely remembered the small valley on Red's map. It had been surrounded on three sides by mountainous ridges with a lower lip on the southeast-
ern side that led to a wider plain. This camp was somewhere on that lip. That
meant scourglings would be spilling from the eruption on the other end of the
valley and slowly filtering in this direction.

Quickly, Arthur searched the cold fire pits. He came out with a hearty branch
with wood too dense to burn easily. It had a bulbous end. Better than nothing,
though he wished he had something sharper.

The memories of how that other group of men was bowled over so easily,
swords and all, were fresh in his mind. It was easy to imagine his cards being
plucked out of his heart and swallowed down the gullet of a scourgling.

He didn't think he was imagining it: The whistles had become closer and had
a sharper tone at the end. It sounded like an excited hunting cry.

Did they smell him? Did they . . . Wait a minute.

He'd seen the scourglings go straight for the cards first. Like the things had smelled the magic in them.

Doshi the silver dragon had smelled his Legendary-rank card. Now Arthur had a Rare card to add to it. What if the scourglings could sense them? What if he had just made it worse?

He had to get out of here.

The heavy branch in one hand, he started down the road, opposite the way the caravan had traveled.

Arthur felt a stab of regret for that. He wished he could go back right now and tell Red everything that had happened—tell the man he was right and that Arthur shouldn't have gone with Second. That he was sorry for . . . well, everything.

But even if he could find his way back to the caravan, Second would kill him. Red was not a carded man. He didn't have the strength to stop Second. He'd pretty much said so himself.

Arthur's only hope was to put enough distance between himself and the valley.

The hunting whistles continued. To his anxious, racing heart, they seemed to draw closer. Worse, Arthur couldn't pick out the exact direction they came from. The trees were all a tall pine variety with thick underbrush that seemed to distort and bend the sound somehow. Or maybe the sounds weren't bent, and he was simply surrounded.

Arthur broke into a faster walk. Then a jog. A prickling on the back of his neck made him shift into a run.

A sharp whistle made him twist to look back. Behind him, a scourge-wolf leaped onto the road. The path it had broken through the brush was already shriveled and dying behind it.

The scourge-wolf's mouth was a mass of teeth stuck out in all directions. Seeing Arthur, it let out a shrieking sound the equivalent of a howl and broke into a run.

Arthur screamed and dropped the branch, sprinting with every ounce of speed he could pull on. He'd been fooling himself. A little piece of wood wasn't going to do any good against something with a mouth like wood saws.

Leaning forward into every step, he ran like he had not allowed himself to since he had first gotten his skill card. Not even when he'd gotten word of Ernie's sickness.

I need a running skill, he thought wildly. But that wasn't within his card's ability. **Stealth** and his **Card Shuffling** skill had saved his life twice already today. He wasn't sure what other trick he had left to draw.

Risking a glance behind, he was shocked to see the scourge-wolf was still loping along at the same distance as before. Arthur wasn't outrunning it, but he was pacing it. If he had better endurance . . .

A moment later, the wolf was joined by another. Then a third. Then, absurdly enough, some of the scourge-bunnies joined in to run him down as a pack.

True wolves and bunnies would never come together like this, but each one of these creatures was a predator.

Whatever luck the Gambler Class had given him had run out. Arthur seemed to be pulling the scourge in from all through the forest.

He panted, legs burning. He could go all day running messages up and back to the moving caravan, but he could only sprint at top speed for so long.

One wrong step and he would fall. Then they would be on him.

One thing wolves and bunnies couldn't do was climb. Hopefully.

Arthur looked around wildly and focused on a large pine with branches low enough for his use.

He turned sharply toward it. The tree was just off the road, but those few steps he took brought the scourglings closer.

Arthur jumped and grabbed a branch, ignoring the rough bark that ripped at his palms. He hauled himself up with strength born out of sheer panic. He used the next set of branches like a ladder, climbing fast.

The whole tree shuddered as one of the wolves hit the trunk. One scourge-wolf leaped upward and hooked a branch with its paws, but then fell back. The branch it touched turned instantly black and started to die.

As did the trunk of the tree.

Arthur kept climbing. His only hope would be to find a spot to leap to another tree.

But there were none within a safe distance. He could try, but he would more than likely fall through the branches. If the hit to the ground didn't kill him, the scourglings would.

He climbed on, hoping for some answer.

The tree was a tall one, with the top ending well above the general canopy. The moment he climbed above the neighboring trees, he was buffeted by a hot wind.

Off in the distance, an orange dragon had summoned a fireball the size of Second's cart. It exploded onto a mass of flying scourglings. Black and gray pieces fell down, and the dragon swooped among them, the rider harvesting the chunks for card shards.

They either didn't hear, or ignored, Arthur's yells for help.

Arthur kept climbing until the branches became so small they snapped under his boots. He clutched the trunk for balance, feeling the tree wobbling. Though he couldn't see it, he could imagine the base of the tree was rotting away under him. He'd have to risk a jump, and soon.

"Boy!" came a girl's voice. "Tess comes!"

He looked up to see a small purple dragon shoot through the sky toward him. Its body was the size of Bella the donkey, discounting the tail. It had four wings: two on each side that flapped so fast they were a blur. It stopped to hover right in front of him like a hummingbird.

"Jump on Tess!" she said. It had been her voice, high and clear like a young girl's. "Tess catch!"

A rider sat crouched low on the space between Tess's wings and her neck, sitting on a tiny saddle like a horse jockey. Their head was encased in a leather helmet, goggles, and a cloth mask over the bottom of their face.

As Arthur felt the tree shudder, the rider extended a hand. They were still too far away for comfort, but Arthur had no choice.

Gathering himself, he leaped from the tree. His hand scraped at the rider's arm for a stomach-dropping second before he caught the wrist. The purple dragon squealed and dipped to the side, thrown off balance by his weight.

Then Arthur's other flailing hand caught Tess's back ridge. With the rider's help, he pulled himself up onto his stomach behind them.

Tess righted herself with a flick that almost sent Arthur tumbling off the other side.

There was almost no space between the back of the saddle and the wings. Arthur stayed on his stomach, legs in the air. All he could do was stick his fingers under the saddle straps and hold on for dear life.

Below him, the tree he'd been climbing toppled sideways to the ground.

"Tess caught boy! Tess caught boy!" the dragon cheered like a girl who had just captured a butterfly.

The rider said something he couldn't catch. Suddenly, the wind screamed as Tess lifted higher—straight up, using her buzzing wings. Then she darted forward faster than any galloping horse.

Arthur never thought he would be afraid of heights, but he was very aware of the sheer amount of sky between himself and the ground. His fingers had a death grip around the saddle straps, every muscle coiled tight as he clung on to the dragon and tried not to die.

Below him, the valley seethed with scourglings, though it seemed the hives were mopping up the aerial battles. Tess shot back and forth, deftly avoiding the last scourgling flyers.

Arthur expected he would be taken to a safe spot: a nearby town or maybe even the caravan if he was lucky.

It took him too long to realize Tess was heading straight toward one of the dark rips in the sky.

Tess was taking him to a hive.

No, wait. Take me to the caravan! Arthur wanted to say, but between fear and the screaming wind, his mouth had gone dry, tongue glued to the top.

The rip loomed larger until it seemed to take up the entirety of the world, the iridescent green dragons still holding it open. It didn't seem real: flat black with nothing he could see beyond, like they were aiming full force for a dark wall . . .

Then, they were inside.

PART 3
THE HIVE

CHAPTER 25

Something very odd happened the moment the dragon took Arthur through the rip in the sky. It was as if he instantly lost all sense of direction. And at the same time, it was so much more.

There was no up or down. He felt like he was falling and yet could feel his stomach uncomfortably pressed against the dragon's sharp spine. Every inch of his body felt like he was on the verge of being ripped apart, yet he was compressed together. He was dizzy and yet stationary. He was out of his body and yet screaming within his own mind.

These were not sensations he could explain to himself. Only feel and endure.

Thankfully, it only lasted a moment. Within the next, they were blasted out in bright sunshine.

Still half convinced he was falling, Arthur scrabbled for a hold, kicking his legs in the air.

The rider turned in her seat and gripped the back of his shirt to hold him still. The knowledge that someone had a hold on him was enough to get himself back under control.

Only then was he able to look around.

His first thought was that they had been in that awful rip for much longer than he had thought. It had been just past noon a few moments ago. Now the sun was low to the horizon. It was almost evening.

Tess the dragon buzzed to the side to give way to another dragon angling toward the rip. As she turned, the view changed.

Arthur's jaw dropped open. They were at the site of another scourge-eruption.

This cone was much, much larger than even the one in the valley. It seemed to dominate the entire sky. Tess was so high up Arthur had no way of measuring it—dozens of tree lengths at least—and yet they only came to around the middle of the cone. It made ants of the dragons near to it.

No scourglings came out of the top. After the first shock wore off, Arthur recognized that this must have been the site of an ancient eruption. So old the crumbled dirt had turned into stone.

Terraced roads had been cut into the deeply sided slopes, winding around and around the cone and leading in and out of cut-through entrances. Vegetation, including entire trees looking like tiny sprigs, dotted different areas. Hundreds, perhaps thousands, of dragons darted back and forth, in and out of arched entrances, and looping around in general chaos.

This must be a hive. Dragons built their hives out of ancient scourge-eruptions.

Ringing the hive on all sides were buildings and streets. There were so many dwellings, in all shapes and sizes, that Arthur found himself boggling all over again. It went on and on, stretching as far from the foot of the hive as he could see.

Two rivers wound through it all. One from under the hive itself, the second splitting off into canals that threaded all through the city. The water blazed like fire in the reflection of the sinking sun.

Tess buzzed down to the base of the hive. An area had been cleared between two large buildings, like the square back in his village, except several times as large.

There were white tents and long tables set up. Shocked and dirty people sat huddled together in clumps, weeping. Some of them were bloodied. Easy to guess that these were the survivors of the scourge attack.

Tess set down with barely a jolt. Her rider unbuckled themselves from the saddle and turned to Arthur. "You still alive?"

She had a woman's voice, though he couldn't have known through the thick jacket, helmet, and covered face.

Arthur croaked out something that was supposed to have been "Yes."

His effort must have satisfied the rider. She slipped off Tess's side and went to her dragon's head.

The dragon was crowing for all the courtyard to hear. "Tess caught boy! Tess caught boy!"

The rider caught the dragon's head between her hands and squealed at her in a sudden high, excited voice. "That's right, Tess. You were a very, very good girl!" She scrubbed her dragon's head as if she were an enthusiastic dog.

The dragon hopped in place, jostling Arthur, who was still hanging on, stomach down. He couldn't seem to force his hands to unclench. He was shaking like a leaf in autumn. He couldn't even make himself sit up.

"What have you got here, Jo?" another woman's voice asked.

The rider, Jo, turned from praising her dragon. Her voice returned to normal. "Tess and I found him at the very top of a pine tree. Trying to escape a wave of scourge, I think."

"Tess caught boy!" Tess called again. "Tess very, *very* good girl!"

The other woman came around, took one look at Arthur, and grinned. She was a short, maternal-looking woman with a kind, round face and fizzy red hair, pulled back. "Spatial rift sickness can be a bear. Let's get you down." She started working on Arthur's clenched hands. "Did you wet yourself?"

This was asked kindly, but it did jerk him out of his shock. "No!"

The surprise was enough to make his hands release the strap. Off balance, he slid off the side, stomach scraping all the way down.

It was only a short fall, as Tess stood maybe as high as his neck. But his body was strung so tight, for a moment he fully expected a thousand-length fall.

Arthur gave a short scream before he hit the ground and crumpled, feeling immediately embarrassed.

The woman came around the other side and thankfully didn't laugh. "There you are, and I see you still have dry pants. Good," she said with a brisk nod. "Are you hurt anywhere? Did the scourge bite or scratch you?"

"No," he said. "I . . ." He held up his hands to show scraped palms. "I climbed a tree."

"You got lucky. Some of them can climb, too."

"They rotted the trunk out from under me," Arthur said, though to his ears it sounded like whining.

However, the woman could not be more sympathetic. She knelt to his level and patted his shoulder. "You poor dear. You're safe now. I know you said you weren't hurt, but we're going to get you looked over and then get you something hot to eat. You'll feel better soon."

"Magda, Tess and I need to go." Jo the rider had finally broken off from praising her dragon's goodness and courage. She had pulled down her mask to show olive skin and a wide mouth. "The fighters just got control of the airspace, but I'm sure there are more people out there."

"Of course. Here." Standing, Magda hunted through a pouch attached to her belt and pulled out a milky green chip with *1* emblazoned on it. "Here's your token."

Arthur wanted to ask what that was about. The token exchange had the air of a transaction. But there was a more important consideration.

Slowly, painfully he stood to his feet. His legs still felt like jelly, but they held. "Thank you," he said to the rider. His words felt so weak and insincere for what she had just done. "I would've died. I—"

"We were just doing our job," Jo said, gesturing to include Tess. The purple dragon blinked empty yellow eyes at him. "And you might have still thought of something. It's not every boy who can keep his head enough to try to signal a flying rider."

He hadn't tried to signal anyone.

Before he could find something to say, Jo put her hand on his shoulder—a familiar gesture that surprised him.

"What direction was your farm?" she asked.

They thought he was a farmer's brat. Made sense. He'd seen the remains of a few farmhouses here and there from atop the ridge.

Arthur shook his head. He still felt too scrambled to make up an effective lie.

Jo must have thought he was still in shock. That wasn't too far from the truth. "How many were in your family?"

This, he could answer. "Just me and my dad. My mom and sister . . ." He choked the next words off, alarmed to find his emotions so close to the surface. "It was just us."

Jo exchanged glances with Magda.

"All the Lobos are to bring their rescues here," Magda said, as if that was supposed to mean something to Arthur. "Don't lose hope yet."

The rider nodded briskly. "Tess and I will look around the area we found you and see if there are other survivors."

"Don't," Arthur said, knowing it was a fruitless task. Weeks of keeping secrets to himself had ingrained the habit, but he couldn't let the rider fly around on a wild goose chase when there might be real farmer families to be saved. A halting story of half-lies tumbled out of him. "I got separated from the rest. There were men hunting for scourglings, and for . . . for . . ." He looked guiltily at the rider and couldn't say it.

Jo, however, finished for him. "Vultures. Looking for fallen dragon riders and their cards."

Behind them, the normally bubbly Tess hissed.

"They thought I might be carded," Arthur said quickly. "They wanted to kill me and check my heart, even though I got nothing. I don't know what's worse: them or the scourglings."

This last part seemed to earn him a bit of favor from the dragon rider, judging by her smirk.

"Then the scourglings came up on us and I ran," Arthur finished. "I think the scourglings ate them."

"Then good riddance," Magda huffed.

Jo turned to her. "Keep an eye on this one. He has some guts in him. Might even be a dragon rider one day," she said with a wink. Then she turned to her dragon and held up the token, taking on that excited voice again. "Tess! Look what I got!"

"Jade stone!" Tess trilled, bouncing from foot to foot. "Tess find more! More! More people for stones!"

"That's right." Jo put her mask up on her nose again and then swung up onto the dragon. In a moment, they were buzzing away.

Magda put her arm under Arthur's. "Let's get you a seat."

She guided Arthur toward the tables, which was difficult for him as his legs were still trembling.

This was ridiculous. He used to face death all the time back in the border village. But something about so many shocks at one time—and that terrible rip in the sky—had nearly undone him.

Arthur took deep breaths and firmly told himself that he was safe. He made himself believe it.

Slowly, his heart rate calmed, though he still felt shaky.

Magda guided him to sit at a table. "Anyone look familiar?" she asked.

She meant the other people who had been rescued. A few had glanced at him, hope that he was their boy dying almost at once. Arthur shook his head.

Looking unsurprised, Magda pulled out a small pile of papers and then took out a wooden pencil. Red had carried one of those, though Magda's looked brand new instead of the stubby thing Red had used.

"Let's get some information down, so when we find your father, we can get you two reunited. Let's start with your name."

"Arthur," he said at once, and wanted to slap himself. He needed to be smarter than this. Then again . . . he had gone by Ernest in the caravan. If Second was looking for him, that would be the name he asked about.

"Your surname?"

"Youngblood," he said, using Ernie's last name.

"Okay, Arthur. You said it was just you and your father at your farm?"

He nodded. She made a note.

"Do you know your father's rank?"

He had no idea what people outside border towns thought was normal. There were no ranks in the caravan either. He decided to just shake his head. "We are just farmers. Not nobility or nothing."

She gave him an odd look. "I meant card rank."

Arthur hoped he wasn't breaking out in a sweat. Quickly, he shook his head. "No cards."

She made another mark. "And how old are you?"

He sensed an opportunity here. "Thirteen."

Magda's gaze flicked from the notes. She gave him a *look*.

"Twelve," he corrected.

She continued looking at him.

He wanted to bristle. He wasn't that small! Well . . . he was growing! But the kids he played dice and card games with never treated him like one of the teenagers. In fact, he had fit in pretty well with the ten-year-olds.

Reluctantly, as if he knew he'd been caught in a lie, he said, "I'll be eleven at the end of next month."

That seemed to satisfy her. It also prickled at his pride a little bit.

"You're almost old enough for your first card," she said.

She really didn't know he was carded. Then again, Tess was a purple, not a silver, and had seemed to be a . . . simpler creature than Doshi.

Magda made a few more marks. Then, turning, she gestured over to someone else.

A lanky teenager wearing a long white tunic edged in blue walked up. He stared at Arthur in a creepy intense way, and a prickle went down his spine.

"Not scourge-touched," the teenager said. "Aside from that black eye, he has some light bruising on the torso, a minor laceration to the throat and both palms."

Magda made another note.

"Are you some sort of a treasure seeker?" Arthur asked. It was the only name he knew for people who could find things.

"More of a sickness seeker," he said with a chuckle. Then, abruptly, all business again, he continued to Magda. "He's suffering from malnourishment with several vitamin deficiencies. Though it looks like some of it has started to be addressed. Good harvest last season?" he said in an aside to Arthur but didn't wait for his reply. "He should have citrus juice with every breakfast and supper meal for the next two weeks. Aside from that, no defects, nothing brewing."

Magda nodded, and the man walked away to visit a woman who was holding a fitful baby.

The whole exchange had sounded uncomfortably to Arthur like someone describing a horse they'd like to sell. He'd practically said Arthur had good teeth and sound hooves.

"What was that chip?" he asked. "The green one you gave to Tess's rider?"

Magda didn't blink an eye as she continued to fill out the form. "Oh, she's on the rescue and evacuation team—we call them the Lobos, as we're the Wolf Hive. Tess isn't a fighter, so she can't compete with the big dragons for shards. Every Lobo gets an extra incentive for a person recovered. Tess and Johanna are some of the best at what they do. Even better than some who have a seeker card."

So, he *had* been sold. Sort of. Exchanged, maybe? Was it a bad thing?

He wasn't sure yet.

Magda rose and went to the tents, returning with a plate heaped with thickly sliced beef, crisp greens, an apple, and a real glass filled with vivid yellow juice.

Arthur tried the juice first. It was shockingly tart and stung a little at the inside of his chapped lips. He loved it.

As he ate, Magda rose from the table to check on more people the dragon riders brought in. Most of these came aboard small purples, like Tess. Though there was a blue dragon so pale it was close to silver in the fading light. It didn't give so much as a sniff to Arthur. Once its rider had collected two jade chips from Magda, they were on their way again.

Magda returned as Arthur finished the last of his plate.

"You ought to grab a cot and lie down," she said, nodding to the largest tent. "They're going to be rescuing people through the night, as the sun is still up over there."

Arthur stared, trying to puzzle out that sentence. "How can the sun be up somewhere else?" he asked, pointing to the now-dim outline on the horizon. It had nearly set.

Sunset . . . there was something important about that phrase. Something which nagged at his mind, but he was too exhausted to work it out.

She chuckled as if he'd just made a joke. "Duke Rockhound's land is behind us by at least five hours."

Arthur's mind spun, but Magda ushered him from the table.

"Get some rest, Arthur. I promise to come to wake you when we find your father."

Yeah, right. That would be a good trick.

But a bed did sound good. He hadn't slept in a real cot since he left his village.

Arthur went to the tent and found a free cot near the middle. The mattress was soft, the blankets thick. Several people were already sleeping nearby—or at least lying down. One wept quietly.

Arthur felt bad for them, but also disconnected from their grief. In truth, he had lost his family a long time ago. He just felt glad to be alive, and so, so tired.

He fell asleep almost at once.

CHAPTER 26

Arthur slept in, hours past dawn, which was unusual for him. Red had started his days early, even if the rest of the caravan would prefer to sleep off the wine and ale from the night before. That had meant Arthur did too.

But when he opened his eyes, it was to find people shuffling around the tent, and half of the beds left empty with rumpled bedding.

Maybe it had been—what had Magda called it? Spatial sickness?—because his mind felt much clearer than before.

He was in a dragon hive. A hive that was probably full of silver dragons who could smell his cards, like Doshi had.

Which made Arthur wonder why they weren't all over him as soon as Tess landed, like flies on a cow pie.

Were they busy with the scourge-eruption? Maybe. Doshi wasn't a fighter, though. They weren't one of the Lobos either, so they couldn't be too busy.

He thought about it and figured Doshi was either really good at smelling out cards, or Arthur was hiding somehow. Maybe there were so many people with cards around the hive that his Legendary rank didn't stand out as much?

Better not to risk it. If he saw a silver dragon today, he was going to give it space.

The other thing he had to worry about—and something he wanted to kick himself for—was his newest card. Return to Start was a Trap card that would activate as soon as someone attacked him with a card power.

Easy enough to avoid if he had been back at the caravan where no one used magic powers willy-nilly. Even the small towns they'd visited didn't have people randomly throwing magic around.

But what exactly defined "attack"?

Here . . . Well, that sickness seeker had just looked at him and determined he wasn't going to fall over dead. Something deep and instinctual from his heart deck told him that counted as a card's power being used on him. Not an attack . . . but what if he didn't want to be checked over for sickness?

Magda seemed like the mothering type. She might want him checked out again to make sure he didn't have the sniffles or anything. It may or may not count as an attack. He knew for certain his Trap card hadn't activated last time because the power reset at sundown.

If someone used it on him today, there was a good chance he could be thrown back in this cot. That would be hard to explain.

Maybe dragon riders had cards, but Arthur was just a kid small enough to make people think he was only ten years old. If they knew he had cards, they'd want to take them. If they knew he had a Rare and a Legendary . . .

Arthur shifted to his side under the thick blankets, rolling over so he faced the wall. Then he pulled down his collar and reached to his chest.

He stopped.

He didn't want to remove the card from his heart. It felt like . . . like removing a nursing kitten from her mother. It felt like abandonment and betrayal. As if he had made a promise to keep the card safe, and now . . .

Arthur squeezed his eyes shut, pulled up every scrap of courage and grit he had, and pulled the card out.

It didn't hurt, physically. But it felt like it should have. Though the Rare card had only been in his heart for less than a day, it felt like it carried a piece of him.

He felt like apologizing to it.

He knew it was stupid. But it also answered a question he'd thought about on and off: Why had Second gone to all the trouble of keeping his set of cards in his cart when he could have just hidden them in his heart? Unless a high-ranked Treasure Seeker looked, no one would ever know.

The answer? Because when you stuck something in your heart, it became part of you.

Remembering the other man, Axel, had lost some of his cards on a bad hand of poker made Arthur shudder.

"What am I going to do with you?" he whispered, fingers tracing over the slick, metallic surface of the card. It was warm, still carrying his body heat.

He didn't have a pocket large enough, nor a pack. And he didn't want it too far away from him, either.

He'd carry it on himself for now.

Arthur tucked his shirt into his pants and then slid the card between the shirt buttons so it rested over his stomach. He was lucky the shirt was a little big for him and wrinkled from sleeping in it. Also, he felt a little better with the card close at hand. If someone were to come at him with a dangerous spell, it would only take a few moments to reach in and shove it in his heart.

It wasn't perfect, but it would do.

The final question was . . . did he want to stay here?

Arthur thought about it as he got out of bed and tried to put his hair back into order before he made his bed.

If he asked Jo or one of the other dragon riders, would they take him back to the caravan?

Did he want to go back?

There was every chance Second died while searching for card shards, and Red never had to know Arthur had two cards. If Second was gone, no one would call him Pissant anymore, either.

But . . . a sense of adventure and curiosity tugged at him. He wanted to see what a hive was like.

Maybe it had more to offer him than being Red's apprentice.

He walked out of the large tent and found a bustle of activity in the courtyard. Several small families were being loaded onto waiting purple and blue dragons.

Magda came bustling up to him. She looked harried and concerned. "Did you sleep well, Arthur?"

"Yes, ma'am," he said, deciding to be polite.

She hesitated for a moment, then let out a sigh. "The scourge has been contained to lines within the valley, and the last of the Lobos have been recalled. I'm sorry, Arthur. We've had no word of your father."

Oh. Right.

Arthur looked down at his shoes, because he didn't think he could fake a convincing sniffle. He thought quickly. If his lie had been true, would he just take her word for it?

"Are you sure?" he asked in what he hoped was a quavering voice. "Did they look really hard?" Magda thought he was two years younger than he was. That felt like a childish thing to ask.

His card must have agreed.

New skill level: Acting (Thief/Performer Class)
Level 6

"Yes, dear," she said, adding gently, "There's nothing left living in that valley. I'm very sorry."

He nodded, still looking down. The best thing to do was to remain silent.

Magda continued. "I know it's unfair to ask this of you right now, but you have some decisions to make. Sometimes, we adults step in when it comes to children, but I think you're mature enough to make them on your own."

He cautiously looked up. "What do you mean?"

Magda gestured to the dragons. They had nets to either side, which were being filled with sacks of provisions. "Your baron is required to rehome all willing families on land that hasn't been touched by the scourge. Arthur." She paused as if considering how to phrase it. "This isn't free. The baron must rehome them by law, but they must pay for supplies to restart their farms on new land. To some, it's worth it. They know the land, and most of the time their friends and neighbors come with them to their new communities. It may take years to work off the debt, but they'll be together."

Arthur did not like that option. These weren't his people, and sooner or later someone would twig onto the fact that no one had ever heard of his father.

Magda continued. "However, your baron requires that all children under the age of twelve have a family to take them in. Do you think anyone would do that for you?"

Arthur quickly shook his head.

She smiled as if she had been half expecting this answer. Likely, she'd made some delicate inquiries from the other evacuees.

"Well, in that case, the Wolf Hive has provisions for cases like yours. We would love to have a smart, brave boy."

That felt off to Arthur.

Magda barely knew him from any other kid. How was she to know he was brave and smart?

Still, he nodded. "Does that mean I get to live in the hive?"

"No, you'll only live there if you become a rider someday. Is that something you would like to do?"

People kept asking him that. He decided honesty might be best. "I don't know."

Magda nodded. "It's a great duty . . . and a burden. You have plenty of time to decide. And of course, it all depends on the cards you earn."

"You can earn cards?"

By the slight smile on Magda's face, she had left that hanging on purpose. "Most of us are carded, Arthur. I'll tell you more about that later. For now, would you mind helping out around here? We must get the rest of the evacuees packed up and on their way."

Magda framed her request in the same way Yuma did back at his village: a polite order.

She directed him to return to the tent he'd woken up in and start organizing. By then, most of the evacuees had woken and been formed into groups: those who were to leave to rebuild new lives in their barony, and those who were to stay.

Arthur folded blankets and placed pillows near them. The cots had hinges on the legs, which allowed them to be folded and stacked up. Then he grabbed a broom leaning against the canvas and started sweeping.

When Magda came to check on his progress, she seemed surprised to see everything stowed in its place.

Well, it ought to be. He had a level 8 in **Tidying**.

She took him outside, where a plate of breakfast foods had been made up for him. By now, the dragons had flown away, and the courtyard seemed huge and empty.

"I want you to eat it all," she said, sitting across the table from him. "And mind you drink all your juice. Meanwhile, I'll tell you how things work around here."

No need to tell him twice. He started in on the heaped food, which was . . . odd. They ate sweet flat cakes, which he would have thought to be a dessert. There was a small mound of fluffy yellow eggs as well as sliced potatoes that smelled like they'd been fried in bacon fat. Those were his favorite.

Magda chuckled at his enthusiasm. Then to his complete shock, she reached into her pocket and pulled out a glittering white card shard. It was triangle shaped—probably one of the inner pieces. And, judging by the cardstock-looking quality, only a Common. He was still stunned a random woman carried them in her pocket. He'd seen men ready to kill for shards.

"By the look on your face, I don't need to ask you if you know what this is." Her lips quirked upward in good humor. "The first thing you should know is that in the hives, these beauties are easy to come by. Keep eating," she added.

He had been so busy staring he'd completely forgotten about the food.

Arthur shoved more eggs in his mouth. Magda watched him for a moment, nodded, then continued.

"In the hives, you're given two options for pay: coins or shards. Boys and girls are taken care of. You won't ever starve, and you'll have a place to lay your head every night. But it's expected by the time you're twelve to start in on a trade. It's also expected that you should have at least a Common card by the time you're fifteen."

"Fifteen?" His dismayed voice was muffled by potatoes. She expected him to wait *years* for a card?

"That's the official calculation for those who do the bare minimum," Magda said, still with that quirked smile. "But a smart, hardworking boy like yourself . . . Well. I wouldn't be surprised if you had several cards by then."

She held the triangle shard up for a moment, tantalizingly. Then she returned it to her pocket.

Arthur hurriedly swallowed the last of his food. There was nothing she could have said that would have sparked more enthusiasm. He suspected she knew it, too, by that smile.

That was fine. The possibility of adding more cards to his deck meant everything. He wouldn't settle for Common cards, either.

Arthur set his fork next to his empty plate. "What do I need to do?"

CHAPTER 27

Arthur stopped in shock in front of the building. His feet planted to the ground in horror.

After they got the last of the evacuees sorted out, Magda had led him through the city, where finally, they had come to this stop.

He hadn't actively practiced his **Reading** skills, but he had gained a level though necessity by reading unfamiliar signage while in new towns.

This was a word he had seen several times before, emblazoned on a wooden archway that led into a small courtyard.

Orphanage.

Technically, it said wolf cub orphanage, but truly, it was the one word that counted.

Magda, who had been leading the way, stopped and turned back, her eyebrow raised. "Is there a problem?"

"You're dumping me in an orphanage?"

She saw his shock and let out a sigh. "I'm sorry, dear. Your father is not coming back. I know it will take time to adjust—"

She thought he was holding out hope. Quickly, Arthur shook his head and backed a step. "I don't wanna live in an orphanage. I can take care of myself."

"Not by hive law, you can't." She walked over and bent to his level. "This is the very best place for you right now. You'll have a roof over your head, food twice a day, education, *and* access to earn your own card shards."

He hesitated, looking up again at the sign doubtfully. "Education? Like classes and stuff?"

"Yes, by law all children between six and twelve are taught the basics. After that, most are apprenticed to a trade, though the scholarly types are offered additional classes. We've had several smart boys and girls attend high classes in the main circle cities."

That meant nothing to Arthur. He dithered for a moment, glancing around warily. "Where are all the kids now?"

She pointed to another, squat building that sat adjacent to the orphanage. "In class, of course. They'll be let out for lunch at noon and then expected to go to their work duties. The older children are off to their apprenticeships. Everyone will be back for dinnertime. Arthur," she said, "I know we haven't known each other for very long, but I haven't led you wrong yet, have I?"

"No," he admitted grudgingly.

She held out her hand.

It took him a moment to figure out what she wanted. Magda wanted to lead him by the hand like a little kid. Then again, she *thought* he was a little kid.

Still, he hesitated. "When I work, I can earn card shards?"

She chuckled. "You have a one-track mind, but yes. That is the main point. When you help out the hive, the hive helps you back by giving you the means to gain magic and skills to become an even more productive citizen. Maybe even a dragon rider. How does that sound?"

He wasn't sure, but for the opportunity for cards . . . he was willing to give this a try.

Arthur put his hand in hers, and Magda led him in.

The inside of the orphanage was about the size of the largest inn he'd seen in the outer towns. Everything was neat, but the rugs and spare furniture in the front hallway had a worn look about them like they had been put through hard use.

"Freyja?" Magda called.

The stairs creaked as a slim woman in a long skirt came down the stairs. Her dark hair was pulled back in a tight bun that gave her face a severe look. Her smile of greeting was warm but small.

"Magda. Are you bringing me a new arrival so soon?"

Magda released her grip on Arthur's hand to squeeze his shoulder instead. "This is Arthur. He's come to us from yesterday's scourge-eruption. I was thinking he might be a good roommate for Horatio."

Freyja's look sharpened. "You don't think he'll pick up his bad habits?"

"The opposite. Arthur's already proved to be self-reliant and a hard worker."

Who in the world was Horatio? And why was Magda springing this on him now?

Before Arthur could ask, Magda went on. "Arthur is very interested in earning card shards."

"Hmm." Freyja looked him up and down. "Well, it's too late in the day for you to join classes. If it's shards you're interested in, we best get you a work assignment first thing. I'll show you to your room, and we can begin."

With one glance at Magda, Arthur followed Freyja's gesture to come up the stairs.

"I'm the head director of the orphanage," Freyja told him. "If you have any problems in the future, you come to me." At his nod, she turned and started walking up the stairs. "Now, the first floor is for boys; the second floor is for girls. You aren't to go up to the second floor for any reason, you understand?"

"Why would I?" Arthur grumbled. There hadn't been any girls his age left alive in his old village, but the older teens had ignored him as much as the boys had. The young girls had been whiny and a lot of trouble.

A slight smile crossed Freyja's face, though she didn't answer. "I won't allow any bullying, stealing, or destruction of orphanage property. Punishment means work duties out in the dragon soil fields. You know what those are?"

Arthur caught himself right before saying yes. He'd worked with dragon soil all his life. "No."

"It's hard, dirty work, ankle deep in fresh dragon shit," the woman continued, the curse snapping Arthur's attention sharp. "Usually, only criminals are put to work in the fields, as long-term exposure can warp your flesh. The most obstreperous boys and girls usually need only one or two days in the field before they figure out it's not for them. Do you understand me?"

She . . . used a lot of big words, but Arthur caught the gist. "I understand. I'm not no thief."

"You are not *a* thief," she corrected. "Here we are." They had been walking down a long hallway at the top of the first landing. She opened a wooden door to show a small room with two cots on either side and a window in the middle. The room was just longer than a grown man was tall.

One cot was laid out with blankets so pristine it looked like no one had ever touched them before. The other was messy, as if his roommate had kicked his blankets down before rolling out of bed and never bothered to remake it after himself again.

With a sigh, Freyja flicked her wrist. Rumpled clothing that had been scattered all through the room was plucked off the ground as if they were attached by invisible strings. They then flew over to the foot of the rumpled bed and dropped down in a pile.

Arthur tried not to gape, and then failed. "What kind of a card spell is that?"

"It's rude to ask people specifics about their cards around here, Arthur. Some may challenge you to a duel over it," Freyja corrected. "But as it happens, I'm proud of this card. It's Uncommon Organization, and it was my first, earned when I was a girl in this very orphanage." She smiled her small, serious smile at him. "If I pushed enough mana into it, I could organize this entire room from top to bottom in a blink . . . but I would rather young men take care of their own tidying, don't you agree?"

Again, she didn't wait for his answer before she walked in and checked the deep chest which sat at the foot of the cot. Arthur caught a glimpse of folded fabric inside.

With a nod, Freyja rose. "You have three sets of clothes in here. Change, scrub yourself down in the bathroom at the end of the hall. Then meet me in the front lobby and we'll start planning your future."

The "bathroom" was an interesting experience. Arthur had heard of indoor privies from the caravan's men. He never expected to live in a place where he had access to one.

There were three privies for the boys on this floor to share, as well as a row of gleaming sinks. When he twisted a tap, water came gushing out, clean and plentiful. No spell card required.

Arthur cupped some in his hands and washed as best he could. It was almost as refreshing as jumping into a stream.

The clothing was by far the nicest he'd ever worn. Plain but thick fabric. His shirt was a cream color, his pants a dull brown. They had creases in them as if they had never been worn before.

The chest didn't have any shoes, but his boots would suffice.

Freshly washed and dressed, Arthur came down the stairs. Freyja gave him a look over. "Let me take a look." Stepping forward, she straightened Arthur's collar and gave him a closer glance over, nodding once. "Acceptable."

Arthur, however, looked around with dismay on his face. "Where did Magda go?"

He assumed that the woman would stick around, though now that he thought about it, he wasn't sure why. But her sudden disappearance felt like abandonment. And he felt a pang of something deeper. A very pale echo of grief, like when he had set eyes on his mother's grave.

Magda hadn't even said goodbye.

Freyja gave him a sympathetic look. "She is a busy woman, and if she is not careful, she becomes attached to the children she helps. Trust me, it is easier like this. No doubt you will see her around. Now," she added in a brisk tone. "Let's you and I talk about your work assignment. Do you have a preference?"

"I want to earn cards," Arthur said at once.

Freyja's lips pursed as if she were trying not to smile. "That's admirable, Arthur. You should know that the quality of cards matters just as much—if not more—than the quantity. One good Uncommon rank is worth three of an average Common."

He decided to play a little dumb. "But the sooner I get a card, the sooner I can get healthy and stuff?"

"Once your body can accept a card, yes. It's not a matter of age, but maturity. Twelve is only the average." Again, her smile was sympathetic. "Girls are usually able to gain cards a little faster than boys. It's why, at this age, they're often the same height. Though don't worry, you'll outgrow them soon."

Arthur didn't give a fig about girls, and he already knew he was mature enough to accept cards, but he nodded along anyway.

Freyja told him to wait and went into her office, which was just down the hall. She returned moments later with a softly glowing white stone in her hand.

She held it up for his examination. An image was burned into the stone of a card, a simple human body dominating with lines radiating around it. It was bordered by a rectangular box, like a card.

"What's this?" Arthur asked, pointing to it.

"A card-mark, of course. I'm sure you've seen enchanted farm equipment with it—it draws the power of a linked card." She held it up. "This will tell me how long you have to wait for a card."

Right. Because they thought he was younger than he was. Arthur hesitated. Would the stone show her that he already had two cards? He wanted to keep that information private. If someone found out, his whole story might fall apart. Worse, they might try to take his cards from him.

"I don't have to know right now," he hedged.

"I promise it won't hurt. Hold still." Before Arthur could form more of an objection, she pressed the flat of the stone against his forehead.

He expected it to be cool, but it was slightly warm.

Arthur couldn't tell what it did but grimaced as Freyja's eyebrows rose. He practically had to bite his tongue to keep from asking if something was wrong.

New skill level: Acting (Thief/Performer Class)
Level 7

Apparently, his card thought it was the smart move.

Freyja recovered quickly and smiled down at him. When she removed the stone, it was glowing as if an invisible candle flame had been lit inside. "Well, it seems you are ready for a card right now."

Arthur didn't have to pretend his relief.

"But you still must earn your shards first." Freyja slipped the card-marked stone into her pocket. "There are two ways to earn a card: purchasing one with coins and putting one together with shards. Both are valid, but for your first card, I recommend you build one using shards."

"Why?"

"Because the card it creates comes from your soul. Generally, the first card you add to your heart deck is the one you end up building your entire deck around. As you grow and advance, you can build multiple decks, but the one you add to your heart"—she tapped her own chest—"is the most meaningful. Some say that it represents who you are, and who you grow up to be. The card becomes part of you, and as you grow, it begins to shape your outlooks and experience."

Arthur frowned, wondering what a Master of Skills card said about him. That he liked to try new things? He didn't build it himself, but it felt like it was part of him.

And as he looked inward, he found a slightly bruised place in his heart where the Trap card used to sit.

Quickly, he pushed his awareness from that, not wanting to linger. It hurt too much.

"That being said," Freyja continued, "I personally recommend you aim as high as you can for your shards. Uncommon rank will put you head and shoulders above many people. It will open up new jobs and opportunities, which will allow you to earn still more cards."

"What about Rare ranked?" he asked.

Her slight smile told him she had guessed the direction of his thoughts. "Uncommon shards will already be a reach. Rare shards are given to highly advanced journeyman work or masterwork. Once you grow in your trade, you are paid in coins or sometimes full cards. Rare ranked are usually sold as whole cards."

Easy to guess that Legendary shards would be reserved for the rich and powerful.

"I guess I'll go for Uncommon," he said, trying not to sound disappointed. He knew he'd been spoiled by the ranks of his current cards, but working hard for something less powerful felt like a step backward.

Still, he had to get his hands on some card as a cover. It was the caravan situation all over again. Especially if a silver dragon came sniffing around.

"The most popular way to gain Uncommon shards is by collecting Common shards and trading them in—they usually go to a three-to-one ratio. That means three Common shards to every one Uncommon."

"So in the time it takes to build an Uncommon card, I could have made three Commons?" Arthur asked.

"Exactly right. That's why impatient people—or those who don't care much, as long as they want a card now—usually carry Commons." Freyja had a note of distaste in her voice.

Arthur, though, couldn't blame people for that choice. He had been that desperate for a card. He still might be, if push came to shove.

Any card meant uncountable riches to those stuck at the border. It was easy to be a snob when you were surrounded by them.

"The other way is by purchasing the shards with coin," Freyja continued.

"Which is better?"

"That depends on what kind of a job we can get you." She folded her hands. "Now, you have some farming experience, and the farms always are looking for good, experienced hands."

Arthur had zero farming experience and no interest in gaining some.

"I worked with the donkeys mostly," he said quickly, wracking his brain to find something that would keep him out of the fields. His list of skills swam up, but he didn't think Freyja would like to hear of his **Card Shuffling** or **Blackjack** skills.

His mental gaze landed on the **Apprentice Meal Preparation**, and his **Acting** skill filled in a story. "After my mom died, I sorta took care of the cooking for the house and the farmhands since Dad could burn water. I got pretty good, too. At least, no one got sick."

She blinked and cocked her head, thinking. "That . . . might work. And it would be convenient."

She didn't explain what would be convenient about it. Instead, she glanced out the window as if judging the time. "Come with me."

Turning, she strode out the door.

"Where are we going?" He obediently matched pace with her.

"To see if I can get you work in a kitchen."

CHAPTER 28

Arthur had expected to see something like the community kitchens back in his village. Thinking of old Yuma and how she sat on her stool and threatened kids with her wooden spoon gave him a pang of homesickness.

Instead, Freyja led him down three winding blocks and turned sharply. Arthur found himself standing in front of a business labeled salt and spoon.

"It's an inn?" he asked hesitantly.

"It's a restaurant," she said, "and despite all appearances, it's the best one in this corner of the city. Come along, Arthur."

With that, she strode confidently forward through the front door.

The inside was much like a lobby of an inn. Only instead of tables for gaming and chatting, people only sat and ate. There were no stairs leading to the upper rooms, either.

Freyja brushed past a lady who asked if she wanted a seat and headed straight back toward the kitchens.

Though the front of the restaurant was quiet with only a few people sitting and eating, the kitchens were a flurry of activity. People ran back and forth, chopping vegetables and meats, and there had to be a dozen different pans simmering with sauces. It smelled amazing, but also overwhelming.

Arthur was used to kitchens by now, but none were so busy or . . . professional. Everyone wore white smocks and looked utterly focused on their jobs. The youngest was a good ten years older than Arthur.

He tried to stay out of the way as Freyja walked up to a rotund man who was peeling potatoes along with three others.

The man saw her coming, put down his potato, and scowled.

"Don't bother, Freyja. I'm full up on dishwashers and garbage boys, especially if this new one is as useless as the last."

"You're having problems with Horatio." This was a statement rather than a question.

The man huffed. "That boy is so sour, I don't keep him near the meat for fear of him putting it off."

Freyja's expression sharpened. "Is he disrespectful? Failing to do his duty?"

The man pulled a face and raised his hand to rub at his chin, but then remembered it was dirty with potato skins. Lowering it, he shrugged. "No, he does the work, though he's surlier than a broken man three times his age. It ain't right to see it in a squirt of a kid."

"Give him time," Freyja said. Then she turned and gestured to Arthur. "Let me introduce you to our newest intake. Arthur says he has experience cooking for a large number of people back at his farm."

That hadn't been precisely what he had said, but Arthur walked forward anyway.

"Arthur," Freyja said as the man looked him up and down. "This is Barlow. He is the head chef here and often takes in young men and women looking to earn shards."

Barlow snorted. "Garbage boys earn one Common shard at the end of every month. You won't find a better deal than that around."

"How many shards does it take to make a Common?" Arthur asked.

The man looked briefly surprised. Freyja hid one of her slight smiles. "It depends on the card and the pieces, but usually it's around twelve. Though more is not unusual. Three times that, or thirty-six for Uncommon shards. Again, these are approximate. Every card is an individual."

A year at least to build a Common card and three times that for an Uncommon. That wouldn't do. Arthur looked at Barlow. "What would it take to earn Uncommon shards?"

"Only cooks earn Uncommon pay." The man rolled his eyes. "What's going on, Freyja? First, you give me a boy who resents all work, and now you're offering me one who's too big for his britches?"

But Arthur wasn't put off. Second was a much scarier man than Barlow, and Arthur had learned to deal with him.

"I can cook," he said.

"It's not about cooking boy. It's about doing it well."

"I can prove it."

The man made a face and then looked at Freyja, who spread her hands.

"Fine, but only because I happen to be short-staffed tonight. It's the only reason I'm helping with the prep. LUK!" he bellowed to a man who was perhaps ten paces away.

The man must have been used to it because he didn't flinch. He turned.

"Yes, Chef?"

"You're on sauces. The kid's taking over your station."

The man didn't look surprised, which showed he had been eavesdropping. By the sudden quiet hush that fell over the kitchen, he wasn't the only one.

"Yes, Chef." Luk hustled off to another roaring woodstove cluttered with pots. Meanwhile, Barlow gestured for Arthur to step up.

"You know what this is?" he asked.

The counter was so high, Arthur had to stand on his toes to look at all the ingredients. "Soup makings?"

He only guessed that thanks to the big soup pot sitting on the stove.

"Chicken soup," Barlow corrected. "Even an idiot can make chicken soup. Are you an idiot, boy?"

"No," Arthur said. "But I can make chicken soup."

This was the plain truth, and he didn't know why the man barked out a laugh. "You have until the dinner rush. Tell Luk over there if there's anything you need."

Arthur could think of something right away. "Do you have a box I could stand on?"

This was a high counter with deep drawers meant to store big pots. He couldn't reach.

Arthur hadn't leaned on his **Apprentice Meal Preparation** skill so hard since that night he first cooked a meal for Red and his father.

Unlike then, he was familiar with the majority of the ingredients. The weeks in the caravan had been instructive, and he had eaten at half a dozen inns since.

In addition, his mother used to make chicken soup for their small family. Arthur had never helped her out at the time, but he remembered the scents and the tastes. She'd had only simple ingredients, but they had been delicious.

He leaned hard on his skills for the rest.

Much like his **Stealth** skill, his meal skills had not gained many levels. It seemed it was easy to grow at first, but unless he pushed himself to learn new things within that skill, the level remained the same.

As a result, he had been stuck on Apprentice level 14 for a couple of weeks. That had been fine when he was throwing prepared ingredients into a big pot for the nightly stew out on the road. Now, he had to stretch his cooking muscles a little.

He started with the pot. It had already been filled with water and set to the fire. The vegetables and meat had been laid out, though none of it had been prepared.

Arthur checked the chicken and pinched off a few pin feathers he found stuck to the skin. Then he split the joints, cleaned out and parted out the rest of the carcass, and threw it in a bigger pan with bacon fat and some salt.

While the meat browned, he cut the potatoes, using his **Knife Work** skill to slice them into equal cubes. He cut up the carrots and the celery the same way. A whisper of wisdom told him that equal-sized vegetables would cook evenly.

The chicken was starting to brown, so he carefully took it off the flame and worked on cutting it up into smaller pieces. It all went into the pot to start a broth, along with the herbs he found lying nearby. And, of course, more salt.

"Did you forget the potatoes and carrots?" Barlow snapped from behind him.

Arthur jumped in place, almost falling off the wooden crate that had been brought in for him to stand on. He hadn't realized the man was behind him.

"No, sir."

"No, *Chef*," Barlow corrected. "Tell me why you haven't added the potatoes."

"Because if I add them now with hours to go, they'll get all mushy. Same with the carrots, uh, Chef," he corrected. "Right now I'm working on the broth. That's why I put in all the chicken, parts, and all. I'll skim out the bones and the skin when it's done."

Barlow stared at him and, trying not to fidget, Arthur continued.

"I'll be cooking some of the vegetables in the chicken fat. Not all of them, but I thought it might be good . . . for . . . variety . . .?" He trailed off, unnerved, as the man continued staring.

"Fancy," Barlow said drolly. "You are focused on textures, but . . ." He let it hang.

Arthur looked around for help. None materialized. All the men and women in the kitchen were busy, and Freyja had long since disappeared, back to her work at the orphanage.

"But?" he asked.

"How does it TASTE?" Barlow practically roared the last word, making Arthur flinch.

"Uh . . ." Hurriedly, he took a spoon and tried the broth. It was fine. The vegetables were next, though he didn't expect much.

Then the combined flavors hit his tongue, and he realized something was missing. A vegetable that even his mother had access to.

"It needs onions and garlic?" he guessed.

"Are you asking me or telling me?"

Arthur straightened his shoulders and met the gaze of the cook . . . though he had to look up, even standing on a crate. "Where do you keep your garlic and onions?"

Barlow pointed, and Arthur scrambled to go fetch the ingredients.

Minutes later, he was frying both in the pan until the onions had turned soft and translucent. After scooping out the skin and the bones from the broth, he cut up the largest pieces left of the chicken and then added the ingredients one by one into the pot, starting with the potatoes. They would help thicken the soup further.

He had barely added fresh peas in by the time Barlow came up again.

Without a word, the man dipped a spoon into the pot, blew on it, and tasted it.

"Needs more ginger and pepper," he said. "Otherwise, it's acceptable."

Arthur let out a breath. "Really?"

"I still reserve the right to kick you back down to garbage boy if you're as useless as SOME brats around here." He roared the word at a dark-haired boy Arthur hadn't noticed before. The other boy was skulking in the back of the kitchen as if hoping not to be seen.

Before Arthur could react, Barlow turned back to him. "Tell Freyja you're hired at half apprentice cook rates."

Immediately, his heart fell. "Half?"

"While in school, kids work only half the day. That's half the pay. It's still five copper a week and one Uncommon shard at the end of every month."

Arthur brightened again.

"You're to report here straight after your classes. You understand?"

"Yes, Chef."

"Good. Now get going." After protecting his hands with a couple of thick towels, Barlow grabbed the sides of the pot and moved it to another fire on a different stovetop. One where the other cooks could easily ladle it into bowls.

Arthur grinned. His soup would be going toward feeding people tonight.

And speaking of food: He was hungry. He had been so focused on his task that he hadn't even sneaked any bites, other than tasting.

He walked out, still grinning, and ignoring the dark looks of the other kid, who was washing pans over a huge sink.

One Uncommon card shard a month. It wasn't much, but those weekly coppers would add up. Thanks to his Gambler Class, Arthur already had plans to make those coins work for him.

CHAPTER 29

Soon, Arthur's days at the Wolf Moon Hive fell into a pattern.

Most of his days went like this.

He would wake at the sound of the breakfast bell. It was a huge metal cylinder that hung at the entrance between the lobby and the communal dining room. The kids who were too young for work duty outside the orphanage—under ten years old—were required to complete kitchen duty in the mornings and evenings instead. It was a reward to be the one who was allowed to take a maul and bash the morning and evening bells. The winner was usually enthusiastic.

Rubbing his eyes, Arthur would sit up in his bed and glance over at his roommate's cot. Horatio slept like the dead and seemed to have trouble waking up every morning. Usually with muttered complaints.

He was also the garbage boy who the chef had complained about so bitterly. After knowing Horatio for a total of five minutes, Arthur knew why.

"Good morning," Arthur usually said. He tried to start the day politely.

Horatio would ignore him as if he hadn't said anything at all.

With a shrug, Arthur would dress and go down the hall to one of the shared bathrooms on the boys' floor. If he was quick enough, he would immediately walk in to start his allowed five minutes (timed by one of Freyja's assistants) to wash and do his business. If he hadn't been quick enough, he would stand in a line with everyone else and wait five minutes for the line to advance.

Breakfast downstairs was a noisy, chaotic affair. Many of the children were orphaned farmers kids, rescued from previous scourge-eruptions. They were used to being up and at 'em at the crack of dawn.

To his dismay, Arthur fit right in with the ten- and eleven-year-olds at the end of the boys' table. Though he knew he was growing stronger by the day . . . he had a lot of catching up to do.

Horatio, who was eleven years old but towered over Arthur, would sit by him . . . if there wasn't any other seat available.

"Pass the juice?" Arthur would sometimes ask.

Horatio would ignore him.

After breakfast, all children under twelve years of age were herded to the building next door, which functioned as a schoolhouse.

School was a novelty to Arthur. There certainly hadn't been anything like formal education in his old village. On balance, he wasn't sure if he liked it or not.

The lessons were a rich source of new skills, but he had never been made to sit in one place for a long period of time before. His teachers often told him off for fidgeting.

But they could not find any fault in the quality of his schoolwork.

Arthur had a head start on his **Reading** and **Writing** skills. Now, before he finished his first week of school, he had pushed past the Basic threshold in both and moved into the Apprentice levels.

The quality of his handwriting improved, too. It wasn't as pin-neat as Horatio's, which was like looking at the print in a book, but it was readable.

Where Arthur truly excelled was in the math lessons.

Within a few minutes of work, he received a message from his card.

New skill gained: Basic Arithmetic (Scholar/Mathematician Class)
Due to your card's bonus traits, you automatically start this skill
at level 3.

Due to your equipped Gambler Class benefits, you have received 5
additional skill levels. These levels will return to baseline once this class
is unequipped.
Current level: 8

He had been able to do basic figuring in his head with his only official skill being **Card Counting**. Unknown to him, he'd also been doing rudimentary multiplication. He understood doubling and tripling on a fundamental level. So when his teacher gave him a multiplication table to memorize, he found it easy. Division was a sort of a reverse of that, and once he learned the steps to long division, it became a snap.

He breezed through his standard Arithmetic tests. Soon, his teacher had him on fractions—easy to learn once he realized it was practically the same as working with portions in recipe books in the restaurant.

His teacher told him that if he kept up his work, he would be ready to start algebra next. Arthur wasn't sure what that was, but since Horatio was the only other boy in their age group working on algebra problems, he wasn't looking forward to it.

Classes ended at noon. After they were sent off for the rest of their day, all students were given thick slices of bread with a slice of random meat and vegetable stuffed in between.

Most of the boys—Horatio, especially—complained that the bread was dry, and the meat was a tasteless mystery. Arthur couldn't believe he was allowed to eat so much regularly. Mystery or not, meat was a treat and bread was to be savored.

After his meal, Arthur would head to the restaurant to begin his work duty. All the ten- to twelve-year-olds did this, and once he finally graduated from classes at "twelve," he'd go to work full time.

Horatio, who worked as the dishwasher/garbage boy, would sometimes walk along with him.

If Arthur ever tried to start up a conversation, Horatio would ignore him.

Thankfully, once Arthur made it to the restaurant, it became easy to ignore Horatio instead.

The other boy kept to his dark corner of the kitchen, scrubbing out pots with a sour expression on his face, as if he would rather be anywhere else. He never started on the garbage duty until someone yelled at him, and most of the time the other cooks practically had to stand close and watch over the boy to ensure he didn't do the scrubbing half-assed.

Arthur didn't know why Chef didn't fire him—he'd heard him complain to Freyja enough. But for whatever reason, Horatio stayed.

Arthur, meanwhile, was kept busy with his own work. Chef wouldn't allow him on the line yet, which meant he wasn't allowed to directly plate the food. Instead, he was put on food prep.

It was an intense experience. There was so much more to learn about cooking than he expected. He learned different ways to cut vegetables, from julienning long strips to carefully mincing into the tiniest uniform bits to even decorative scouring.

His **Knife Work** skill climbed to Apprentice 15, and Chef said if he kept it up he would teach Arthur how to cut radishes into flowers.

He gained two more valuable skills as well.

New skill gained: Butchering Meat (Cooking Class)
Due to your card's bonus traits, you automatically start this skill
at level 3.

New skill gained: Basic Baking (Cooking Class)
Due to your card's bonus traits, you automatically start this skill
at level 3.

Every time he added a new one, he hoped for the option to combine them into an actual Cooking Class card, like his Gambler Class. It hadn't happened yet, but he could feel it was close.

Finally, after six hours of work, Chef let Arthur and Horatio out for the night. As children under twelve, there were strict rules about how much they were required to work.

They walked back, with Arthur trying to strike up a conversation and Horatio ignoring him, and would arrive at the orphanage in time for dinner.

The younger kids had been working hard on the meals, if not expertly. Dinner was usually a bland but hearty soup with more crusty bread and a piece of fruit for dessert. Due to the sickness seeker's diagnosis, Arthur was allowed two bowls every night.

Soon after dinner, it was lights out for the younger kids—of which Arthur was one.

That last part stuck in Arthur's craw. If people believed him when he'd said he was twelve years old, he might be able to go out again.

His fingers itched to practice his Gambler Class. He had left his deck of playing cards back in his pack at Red's caravan. He wished he could at least spend those hours practicing his **Card Shuffling**.

He'd received five coppers in payment after his first week. If he were allowed to go out, Arthur just knew he would double his money—maybe even earn himself a card shard or two.

The room he shared with Horatio had a window that opened wide to let in the night air. A drainage pipe was bolted to the outside wall within arm's reach. Perfect for climbing up and down if he sneaked out.

But he didn't trust his roommate not to snitch.

True, Horatio didn't say much, but Arthur had caught him staring with a resentful expression during classes and while cooking. His gut told him if Horatio thought he could get Arthur in trouble, he would.

Arthur gritted his teeth and resisted the urge to sneak out. But he wasn't sure he would be able to do so for much longer. The sounds of the city floated in through that window. It called to him.

Thankfully, he had other things to occupy his mind. His favorite topic in class by far was Card Lore.

It was held during the last hour of the day, right before school was let out for lunch. Judging by the hushed silence that fell over the class during this time, he wasn't the only one who looked forward to it.

One day, he knew he was in for a treat. It was all in the sly smile of the teacher who brought out a slim glass case from her desk drawer.

A card was suspended inside.

She held it up before the class, who all leaned forward as if subtly pulled in. Judging by the silver metallic sheen of the card, this was an Uncommon rank.

"Today, we will be going over crafting cards," the teacher said.

Instantly, the tension was broken. A low groan passed through the boys and girls.

Putting down the case, she shook her finger at them.

"I know they aren't the flashiest of cards, but crafting is the unbroken spine of any city. Any Common-rank cards will get you a foot in the door to a good trade. Most guilds will accept a crafter with an Uncommon rank or higher without question. Now," she said, looking around at the class, "who can tell me which category crafting cards fall under?"

Several hands shot up. Arthur kept his down, listening intently.

Horatio didn't wait for someone to be called upon. He drawled out, "Utility Class."

The teacher nodded, and Arthur had to resist the urge to turn around in his seat and glare at the other boy. Horatio didn't often speak up in class, but when he did, he never waited his turn.

Worse, none of the teachers told him off for blurting out answers without waiting to be called on, like they would for everyone else.

Arthur didn't get it. Even Chef, who tolerated no nonsense or subpar work, only grumbled about Horatio's work ethic. Nothing was ever done.

"Correct," the teacher said. "Crafters are a subcategory of a Utility Class."

"No good for dragon riding. So what's the point?" Horatio grumbled.

Again, the teacher didn't yell at him, even though she normally tolerated no backtalk in her class.

She only said, "Remember, a functioning hive needs on average at least five support personnel for every active dragon rider. That means meal preparation for man and beast, laundry, cleaning, and every aspect of ensuring a hive runs smoothly so they can focus on fighting the scourge."

Arthur hadn't had the chance to set foot inside the hive. Non-riders weren't allowed unless they had a permitted job. But from the outside, the hive was a constant bustle of activity. He could just imagine how it must be on the inside—and how many people it must hold.

"Common-rank craft-based cards," the teacher continued, and there was a general rustle of activity as the students readied quill and ink to take notes, "usually enhance one aspect of a crafting skill within a narrow scope. For example, a minor woodworking ability may allow its wielder to manipulate wood into a particular shape. Or for farriers, the ability to size horseshoes to perfect accuracy. I once knew a man with the Common ability to drive nails into a board with a gentle tap of his thumb."

She paused for a moment to let the slower students finish their note-taking. Then she continued, picking up the encased card.

"Uncommon-rank crafting cards like this one are usually broader in scope. Who can tell me how to identify an Uncommon card?" she asked.

Hands went up all around. She picked one at random.

"It will say 'Uncommon' on the description," said a girl.

Arthur rolled his eyes and kept his hand up.

"Correct," the teacher said. "Arthur?"

"They're usually a base metallic color. Iron, silver, or copper," he said. The teacher had shown several example cards already—all strictly encased in glass and watched over by an assistant when it wasn't in the teacher's hands. Not that he'd been tempted to steal it. Much.

"That is correct," she said. "They have also been compared to polished steel. However, some Rare cards have a metallic appearance, so it's important to look closely. Anyone else?"

Horatio snorted. "Only an idiot would mix up a Rare and an Uncommon. Rares have moveable images. Uncommons don't."

Wow. Horatio was chatty today. Arthur also noted that he seemed to know what he was talking about. He had seen Rare cards before.

The teacher ignored his snark.

"Uncommon-rank cards are broader in scope than Common cards. An Uncommon crafter may not only have the ability to manipulate wood into shapes but can shave it down with their bare hands. Uncommon cards regularly have mana abilities or use mana at a reduced rate rather than Common cards."

She nodded at her own words. "Someone with a Rare card in their heart may be skilled in multiple disciplines within the same craft. For example, someone may have equal talent in carpentry as well as general woodworking. Any mana cost would be significantly reduced. They may be able to slick planks with their bare hands as well as create works of art."

She turned to the card. "Now, what other crafts—"

Arthur held up his hand.

The teacher paused. "You had a question, Arthur?"

"What about Legendary-rank cards?"

He heard a scoff that came from Horatio's direction.

The teacher smiled sympathetically at him. "Not much is known about Legendary crafting cards. There are rumors that some of the highest guild leaders hold one, but they keep their secrets close."

Arthur wasn't surprised. Her lectures always went over the general aspects of Common, Uncommon, and Rare cards. Legendary rank was seen as too far out of reach.

It was a shame. He would have liked to see how his card stood up to the rest.

Still, it was during this card class that he first got to see a new card born into the world.

It happened the very next day after the discussion of the Craft Cards. An announcement must have gone out to the teachers, because the entire class was herded out to the courtyard. There, they were joined by the littler kids from other classes. They were arranged into groups according to age. Arthur's group, as the oldest, was near the front.

Standing pride in place was a girl in his class. He hadn't had much to do with girls and didn't know her name.

Freyja stood next to her, a proud hand on her shoulder as she addressed them all.

"Today, we recognize the achievement of Olive Sansbury. Olive came to us two and a half years ago and has worked diligently ever since. And today, she creates her first card."

Arthur craned his head to see. There was a table set up with the card pieces laid out upon it. "What's the rank? Can anyone see?"

He fully expected an Uncommon- or Rare-rank card for all this ceremony and effort, so he was surprised by the answer.

"Common," said a boy next to him.

"A Common took her over two years?"

"Well, she had to trade for the corner pieces, didn't she?" the boy scoffed.

Arthur wasn't sure what that meant. Standing on tiptoes, he was able to see just over the shoulders of the boys in front of him. The card shards were placed together like an almost-completed jigsaw puzzle. However, most of the pieces were alike—uniform triangles that fit together.

The exception was the corner pieces, which were also triangles but rounded on one side.

The card was mostly complete except for the upper-right corner triangle.

Olive clutched the last piece tightly between her fingers like it was the most precious object in the world.

Interesting how Freyja never mentioned *that* complication when she was selling him on the idea of card shards.

Freyja continued speaking. "When you create your own card, it's important that you are the one to arrange the pieces. The resulting card comes from your knowledge and will return to your heart." She turned to the girl. "Are you ready, Olive?"

The girl nodded and stepped forward. She was so pale that her freckles stood out from her cheeks, and Arthur caught the hint of a tremor as she slid the last pieces into place.

"Think about what you want out of the card," Freyja coached. "It may help guide the creation."

"I want to be a dragon rider," Olive murmured.

As the corner clicked into place, a shining white light suddenly glowed up between every single piece. It was so bright Arthur had to blink quickly.

It faded, and the blank white card now had script on it.

All the kids leaned forward, though no one crowded around Olive. They gave her space.

Staring down at her new creation, Olive broke into a grin. "It's an illusion! Minor camouflage," she said, took the card between her hands, and hugged it. "I'm going to be a dragon rider!"

Around her, people clapped. Arthur did, too.

Behind him, he heard a scoff.

"I hope she likes delivering messages back and forth to nobles the rest of her life."

Arthur turned and was unsurprised to see Horatio standing behind him. The other boy was so tall, that he practically loomed.

Arthur glared up at him. "What do you mean?"

"Sure, it's not some useless utility card, but it's not exactly a combat card, is it?" He made a dismissive gesture. "I'm sure there's some Common purple desperate enough—they'll match to anyone."

Privately, Arthur wasn't impressed with Olive's new card, but she had worked hard for it. Horatio's attitude rubbed him the wrong way. "Have you ever thought of just trying to be happy for her?"

Horatio gave him a look like he was an idiot and walked away.

A boy next to Arthur gave him a sympathetic look. "That guy is your roommate, right?"

"Yeah," Arthur said.

"That's bad luck."

"No kidding."

However, that seemed to be a watershed moment, because Horatio voluntarily spoke to Arthur again that day. This time, in a rare lull in the kitchen.

"You won't be seeing your girlfriend again."

"What?" Arthur asked, looking up from his pile of chopped onions. Unfortunately, there wasn't a skill to keep his eyes from watering.

Horatio shrugged and bent to empty the pail of vegetable leavings.

"She went off to the hive. I saw Freyja walking her out just before I came here."

"Just because she went doesn't mean she'll get chosen," Arthur said.

"Nah, there's always more Common hatchlings than there are people willing to take them. They're scourge fodder. Why do you think the adults sell us on the idea of being a dragon rider so hard?"

Before Arthur could think of anything to say to that, Horatio slumped away.

CHAPTER 30

Arthur chewed over what Horatio had said for the rest of the evening. So much so that he chopped a pile of onions so roughly, that Chef told him to throw his work in an onion soup and start again—and do it right this time.

Grumbling to himself, he did. But he couldn't keep down his spinning thoughts.

It was obvious to anyone who had eyes that everyone from Headmaster Freyja to the teachers wanted their students to be carded. A carded person was healthier and more productive. He'd heard Freyja say that with his own ears.

A Common card gave just as many health benefits as someone with a higher-ranked card. It didn't mean Commons were bad. Anyone in his last village—including him—would have given all the toes on their left foot to have a shot at any card, Commons included.

But now that Horatio mentioned it, he did realize the adults pushed the idea of becoming a dragon rider with subtle encouragement.

Was that a good or bad thing? Arthur didn't know.

He tried not to think about the pink dragon's death. It had been awful and violent, and it made him think that not everything in the hive was as sunny as the teachers liked to believe.

But . . . he hadn't seen any dragon fights over the last couple of weeks here. There was always activity around the hives—dragons were constantly coming and going from the hive slopes. He'd seen several almost-collisions as different dragons swerved to avoid midair crashes.

But he'd never seen one snap at another while at the hive.

Anyone with brains would know that fighting scourglings was dangerous work. If vultures like Second and his friends regularly looked for fallen dragon riders, it made sense they'd need new hatchlings to fill out the ranks.

It was grim, but aside from the pink's death, not suspicious.

Horatio might be his normal crabby self. Or he might have a point. That was fine, because Arthur wasn't entirely sure he wanted to be a dragon rider . . . Or if it was even possible.

Doshi's rider had to wait five years for Doshi to hatch, and he was a Rare rank. Arthur had a Legendary card under his belt.

With a shake of his head, he put the problem of dragon riders to the side.

No, what really bothered him was the length of time it took to make a card from shards.

As subtly as possible, he reached down to scratch his side. He'd taken to winding a strip of bandages around his middle, then tucking the Rare Trap card under. That way he kept it close and didn't have to worry about it falling out of his shirt.

Over the last few weeks, the bruised spot in his heart had healed over. He didn't even miss the card being there. Much.

He needed another card. Uncommon, if he could get it. That would keep him under the notice of anyone important.

Assembling a card piece by piece would take too long. Freyja had been wildly optimistic when she'd been selling him on the idea of living at the orphanage.

He wasn't willing to wait years.

Either he would have to try to sell his Rare card for several Uncommons, or he was going to get card shards another way.

He knew which one he wanted.

One good thing about having Horatio as a roommate—and coincidentally, the thing that annoyed him the most now—was that the other boy didn't snore.

So Arthur couldn't reliably tell when he had fallen asleep.

Arthur stayed as still as he could while in bed, listening to the dark, quiet room around him. Lights out had been over an hour ago, and Horatio's breathing was deep and even. Or was he pretending?

Why would he be pretending? Arthur scolded himself. The other boy never paid attention to him and had, in fact, ignored Arthur as usual when they walked home from the restaurant together.

He was overthinking, and the night was passing him by. City noise drifted in from the window. It called to him.

Slowly, Arthur pushed his blankets down and slid out of bed. He'd gone to bed in his clothing and so only had to lace up his boots.

Using his **Stealth** skill, he crept to the window. It was the type that swung outward, and he had checked the hinges earlier to make sure they didn't squeak.

Leaning out, he reached for the drainage pipe.

Climbing down was a lot harder than he thought it would be. His fingertips were sore by the time he made it to the ground. But after that, he was free.

Grinning to himself, he walked down the darkened streets toward the sounds of people.

The city had different energy after the sun set. Lights blazed from lamps of a hundred different colors. Vendors sold food and drink from temporary booths.

Arthur stopped and watched in amazement as a man stood on a street corner and ate swords burning with flame in front of an admiring crowd. He wasn't sure if it was a weird talent or a card skill, but he was impressed either way. So was the crowd, judging by the amount of tips.

He privately made a note to keep an eye out for a "swallowing fire" card.

He walked on, keeping a sharp eye out for card dens, saloons, or even dice games. He wasn't sure how he'd talk his way into playing a hand of cards, because everyone around him was a grown adult, but maybe if he hung around long enough, he'd see an opportunity.

His attention was drawn by a man who set up a simple table by a meat-stick vender. He was introducing a young couple to an odd cup game.

The idea was that he slipped a card shard under one of the cups and mixed them around. If either the man or the woman could guess the cup it was under, they would win the shard. Of course, they had to pay to play.

Arthur didn't need his **Card Shuffling** skill to know that this couldn't be as obvious as it seemed. Sure enough, the couple paid three times in a row and guessed the wrong cup every single time.

There had to be a card-enhanced skill at play here. Was the game master hiding the shard? Making it invisible? Throwing an illusion over the table?

No . . . Arthur wasn't certain how he knew, but it felt like there was a skill being used. As the game master shuffled the cups around, it was as if his heart throbbed in sympathy.

Somehow, the game master convinced the couple to try again. This ended up in yet another wrong guess from the increasingly frustrated couple. Just when the man started to bluster and grow annoyed, the game master offered his money back from the last round.

The man huffed, but it was clear his injured pride wouldn't allow him to accept. Thankfully, the woman tugged him away before he made a fuss.

The game master tipped his hat sarcastically at their backs. Then he turned and looked directly at Arthur. "This ain't a free show, kid. You either play or you get outta here."

Arthur was startled. He hadn't realized the man had noticed him.

"Cups aren't my game." Arthur paused. "Say, you know where they like to play dice around here?"

"Dice? What do you know about dice games? You look about ten years old."

"I'm twelve," Arthur snapped. This was getting old.

The man rolled his eyes. "Sure, kid. Look, go through there, between that next alley and around the corner to the left. You'll find what you need. Now leave me alone. You'll drive away the marks."

Marks? Arthur wondered but shrugged and did as he was told.

He figured the man had either sent him through the alleyway on a shortcut, or at worst, a wild goose chase.

It wasn't until he was partway down the dark alleyway that it occurred to him that someone who called customers "marks" might send him into danger.

He stopped and began to turn. That's when he registered the presence behind him.

Arthur caught the man following him out of the corner of his eye. He gave an involuntary yell and jumped back.

His hand fumbled under his shirt for the card. If someone used a card of their own, he'd be home in a snap. Though if they stabbed him or something, he would be screwed.

He didn't manage to get the card free before his brain caught up with his eyes. The figure behind him was tall, but not as big as a full-grown man.

Sure enough, a familiar voice grated out, "If you're going to bother sneaking out of the orphanage, you should at least stay out of the slums."

It was Horatio.

Straightening, Arthur lowered his hand from the bandage under his shirt. Hopefully, Horatio would think he had been going for a belt knife instead.

"What are you doing here?" he asked, though he already knew. "You were following me?"

Far from looking guilty, Horatio rolled his eyes. "I wanted to see if perfect Arthur knew his way around the town like everything else."

Perfect Arthur? His eyebrows knit together, and he opened his mouth to reply.

Horatio beat him to it. "Instead I find you walking through one of the most dangerous parts of the city. You oughta thank me for stopping you before you went too far."

"This place doesn't seem too bad."

It was dark inside the alleyway, but he still caught the sneer on Horatio's face. "You really are a bumpkin, aren't you?"

"What's your problem?" Arthur demanded. He was sick and tired of Horatio's attitude. The other boy clearly didn't like him and acted like he didn't want to be around him. But instead of snitching when Arthur snuck out, he'd followed him and risked punishment, too. It made no sense. "Why do you act like you're better than everyone else?"

"Not better. I just know my ass from a hole in the ground." Horatio looked around. "Why did you sneak out, anyway?"

Arthur was not going to tell him that he was after gambling huts. "I don't know. I was just looking around."

Horatio rolled his eyes.

Arthur sort of felt like hitting the other boy, but he was about a foot taller than himself. It might raise questions if Horatio went down to the breakfast table tomorrow with a black eye. Especially since, for some reason, Horatio was the teacher's favorite.

"Why did you follow me?" Arthur asked again.

"To see if you had taste. You don't . . . but I suppose it's not your fault." Horatio turned. "Come on, let's get out of here before we're mugged."

He went back the way they'd come in. After a moment's hesitation, Arthur followed.

Once they hit the street, Horatio kept walking in a direction opposite from the orphanage.

Arthur hurried to catch up, though he had to step twice to keep up with every one of Horatio's strides. "Where are we going?"

"Looking for some real fun," Horatio said. "Or whatever this dumb little hive town can provide."

For the first time, Arthur wondered if Horatio came from a noble family. He sure acted snooty enough.

They walked down one street after another, all filled with nightlife. Arthur looked around with greedy eyes. They passed by bars so full that adults were spilling out, laughing drunkenly. Through the wide-open windows, he saw some playing poker.

All of those playing cards had a hard-edged look about them, though. There were no kids in there, either. Not even as waitstaff. Arthur would have a tough time talking his way into one of those.

More booths lined the streets, selling everything from clothing to food. One vendor yelled out that he had card shards for sale. Arthur would have stopped, but Horatio seemed determined to keep walking.

"Is it always like this at night?" Arthur asked half in awe.

Horatio gave him a weird look. "They don't do harvest festivals where you're from?"

Whoops. Though it explained the air of celebration in the streets. He hadn't walked far enough to see signs, though.

Arthur shrugged. "Most seasons, we didn't have a lot of reason to celebrate." That was the truth. "What about you?"

"I didn't have much to do with farmers," Horatio said.

Mentally, Arthur ticked another box next to "noble."

Maybe Horatio had been the last son of a minor noble, like a baronet. Someone who was in charge of a couple of small towns and thought he was king of the world. He'd heard Red talking about them once or twice.

Only then did he realize the crowd was growing thicker as they went on. Horatio didn't slow down and instead wound around clumps of people. Arthur had to half jog to keep up with him.

Looking over his shoulder, Horatio scowled. "Come on. I don't want to miss more than I have already."

"Miss more of what?"

"What do you think?" Horatio asked, annoyed. Then his expression blanked. "Wait, you weren't playing before? You really don't know?"

Arthur scowled. "What are you talking about?"

"Card duels."

"What?" Arthur gasped.

At that moment, a burst of multicolored sparks lit an area down the street. The crowd *oohed* at once.

Others were hurrying down the street, too. All were heading to the same place.

Horatio was a man on a mission and seemed to navigate the increasingly thick crowd. This many people was intimidating to Arthur, but the other boy didn't seem fazed at all.

Swallowing his ego, Arthur grabbed the tail of Horatio's shirt like a little brother who hoped the elder wouldn't leave him behind.

Horatio glanced over his shoulder again, smirked, but didn't say anything.

Another corner, and then the street ended at a massive building at least four stories tall. A glittering, spelled sign above announced it was the Wolf Arena with pictures of wolves tipped back and howling at either end.

"This isn't a proper fighting arena like you find at one of the big hives," Horatio said, raising his voice to be heard over the crowd. "But you should see what a real card artist can do. Not the trash the orphanage tries to get us to accept."

He hurried forward again before Arthur could reply.

There were several oval entrances at the base of the arena, and people were streaming in. From inside, an echoingly loud voice called out. The walls muffled the words, but it sounded excited.

An attendant held out his hand as they tried to pass by. "That will be one copper each."

Horatio looked to Arthur. "Go on. You make twice as much as I do."

"I've only gotten paid for a week," Arthur said.

Horatio shrugged and looked at the attendant. "Price is the same for kids and adults?"

"Who cares if you're kids," the attendant said. "You want me to flag down the authorities because you're breaking curfew?"

Grumbling, Arthur reached into his pocket where he kept his precious copper coins. He paid, and the attendant ushered them forward.

Instantly, Horatio was speed-walking again.

They climbed staircase after staircase, and despite the number of people around them hurrying to get seats, they were able to find two easily.

Arthur looked down on a vast oval space. Bench seats went from the soft earthen floor of the arena all the way to the top.

"This is all for cards?" Arthur asked.

Horatio scoffed. "No, this is a minor hive, so it's not like they have their own arena." He must have seen Arthur didn't understand, so he went on. "It gets used for ceremonies, dragon groundwork training, and other stuff. Ooh, here they come."

Three people walked out from an underground tunnel into the arena proper.

One man and woman went to stand on either end of the oval. The woman, who was closest to where they sat, wore a sparkly black gown that was cut so low that Arthur couldn't help but stare a little. The man on the other end wore fancy clothing too—a vest and a top hat like he was a grand performer.

The third person was a portly man who stood in the middle. He waved to the crowd and put a hand over his throat. When he spoke, his voice boomed out under a card's power.

"Ladies and gentlemen: Betting for this next Uncommon Rank Duel will close in two minutes. Shawna Shadow Sorceress versus the Master of Multiplication. Please get your final bets in quickly for this illusionist versus illusionist showdown!"

Horatio groaned.

"What? You don't like illusionists?"

"If they're both camouflage illusionists, we'll be staring at an empty arena until one finds and stabs the other."

"They stab people?" Arthur asked, horrified and a little intrigued.

"Sure, to first blood."

Arthur looked down at the woman. "Why isn't she wearing armor or something?" Then he caught the sly look on Horatio's face. "You're messing with me."

"They get markers." Horatio rolled his eyes. "Blue on her side, red on his. See the colors?" He pointed to the square of fabric hanging over each competitor's side. "First to mark the other wins. Why do I have to explain this? They *really* don't have duels in your city?"

"Where I'm from, people were lucky to have one card," Arthur said.

"Well in *proper* cities, most people get starting cards from their parents or their master, if they're apprenticed. They don't string kids along with shards in some kind of work scheme."

Did he have to complain about everything? Didn't he realize what kind of an opportunity they'd been given? "Olivia made a card," Arthur snapped. "You saw it."

"Maybe you want to be Common fodder, but I don't," Horatio sneered. "Anyway, most people who are worth a damn—even people in minor hives like this—have decks. There are some nobles and important dragon riders who have entire libraries of cards."

Arthur's father had said something similar, but he had been so new to being carded he hadn't realized the implications. "But . . . doesn't it hurt to take them in and out of your heart? Why would you stuff them in a library?"

Horatio looked at him like he was insane. "Do you just swallow anything you want to carry around? No? Then you don't stick things in your heart unless you want them to become a part of you." He shook his head. "This is why I hate this place. No one knows anything."

"But how—" Arthur started.

"Ladies and gentlemen," the announcer boomed out, "final betting has closed. Please take your seats. This duel is about to begin."

"Watch," Horatio said. "You might learn something."

CHAPTER 31

In the red corner," said the announcer. "Shawna Shadow Sorceress."

The crowd cheered, and Shawna turned and waved. As she did, Arthur noticed she held a stick in her hand about a foot long with a painted red end on it. This must be the marker Horatio talked about.

"And in the blue corner, we have the Master of Multiplication!"

The man on the other end was a little harder to see due to distance. However, as the crowd cheered, he took off his top hat and bowed to them all.

"Tonight we battle under normal Uncommon dueling rules: the first one to mark the opponent's skin wins. Now . . . fight!"

With the last word, the announcer dropped his hand and quickly backed to the far wall, presumedly to stay out of the way.

Shawna Sorceress reached for her left forearm. There was a dark rectangular mark on her skin. Arthur couldn't see the fine details, but Shawna seemed to pull out a card from her skin.

She held it out in front of her. "Shadow Veil!"

Instantly, a cloud of shadow engulfed her half of the arena. It was inky black and impossible to see through. For a moment, it seemed the cloud would roll up to engulf the audience, but at an angry buzzing sound, the cloud sank back again to puddle on the grounds.

"What did I tell you?" Horatio sighed. "If there's any fight in there, we won't be able to see it."

The Master of Multiplication hadn't been resting on his laurels. With the hand not clutching his own marker, he reached under his long, flowing jacket and held up his own card.

"Baker's Dozen!"

Instantly, a crowd of exact copies of him sprang from where he'd been standing and charged headlong toward the darkened half of the arena. Arthur could not tell which was the original, which was likely the point.

Before the first of the copies reached the shadow cloud, Shawna's voice called out, "Dark Tentacles of Power!"

The shadowy clouds boiled and coalesced into long whip-like arms that slashed at the oncoming copies. All that struck passed through, proving that the copies were insubstantial illusions.

The dark tentacles couldn't reach all the copies. Several plunged through and disappeared into the dark cloud.

Arthur half stood, desperate not to miss a thing. "What's going on? I can't—" He stopped himself before he blurted out that he couldn't see anything.

Horatio laughed. "Told you."

He didn't have to worry. A moment later, the dark clouds thinned and boiled away in patches, revealing copies of the Master of Multiplication holding up identical cards that beamed bright light.

It seemed to break Shawna Sorceress's illusion spell entirely, and as the clouds shrank back, she was revealed looking caught off guard.

Shawna reached for the black mark on her arm, pulling out one card after another and looking a little panicked.

"She's either arrogant or she's planning something," Horatio said.

Three of the Master of Multiplication spotted her at the same time and ran at her. Only one held a stick tipped with blue at the end—his marker. That likely meant he was the real version.

He lunged at her, thrusting the marker like a saber.

Shawna cracked into a hundred pieces and fell away—she had been an illusion, too.

"Trap illusion!" Horatio cried, and the crowd applauded and whooped.

Suddenly, the bare edge of the shadows boiled away to reveal the real Shawna standing not six feet away from the Master.

She plunged forward with her red stick.

Several of the audience members screamed out a warning, but they were drowned out by the still-exuberant crowd.

The Master must have sensed something, because he began to turn. But not before she swiped the end of her red wand against the back of his neck.

. . . Only he puffed away in illusion smoke as well.

A look of pure fury crossed Shawna's face. The crowd, however, went wild.

Meanwhile, the real Master stumbled out of the last cloud bank shadow and pulled out his card.

"Baker's Dozen!" he yelled again.

This time, only four copies showed up.

"He's running low on mana," Horatio said. "Uncommon cards are mana hogs."

"Then how is she able to do that?" Arthur pointed to Shawna, who had called the last of her inky clouds to her. She disappeared into the middle, and the whirling dark ball split into two separate clouds, which advanced on the Master and his illusions.

"All her card powers are alike. I bet she has part of a set—mana costs usually go down when you add a Special card into the mix."

Either way, Arthur could tell this duel was coming to a close.

The two clouds moved with eerie—though slow—grace toward the Master. Meanwhile, some of his doubles were visibly illusions. The colors were washed out, and one looked like a walking painting, flat and unreal. It dissolved, leaving four others and the real master.

They approached the oncoming dark clouds. By the frown that crossed their identical faces, Arthur saw they were facing a choice. Which cloud was Shawna hiding in?

It reminded him of the shell game. If his illusions were more realistic or better formed, maybe they could have searched both.

As one, they surged for the cloud to the right.

But then both clouds seemed to grow sharp teeth. They opened their dark mouths in a silent roar that gusted such fierce wind, three of the Master's illusions popped, and the real man was pushed to the ground.

Abruptly, Shawna staggered out of the left cloud and clumsily swiped her red-marked wand over his arm.

She collapsed a second later and so did the final wisps of both clouds, but it was enough.

"The Sorceress of Shadows is the winner!" called the announcer.

Arthur cheered and clapped along with the rest. When he thought he could be heard over the roar, he turned to Horatio.

"Each one of those powers came from a card? You think she had more than him?"

"It's not about the number of cards," Horatio said. "My dad used to say it was the synergy between 'em."

"Synergy," Arthur repeated, committing that word to memory.

Down below, Shawna and her opponent were picking themselves up and being ushered off to clear the room for the next duelists. As they did, Arthur saw them put their used cards away—the Master in his jacket and Shawna in the mark of her arm.

Was there such a thing as an arm deck?

Arthur turned to ask Horatio, but he was busy signaling a vendor who was selling bags of popped corn.

"Hey, popcorn guy!"

A minute later, Arthur found himself paying for a bag of popcorn. Horatio paid for his own, though he grumbled about it.

"How did she pull cards out of her arm?" Arthur asked between handfuls of popcorn. It was the first time he'd had it—he'd eaten corn before but had no idea it could be made like this.

Horatio rolled his eyes. "How have you gone this long being so ignorant? Yeah, it's a card anchor mark. Kind of a false deck so you're not shoving powers into your heart. Fancy ladies have it on purses, and you can get tattoos and stuff."

"Why doesn't everyone use a card anchor?" Had Second known about them? If he had, why would he have gone through the trouble of hauling tobacco?

Horatio grabbed another big handful of popcorn and chewed obnoxiously around his answer. "'Cause that's how people get cards stolen. Can't steal from here." He tapped his chest.

Made sense. And a card anchor might be exactly what he was looking for: a place to hide his Rare Trap card without it accidentally triggering on him.

The next fight was called. It was to be a duel between Common Earth card artists.

Horatio perked up. "Elemental duels are always good, even if it's just Commons."

"You've seen a lot of duels, then?" Arthur asked, trying and failing to keep the jealousy out of his voice.

"Oh, yeah. It's great fun in the winter when it's too damn cold to go riding—" He stopped and shook his head. "Anyway, maybe they'll show a fight between Rares. They usually have enough mana to fill up the arena . . ."

He chattered on until the next duel started.

The earth duel was a slugfest between a man who had an earth golem and a man who seemed to have control of stones the size of his head. After that was another illusionist, though he faced a man who could juggle anything—even knives.

As exciting as the duels were, Arthur found himself yawning by the end. He had a long walk back, as well as class and work duty after that. He wasn't looking forward to climbing up that pipe back to their window, either.

Even Horatio didn't complain as they made their way out.

The streets outside the arena were as festive as ever. Not everyone wanted to watch duels, and several bands of musicians—carded and otherwise—started trying to outplay each other on different street corners.

Arthur looked around, tired but still entranced.

That was likely the reason he didn't notice the dragon.

"A silver's on the hunt," Horatio said casually.

It took Arthur a beat to register his words, as he was watching a carded man play the guitar using only wind and not his fingers. Then it hit him, and he glanced up. "Huh?"

Horatio jerked his chin to the right.

A silver dragon roughly the size of Tess was hopping down the street, long ungainly wings threatening to knock people over. Something about its proportions, from overly large feet to the big luminous eyes, made Arthur think that it was very young.

The girl following after, practically begging him to stop, seemed inexperienced, too.

"Marteen, stop! You're going to knock someone over. Marteen . . . listen to me!"

"I smell one!" Silver Marteen insisted in a high, young voice. "There are good cards here. I can tell!"

"Marteen!"

Horatio snorted. "First time out of the hive and it probably smells a noble brat's first card. This should be fun—hey!"

"We need to go." Arthur grabbed his elbow and pulled him aside.

Marteen and her rider were still several shops away, and Marteen was casting around—likely confused by all the scents and carded folk—but he had no doubt she smelled him.

He was surrounded by strangers. If someone knew he had a Legendary card—

"Here he is!" Marteen trilled.

Sure enough, the silver had stopped short next to a very well-dressed family and was currently sniffing one of the children up and down. They did not look amused. Marteen's rider was beet red and mortified.

Horatio shook his head. "That dragon's got to learn there's a time and a place to sniff out good cards—all right, all right, I'm coming. Stop pulling me."

He started walking, which was a good thing, because Arthur was at the point of ditching him completely.

As he rounded the corner, he heard Marteen tell her rider, almost plaintively, "But I smelled *two* good ones . . ."

Arthur kept walking, ignoring Horatio's gripes about being in a hurry to get back for no reason.

Luckily, the young silver didn't follow.

CHAPTER 32

By all rights, Arthur should have woken up at the morning bell dead with exhaustion.

Instead, it was as if his limbs were charged with bits of lightning. What he had seen last night—real demonstrations of what cards were capable of—had set his mind ablaze with possibilities.

He wanted a card that worked like that, but even more . . . He wanted to find out what his own card could be capable of. The wonders he'd seen came from Uncommon cards. He had a Legendary.

Would he be able to out-skill someone in the arena?

He would never find out if he didn't push the limits.

So, even though Arthur disliked his **Tidying** skill, the moment he got up, he started making his bed. He had advanced **Tidying** more or less accidentally up to the threshold between Basic and Apprentice. As a result, when he was finished, the blankets were tight on the frame, and the pillow neatly placed without so much as a wrinkle. It was as if he hadn't slept there at all.

Horatio still lay in his bed, looking like a wrung-out rag.

Arthur reached out to poke the other boy. "Come on, Ray. It's breakfast time."

Horatio cracked open one eye and scowled at him. "Don't call me Ray. I am *not* a ray of sunshine." With effort, he sat up. His dark hair was a mess, and there were shadows under his eyes. Squinting, he looked at Arthur accusingly. "Speaking of, how are you so bright and cheery?"

Arthur flashed him a smile. "Because there are still two more days of the Harvest Festival."

He had gotten that factoid out of the other boy during their walk back to the orphanage last night. Harvest Festivals around the hives usually lasted three days in total. It was something to do with the full phase of the moon. "You're watching the duels with me tonight, right?"

"You're paying?"

"Yeah." That was an easy promise to make. He had plans to make that money back.

Horatio instantly brightened.

That night, Arthur let Horatio claim seating in the arena's stands. Arthur himself went by the betting booths to see what his Gambler Class could do for him.

A list of each of the upcoming duels were on a painted board behind the booths. It listed the name of each of the competitors, a win/loss ratio, and the current odds.

The first duel was to be between two men with body enhancement cards: Hammerhead Harry versus the Destroyer.

The Destroyer had won five of his last duels. Hammerhead Harry hadn't ever dueled before. So the officials had given the Destroyer a three-to-one odds to win.

Arthur bit his lip, considering.

The smart thing to do would be to place his hard-earned coppers on Destroyer. But he didn't like the miniscule payout.

Besides, Hammerhead was brand new. That meant he was a complete wild card. Plus, he had an intimidating name.

He hoped this was his Gambler Class whispering wisdom in his mind and not a moment of foolishness.

"Two coppers on Hammerhead," Arthur said, giving it to an official at the booth.

The man pocketed the coins and wrote his receipt on a slip of paper before stamping it and handing it back to Arthur. "Good luck, son."

Grinning, Arthur went to find Horatio, who had gone off to find them seats.

"They actually let you bet?" Horatio asked. "Didn't give you any trouble over you being a kid?"

"I told you," Arthur said. "Coins talk."

Horatio rolled his eyes. "A decent city wouldn't allow it, but whatever. Are you going to buy us popcorn or what?"

"Sorry," Arthur said cheerily. "Those were my last two coppers. You better hope I win."

Moments later, the competitors were announced.

To Arthur's intense disappointment, Hammerhead Harry had a completely normal-looking head. He also came out looking like a farmer, overalls and all.

Horatio noticed, too. He whooped in laughter and elbowed Arthur on the side. "That's who you bet on, right? Is he your kin?"

"No. Shut up."

The Destroyer, in complete contrast, wore almost no clothing at all save for brilliant red shorts that seemed much too small. He was a mountain of a man with bulging muscles. Arthur had to admit to himself, that unfortunately, he looked exactly like a destroyer should.

Because this was a duel between two body enhancers, each competitor was given a bag of colored chalk dust wrapped in a cheesecloth. Letting the bag drop from his hand would create a small cloud of chalk dust. That would mark the loser.

The moment the sign to begin was given, the Destroyer charged at Hammerhead full speed.

Hammerhead put up an arm as if in surprise but did not attempt to dodge.

He was hit and was sent, literally rolling, across half the arena.

But Hammerhead kept his hold on the chalk dust bag. And when he climbed to his feet, he only brushed himself off with his free hand. There wasn't a scratch on him.

With a roar, the Destroyer charged again.

That set the tone for the rest of the duel. The Destroyer batted Hammerhead twice around the arena, resorting to punches and kicks when full-body tackles proved to have no effect.

Hammerhead took every hit easily. Not once did it seem he was about to drop his bag.

Soon, the Destroyer was sweaty, red-faced, and looking winded.

"Do you think they're using mana?" Arthur asked.

"Dunno," Horatio said. "Usually body enhancement works on stamina—your own strength. Though Hammerhead might be." He squinted. "Maybe at the point when he gets hit?"

With a frustrated yell, the Destroyer ran at Hammerhead again.

For the first time, Hammerhead moved. He grabbed the tired man, stopping him in his tracks, which was a surprise considering how big he was.

Then Hammerhead leaned back and head-butted the other man.

There was a crack of light as their foreheads connected.

The Destroyer fell like the strings had been cut from him. His chalk dust bag rolled free in a cloud of red.

Hammerhead had won.

"Now *that* was mana," Horatio yelled over the cheers of the crowd.

Arthur was cheering, too. He had just turned his last two coppers into six.

"I'm going to place another bet," he told Horatio before the crowd had even settled.

* * *

They left the arena after the last match of the night.

Horatio gave Arthur a disgusted look. "I can't believe you turned two coppers into a whole silver. You must have the luck of a Rare dragon."

"I didn't win all the bets," Arthur said modestly.

Though he had won enough to come out substantially ahead. It had also given him the experience he needed to add a new skill.

New skill gained: Game Proficiency: Duel Betting
Due to your card's bonus traits, and your Gambler Class bonus to skills
with an arithmetic foundation, you automatically start this skill
at level 8.

The card had also given him an option to add it to his Gambler Class, but Arthur had declined. His Gambler Class was made up of an average of all of those class skills, so he wanted to fatten **Duel Betting** up before he added it.

Still, he was riding high on his own success . . . even though he was so exhausted from two nights of lost sleep that it felt like bees were buzzing around in his brain.

He and Horatio were walking out with the bulk of the crowd when a strident, annoyed voice caught Arthur's attention.

"Marteen! Stop!"

Arthur turned on his heel, his stomach dropping down to his shoes.

Sure enough, Marteen the silver and her hapless rider were again searching the square.

Seeing them, Horatio chuckled. "Come on, if we don't get back soon, you'll have to carry me the rest of the way."

But that direction, and the flow of the crowd, would take him past the silver.

Arthur stayed rooted in place. "Isn't there another way home?"

"What? Are you kidding? I'm dead on my feet. I'm not going the long way. Come on." He hooked Arthur under the arm and tugged him forward.

Arthur tried to bully his brain into making an excuse, but nothing came. Just the sound of bees. All that came out was, "I can't."

"Why not?" But Horatio was grumpy, not an idiot. He followed Arthur's gaze to the silver dragon, who was sniffing hopefully at every passing person.

His eyes narrowed, and to Arthur's shock, he hauled Arthur across the crowd—away from Marteen, and to a dead end. They stopped in the shadow of some hastily erected stalls, now empty thanks to the late night.

Horatio looked him up and down. "You don't have a gambling card," he said flatly. "One of the official's Trap cards would have caught you cheating."

Arthur started to open his mouth to deny everything, but then he blinked. "They have those?"

Seemed like enhanced skills didn't count as cheating. Though, it had been mostly luck that had helped him guess the winners. It wasn't like he had used mana to tilt the odds or see the future.

Horatio glared down at him. "You haven't said you *don't* have a card."

Well . . . damn.

"Don't tell," Arthur said. "It's not like I don't want to be a dragon rider. I just . . ." He trailed off, unsure how to say it.

"Yeah." Horatio ran a hand back through his hair, glancing over his shoulder in disgust at the silver. "There's a difference between wanting that future and being dragged into it."

Arthur looked at him in surprise. "Yeah. That's it. Exactly."

Horatio turned his scowl back on him. "Judging by the way that silver came back, you've got a high card."

Arthur didn't say anything, but the look on his face must have confirmed everything.

Horatio let out a long breath. "Of course the stupid kid has a high card," he muttered.

Arthur flared up. "I'm not a kid. I'm older than you, I bet! I'm going to grow soon, just you watch. But I have to . . . I have to get a low card in me, because if someone finds out what I have . . . I have no parents to protect me." His voice broke. He hadn't meant to say any of that, but it was as if telling Horatio just a little bit of the truth had cracked open a dam to all of his fears. "During the scourge-eruption, I saw a dragon rider die. I don't know if I want to be one of them."

"They die all the time," Horatio said, his voice flat and dead. "Why do you think they're always pushing kids at new hatchings?" He sighed. "Give me your silver coin."

Arthur looked up at him, stunned. "Why?"

Horatio was going to rob him? Blackmail him for the knowledge?

Horatio rolled his eyes. "Hurry up. We need to get some scent on you before the crowd thins too much. I can walk past it—I never got my card," he added sourly.

Arthur hesitated, but he didn't have much of a choice.

Taking the hard-won silver out of his pocket, he pressed it into Horatio's hand.

Horatio spun and without another word, marched down the block confidently past the silver. The young dragon didn't give him so much as a sniff.

Arthur stayed in place, pressing up against the side of the stall to stay in the shadows. What if Horatio didn't return?

But less than ten minutes later, he did, carrying a tin of something in his hands. He opened it, and Arthur found paper-rolled cigarettes.

"Tobacco?"

"Yeah, and some matches. Here's your change." Horatio passed both items to him, as well as two coppers.

Sticking one of the rolled cigarettes in between his lips, Horatio showed him how smoking was done. Arthur coughed like his lungs were trying to jump out of his mouth. The smoke tasted disgusting, but the spicy, complicated scent of tobacco was soon thick in the air.

With Arthur still coughing, the two boys walked on the other side of the street from the silver. He didn't dare look at Marteen, but no one called after him.

After rounding the corner, Arthur threw his cigarette down. He felt nauseated but also exhilarated.

Horatio took a practiced drag of his cigarette and then tapped the ashes. "It's a bad habit, but there's something about tobacco that confuses magic."

"Thank you," Arthur said.

"Don't thank me," Horatio said. "You owe me."

A cold feeling wormed its way into Arthur's gut. Owing Second had almost gotten him killed.

"What do you want?"

"You don't want anyone to know about your high card? Fine. On one condition."

Horatio gave a final drag to his cigarette and then threw it down and crushed it under his shoe. "I need a Rare card of my own."

CHAPTER 33

Arthur recoiled in horror, hand halfway up to his heart, even though he didn't keep his Rare card there anymore. It was pure reflex, and the bruised spot where he'd taken it from his heart throbbed.

"I don't want *your* card. What do you take me for?" Horatio snapped.

Arthur glared up at him. "People have tried before."

Horatio's lips tightened. "Look," he said, and took a breath as if to steady himself. "Look, I need a good high card. I don't want yours, but I figure . . ." Again he seemed to collect himself, as if his next words hurt to say. Maybe they did. Horatio was a proud boy. "I figure you got a line on one since you're already Chef's favorite and will have at least an Uncommon this time next year on top of what you already got."

Slowly, Arthur relaxed.

Having Second turn on him had twisted him up inside more than he thought at first. Hadn't Horatio already helped Arthur out once just by getting him the tobacco? He could have taken the silver coin and left. And yesterday, he could have easily gone to Freyja or one of her assistants instead of following Arthur and taking him to the arena.

With his constant dark cynicism, Horatio wasn't the easiest person to like . . . but he wasn't a bad guy, either.

"Why do you need a high card?" Arthur asked. Most people wanted a high card, of course. It led to a better life and more power and opportunities. That was a no-brainer. But if Horatio was willing to humble himself enough to ask, then it was more than a simple want. It was a need.

Horatio's lips pinched, and he screwed up his nose as if he tasted something bad. He glanced around as if to make sure there weren't any listeners nearby.

Finally, he blurted, "I come from a long line of high-card dragon riders."

"Not nobles?" Arthur was surprised.

"In the hives, it's practically the same thing. My great-grandmother had a Legendary white dragon, grade-A shimmer and everything. You know what that means?"

Arthur shook his head.

"She could put thoughts into people's heads, twist their dreams around. She could probably read minds, too." Horatio sighed so hard his whole body seemed to sag. "I was supposed to be someone. My dad was a rider, too. He was saving a Rare up for my birthday. Then he died fighting a scourge-eruption—some vultures found his body before his flight-mates did. They stole his cards."

An awful suspicion swept through Arthur. "What color was his dragon?"

Horatio gave him an odd look. "Sams is yellow—light aspect. Why?"

Yellow. Not the dragon he'd seen die.

"I told you, I saw dragons . . . fall," Arthur said awkwardly.

"No, this was months back." Horatio seemed remarkably casual about his father's death. Either he hid it well, or the loss of the cards bothered him more. "Anyway, Sams got cut up, but he lived. The admin—they're the hive leaders—wanted him to link his card with another. He refused. He said—" Horatio's voice went thick, and he hurriedly cleared his throat. "He wanted to wait for me. But Dad's cards were gone. So as punishment, the hive admin separated us—sent me across the continent to this podunk hive where people think Uncommons are a big deal. They think if enough time passes, or someone waltzes up with a perfect Rare, that Sams will link up with them instead."

From the pinched look on Horatio's face, he worried about the same thing.

"I . . . I'm sorry." Arthur wasn't sure what to say.

"I didn't tell you my life story to make you sorry for me. I wanted you to understand."

"I do," he said, and then had to admit, "Well . . . no. I don't know anything about the hives."

"They're great," Horatio said automatically. "If you want to make a difference, that's where you want to be. You're the front line in the fight against the scourge, and that's no small thing. Not many people can say they've saved lives apart from those with healer cards. But if you become a dragon rider, you save lives almost every time there's an eruption."

Arthur stared at his friend. He hadn't seen Horatio this enthused about anything, even the duels.

"And you're treated well, to boot," Horatio went on. "You work hard, but you play hard too, you know? You don't have to worry about enough to eat, or impressing a master or teacher, or even doing your own laundry. All you worry about is your dragon and killing enough scourge to earn shards and hive points."

"Hive points?"

"They're like coins, but better," Horatio said impatiently. "You bank enough points, you get privileges like bringing your family into the hive so they can get pampered while you fight." He poked his thumb into his own chest, but Arthur's imagination was caught.

He had promised his father, and himself, that he would come back to the village. Now, for the first time, he had an idea of how to get his father out.

If he could link up with a powerful dragon and earn enough hive points, he might be able to set up his family for life. They didn't even have to live in the hive—if he had a high-card dragon, which Horatio said were treated like nobles . . . who could stop him?

Well. Quite a few people, possibly. And this wouldn't be an easy task. For one thing, Arthur would need to wait until a Legendary dragon egg was laid. And he doubted the hive would let just anyone try for one of their most valued dragons. He would have to prove himself first.

The more he thought about it, the more difficult his idea seemed. But now, he had at least a glimmer of hope.

Horatio was looking at him expectantly, so Arthur shoved those thoughts to the side and focused on his friend's issues.

"So, not only do you need a Rare card . . . you need one that can link up with Sams?"

"Basically. He has a Mirror Light card. It enhances any Light-based spell or illusion. He can conjure up mirrors in midair. Dad had a Rare light-spike card that used to shoot beams of sunlight and heat with practically no mana cost at all. They used to be able to sweep a whole field of scourglings together."

Horatio's shoulders were so slumped it looked like he was carrying a thousand pounds of weight on his shoulders. "So even if I collect enough Rare shards, if the card ends up something like creating earthquakes, it'll still be useless."

"You could always trade for a light card," Arthur suggested. "Farmers would want something to move a lot of earth at once. Cheer up." He knocked his shoulder against Horatio's, though he had to stand on a nearby curb and on his tiptoes to do it. "There might be a way."

Because he felt safe with Horatio now that he knew his card would be useless, he shared, "Mine's a Trap card, and it's sort of useless."

Horatio looked startled, then confused. "How can a Trap be useless?"

"When it transports you somewhere else the moment someone uses a card's power on you."

"Oh . . . ouch." He looked sympathetic. "That might work if you got the right dragon. Though you'd probably just be put on the dangerous front lines and expect to be transported away if you got hurt."

"No thanks. I'm working toward another Rare." He didn't mind opening up to Horatio, but he wasn't going to be stupid about it. His Legendary card would remain a secret.

"How?" Horatio asked.

They had been walking all this time and had finally come up to the orphanage. Climbing up the drainpipe was a difficult task, and they had to be quiet. That gave Arthur the time he needed to think about his answer.

They made it back up to their open window with no one the wiser. Turning to Horatio, Arthur lowered his voice.

"If you want a Rare so much, why don't you put in the work in the kitchens?"

It was hard to tell in the dark, but he thought he saw Horatio blush. "I don't like it there. I never had to do anything like that before."

"You mean work?"

"Dad got enough hive points to take care of things like that. Now I'm on my own, and I hate it."

Spoiled, Arthur thought.

He shrugged. "I came across my card by luck. Scourgling the size of a horse cart fell out of the sky in front of me when I was running for my life. I think a dragon must have killed it but didn't follow it to the ground. It had a card on it. So it was just luck. But my next card . . . my next I want to earn through my own work. And I think if you want Sams to respect you, you've got to earn it too."

Horatio made a face, but he didn't argue. "Even if I become Chef's pet like you, he only pays in Uncommon shards."

"I turned a couple of coppers into a silver today," Arthur said. "You think you can turn some Uncommons into a Rare?"

Horatio started to reply and then stopped, looking at him with narrowed eyes. "How?"

"Dunno," Arthur admitted. "First step is making you a cook, not a dishwasher. But you gotta work for it."

With that, he turned and started changing for bed. Dawn was only a few hours away, and his body felt heavy with weariness.

Horatio was silent too. It wasn't until they slipped under the covers of their separate cots that he spoke again. "All right."

Arthur smiled to himself. The moment he lay down, he started to drift off.

The last thing he noticed before he fell asleep was a slight shift in his mind, as if something was being tallied up and reordered. He'd felt it before. It felt a little like when he was on the track to gain a new skill.

The evening of the next day, Arthur was set to the task of baking bread. Kneading was exhausting work, especially when he was going on a few days of little sleep. He only meant to sit down for a moment's rest when the bread was rising. He woke what felt like a second later with Chef snapping at him that the dough was now over-proofed.

Sure enough, the sides of the dough were spilling out of a giant bowl.

He had to start the process all over again and wasn't too surprised when he didn't receive a skill for it.

Horatio, who'd come to help toss the mess in the trash, caught his eye and smirked. A few days ago, Arthur would have taken offense or thought the other boy was mocking him. Now he was certain Horatio was mocking him . . . but he didn't take offense.

Horatio hadn't exactly found a new enthusiasm for his job, but at least he acted with a bit of competence. Neither Chef nor any of the other cooks had to tell him to do his work. Horatio even picked up a mop and started cleaning without someone ordering him to do it first.

Arthur waited until he had gone over most of the floor. Then, as casually as he could, he said, "After you clean up, do you want to give me a hand with the kneading?"

Horatio gave him a look. "Won't Chef mind?"

Arthur shrugged. The chef was currently berating one of the other cooks who had oversalted the stew.

"I already fell asleep once. Can't see how it would hurt. It's just punching some dough into place."

Horatio nodded, and after quickly washing his hands, he came over. Arthur showed him the technique, and they got started.

He caught Chef glancing over once or twice, an unreadable expression on his face. But as neither boy was making trouble, and Horatio's work had already been done, he didn't say anything.

After kneading the bread, Arthur set the dough to proof in several big bowls. He started cleaning up the extra flour on the counter, and Horatio did as well.

This time, Arthur did not fall asleep while waiting. Then he and Horatio kneaded it one more time before shaping the dough into individual loaves.

It would still have to wait overnight, but the bulk of the work was done.

"Make sure that you crack an egg and wash it over the top of the loaves," Chef said as he came up to them.

"Yes, Chef," Arthur said.

Chef looked at Horatio. "I saw you helping out. You have thoughts about being a baker?"

Arthur caught a flash of Horatio's old self—the one who did not like the idea of working. But it was gone again in the next moment. He straightened his shoulders and nodded. "Whatever gets me out of garbage duty . . . and pays better," he said boldly.

Arthur winced inwardly, but Chef just chuckled. "That's why we reward more responsibility with higher pay, my boy. We want to encourage ambition here. Keep up the good work, and I'll see if a baker's position opens up soon."

Arthur knew for a fact that they were down one baker. If Horatio was halfway competent, he'd probably get the job.

But the moment Chef walked away, Horatio turned to him, his eyes bright. "You think the baker position pays in Uncommon shards?"

"I think so," Arthur said. "That's a step closer to a Rare card, right?

"You're damn right. Now, what is an egg wash?"

New skill gained: Basic Career Counseling (Empath Class)
Due to your card's bonus traits, you automatically start this skill
at level 3.

The message surprised him, but it also made him feel gratified. As corny as it was, it felt good to receive a skill for helping out a friend instead of just doing something for himself.

It also made him wonder what it would take to level the skill up. What was an Empath Class?

CHAPTER 34

The day after Arthur was paid his first Uncommon card shard was a break day.

These came once every six days, with the seventh being a day of rest. However, for those with lower positions, such as Arthur, he was usually required to work them anyway, even though he got a break from classes.

But Horatio had surprised him and offered to take his usual shift to help bake bread loaves. He had assisted Arthur throughout the last week and now knew just as much as he did. When they ran it by Chef, the man seemed pleased and even offered to teach Horatio how to make a different kind of savory pastry.

Privately, Arthur thought Chef might be testing Horatio for advancement into a baker position. He hoped his friend took advantage of it. Meanwhile, Arthur had copper coins in his pocket, an Uncommon shard, and the rare luxury of free time.

He knew exactly how he was going to spend it.

After some careful questioning, he learned there were three card shops within the city. One was on the complete opposite end of the hive and was too far away for walking distance. He got recommendations for the other two.

He decided to aim for the one farthest away . . . just in case the shopkeeper recognized him later.

It never hurt to be too cautious, and he had grown used to secrecy.

It was a clear-sky day. Above, dragons flew back and forth, the tiny purples fastest of all. Arthur tilted his head up and watched them dart across the sky.

The shop itself was located near one of the canals that shunted water from the glittering river. The whole area had a swampy smell to it, and he wondered if the humidity was bad for cards.

The card shop itself had no windows, and the outside walls were reinforced with thick metal bars with some kind of weird runic script on them. It seemed the shopkeeper was very concerned with keeping thieves out.

As soon as Arthur stepped in, he saw why.

The shelves were tucked tight against the wall. Lining them and sandwiched between thick panes of glass were cards. Hundreds of cards.

There was a taste in the air, metallic, yet flowery and sweet at the same time. It wasn't unpleasant, but it was powerful. He thought it might be the taste of magic leaking out from the cards.

Eyes wide, Arthur stepped to the nearest shelf.

These were Common-rank cards with scholarly attributes. One allowed its user to read at a quicker pace, with slight bonuses to comprehension. Another gave benefits to learning a language Arthur had never heard of. Come to think of it, he never encountered anybody who spoke another language. As far as he knew, all the other kingdoms had long ago fallen to the scourge. That likely meant this card wasn't valuable for its magical skill, but for the health benefits it gave its user.

He stepped to a different shelf and saw that these Common cards contained aspects of water magic. There were minor charms to seek out deep wells within the earth, another card to change fresh water to salt water and back again at need. There was even one that reminded him of the card Hivey had: the ability to conjure drinkable water from the air, though this one used a lot of mana.

Arthur glanced to the front of the store and saw there were more shelves where only the employees stood. These had flashier-looking cards—the Uncommons.

If the shop had Rares, they were probably locked safely within trapped cases.

One of the shopkeeper assistants saw Arthur looking and snapped his fingers at him. "What are you looking for, kid? Do you need a test?"

Reluctantly, Arthur peeled himself from the shelves and walked up to him. "A test?"

"To see if you're ready for a card." The man reached under his counter and pulled out a glowing white stone—just like the one Freyja had used on him.

"No, I know already. I'm looking for a card anchor."

The man looked Arthur up and down as if judging if he was wasting his time or not. "There are tattoo places that'll do that for you."

"I don't want that." He didn't want a mark that anybody could see. His imagination had been caught by the Master of Multiplication, who had seemed to pull cards out of his jacket. "Do you have a bag or clothing with an anchor on it?"

The shopkeeper's eyebrows raised. "Yes, but it's not cheap."

Arthur didn't flinch. "Show me what you have."

Maybe it was his calm certainty, or maybe the shopkeeper was just curious by now, but he waved Arthur to follow him past the counters to a room in the back. This was clearly where they kept their higher-rank cards. There was yet another room beyond, barred by a thick metal door with a ringed lock on it. Two burly men stood on either side of that door and glared at Arthur with hostile expressions.

The shopkeeper ignored them and the door. Instead, he walked to another set of shelves that had several items.

A few of them were lady's purses, with delicate straps and gems crusted on the tops and sides. There were more masculine bags, too, made of dyed canvas fabric.

Arthur looked them over for a moment, then pointed at the simplest of them all. A small drawstring bag that looked barely big enough to fit a card.

The man took it out for Arthur to examine. It didn't look much different than his own coin pouch, except for the rectangular mark sewn into the fabric.

"How much?" Arthur asked.

"Three silvers."

Arthur dithered for a moment, but he needed something like this. With a regretful sigh, he pulled out his Uncommon shard. "And how much for this?"

The man looked at it, seeming faintly surprised. "That's a middle piece of the card, so I can give you two silvers for it."

That price felt a little low. The man reached for the piece as if this was a done deal, but Arthur drew his hand away. "How about a straight trade between this card shard and that anchor?"

The man didn't hesitate. "That card shard, and either a half silver more or five coppers, and I will throw in the charm to link you and the anchor for free."

Arthur hadn't realized that would be an extra cost. He considered for a moment, but either he took the deal now or he waited until another free day to visit another shop.

"Deal," Arthur said.

New skill gained: Haggling (Merchant Class)
Due to your card's bonus traits, you automatically start this skill at level 3.

Reluctantly, he pulled out five additional coppers to go with the shard. That was the entirety of his pay, gone in a moment. Hopefully, it would be worth it.

After taking his money and writing up a quick receipt, the man led him into another side room, where he directed Arthur to sit in a chair.

A moment later, a woman in her twenties entered from another side room. She took a look at the draw-bag anchor and nodded. "That is a good starter purchase for a young card wielder."

"Who are you?" Arthur asked.

She smiled. "I'm the one who sewed the anchor in, so I have to be the one to activate it. Now, you may feel funny for a moment, but it will be brief and there should be no pain. Are you ready?"

Arthur nodded, sitting up in his seat and trying to look brave. "I'm ready."

"Pull down your collar for me."

The woman used two fingers to touch the anchor mark on the pouch. With her other hand, she touched right over Arthur's heart.

He felt a sharp snap that seemed to echo inside his head.

She lowered her hands and smiled. "See? That didn't hurt, did it?"

"That's it?"

"That's it," she confirmed. "This bag is keyed into your heart deck. When you wish to upgrade it, come back here, and I will move the anchor to the new container."

She left soon after, drawing a curtain across the small space to give him privacy. Arthur knew why. The moment she was gone, he reached for the Rare Trap card, which was tucked under the bandages against his waist.

He slipped it into the draw bag and pulled it shut. As he did, a message appeared in front of his eyes.

Secondary Deck 1/3
Do you wish to activate Return to Start (Trap) now?

"Yes," Arthur said.

The card immediately prompted him to key in a location point or object. He declined.

Then, as an experiment, he mentally reached for the secondary deck option again.

Do you wish to deactivate Return to Start (Trap) now?

"Yes," he said with a grin.

Now, if he found himself in a bind, he could activate and deactivate the trap card at a moment's notice. Much easier than shoving it in his heart. The only catch was he had to have the bag with him. He felt that instinctively. After all, it was now connected with his heart.

And there were two more slots available.

CHAPTER 35

I've created a monster, Arthur thought fondly as he walked down the streets of the hive city. For once, he was not heading back to the orphanage after work . . . and he was alone.

Horatio had passed Chef's test/orientation with flying colors. It turned out he had a real flair for working with breads and pastries. Arthur didn't get it. Bread was good to eat and all, but it was a pain and a half to make, even with his **Baking Skill** to help him.

He much preferred making entrées full of meats and vegetables in new ways. It allowed him to experiment on the go, whereas baked goods had to follow a recipe practically to the letter, or else something would go wrong on the other side.

Horatio felt the exact opposite. He enjoyed having the recipes laid out for him—a structure that, if he followed it, he could depend on something tasty for his hard work. He could experiment with decoration and arrangement.

Arthur was happy to leave him to it.

In any case, now that Horatio had stepped into a position as a baker, with a generous pay in Uncommon shards, he was much happier—though he still kept his cynical sense of humor. And he still had almost zero respect for what he thought of as an inferior hive.

He had volunteered to stay late tonight to try out a new pastry idea, certain that Chef would reward him if he came up with something spectacular. Possibly even a shard. That wasn't a bad plan, and Arthur might take a page out of his book . . . but today, he needed to think.

He had to decide if he was going to become a thief.

It had started innocently.

Arthur had been finding himself hungry more and more often. Hopefully, it was his long-awaited growth spurt about to kick in. However, being surrounded by food while his stomach was growling was pure torture.

So, he started to sneak bites that weren't necessarily for tasting.

He didn't think much of it since the restaurant threw away more food in a night than could probably feed his entire village. Then he had gotten a new skill.

New skill gained: Embezzlement (Thief/Merchant Class)
Due to your previous experience and your card's bonus traits, you automatically start this skill at level 7.

That was plain unfair.

Though . . . he admitted to himself he did have experience thieving. It had been the only way not to starve in the borderland village.

Technically, every time he and his father planted secret gardens where they shouldn't be, they were stealing the baron's land. He had also snuck out knives and common garden equipment when dragon soil shipments came. It's not like those tools were given to them, seeing as they weren't supposed to grow their own food. And yes, he had skimmed off the top of harvests for the same reason.

Arthur didn't regret any of it, and he resented the fact that his card gave him thief experience.

But the worst, and most discouraging of his new skills so far, had been his **Sleight of Hand** skill.

He had gotten it just this morning, and he still wasn't sure how he felt about it.

It started when, as a thank-you present for helping him get the baking job, Horatio bought Arthur a used deck of playing cards.

"How did you know I'd wanted one?" Arthur asked.

Horatio shrugged. "You're always complaining that kids aren't allowed in the gambling halls. So I figure this will tide you over until you grow another foot or two."

He had to duck as Arthur mimed a punch in his direction.

Horatio had to do a lot of ducking . . . and Arthur had to punch up.

Anyway, the playing cards were a good replacement for the ones he had left behind in the caravan. They were old with some marks on the back to give away what would be on the other side of the card if someone was observant enough.

But they provided an excellent way to practice his **Card Shuffling** skills.

Arthur had grown used to waking up around the time of the morning bell. So when he woke a few minutes early this morning, he spent them quietly practicing the shuffling tricks he knew.

Remembering the tricky man with the cups, he started playing around with the idea of hiding a card in the curve of his palm and then sliding that same card into the deck at a later point.

He wasn't very good at it and nearly bent the card he was trying to hide several times before he figured out the method. He didn't plan on cheating anyone with this trick. Honest. It was just something to do to pass the time.

But his own card did not agree.

New skill gained: Sleight of Hand (Thief/Gambler Class)
Due to your card's bonus traits, you automatically start this skill
at level 3.

New Class!
You have learned five skills that contain unusual synergy.
You may combine these five skills into one basic class:
Lock-Picking
Apprentice Stealth
Acting
Embezzlement
Sleight of Hand
This class will be the average of all added skill levels. Newly learned compatible skills may be added to the Thief Class. However, an added lower skill level contributes to the overall average, possibly lowering the overall skill level.
Thief Class (Basic: Level 6) 5.6 average with a one-time rounded bonus.
When equipped, card wielder will learn all Thief Class levels at a 1.25 times rate in addition to existing skill bonuses.
+3 to Dexterity
+3 Perception
Do you wish to combine these skills now?

He froze. This wasn't what he wanted.

"Can I erase a skill?" he hissed.

Horatio shifted around on his own cot, on the verge of waking. Arthur pinched his lips shut.

His card, of course, did not give an answer.

Now he was faced with a choice. Well, three choices, and he wasn't sure what he wanted to do.

He could always move his new **Sleight of Hand** skill into his Gambler Class. But only if he intended to cheat people.

Yes, he intended to make money with his Gambler Class—as soon as he looked old enough to be let in—but there was a stark difference between outwitting someone by skill or paying attention to the numbers than . . . sliding a card into the deck to give himself an advantage.

No, he didn't want his **Sleight of Hand** going into the Gambler Class.

His second option was to consolidate it into a new Thief Class.

That was even worse, wasn't it? Arthur did not want to be a thief. Yes, he stole to live, but that had been out of necessity. If he was uncomfortable with cheating people, he didn't want to steal from them.

Plus, his Master of Skills card was in his heart. Did that mean adding a Thief Class might change his nature?

But . . . the Thief Class would have his **Stealth** skills, too. What if something bad happened and he needed the combined skills of a thief to get out? **Stealth** had saved his life by allowing him to hide from the scourglings. And he couldn't forget that Second would likely kill him if they ever crossed paths. Not to mention, if anyone discovered he had a Legendary-rank card . . . he'd have to get away, by any means necessary.

His Gambler Glass had given him a bonus to his luck status. Arthur was certain that had saved his life already.

What would a Thief Class give him?

Glancing at his class stats, he noticed that Thief was another basic class. He could equip three basic classes at one time. That meant there would be room for another active one after Thief. He hoped it would be cooking.

The last option was to do nothing at all. To keep **Sleight of Hand** as a regular skill and not add it to Gambler or create the Thief Class at all.

That last option felt like the worst out of the three. Arthur didn't like the idea of not using any advantage he could get.

His wandering path took him, at last, to the edge of one of the canals that ran through the city. This wasn't a large one. He could cross it with a running jump. But it was deep enough that he didn't want to risk falling in.

Standing at the edge, he looked down into the water. His reflection looked back at himself. Maybe it was how the water rippled, but he thought he looked a little bit like his dad: stern but responsible. Even though inside, he was troubled.

What would his dad do?

His father had been the man everyone in the village could trust. He went out of his way to help families who couldn't scrape up a meal from somewhere—even if that meant dipping into the harvest storehouses that the baron's men guarded.

Arthur wasn't supposed to know about that. But his father had sometimes disappeared at night. Then within a few days, the baron's men complained about losses or harvests coming in under what they thought they should be. Some of it had been them skimming off the top themselves, no doubt. But Arthur knew that some of those "losses" had ended up in the bellies of hungry borderland families.

So his father had technically stolen from the baron. But everyone did, and it had been a little fun because the baron would rather let families with children starve than give them a scrap. The choice had been easy. Not like now.

What would his father tell him to do?

He had told Arthur to find another card. To steal it if he had to.

Arthur was working on getting another card, but doing it the legit way was a slow process.

If he activated his Thief Class, could he get one sooner?

He had a feeling that, no matter what, his father wouldn't want him to sit on any opportunity. And just because he had, it didn't mean that he had to be a bad person.

Arthur nodded at his own reflection and then brought up the card dashboard again.

Inhaling a breath to steady his nerves, he accepted the Thief Class.

Thief Class
(Basic: Level 6)
Skills:
Lock-Picking
Apprentice Stealth
Acting
Embezzlement
Sleight of Hand
Bonus
+3 Perception
+3 Dexterity
Would you like to equip the class now?

"Yes," he muttered, bracing himself.

Immediately, the world felt different. As if it had become just a bit more real. The wind that blew off the canal felt a little colder against his skin. It carried with it an acidic tang that reminded him of home. It was dragon soil.

He heard there were dragon soil fields, though he had yet to see them. They weren't the type of place people went for fun.

He looked up to see dragons wheeling and darting in the sky and noticed for the first time that not all of them had riders on their backs. Were they riderless, like Sams? Or were their riders just busy and they were having a nice flight by themselves?

It didn't matter. His new perception seemed to sharpen his hunger as well.

It might be too late to get dinner at the orphanage, though he would have to check in with Freyja before he went to bed. That was one of the rules. He would just buy something on his way back.

Turning, Arthur retraced his path through the streets. His steps felt more fluid, as if he was more aware of how his body was constructed, how his joints moved with each other. He rolled his shoulders and realized he had been slouching. That was normal in the borderland village, where he didn't want to bring attention to himself. It made him look even smaller than he had been before.

He had no reason to hide here.

Arthur straightened up and made the effort to square his shoulders. Though he didn't stride down the road, he walked with more confidence.

His enhanced perception caught the scent of cooking food not far away. One of his favorite vendors manned a booth here where he sold mincemeat pies.

Arthur made a line toward him. As he did, he passed by a fruit stall. A bushel of apples sat on the edge of the table. One apple was so precariously balanced it was in danger of tipping off.

Out of the corner of his eye, Arthur saw the vender was busy talking with a customer.

Neither were paying attention to him.

Concentrating on his **Sleight of Hand** skill, he reached out and plucked the apple from the edge of the table. Then he smoothly shifted it to his other hand, using his body to block the motion.

The vendor didn't even glance his way.

New skill gained: Shoplifting (Thief Class)

Due to your card's bonus traits, you automatically start this skill

at level 3

Do you wish to add this to your existing Thief Class?

"I was going to put it back," he muttered.

Pausing, he pretended to examine some lush orange fruits he had recently learned were just called oranges. As he did, he replaced the apple exactly where it had been, with no one the wiser.

New skill level: Sleight of Hand (Thief Class)

Level 4

Too bad he couldn't get rid of the stain of his **Shoplifting** skill.

With a sigh, he added **Shoplifting** to his Thief Class.

Then he headed to the pie shop.

He had just purchased a mincemeat pie—though the cooking snob in him noticed that the vendor never mentioned what kind of meat went into the pie. Whatever it was, it was pretty tasty. The price was right, too. He was able to get two hand-sized pies for a half copper.

With his new perception, he heard a burble in the crowd. Arthur was too hungry to care. The vendor had already taken his coin and was about to hand the pies over. The vendor looked up just past Arthur's shoulder, his eyes wide.

A hot gust of breath blew across the back of his neck.

"You're the one," said a feminine, but very loud, voice behind him.

Arthur whipped around.

Marteen the young silver dragon stood right behind him.

He'd always thought of her as a smallish dragon, but she loomed large from only a few inches away. So did her teeth.

In the sunlight, her silver scales glittered like polished metal.

"I . . . I . . ." He backed up a step, but his butt hit the pie stall's counter, and he couldn't go any further.

"You're coming with me," Marteen said cheerfully.

Arthur turned to run. He didn't get the chance to start.

With shocking delicacy, the dragon reached to his collar with her teeth and yanked him up off his feet. Arthur heard something in his shirt tear, a few seams popping. As he was lifted off the ground, the front of the collar cut against his neck, half choking him.

The world spun wildly around, giving Arthur a quick view of the people gathered around to watch. Some were curious and a few were outwardly amused.

Then, as the dragon twisted her neck, he found himself hovering just over her silver back.

Marteen dropped him, and he hit hard, feet missing completely and breath whooshing out as his chest hit her back. Her scales were exactly as hard as they looked, like rivets of metal dovetailed over one another.

"Sit up straight and hold on." With that, Marteen spread her wings, making the gathered crowd quickly back up.

Arthur thought about dropping down and running, but he figured the crowd wouldn't let him.

"I'll hold on to your pies for you!" the pie vendor called, not so helpfully. "Come see me if you make it back."

Marteen shifted under him, so Arthur had only seconds to find a seat, straddling her back like he would a horse. She only had two wings to Tess's four, so at least there was more room.

But there was no saddle and no ridges along her spine like he'd seen with other dragons. There was nothing to hold on to.

Marteen pumped her wings. They were long enough to almost touch either side of the building.

"Wait!" Arthur said. "No, what are you doing—"

Marteen jumped into the air . . . and immediately started to fall down again.

But her wings caught her before her claws scraped the stone road. In a heavy, bobbing rhythm, she wallowed up into the sky.

Arthur clenched his legs on either side of her shoulders. Crouching, he pressed his arms to either side of her neck, clamping his hands uselessly over the hard spread of her scales. He even clenched his jaw and his butt cheeks for good luck.

Marteen was already above the rooftops and didn't seem ready to stop soon.

He held on and tried not to fall.

CHAPTER 36

Don't shift your weight around so much. You'll tip me over," Marteen called, which didn't help Arthur's nerves. Especially since he didn't think he had been shifting his weight.

Arthur froze, every muscle clenched so tight he was in fear of getting a cramp. Then he would likely fall off on his own.

By this time, they were several house-lengths above the roofs of the city. He caught sight of a large squarish building that might be the orphanage. For a second, he allowed himself a hope that Freyja or someone would come out and wave the dragon back down . . . but of course, that didn't happen.

Dragons came and went all the time near the hive, and he was so far up, there was no way anyone would recognize him.

New skill gained: Dragon Riding (Animal Husbandry/
Dragon Rider Class)
Due to your card's bonus traits, you automatically start this skill
at level 3.

With the new skill came a trickle of knowledge. Arthur was aware of how stiffly he sat, and how by grabbing on to Marteen's neck, he was surely shifting her center of balance. He was in danger of her tipping forward, not side to side.

Though every instinct screamed to wrap his arms around the dragon's neck and hold on tight, he instead eased his weight back so his legs and torso were angled toward her wings.

He thought he heard Marteen sigh in relief—or maybe she was just puffing for breath. Flying seemed to take a lot of work. Every wingbeat bobbed them up and down in the air. Either Marteen was not very good at flying or just young and inexperienced.

But she didn't seem to be in danger of falling. Slowly, Arthur started to relax.

Up above, adult dragons in every color flew to and fro the hive itself. None so much as glanced down at the floundering silver and the unauthorized rider.

Arthur wasn't about to let go of his precarious hold to try to wave one down, either.

But as terrified as he was, a part of him was crowing in delight. Last time, he'd been too shocked by Tess's rescue and possibly the spatial sickness to take in the view.

Now he could properly appreciate the sheer size of the city. It ringed the hive cone, which was in itself the largest thing Arthur had ever seen. The streets and buildings seemed to go on and on, with only the winding rivers and the off-shoot canals to break them up.

Horatio had complained many times that this was a small hive, but he couldn't imagine anywhere bigger than this. The sprawl only stopped at the edge of rich brown fields. Thanks to his new perception and the scent in the air, Arthur guessed that was dragon soil left to bake out in the sun for a year and a day. From there, it would be sent to the border to help reclaim the scourge-lands.

Maybe he was looking at the soil that would go to his old home.

Speaking of home . . .

"Where are we going?" Arthur had to yell to be heard over the rush of wind.

"Where you belong!" Marteen said, which was no help at all.

Within a few more wingbeats, she had stopped climbing and leveled off. This made it easier for Arthur to shift his weight to her center, since he no longer felt like he was going to slip off over her tail.

New skill level: Dragon Riding (Animal Husbandry/
Dragon Rider Class)
Level 4

Still, Marteen breathed heavily, and her wingbeats were laborious—not at all like Tess, who buzzed back and forth. She seemed to fall and catch herself with every wingbeat, making Arthur's stomach flip-flop.

"I don't belong at the hive," he called back.

Marteen ignored him, still breathing hard.

As they drew closer, he realized what he'd always thought were bushes hanging off the side of the hive walls were full-grown trees. From top to bottom, the cone-shaped structure had been cut into terraces to plant gardens and allow for roads. Thousands of tiny entrances dotted up and down the slopes, making them look like the cells of a beehive.

Soon, they'd drawn so close that he was able to pick out more levels of detail. Some of the entrances were decorated with bits of fabric and signs.

Commissary – Level 4
Mail Room – Level 4
Chip Exchange – Level 4
Level 4 NW Egress Point

Arthur had a funny feeling they were at level four.

A girl stood on an open-air balcony. From her pinched, angry expression and her hands on her hips, Arthur guessed this was Marteen's rider.

He had never gotten a good look at the girl before, other than to notice she was older than him, at seventeen or eighteen. With dark hair, eyes, and skin, she had her tight curls bound up in a no-nonsense bun. The expression in her eyes was stormy.

Making a happy burbling sound in her chest, Marteen headed right for the balcony. Very, very fast.

Arthur braced himself, but the landing was exactly as bad as he feared. The rider stepped to the side just in time for Marteen to hit heavily and skid to a stop.

Arthur was launched forward, flipped end over end, and landed on his back on the rocky terrace. The air was knocked out of his chest.

Over his wheezing, he heard the rider say, "I can't believe you did this—that you flew off without me. Who is that? What have you done?"

"I found him! The one that had smelled so good. The one I've been looking for!" Marteen danced from foot to foot, a little like Tess, but much heavier.

Arthur curled up, trying not to get stomped. He might as well have not bothered. Marteen reached down and once again gripped the back of his shirt—more seams popped, and this time he heard a rip as he was heaved up like a prized toy.

"Marteen! Drop him!"

The girl came around the other side of her dragon and helped catch Arthur as she dropped him. Luckily, he only fell a few inches and was able to stay on his feet.

"I am so sorry!" Looking horrified, the rider began brushing the dust off Arthur's torn clothing. Before Arthur could say anything, she turned to her dragon. "You just kidnapped a child from the city? We are in so much trouble..."

Arthur sensed an opportunity. "I won't say anything," he rasped, having gotten most of his breath back. "Just point me the way home. I'll go."

"You can't go!" Marteen objected. "You just got here."

The rider sighed. "I'm sorry about her. Silver Mystics tend to think the rules of society are more like suggestions, you know what I mean? Oh . . . your shirt's ruined."

Now that he was upright, he could feel air in the rips in his shirt. But Arthur had more to worry about. If someone high up, someone he couldn't say no to, learned he had a Legendary card . . .

Arthur reached for his **Acting** skill.

"I just want to go home." The wobble in his voice came naturally, like he was a child on the verge of crying.

The rider frowned at him and then turned to Marteen. "He's just a kid. Are you sure?"

Marteen nodded in an extremely humanlike fashion. "This is a good one."

"Okay." She took a deep breath and aimed a smile at Arthur. It looked fake but not like she was hiding dangerous intentions, more like she was trying to get herself under control. "Let's start over. I'm Kenzie, and that's Marteen. If you haven't guessed, she's my dragon. What's your name?"

"Arthur." He looked down, as he couldn't summon any tears. "I just want to go home."

"What about your shirt, Arthur? Won't your mother or your father be upset if you come home with it all ripped? I can get you a replacement—"

"Don't have any," he interrupted. "I live at the orphanage, and I gotta report in before nightfall. It's a rule. They don't care about the shirt—I can buy another one. I just need to go back." The anxiety in his voice wasn't completely faked.

Kenzie frowned briefly, then brightened. "Well, that's one problem solved. Marteen?"

In answer, Marteen rose on her haunches and let out a fierce bellow to the sky. Arthur cringed back, but Kenzie put a hand on his shoulder.

"It'll be all right, Arthur. Watch."

Sure enough, within half a dozen heartbeats, a purple dragon had zoomed down from a level above. It was about the size of Marteen, though side by side, the proportions couldn't be more different. The purple's four wings beat so fast that they practically blurred into invisibility. It was racing-dog thin with a sharp skull and big, dim yellow eyes. The rider sat half crouched, like a jockey with almost no room to spare.

"Who's the recipient?" the purple rider called. They hadn't bothered to land, just hovered in the open sky a few feet back from the terrace.

Kenzie turned to Arthur. "What's the name of your orphanage?"

Had Arthur been less surprised, he would have claimed not to know. Instead, he blurted out, "Wolf Cub."

"I know them. They had a girl link up a Common last month." Kenzie looked at the other rider. "Tell Freyja at Wolf Cub Orphanage that Arthur will be staying at the hive overnight."

"But—" Arthur protested.

Kenzie flipped the other rider a wooden coin, which was deftly snapped out of the air. With a salute, the purple and rider buzzed away.

Arthur watched them go, feeling sick.

"There now, that's all settled." Kenzie heaved a sigh and aimed a bright smile down at Arthur, showing a large number of teeth. "Let's get you some new clothing and talk about what's got Marteen in such a tizzy."

Placing her hand on Arthur's shoulder, she led him into the tunnel. He felt, roughly, like he was stepping toward his doom.

The tunnel inside was made of polished stone, which surprised him. White was the predominant color, with swirls of brown, jade green, and rust red. He had never seen anything quite like it before.

The air was noticeably cooler, too, and blew outward as if the breeze originated from the heart of the hive. Though Arthur couldn't figure out how that was supposed to work.

And they weren't alone.

They passed a young red dragon a few dozen feet in the tunnel. As dark red as a drop of blood, it was roughly Marteen's size. However, again, the proportions were much different—more like the red that had given Arthur his Legendary card. Standing low to the ground with elbows and knees thrust out, it walked with an ominous sway. Its neck was short and thick, leading up to a blocky head, and sharp black ridges stood out along its back, pointed up like knives.

Marteen showed her teeth at the red dragon as they passed. The red looked briefly surprised, pumpkin-orange eyes widening, before it showed teeth back and slunk away.

"That was rude," Kenzie commented.

"This boy is *my* prize, not Roody's," Marteen sniffed.

"Prize?" Arthur asked.

Kenzie smiled down at him. "Sorry, she'll probably think of you as her property until you link with a dragon of your own. Hang a right here." She pointed down another tunnel.

This led to a sort of General Store labeled commissary, level 4.

Several assistants were helping other dragon riders. Arthur hung back by Marteen as one came up to Kenzie.

Arthur looked around, more interested in the other dragon riders standing nearby gossiping about the latest scourge-eruption than the clothing and jars of goods for sale . . . at least until his gaze landed on several cards.

They were placed in the middle of the store on thin, bent pieces of metal to display them upright.

The cards were ripe for the picking.

CHAPTER 37

Arthur's mind was split three ways. He had just promised himself he would not allow the Thief Class to change him. Yet here he was, tempted to put that **Shoplifting** skill to good use.

The second part of his mind was occupied by the voice of his father.

"Get your hands on a low-ranked card—any card. Save up your money or steal one if you have to."

The third part knew there was virtually no chance of him getting away with this. Yes, these cards had been placed out in the open. Several anxiously diligent shopkeepers attended to who Arthur assumed were dragon riders. But no one looked his way.

Whatever leftover brain power was in his mind flashed back to that moment Second had yanked the card from his fingers. How he had promised himself he would not be so slow to act in the future.

Arthur stepped forward, casually looking around at the items stacked on nearby shelves: jars of spices, long stripes of leather, and soft rope he assumed were used for the construction of dragon saddles. Decorative quilts in a geometric design. All simple items with a touch of luxury—things a dragon rider would need to furnish their living space.

Kenzie had stepped forward to get the attention of one of the shopkeepers. For a moment, her body blocked the closest shopkeeper's view.

Arthur's hand flashed out. He snatched one of the cards at random. He didn't have time to look at it other than to note that it, and the rest, were Common rank. The card was a little too big to hide in the palm of his hand.

In one smooth motion, he stuffed it in his card anchor bag. Not in his heart deck—not until he knew what he was dealing with.

The deed was done. Arthur continued stepping forward as if interested in examining one of the oil paintings hanging off the wall. It displayed an impressive midair battle between a gleaming tan dragon and a massive scourgling.

No outcry went up from behind him. No one had noticed. Yet.

He didn't expect that to last.

The die is cast, he thought grimly, heart pounding. Now he had to figure out what to do next.

"Arthur," Kenzie called.

Turning, Arthur stepped over to her. The shopkeeper tsked under his breath when he saw the state of Arthur's shirt. A short discussion followed, ending with Kenzie handing the man a wooden chip.

In return, Arthur was given a well-made shirt and a heavy leather jacket to go over it.

He was a little stunned. One feel of the shirt's thick fabric told him it was much better quality than anything he'd been able to buy himself. Despite being brand new, it wasn't scratchy at all. The stitches were so small they weren't able to be seen.

The leather jacket was even more of a prize. His father once had something like this, but it was eventually worn to sinew in the harsh borderland winters. A whole jacket would keep him warm in any weather, he'd bet.

The value of these two items might be equivalent to a Common card shard.

Arthur looked up at Kenzie. "You're . . . giving this to me?"

The girl smiled. "Yeah, Marteen ripped up your other one. Plus, you're Marteen's first official recruit, so that's worth a celebration, don't you think?"

She briefly put an arm across his shoulders. "Let's go."

Squashing guilt, Arthur nodded. The stolen card seemed to burn against his skin.

Marteen, who'd been waiting outside, burbled happily at their arrival, sniffed over Arthur's new jacket—he held his breath, but she didn't seem to notice the card—and then trotted along beside them back down the tunnel. Thankfully, the tunnel was wide enough to accommodate her.

Arthur glanced around, hoping to spot a bit of trash or debris to ditch the card under. He couldn't afford to carry it with him in case there were Treasure Seekers.

Unfortunately, the tunnels were clean and well-kept. Aside from doors leading off here and there, the only other feature was lighted sconces. The stone base sat nearly flush against the wall, with the plinth jutting out as the tunnel curved. The top emitted a white light that didn't seem to be made of fire and yet glowed.

Focusing on his **Sleight of Hand** skill, Arthur grabbed the card and slowed his step just as they came to a curve lit by a sconce. He sidestepped and used the pretext of gazing up at the light to slide the card between the plinth and the tunnel wall.

It took a few seconds for Kenzie to notice he wasn't walking with them. When she looked back, Arthur's hands were behind his back as he gazed up at the sconce. "What is this?" he asked innocently. "It's not fire."

She gave him an odd look, then nodded to herself. "Just a card-lit crystal. You've never seen—Oh, you're from the orphanage. Right." Kenzie stepped beside him, apparently as interested as Arthur was pretending to be. "The hive pays all sorts of service staff who have utility cards. One guy's entire job is to go around and refresh these crystals through every public tunnel—on all levels. I heard it takes him two days to go around the hive. By the time he returns to the point he started from, the light's already dimming." She shrugged. "Sounds frustrating. He gets paid well for it, though. Come on."

Arthur let himself be dragged away.

He carefully counted the curves and the number of sconces to memorize where he had left the card.

There was every chance a Treasure Seeker or just bad luck, would have it discovered before he could return. But if not, he intended to collect it himself at the first chance.

He supposed he should have felt guilty about stealing from the hive. But really, who in their right mind kept their cards out in the open?

Kenzie led him through five more turns. His sense of direction told him they were heading deeper into the hive.

Finally, she stopped at an extra-wide door. A sheet of slate above it was marked in chalk with *Kenzie* and *Marteen* in flowing script.

"This is me," Kenzie said cheerfully.

The inside was a nice space, though there was no access to the outside. Instead, it was lit with slightly orange-tinted sconces that gave the room a warm golden feel. A simple bed about twice the size of his cot was shoved up against the wall. Loose straw bedding covered in thick blankets dominated the other half of the room. Marteen went there to curl up, looking satisfied.

A second door to the side likely led to a private privy.

"It's not much," Kenzie said, "but it's home. At least until Marteen and I earn ourselves a better apartment." She sent a fond look to her dragon. "We'll have to soon, or she'll outgrow the door."

Arthur didn't mention this room alone was likely as big or bigger than the cottage he'd grown up in.

Kenzie gestured to the single chair set against the wall. "Have a seat. Let's talk."

He sat, hugging the folded shirt and the jacket close. He looked down, not offering information and pretending to be shy. They wouldn't want to recruit a shy boy, would they?

Kenzie sat at the end of her cot and just . . . looked at him. As if she were waiting.

The silence stretched until Arthur couldn't take it anymore.

"Why did Marteen grab me?" he blurted. "Am I really the first she's . . . found?"

This second question was a test, because he knew it wasn't true. He had been outside the arena when he saw Marteen practically bowl over a noble family.

Arthur wanted to see how honest Kenzie would be with him.

"Well, you're the first one she's been able to bring back to the hive," Kenzie said with a laugh. "Marteen is turning out to be a very sensitive mystic."

"What does that mean?"

"You're from the Wolf Cub Orphanage, right? I know they funnel likely boys and girls to the hive. But what have they told you about dragon riders?"

She hadn't answered his question, but Arthur played along anyway. "That you have to have a card to be one."

"That's right. All silvers have a special relationship with magic. Some are attuned to natural magic in the air, some concentrate on areas of magic called ley lines, and some focus on magic generated by cards." Kenzie gestured to Marteen at the last bit.

"We see magic," Marteen added. She seemed content now that Arthur was in her home. "Some dragons see much better than others."

"It's an inborn gift, nothing to do with mine or Marteen's card. All dragon colors have different inborn gifts. That red, Roody? They generally have flame-based or transformative magics."

"What about the purples?" Arthur asked.

She lit up. "You like those, don't you?"

He hadn't said that, but it was true. "I got saved by Tess. She was . . . nice." He didn't say that the flight was smoother and faster than Marteen had managed.

By the upward tilt of Kenzie's mouth, she read between the lines.

"Purples have the inborn gifts of flight. They manipulate air so they're more efficient. Most also have a strong sense of direction. Once a purple knows where the rider wants to go, they'll know the fastest route through the air currents. Usually, purple hatchlings look for people with speed-based powers to link with their own. That's why they make great couriers and rescuers."

Arthur decided to be brave. "So . . . what's yours and Marteen's cards?"

"I'll show you mine if you show me yours."

There was a certain lilt to her voice, and Arthur felt a little . . . funny. The tips of his ears were very hot.

Kenzie broke out laughing, clutching her knees and rocking back on her bed.

"Kenzie," Marteen said. "That was mean. His face is on fire."

"I'm sorry," Kenzie said, grinning. "Here, I'll give you a hint: Marteen here is an Uncommon, B-rank shimmer. That means her powers are fairly strong. Generally, the more shimmer that you see on a dragon, the more innate power that they have."

Arthur nodded. Horatio had mentioned something about shimmer dragons before.

"So," Kenzie added with false casualness. "What card do you have?"

He had to try. "I . . . don't have one."

"Yes, you do," Marteen said. "It smells delicious."

Well, it had been worth a shot. Arthur sighed. "It's not what you think. It's . . . it's not very good, and I don't want people to know about it, because where I'm from, more powerful people will kill you if you have a high-rank card and won't give it up. My card isn't enough to keep me safe."

Kenzie and Marteen exchanged a look, but neither tried to dissuade him. Apparently, this wasn't shocking.

"All cards have their value," Kenzie said. "And we won't force you into a decision, but I need to know what Marteen is capable of sniffing out. She is still in training. And . . . if you have a high-rank card like I think you do, we might be able to help. The hive wants dragon riders."

That much was clear.

Arthur sighed again, as if he was reluctant to give out this information, though he had already made his decision.

"But Rares don't hatch out that often, right?"

Kenzie sucked in a sharp breath, and Arthur knew he had her fooled. She must have suspected her dragon had sniffed out an Uncommon card. Now that he had let slip that he had a Rare, she would not be looking for a Legendary.

It was sheer luck that Marteen was too inexperienced to know what she'd found. Doshi had, but Doshi had also been a Rare-ranked dragon himself.

"Yes," Kenzie said. "This hive hatches out a few a year. But that means we want a good pool of boys and girls to be available for them."

Arthur shook his head. "You wouldn't want mine. It's a Trap card." Then, with a show of reluctance, he pulled his draw bag out from where he had tied it to a string under his ripped shirt.

Kenzie gave Marteen an odd look.

"You were able to smell the card when it was in the bag?"

"No, the card magic is in his heart," Marteen replied.

Arthur thought fast. "It used to be in my heart. I took it out a few days ago."

Kenzie whipped around to stare at him. "You took it out of your heart?"

"Yeah. It . . . hurt." Not physical pain, but by the way Kenzie winced, she understood. "It's just . . . Well, look at it." He took the Trap card out and faced it in her direction.

Kenzie leaned forward to read it, her lips compressed. "That's the thing about Trap cards. Sometimes they can come with catches. But Arthur, that is not a bad card. If you are ever in trouble—"

"It'll save me, sure. But if a healer ever scans me for sickness too rough, I get flung across the city." Arthur did not have to fake the bitterness in his voice. "And I have a friend who used to live in a hive. He said people with Trap cards like mine get sent to the most dangerous part of the eruptions. I want to help, but I've seen the scourge kill people, and I don't want to die like that."

Kenzie's compressed lips turned into a frown. "I see." Now it was her turn to sigh. "I suppose I can't blame you. Marteen's not much of a fighter, either. Okay, Arthur. Fair's fair."

With that, Kenzie gestured to her own chest. A depiction of her card floated up between them, much like the way Arthur's father had shown him.

Aura Eye
Uncommon
Body Enhancement

This card allows the wielder to view the auras of other people and sentient beings, which reflects basic personality characteristics and strong emotions back on the world. Mana may be used to obscure the wielder's own aura in order to hide in plain sight.

Marteen did the same.

Unusual Empathy
Uncommon
Body Enhancement

This card allows the wielder to share the surface emotions of a targeted individual. Mana may be used to sense deeper or hidden emotional states.

Arthur's stomach dropped down to his shoes. Kenzie could read auras. Marteen could read emotions and had linked with Kenzie. Did that mean . . .?

Kenzie smiled as if she were reading his mind. Based on her skills, she might as well have been.

"Yes, I know about that little trick you pulled earlier. What did you take from the commissary?"

"I . . . I . . ." Wildly, Arthur wondered if he would make it if he sprinted for the door.

"Ohh. That good, huh?" Again, she gazed at him, and he got the uncomfortable feeling she was seeing down to his core.

"Don't be mean," Marteen chastised gently. "You'll scare him away."

To his surprise, Kenzie laughed.

"Sit down. The shopkeepers didn't catch you, did they?"

Only then did Arthur realize he had been half standing, tense and ready to bolt.

Kenzie reached over and patted his knee. "I came from a farming town up north, where the ground is too hard half the year to even try to plant in. If you think I came across my card easily or honestly, you're mistaken."

Arthur's mouth worked several times before he settled on, "Oh."

"Oh," she repeated. "But I'll tell you the truth: This is by far the best place I've ever lived in. I have an idea of what you took, and I can't blame you. But . . . you're not a Common-card type of boy, are you?"

She had him to rights.

"I didn't want it for myself," he admitted. "I didn't even get a good look at it. I just wanted to sell it. I'm aiming for a good Uncommon or another Rare."

She looked surprised. "That's not a bad idea. How old are you?"

"Twelve."

Kenzie nodded. "I thought you might be a little older than you look. Do you want to be a dragon rider?"

He thought of the affection he'd seen between Tess and Johanna, how Doshi spoke so highly of Chancy, and the fast partnership between Kenzie and Marteen. How their cards linked perfectly together to create a stronger whole.

And he couldn't ignore that things were better made in the hive, that he'd have the opportunity for card shards and to help people during the eruptions. That, if he became high enough ranked within the hive, he might be able to help his father and the rest of the border villagers.

"Yeah," Arthur said. "I do."

"Then you and I need to strike a bargain," Kenzie said, her eyes sharp. "You need me to keep quiet about what happened in the commissary." Marteen made a sound of protest, but Kenzie held up her hand, forestalling her. "More importantly, there is no better place than the hive to buy and trade cards. We are where most raw card shards come from. Card shops will overcharge you, and trading in the back alleys is a good way to get stabbed in the kidney. But here." She waved a hand around. "This is the cheapest place you'll find for trade. And you have to have a connection with a dragon rider to get in."

Carrot and stick. But it was a juicy carrot. "What do I got to do in return?"

"It's easy: you officially register as Marteen's recruit."

"Why?" Arthur asked bluntly.

She tilted her head back and forth in a so-so gesture. "For silvers, recruiting people earns you a kind of second currency in the hive. I can put it toward better lodging and more benefits. Marteen and I might be able to move up to level five just from you alone because you have a Rare card."

"But I don't want to tell anybody I have a Rare," Arthur said.

She waved his concerns away. "Oh, the list is kept secret. You aren't the only one. The hive has noble brats coming in all the time for this sort of thing. Plus, being here even part-time will be good for you. Prices for goods are less when you buy from the hive, work pays better, and you can visit the hatchlings whenever you want to get used to the idea of being a dragon rider for when a Rare egg is laid." She must have seen that Arthur looked uncertain, because she added, "None of the lesser ranks will give you a sniff, even if you're holding a dozen Commons in your heart, because of that Rare."

Arthur was tempted. Extremely tempted. But he also knew he still had a card to play: Kenzie needed him to say yes.

"I have one condition," he said.

"What's that?"

"I have a friend who's working toward a Rare card, too. You give him the same deal, and I'll say yes."

"I can get him a discount on card shards," she said. "But only if he promises to let Marteen recruit him when he gets that Rare in his heart." She eyed him. "You've got to put yours back in your heart deck, too. Trap or no trap."

"I will," he lied. Marteen wasn't smelling the Rare. She was smelling the Legendary but didn't know it. "And I'll make sure Horatio knows the deal, too."

She eyed him for a moment, and he imagined she saw something off in his aura but couldn't quite figure out what. After all, Kenzie was getting a better deal than she thought. If recruiting a Rare could get her moved up a level in the hive, a Legendary must be loads better.

Not that he'd let that slip—not until he was good and ready.

Finally, Kenzie spit into her hand and extended it to him. "You've got yourself a deal."

He did the same, and they clasped hands.

Signing up was scarily easy.

Leaving Marteen to nap in the room, Kenzie led Arthur through the twisting and turning halls.

They finally came to a set of administrative offices, which had a spectacular outside view of the last sliver of setting sun.

At Kenzie's prompting, Arthur gave his name to a man at a desk. Then, haltingly, his card rank.

Several documents were signed, with Arthur growing more and more nervous that they would have a way to check the card in his heart. But the official merely disappeared into the back and returned a few minutes later with a small disc of jade.

It was smooth and polished with a hole in the middle so he could string a piece of ribbon through it. Carved in black on one side were: Kenzie and Marteen. The other side was Arthur's name.

"You take this." He handed it over to Arthur. It was still warm from whatever magic had been used to carve the names on it. "Carry it with you at all times. If you are ever approached by another silver and their partner, you will show them this chip so they know you're already recruited. You will also show this chip whenever you want to enter or exit the hive." His gaze turned stern. "So, make sure you do not lose it."

"I understand," Arthur said.

Kenzie was beaming as they walked out.

"That's it?" Arthur asked. "They didn't even check to see if I was old enough for a card."

"Did you want them to?"

"Well, no. But—"

She laughed loudly and clapped him on the back, making him stagger forward. "I told you, they're used to dealing with nobles who keep their cards close in their chest. So, they trust the silver partners to check on that sort of thing. I'm made responsible if you were trying to pull something." She grinned. "You aren't, are you?"

Only the knowledge that she was getting a better deal than she knew allowed him to smile back. "No."

"Then we're good. Now, we've got some extra apartments for guests. You can head back to the orphanage in the morning."

"No," he said quickly, looking around to make sure no one was listening. He lowered his voice. "Could you point me back to the commissary?"

Kenzie stared at him, and he was certain she could see the nervous energy roiling around in his gut. "Are you sure?"

"Will they take my chip away if I'm caught?"

"Not hardly. Not with a Rare, but you'll get a few days in the dragon soil fields."

He nodded. "I can take care of myself."

To his surprise, she grinned again. "I can appreciate a good angle." Then she pointed down a tunnel. "Those are color coded. The blue will take you to the tunnel that leads back to the commissary, the red will take you out. Good luck."

Arthur did as he was told. As soon as he was around the first bend and safely alone, he reached into his draw bag.

Do you wish to activate Return to Start (Trap) now?

"Yes."

CHAPTER 38

There was trouble ahead.

He had followed the tunnel through so many twists and turns that he was completely turned around. No windows or balconies led to the outside to tell him what direction he was heading. Only large wooden doors he assumed were dragon-rider apartments. The tunnel just kept going on and on.

The only thing that kept Arthur from retracing his steps back was that it was in Kenzie's best interest to keep him in good standing with the hive. She wouldn't mislead him.

Then again, it might be in her best interest to keep him contained within the hive. Getting lost for days within the bowels of the complex would do that.

Arthur shook his head. He carried her chip now. He was her recruit. That had to mean something.

And if luck was with him, he might gain some kind of Directional skill.

After what felt like an age, the tunnel split off into a Y junction. The marbled walls turned predominantly white on one side and red on the other.

White marble had led to the commissary.

With intense relief, Arthur stepped forward. He hesitated at the sound of booted footsteps coming up from the white tunnel.

Hesitation would only make him look guiltier, so Arthur continued onward.

Shortly, he came upon two large men with frustrated looks on their faces. They each had a decorative pin of a dragon on their pressed shirts. Arthur guessed it meant they worked directly for the hive.

Upon seeing him, the men stopped.

"What are you doing here, kid? Why are you outside the family levels?"

In answer, Arthur held out the jade chip. "I was just seeing my recruiter."

The man glanced at it briefly and then nodded. "Marteen finally got one to come to the hive, eh?"

Not knowing what to say, Arthur shrugged.

The first man seemed relaxed, but the other was not so easily swayed. "Scan him, just to be sure."

Oh no. "For what?" Arthur demanded.

"None of your business. Arms out."

No time to switch his Trap card off. Arthur had to hope that whatever this scan was, it wouldn't count as an attack.

He held out his arms and tried again. "What's this about?"

"You have a Common card, right?"

They were looking for the card.

"No," Arthur said.

The uptight man snorted as if he didn't believe him and pulled out a red card-marked stone. He swept it in a slash from Arthur's forehead to his stomach.

It was as if a cool breeze lifted through Arthur, but his Trap card didn't activate.

Neither did the red stone.

The uptight man's eyebrows lifted. Apparently, Arthur had struck him as Common as mud.

"Come on," the first man said to his friend. "Our section's going to take all night at this pace."

The uptight one leveled a stern gaze at Arthur. "This isn't the night to be getting into trouble, you hear?"

"I understand, sir."

Arthur must have looked contrite enough, because both moved on.

That had been close.

For a moment, he considered abandoning the retrieval of the card. It was only a Common. Was it worth all this?

Ha. *Only* a Common. He grinned to himself. When had he become such a card snob? Of course, getting his hands on a card was worth it.

He continued down the tunnel, but now he paused to check behind every sconce. He'd counted them after he hid the card, but he had become so turned around that he could no longer trust his count was accurate.

He found it behind the ninth sconce down on the left side of the wall.

The card had slipped neatly into a crack between the high plinth and the curved tunnel wall, with only the bare edge sticking out. For a sick few moments, Arthur wasn't sure if he'd be able to retrieve it without tools.

For once, small hands were a benefit. His longest middle finger was just able to poke the top corner of the card, rocking it back to the other side. After a couple of flicks, the card fell free.

Arthur pounced on it at once and slipped it into his bag, ignoring the description that popped into his mind. He would have time for that later.

Now he had to find a way out of here without being scanned again.

He kept going. The tunnel curved into an S bend, with the doors to the Level 4 commissary on the outside of the curve. A sign over the tight shut doors stated it would reopen at sunup.

He guessed that the missing card had been discovered after they shut the doors, or just before closing. Sloppy of them. Why wasn't the card better locked up? Why wasn't there more of a search? Yes, he had seen two men prowling around for anyone suspicious, but it was nothing compared to what the baron had done when he'd recovered his Master of Skills card.

With a shake of his head, Arthur continued past the next bend down the tunnel.

He came upon a pink dragon sitting alone at the next bend. Smaller both in size and stature than Marteen and Tess, it had positioned itself near a lit sconce and seemed to be reading a book.

Arthur stopped in surprise. Yes, that was definitely a book it clutched in long, twig-like claws. Though the cover was so flaked with age he couldn't tell what it was supposed to be about.

The pink lowered the book slightly and gave him a *look* over a long, thin nose.

"Oh, um. Do you know the way out?" Arthur asked.

Doshi had told him that dragons spoke to children, but the pink didn't seem to get the message. It pointed one very long finger over its shoulder then crooked it to the right.

"Thank you." Arthur broke into a jog. Sure enough, at the next bend, the tunnel split yet again. He took the right-hand passage.

He smelled fresh night air. That had to mean he was close. Once he got to the terrace, he could make his way back to the city. Freyja might be upset with him coming so late, but hopefully she would understand after receiving the purple courier's message—

"You there!" a voice yelled behind him. "**Freeze!**"

That last word swept through him with power. Arthur involuntarily stopped mid-step, arms and legs locked.

Trap Card conditions met.
Return to Start: Activated.

There was a cut-off shout as the world flashed white around him.

And in the next second, he found himself not standing upright but lying on his back on a semi-uncomfortable bed.

Arthur let out a gust of air. With it, his muscles loosened and fell back under his control. The caster's spell had either a time or distance limit.

The room was dark. Sitting up, Arthur fumbled for the lamp light before it finally flared to life.

He was alone in his room. Horatio's bed was empty. Judging by the muffled noise downstairs, the kids were still at dinner.

Arthur would miss the meal, but it wouldn't be the first time. It would be worth it not to face Freyja and make up some excuse for why he had come back early.

Finally, he had time to see if all the trouble had been worth it.

He reached into the bag and pulled out the Common card.

The answer was both yes and no.

Bubbles Bubbles Everywhere!
Common
Charm
Use mana to create small clouds of rainbow sheen bubbles. Depending on the amount of mana added, bubbles may provide a stinging sensation when popped against the eyes and skin.

Arthur stared at the card. "I found something worse than the Tidying skill."

There was a small handwritten label stuck on the back: 7 silvers.

Though items were cheaper in the hive, they couldn't be *that* cheap. It seemed even the commissary thought this card was useless.

On the other hand, Arthur could see some slight utility in creating stinging bubbles. It wouldn't win him a duel, but a cloud of rainbow bubbles might surprise an attacker at a critical moment.

Or cause them to die of laughter.

This would be the perfect gift for a girl child who loved pretty ribbons and ponies. He could think of a few in the orphanage who fit that bill.

. . . And a few back in his old village. Even a Common was fabulous wealth, and they would never worry about being sick from scourge-dust again.

Arthur's lips twisted into a grimace. No, the card wasn't for him, but that didn't mean it was useless to everyone.

Now he had to figure out how to sell it. Kenzie was out. She had offered to get him a good deal on shards, but the hive officials would know to look out for this card.

He would have to pursue . . . other means.

"Chef, can I speak to you?" Arthur asked, the next day.

Chef Barlow glanced down at him, and a stormy expression briefly crossed his face. Arthur half expected to be told off for interrupting. The man was busy, and right now he and the rest of the workers were prepping for the usual dinner rush. He didn't have time to glad hand his apprentices.

Instead, Chef jerked his chin to a shadowy nook set in the corner of the kitchen. "Come to my office, then." He turned and stomped over there before Arthur could react.

The office was cramped, the single desk so covered with paperwork that there didn't seem to be free space available. There was no chair or stool to sit on. Instead, Chef leaned his weight on the desk and crossed his arms over his barrel chest.

"Well, let me have it," he said just as Arthur closed the door to give them privacy. "How much are they paying you?"

"Excuse me?" He was lucky that polite question had slipped out, mostly thanks to Freyja's training, instead of a less intelligent "Huh?"

"The hive," Chef snarled. "Word is, you were scooped up on the wings of a dragon yesterday. Frankly, I'm surprised that they let you out. Usually, they find a way to link up anyone with a halfway decent card before they can think better of it. All talent goes to the hive." His voice was filled with exasperation. "But they let you out, I see. So, how much did they say they'll pay you to work?"

Now he seemed resigned.

Arthur realized that the man expected him to quit on the spot.

He hesitated for a moment, reordering his plan in his mind. "I don't mean to quit here," he said carefully. "But I may stay part-time. There's good work in the hive, like you said, but I'm still . . . figuring out what I want to do."

Chef narrowed his eyes. "I can't pay hive rates."

"No. It's just . . . You pay in shards, so I thought you might have someone you trust, or . . . know someone who does."

Chef just looked at him.

Arthur took a deep breath and then pulled out his Bubble Card.

"I need to sell this. And I want a better rate than I'd get in the shops."

And he needed it not to be linked back to him. He had watched enough transactions between the men in the caravan to know how to leave enough dangling so both parties could read between the lines. He hoped Chef Barlow was one of those perceptive people.

The man's eyes narrowed again, and he took a quick look at Arthur's card anchor bag, then nodded to himself. He didn't look too surprised that Arthur had other resources. He had, after all, been scooped up by a dragon.

"Card shops will stiff you," he said. "They'll call it a trash Common—but we know there's really no such thing as trash."

Arthur nodded. He understood that much.

"On the other hand," Chef continued, "my card connection can take some time. You get good coin for the exchange, but it's a wait."

Arthur bit his lower lip. "I would rather get this over with as soon as possible."

"That's what I thought." Barlow sighed and reached into the shirt of his apron. There, tucked against his heart, was his own card anchor bag. It was made of purple velvet and was larger and much more ornate than Arthur's. It also bulged like a full sack of grain, though there had been no visible bump in his shirt.

"I can take that card off your hands," Barlow said, "and while my price isn't top, you'll find it more than fair."

He dug around in the bag for a moment and then pulled out two card shards. From the sheen, Arthur identified them as Uncommon rank.

They were also rounded on one end. Corner pieces.

His **Haggling** skill poked at him. Arthur pretended a look of confusion. "Two shards for one card?"

"Two Uncommon corner shards for a Common card you don't want to be caught with," Barlow said slyly. "And the promise that if someone tries to get you to work in their kitchen, you talk to me first."

Was he worth that much as an apprentice? Arthur thought he could use that as an advantage, but how?

"Those two corner pieces, three regular Common pieces—I know it's a three-to-one ratio, and this is a whole card—*and* you'll let me look at the recipe book during any downtime."

Chef guarded the recipe book, which had been passed down through his family. When he wanted to teach Arthur something new, he copied it from the book and handed it to him instead.

Arthur wanted that Cooking Class, and he had a feeling that memorizing more recipes was the way to get it.

Chef made a show of thinking about it. "If you're doing your job right, you won't have downtime," he said. "But you are free to look at the recipe book on your own time—if you come in early or stay late. And only here, in this office. I don't want any risk of burning or food splatters."

"Deal," Arthur said, and stuck out his hand.

As he and Chef shook, he realized this was the first time he'd made a deal man to man.

He could get used to it.

CHAPTER 39

A month later and Arthur had still not gained his Cooking Class. He couldn't figure out what the problem was.

His **Knife Work** and **Meal Preparation** skills had stalled out at levels 18 and 19 respectively, but they were well advanced. His **Butchering Meat** made it to Basic 9. No one had any complaints about the dishes he sent out.

In fact, it was the exact opposite. Chef Barlow had been slowly adding more and more work duties to his station. By now, Arthur could cut vegetables as well as men who had worked there for years. He had all the techniques down pat: from mincing to julienning. Chef even had him working on decorative little designs to make radishes into flowers and tomatoes into artful representations of animals.

These were for the fancy parties that Chef sometimes catered in a big hall upstairs. Those included nobles and city administrators. As those events earned Chef the most money and prestige, he reaped the benefits and passed them down to his workers.

Just last week, Arthur earned an additional Uncommon shard for his help. It went into his growing pile.

Card shards weren't the only benefit. He also gained a new skill: **Basic Meal Decoration**.

And he had earned a new nickname from the rest of the staff: Golden Boy.

It was said with just as much derision as Pissant had been. The older cooks didn't like the fact that Arthur learned so quickly and had become Chef's clear favorite.

They couldn't move against him directly, but Arthur now found himself excluded from all conversation. No one offered to lend him a hand when he became overwhelmed during meal rushes. When he offered to lend someone else a hand—and possibly learn a new style or technique—he was rudely rebuffed.

Soon, his only ally in the kitchen was Horatio. But the other boy was busy learning the techniques of being a successful baker. He couldn't help Arthur directly; he could only offer sympathy.

Arthur might have been less annoyed about all this if he'd been able to gain a Cooking Class and a bonus to his skills. Since he hadn't, it felt like he was pushing himself for no reason.

While he lay in his cot at night, Arthur wracked his brain trying to think of what else he could do. He had to be missing an important cooking skill in order to complete his class, but he had no clue what it could be.

True to his word, he had read Chef's recipe book from back to front. None of it had provided a revelation. He already knew most of the recipes, and the big differences were alterations to dishes they already served.

The only thing he'd gotten out of the experience was Chef's goodwill and a new level to his reading level.

At level 17, his **Reading** level progress had slowed significantly, too.

He needed a way to break through and learn more.

Out of pure desperation, Arthur had tried his hand again at—shudder—**Baking**. Horatio, at least, was happy for the help.

He got that skill to level 8 without any new revelations. His Chef Class remained out of reach.

"You look like someone pissed in your oatmeal," was Horatio's helpful observation over breakfast the next morning. "What's wrong? You worried about the history test?"

Arthur shrugged. "No, I'll probably pass that." Out of all his classroom subjects, history was by far his worst. He started behind and had almost no worldly context for any of the lessons. He was more ignorant than a newborn lamb when it came to the rises and falls of kingdoms, duchies, and scourglings. Also, he hadn't received a skill, which hadn't helped.

Horatio was still looking at him. Arthur sighed and glanced down at his mostly full bowl. It said something that he hadn't gulped down the bland oatmeal like a starving man.

"You ever feel like you're running in place but never getting anywhere?"

Horatio gave him an annoyed look. "Why do you think I'm so focused on getting out of this tiny hive city? Why? Are you getting itchy feet to move on, too?"

His words had an uplift at the end. If it wasn't Horatio, Arthur would have thought he heard hope.

"What hive does Sams belong to again?" he asked.

"Buck Moon. It's to the south, right on the edge of the big Corinne Desert. Buck Hive is easily three times the size of this one." Horatio scowled. "But Sams will probably have to move over here if I ever get a card worthy of him." He gave Arthur a sly look. "Think Kenzie will let you go to another hive?"

"No, it's not about that. I just feel like I'm not getting anywhere with cooking. It's just the same meals over and over again."

"Well . . . yeah?" Horatio shrugged. "Chef's place is more of a rundown tavern than a fancy restaurant. A place where people want hearty, cheap food." He slanted Arthur a cynical grin. "Maybe you should take over the kitchen here." He hooked a thumb back over his shoulder to the entrance of the orphanage's kitchen.

Even from across the room, it was a complete mess. The kids who worked in it as part of their room and board were too young for official work duties. They also liked to throw flour at one another when adults weren't looking.

Arthur made a face. He wasn't sure if gaining his Chef Class was worth that.

But . . . if it gave him a boost to his skills, he could use it as a stepladder to get more work in expensive restaurants. And that would give him access to more card shards. Possibly even entrance to a guild. That would lead to more full cards. And—

"I was kidding!" Horatio's voice was edged in panic. Clearly, he could see Arthur was considering it.

Arthur shrugged. The kitchen kids worked on basic meals, which were focused on quantity rather than quality. He now ate regularly enough to figure out the difference. It was doubtful he would learn something by working there.

A bell rang twice, indicating a ten-minute warning to classes.

Arthur scooped up the remaining oatmeal into his mouth and forced it down. "Come on," he said thickly, rising. "Might as well get a good seat for the test."

The first part of his day went by easily. He spent most of it still turning over the problem of his Cooking Class. He was so absorbed, in fact, that he was taken completely by surprise when Freyja stopped him from leaving at the end of the school day.

"Arthur, stay here. I need to speak to you. Horatio, tell Chef Barlow that Arthur will be running late, on my request."

Horatio gave Arthur an uncertain look, but of course, he couldn't go against Freyja. With a nod, he took off toward the restaurant to begin his workday.

"Am I in trouble, ma'am?" Arthur asked.

Freyja looked down her long nose at him. "How interesting that is where your mind automatically went. Do you have a guilty conscience?"

Yes.

Arthur shrugged. "I just don't see why you would need to speak to me."

"Is that so?" The look she gave him was piercing, but then she nodded. "Well, follow me, please."

She led him out of the classroom and across the small courtyard back to the orphanage. From there, she walked to her personal office, which was located on the main level. It was both larger and neater than Chef Barlow's.

"Have a seat," she said, and took one herself. A pristine pile of paperwork sat on the desk, but Freyja tapped it into a neat pile anyway.

Arthur sat, trying not to look extra guilty. Did she know about the stolen Bubble Card? That had been a couple of weeks ago, but Freyja and Barlow did talk. Maybe he had dropped a hint?

He struggled not to fidget with nerves.

"How long have you lived here with us?" Freyja asked.

His answer was instant. "Just over five months." That was easy to remember, as he'd marked time by card-shard payments.

"Not very long. But it seems you've already made quite the name for yourself."

Uh-oh. "In . . . what way, ma'am?"

The corner of Freyja's mouth ticked up as if she thought Arthur was making a joke. "For one, Barlow keeps bothering me to release you from classes so you can work full time in his kitchen. Meanwhile, we received official word that you were recruited by a silver. Rumor has it, you are looking to gain yourself an Uncommon dragon . . . or above."

Arthur ducked his head, both in acknowledgment and to hide a stab of fear and frustration. Kenzie had promised that the recruitment list was to remain a secret!

But . . . no one had come for his card yet, and Freyja still looked more amused than anything.

"And now we have the issue with your schoolwork," she continued.

Arthur jerked his head up to stare at her. "What's wrong with my work?" Yes, he didn't think he had a perfect score on today's history test, but—

Freyja snorted delicately and laid the papers out. From the titles, they were reports from his recent teacher and his grades.

"Just the opposite. You lead the class in every subject, except for history, where you come in second place. In fact, you are in danger of running up against the limit of our standard algebra exams. And we only give those to the most advanced students."

"I . . . Math has always been easy for me," he said lamely. That, and his **Arithmetic** skill had never hit a roadblock between Basic and Apprentice. It now sat at a healthy level 12.

"That much is obvious. Regardless, several scholar's guilds have made inquiries."

His eyes widened. "What?"

"They often keep an eye on the city rolls for up-and-coming stars. Arthur . . ." Freyja leaned slightly forward, as if trying to convey something important. "People are starting to take notice of you."

Pride flashed through him. He found himself sitting up straighter in his chair. He never thought he would amount to anything, and now people of importance were asking about him.

But that feeling only lasted for a moment. With it came the realization he might be in over his head.

Someone in charge might suspect he had a powerful card to help him along. It was the truth, after all.

Just like that, his pride popped like an overfilled big bladder ball.

"What are the scholar's guilds?" he asked cautiously. "What do they do?"

"There are nearly as many scholar's guilds as crafter's guilds, though most are based in the kingdom's great inner cities." She paused for effect. "The most prestigious work directly for the high nobles and the royal family."

Arthur's knee-jerk reaction was to blurt out: No.

He had zero desire to work for the people who had taken his father's land away from him.

But he also sensed an opportunity. And possibly a way out.

"I'm not sure being in a scholar's guild is right for me," he said carefully. "But I like learning." Especially when that learning included more skills. "Aren't there books or something? I haven't learned all the math there is in the world, have I?"

"I surely hope not," Freyja said. "But you are coming up against the limits of what is generally taught to the populace. We can issue you additional books of geometry and primers to beginning calculus, but the teachers must focus on bringing the current students up to standard. You would be working alone."

"Oh." He thought for a moment and nodded. "I'd like the books."

"You should know the scholar's guilds have more resources available to them than one person can reasonably expect to learn in a lifetime. You don't have to make a decision now, but you should know what to expect . . . in case you are approached."

Swallowing, Arthur nodded.

"In any case," she said, "you have a couple of important decisions in front of you. While you technically have one year of schooling left, advanced children are allowed to test out." She folded her hands in front of her and gazed at Arthur. "All children without parents are allowed to live in the orphanage until they are fifteen. However, if you are not taking classes, you will be expected to pay rent, which includes your room, boarding, basic clothing, and two meals a day. It should be affordable, especially if you work full time."

Chef Barlow would like that. But Arthur wasn't sure he would. He chewed on his lip, thinking.

Freyja took pity on him. "My advice is to take this time to . . . expand your horizons."

Just like that, it clicked. He *knew* exactly what was holding him back from finally gaining that Cooking Class.

He had been working with what Horatio had called tavern slop over the last few months. Yes, he had mastered it, but there was so much more to cooking than that.

He needed new experiences. Not just fine fancy dining, but a whole range of new things.

If he was quick, there might be a solution to two of his problems.

He sat up straight. "Freyja? Is the orphanage hiring for the kitchen?"

CHAPTER 40

Arthur woke to the tinny chime of a card anchor alarm.

Groaning, he rolled over. Through bleary eyes, he saw a small light pulsing by his bed. His new alarm stone.

Horatio groaned from the next cot over. "I hate you."

Arthur kind of hated himself, too.

He reached over and pressed one finger against the stone. It silenced immediately, and Arthur had to fight the urge to close his eyes and fall back asleep.

From the deep, rhythmic breathing on the other side of the room, Horatio had already done it.

Arthur spared a moment to be intensely jealous of his roommate. But only a moment.

A half-open book slid away as he sat up. He had stayed up last night reading one of the math books Freyja had loaned him. It went into more complicated aspects of geometry than was normally taught in class as well as a basic introduction to calculus.

It had made as much sense as trying to learn a new language.

However, Arthur knew all he had to do was keep working at it. Once he puzzled out the basics, his skill would kick in at level 3, giving him a boost to start on the rest.

For now, he didn't have time to think about math. He had a much more difficult task ahead of him.

Arthur reached for the new long-sleeved shirt he had folded on top of the storage chest. Starched white with thick, durable fabric, it was on par with hive-quality clothing. A chef's jacket.

He put it on and fastened the odd buttons on the side. The well-made fabric gave the illusion of broad shoulders . . . or perhaps he was growing at last. His birthday wasn't too far away.

Arthur threw on a clean pair of pants and shuffled off to the bathroom. Only the barest hint of dawn cracked through the window.

Another benefit of waking up so early was that the bathroom was mostly free.

When Arthur made his way down to the orphanage kitchen, he was unsurprised to see it in a state of minor chaos. Upon hiring him as a morning kitchen manager, Freyja had warned him the kids had gone through the last few months without regular adult supervision. Her assistants had filled in to keep an eye on things, and none had been enthusiastic.

That explained why they were served bland oatmeal in the morning, every morning. Arthur had figured that was just how things were done.

As he walked in, he saw three of the kids in an intense squabble. No one had cleaned the deep pot they used for oatmeal. Now the food had practically calcified on the bottom overnight.

The bickering stopped as Arthur stepped in.

He stood only a little taller than the tallest of them, but the fact he was older, and his white chef's shirt, spoke volumes.

"Who're you?" one of the girls demanded.

"I'm Arthur, and I'm the new morning kitchen manager." He looked around at them all, counting nine kids in total. There were supposed to be ten. But just as he opened his mouth to ask where one had gone, a sleepy-eyed boy scurried in to join with the rest.

"All right," Arthur said. "Tell me what you normally do in the morning. Who preps—"

Immediately, most of the kids began to speak over one another. The voices blended into nonsense. That developed into another squabble with one calling another a liar.

The tallest boy reached for a handful of flour as if to throw it.

"That's enough," Arthur said. "You, flour thrower. What's your name?"

"Neddy," the boy said.

"Neddy, you're in charge of cleaning the oatmeal pot."

Neddy looked like he was considering throwing the flour at Arthur. "That's not fair! No one filled up the wash buckets from the well yesterday, either. I can't do everything."

"You and you." Arthur pointed to the next tallest two, a boy and a girl. "Fetch water from the well. Neddy, loosen what you can, and as soon as the first bucket of water comes, pour it into the pot and set it on the stove to boil. That should get the worst of the gunk off the bottom. Hurry up. The faster we get this done, the sooner we can eat our own breakfast."

The kids grumbled, but the ones Arthur picked out went to go do what they were told. The others went to do their normal chores, which mostly included setting out the dishes on the table.

Breakfast at the orphanage was nothing as complicated as a dinner rush at the restaurant. The oats had been set to soak all night. All that needed to be done was to boil them, lay out the fixings, and make sure the dishes were washed.

Arthur thought that the task ought to take no more than three adults working together. With a shift of ten, he eventually planned to have pancakes, eggs, and toast as well.

One thing at a time, though. Today, they just had to get through serving oatmeal without disaster.

Most of the kids were sullen but obeyed his orders easily enough. Their spirits lifted when Arthur promised them the first crack at their favored side fixing, including raisins and nuts if everything was done before the morning wake-up bell.

Once the big oatmeal pot drama was taken care of, Arthur watched the progress. He only stepped in when his expertise was needed . . . such as fixing the bland oatmeal.

"You'll want to add salt to that," he told the girl who was currently stirring the pot. "Three pinches should be enough."

She looked at him like he was insane. "You don't want to make oatmeal salty." She made a gagging motion.

"Salt clarifies taste," he said. "You don't want to make it as salty as the bottom of the ocean." That was one of Chef Barlow's favorite sayings. "But a few pinches won't hurt."

The girl did it, though she looked doubtful. Arthur caught her sneaking a taste a few minutes later. Her doubt vanished.

When the work was almost done, Arthur broke out the supply of raisins, which were sweet enough to be treated like candy. He quickly learned he had to watch the bowl or else the kids would steal from the top. It was only a few here and there, but with ten people it added up quickly.

Finally, with the oatmeal ready, the fixings dished out to the separate tables, and the dishes more or less organized, Arthur considered it a job well done. They had ten minutes before the morning bell was to be struck—an honor he gave to Neddy, as the boy had washed out the giant pot to his satisfaction.

As the kids under his watch served themselves, Arthur was granted two additional skills:

New skill gained: Basic Teaching (Leadership Class)
Due to your card's bonus traits, you automatically start this skill
at level 3.

New skill gained: Kitchen Management (Cooking/Leadership Class)
Due to your card's bonus traits, you automatically start this skill
at level 3.

He waited a moment, but there was no additional offer to consolidate his skills into a Cooking Class.

Not a big surprise. It was his first day, and they'd only made oatmeal. Two additional skills would be useful.

He put the **Kitchen Management** skill to use right away. As the early morning shift cleared out, the mid-morning shift came in. These were the youngest kids in the orphanage and could only be trusted with washing dishes and putting them away. They would be served breakfast after the older kids were finished and then go to their classes.

Arthur reserved some of the prized raisins for the ones who did well.

Freyja stepped into the kitchen as the dishwashing crew was finishing up. She stood next to Arthur and watched in silent observation, then nodded.

"I must say, that was some of the best oatmeal I've had in some months. Did you finally teach them to add seasoning?"

Her casual question surprised him. For the first time, an adult had just addressed him as if he were a part of their team. A near equal.

He nodded. "Added some salt and a dash of other spices, but we're almost out of everything, except more oats."

"Another delivery from the hive should be arriving soon. Later this week, you and I will work together to plan out a budget for your morning shift. Eventually, I'll expect you to take it over entirely."

Though Arthur's new duties only lasted a few hours a day, it was a lot of responsibility for not much money. Freyja and Arthur had worked out a deal that his morning kitchen management would pay for his room and meals plus two coppers every two weeks. The orphanage couldn't afford to pay him card shards.

But he knew this opportunity would make him rich in new skills.

Arthur nodded and stepped forward to help towel the last of the dishes dry before he sent the final kids off to their classes.

Freyja waited for him, and when he was done, she asked, "Are you ready?"

He let out a breath. "Yes."

For the second time in a week, he was led to Freyja's office. True to her organizational skills, the papers he needed were already set out on a second, smaller desk, ready for Arthur to pick up and work.

Freyja took a seat on her own and pulled out an hourglass filled with sand.

"You will have two hours to complete the test. Do you have any questions?"

"No, ma'am."

She turned it. "Then begin."

This was the exam Arthur was required to take to be graduated from classes early. The test he had been anxious about for the last few days since Freyja had first told him about it.

He turned over the papers to look at the first question and nearly sighed in relief.

It was a basic multiplication question. He could have simply written the answer down but spared a moment to show his work.

Then he started on the next question.

Forty-five minutes later, Arthur finished a required written paragraph detailing what he planned for the next five years of his life. He concocted a tale of using his talents to help the hive and city with such a flourish he was surprised he didn't earn another level in **Acting.**

Freyja looked up as he set his quill down.

"Do you have a question?"

"I'm done."

She looked at the hourglass. "Are you certain you don't want to take any time to double-check your answers?"

Arthur hesitated, but all of the questions had been so easy that it would be a waste of time.

"I'm sure."

Freyja held out her hand for the papers. Then, to his surprise, she started looking them over on the spot.

Suddenly Arthur wasn't so certain of his answers.

He stood in awkward silence as she checked a few of his numbers and made a few remarks.

"You pass," she declared, after what felt like an age. "With an almost perfect score."

"Almost?"

She tapped one line of his paragraphed answer. "You used the word 'can't' when 'cannot' is more acceptable. This is formal writing, Arthur. Not a letter to a friend."

Arthur huffed and opened his mouth to complain. But Freyja continued.

"I thought you weren't interested in attention from the scholar's guilds?"

That made him pause. Then after a moment, he nodded. Perhaps achieving a perfect score wouldn't be for the best.

The important thing was that he passed.

A slow grin spread over his face. He wouldn't have to go to mandatory classes again. Now, any additional learning would be the subjects he wanted to pursue, like the math books.

Freyja smiled back at him. "You never gave me an answer on what you plan to do now you're at liberty from classes. Will you work for Barlow full time?"

Arthur shook his head. Barlow wouldn't be happy, but he'd still help out for the evening shift. "I want to see what else there is for me."

After all, cooking was just one set of skills. There may be other masters look-ing for a part-time apprentice.

He wanted to see what life was like in the hive, and what skills he could learn there.

CHAPTER 41

The city streets had a different feel to it in mid-morning. They were quieter than he had seen before. The children were in school or apprenticed in their future trade. The adults were either working their trade or craft or else caring for their households.

Arthur received a couple of long looks, but after passing his graduation tests, Freyja had given him a new chip to carry.

It was a circle of black polished stone with a hole carved in the middle. It now sat strung on his necklace next to the one Kenzie had given him. Now all who saw it would know he was graduated and could be out during school time.

Arthur found the nearby canal and walked along the path beside it without being stopped. Soon enough, the canal joined the main river. Following the edges against the current, he bypassed shops that grew fancier.

Finally, Arthur came to the entrance of the hive.

Well, one of the entrances.

Eight ground-level entrances ringed around the hive in total. This one, Southeast, was impressive. It was an arch of marble cut in blocks of rainbow colors from white on one end, shading slowly up the spectrum through yellow, and reds in the middle. From there it darkened on the other side through the purples and a blue so dark it was almost black.

Several guards in impressive-looking outfits stood on either side of the large arch. They were the ones who examined and approved all traffic in and out. There was a line each for carts and people on horseback going by in either direction, and a line for individuals on foot.

By the way some of the guards held out hands and murmured to themselves, they must have a Seeker card and were looking for contraband. He was glad he had the foresight to deactivate his Trap card.

Arthur joined the end of the line for the people on foot. He stood out because he was one of the few who was not carrying a pack.

When he got to the front of the line, the guard frowned down at him.

"Are you coming to see your parents?"

In answer, Arthur pulled out the necklace with Kenzie's chip strung on the end. "I'm here to see my recruiter."

The man looked over it carefully.

"Kenzie and Marteen, eh?" He turned to an assistant who held a thick bundle of papers. "Ah, here she is. Level five, apartment 103."

So, Kenzie had been promoted up a level. Was it because she had recruited him?

The guard continued, "Go straight up there with no dawdling. I'll send a message on ahead."

He nodded to a younger teen, who wore a much less decorated uniform. The teen rushed off to a nearby hut. Likely to activate some card anchor device.

"No dawdling," Arthur repeated, nodding once.

That, of course, was a lie. He intended to meet Kenzie and exchange his card shards, but he intended to take his time about it.

The guard gestured him in.

Like the rest of the city, the area inside the hive seemed empty of activity. Most who were visible were workers getting on with their duties.

By now, Arthur had seen the sheer amount of mind-boggling work when a new scourge-eruption was announced somewhere within the kingdom. During those times, the hive became—well, a hive of activity. People and dragons boiled out of the hive through portals that the shimmering dark-green dragons opened. All support staff inside and outside were on high alert. When the dragons returned, card shards flowed into the city, bringing wealth and the promise of new magic.

And dragons and their riders died. People didn't talk about that much in the orphanage, but the teachers and staff were sure to prod the kids about interest in the hive after a difficult eruption.

Arthur wasn't afraid of the scourglings. Not much, anyway. And he knew that working with the hive was the best path to more shards and full cards.

But he was grateful that Legendary eggs were rare. He still had time to grow and develop more skills. More time to decide what he wanted to do with his life.

The ground level of the hive was level 1. Arthur briefly glanced around before he found a staircase upward. The Level 1 commissary held only the most basic of supplies, with prices no different than what he would get in the city.

Arthur's new morning job working in the orphanage kitchen would take care of his basics. He walked on.

Level 2 had a greater range of supplies for sale, including some new shirts and a quilt that tempted him. But surely the higher levels would have a steeper discount.

The third level was better still, though there was no sign of trash-tier Commons cards for sale. Those would be on the fourth level.

However, Arthur passed by the fourth-level commissary completely. He didn't think anyone had managed to connect him to the missing card, but he didn't want to risk it.

The fourth level must have represented a significant barrier. When he got to the top of the staircase there, he had to show his recruitment chip to another pair of guards who barred the way. They glanced at it before letting him through.

The tunnels were busier with people, too. Most had depictions of dragons emblazoned on their jackets or clothing.

Arthur walked by a small group of men and women chatting clustered in a knot—and taking up the entire tunnel. He scooted up against the wall to get past them.

A hand landed on his shoulder.

"What's this? A little Common trying to get past without acknowledging his betters?"

Arthur looked up to see a tall young man with a streak of sunshine-blond hair. He had the build and healthy, clear skin that screamed he was carded.

"Decan, what are you doing?" one of the man's friends asked.

"I tire of these Common trash riders sneaking by without acknowledgment. It's rude." The man had a strange, formal way of speaking. Some phrases clipped as if they sat on the end of his lips.

"I'm not a rider," Arthur said cautiously, unsure if this was a joke or not.

"What are you doing in the dragon rider tunnels?"

"Seeing my recruiter."

By the way one of the men's friends snickered, that had been a mistake.

Decan's blue eyes lit up. "Ah, you must be new. I suppose your recruiter never told you about the toll?"

"The . . . toll?"

"To be among us. What do you have in those greasy little pockets of yours?" The man snapped his fingers impatiently. "Come on, now. Coins or shards?"

Arthur shrugged the restraining hand away. "I don't got nothing."

The man clicked his tongue. "Lying to a dragon rider. That means punishment. Now you owe me double."

Twisting, Arthur turned to run.

He got two steps before an invisible force pushed him as if he had been shoved from behind. He took his next step long and landed hard. The invisible push crashed down on his head, and Arthur was knocked to his knees.

It only took a moment for Decan to reach him and haul him back to his feet. This time the force pushed him against the tunnel wall. Arthur's mouth opened in an involuntary grin as the skin from his face was pulled tight with the force.

Decan didn't look concerned. He turned to his friends, who were frowning but didn't object. "Tell me he has something worth my time." He looked at Arthur. "Else you'll be shoveling my dragon's shit to the fields for the next week."

The male sighed. "He has something heavy with magic under his jacket. Right side."

Arthur's card anchor bag.

Decan reached for it. Even struggling against the invisible force, Arthur tried to fight him back. But the man was stronger and taller. And Arthur had no skills to help him. Combat was outside his card's capabilities.

"What's going on?"

Arthur's heart leaped with hope at the familiar voice. Decan stepped away, and Arthur turned his head to the side to see Kenzie standing not too far away.

"My, if it isn't little Kenzie. The silver who wants to be a white," Decan sneered.

Kenzie's hip cocked. "Are you hassling my recruit, Decan? That's worth a duel." She smiled. "How long did it take you to stop crying the last time?"

Abruptly, the weight pressing Arthur back vanished. He inhaled a surprised breath, tipping forward.

Decan caught him, all sweet and pleasant. "I don't know what you're talking about. I was just helping your little pet find his way through the tunnels. It's a real maze in here."

"Uh-huh." Kenzie jerked her head to the side.

To Arthur's shock, the three walked away. They threw venomous looks at her, but if they had tails, they'd be tucked under their legs.

Kenzie gave Arthur a quick up and down. "Did he steal anything? Are you okay?"

He appreciated the pragmatism that made her ask about the shards before his health.

"No and yes." He looked at their retreating backs and then at Kenzie. "I thought the hive was safe."

"Well, you won't get mugged by a criminal, but you may get a shakedown by some reject nobles with an attitude problem. Come on." She gestured for him to follow her. Then she turned and strode in the opposite direction of where Decan and his group had gone.

Arthur hastened to catch up. Questions tumbled out before he could help himself. "How did you find me? Were those nobles? What did he mean about Marteen? Did you really beat him in a duel? How?"

She rolled her eyes. "Does he look like he could beat me in a duel?"

"He used card magic on me. I couldn't move—I was glued to the wall."

"He rides an orange." She tipped her hand back and forth in a so-so gesture. "They don't go for the destructive/transformative cards like reds, or the

Light-based stuff like the yellows. Decan repels people away—like his personality doesn't do that enough. His dragon is the opposite. Sucks you in."

"And you beat that?" He couldn't keep the surprise out of his voice. "How?"

"Same way I found you. I saw a whole lot of emotion coming down this tunnel."

"But—"

Kenzie flicked two fingers in a twisting motion, and suddenly Arthur was laughing. Hysterically. It was a little like being tickled, in that there was no real joy in it, just a bodily reaction as if something had their thumb pressed on a button where everything was funny, but at the same time, nothing was at all because he could not stop. He couldn't tell if he was screaming or laughing or on the verge of sobbing.

And just as suddenly, and all at once, it did stop.

Doubled over, Arthur heaved for breath. When he looked up, Kenzie gave him a sympathetic smile.

"What did you . . ." he started to say, voice raw. "What . . ."

"I've collected a few cards that have synergized with mine and Marteen's," she said. "It's not a set, but it works for the two of us. That's why Decan's pissy. White dragons mess with the mind."

He had been warned about white dragons, Arthur remembered. Now he knew why. He licked dry lips. "Can they—can you—?"

"Read thoughts?" she asked lightly. *Too* lightly.

Arthur jerked back in surprise.

Now her smile had a definite tinge of sadness. As if she had said this many times. "Just emotions. I'm Uncommon, not Rare."

He spent a moment wondering if that were true. Could she change his thoughts?

No. If she could read his thoughts, she would know about his Legendary-rank card. If she could change his mind, surely she'd make him give it up.

Arthur nodded. "You made Decan cry in the duel."

"Like a baby who had his rattle taken away," she said in satisfaction. Then, unexpectedly, she rested an arm across his shoulders in a big sisterly way. "You're my recruit, so it's my job to teach you to defend yourself, too."

"Really?"

"Sure."

Then she turned him to the right, and they came to large double doors. Kenzie pushed them open and then walked into an apartment easily twice the size of her last.

"So," Kenzie said, perching on the edge of her bed, "why haven't you stuck that Trap card back in your heart yet?"

Arthur froze with a feeling like he had just been caught stealing raisins from the bowl. His first fleeting thought to deny it died when he saw the certainty in Kenzie's face—and remembered the feeling of out-of-control hysterical laughter.

Suddenly, he understood why Decan and his friends had left so quickly after she showed up.

"How did you know—Oh." He stopped as it came to him. Of course. His Trap card would have activated the moment Decan used magic on him. That it didn't was all the tell Kenzie needed.

"I get why it's inconvenient," Kenzie said. "You don't want to be transported somewhere at the drop of a hat. But keeping a Rare in a card anchor bag—especially a cheap one like yours—is a recipe for disaster. You're supposed to be some sort of cook, right? You know recipes."

Yes, he was supposed to be a cook. Too bad he didn't have the class for it.

"I told you, I'm aiming for another type of Rare card." He rolled his shoulder in a shrug. "Besides, if I stick that card in my heart, then will I grow up to be the type of guy who disappears when the going gets tough?"

That seemed to stump her. She cocked her head to the side. "There's something to be said for bravely running away. But it's your card. If you're going to keep it in that bag, you need to learn how to defend it."

Arthur started to perk up, but then almost as quickly sagged again.

His Master of Skills card didn't include combat or any techniques that would enhance his body. That meant he would have to do it the hard way.

"I'm not any good at fighting," he said.

"That's what practice is for. Even us dragon riders learn a few defensive moves. Here, I'll show you."

She stood, and Arthur backed up a step, shaking his head. "How will that help against someone who can stick me to a wall with magic?"

Her dark eyes flashed. "Because until you have cards to help you, you gotta use every tool you have. Why didn't you yell for help? Decan wasn't squishing your lungs, was he?"

"Well . . . no," he admitted. "Would it have done any good?"

"All dragon riders love getting new cards, but not everybody around here will go as low as to rob a little kid," she snapped as if offended. "Besides, what if somebody ran up to see what was going on? That might have given you a second to escape."

Again, escaping from somebody stronger and larger who wanted what he had . . . Well, it hadn't clicked to Arthur that it was possible.

Back in his old village, the baron's men took whatever they wanted, whenever they wanted. They took from people who had next to nothing, and everybody just had to grin and bear it.

Nobody had stolen from him in the caravan, but he was well aware that Red probably could not have stopped them if they tried.

But he wasn't in the village, and by now he had lived longer in the orphanage than he had with the caravan.

The hive wasn't perfect, but it was both fairer and freer. And he was growing up. Soon, he wouldn't be a little kid who had to take whatever unfairness an adult dished out.

He met Kenzie's eyes. "Okay. Show me."

He and Kenzie spent the next half hour or so going through three twisting maneuvers to break different holds. They practiced them several times, with Kenzie gripping his arm and Arthur twisting out of it using various angles. Kenzie advised him to go for a man or woman's weak points. The eyes, the nose, and between the legs.

It felt strange to practice diligently at something and not receive a skill for it. Arthur felt rusty and a little frustrated with himself that his practice came with no level indicators or random bursts of wisdom to help him out.

Still, Kenzie said he was doing good and promised next time to teach him some knife tricks if he purchased a good one.

When they stopped for a quick break, Arthur bit his lower lip in consideration. "Kenzie, you said there are people who can mess with others' minds? The white dragons?"

She waved a hand. "You'll probably never meet one. They live on the higher levels. People who can alter thoughts scare the nobles and the king, so there are all sorts of restrictions on them."

"Why do the nobles put up with them at all?"

Her expression turned grave. "They're mostly pulled out when an eruption happens under a big city. You need a mind mage to keep people from panicking, stampeding over one another, or tearing each other to bits to get away from the scourge."

That painted a picture he had never imagined before. Arthur shuddered.

But his curiosity grew. Was it possible to block that type of magic? And if it was, would that be considered a body enhancement skill, which would be out of his reach? Or a learned skill?

"When you made me laugh earlier . . . it was horrible," he confessed. "But in the end, I felt like I was close to throwing you off."

She gave him an odd look. "What do you mean?"

There was no point dancing around the subject. He decided just to ask. "Could you do it again?" *Two or three more times*, he added silently. That should be enough to learn if he could develop a skill against it. "I want to see if it's possible to toss you out of my mind."

"I'm not really in your mind. It's more like I'm pressing down on your aura," she said. "And why? It's not like many people can do what I can."

He shrugged. "It's not all that likely I'm going to be mugged by someone with a knife in the hive, but I'm still practicing."

She stared at him for a moment. "Are you worried that I am manipulating you? Because I'm only an Uncommon. My powers are a little like hitting you with a mallet. It's not subtle. People can tell when I'm using it. That's why I'm not up there with the mind mages." She pointed upward.

"I'm not worried about that," he said. "I just want to see if I can fight against it."

Again, she stared at him, and he got the impression she was looking deep into his aura. Well, if she was, she would only see his curiosity. He wasn't afraid of her. He wanted to see what he could learn from her—and what he could learn about himself.

"Fine." Kenzie sounded vaguely exasperated. "But I'm not going to use fear or make you cry, you understand? Messing with emotions like this can get ugly."

"That's fine," he said quickly, and would have said more to reassure her, but in the next second, it was as if all of the breath had been punched out of his lungs. His next inhale came out as screamed laughter.

And this time, it was more of a *scream* than a laugh. It was not fun at all.

Kenzie cut it after a few seconds, leaving Arthur doubled over.

"Had enough?" she asked.

Gritting his teeth, he forced himself to shake his head. "No. That took me by surprise. Let me try again."

She looked doubtful, but this time waited for him to nod before she mentally pressed down on his aura.

Once again, Arthur was caught in the throes of hysterical laughter. And it hurt, physically. He was belly laughing and trying to stop at the same time, and it felt like the muscles in his core were trying to tear themselves apart.

Kenzie cut it off and said something that Arthur missed, because he got a message from his card.

New skill gained: Basic Empathic Resistance (Shield Class)
Due to your card's bonus traits, you automatically start this skill
at level 3.

Shield class?

That was new. And he got the impression, through the link in the card that rested in his heart, that this was a borderline case. If Kenzie were a true mind mage and not a silver mystic, he wouldn't have been able to develop the skill.

He focused on what Kenzie was saying. "People are going to call the guards, thinking I'm torturing you in here. And they'd be right."

"No," he said. "One more time. I almost have it."

"You're crazy. Wait, you don't like this, do you?"

He shook his head. "It's terrible. That's why I have to figure out a way to stop it."

Once again, she stared at him as if trying to read his emotions. And one more time, she was reluctantly convinced.

This time . . . Arthur still laughed, but it wasn't as close to a tortured scream. It was more like near hysteria. That was a shade better.

He even got a new level out of it.

New skill level:
Basic Empathic Resistance (Shield Class)
Level 4

Kenzie cut off her influence and looked at him. "You know . . . I felt something there. Almost like you were pushing back a little. I didn't think that was possible." Her expression darkened. "But I'm not doing that again for a while."

Arthur, who was heaving in gusts of breath, nodded and wiped at his cheeks with the back of his hand. It came away wet with laughter tears. "That's fine. I'm ready for a break, anyway."

He had gotten what he wanted—a new skill. And the hint of an interesting class.

Once he could stand up fully, he reached into his vest and pulled out his card anchor bag. "How about a trade?"

He had seven Uncommon shard pieces in total, which included Horatio's pay. The other boy had trusted Arthur enough to trade on his behalf.

Kenzie, true to her word, exchanged them. Arthur got two regular Rare pieces for his four Uncommon, seeing as one of his had been a treasured corner piece. Horatio got one Rare for his three regular Uncommon pieces.

This was still a much better exchange rate than they would've gotten in the city. Even from Barlow.

Kenzie sighed in mock regret, as she got the worst part of the deal. Her half of the agreement was that she would get both Arthur and Horatio as recruits. From the hints she had dropped, Arthur suspected she would also gain an additional bonus if and when they linked with a dragon.

"I'm looking for another job, too," Arthur said as he put his new shard pieces away.

"A third job? Geez, kid, do you ever plan to sleep?"

"I worked harder as a farmer," he said, which was only a small lie. Working the dragon soil fields had been difficult and deadly, and starving was even worse. Arthur didn't mind working hard to get skills and food at regular times. "Do you know anyone who's hiring for kitchen work in the mid-morning? I'm good at meal prep."

Kenzie opened her mouth, hesitated, and shut it with a shake of her head. "No. I mean, I know a place, but . . . it's not really for kids."

That got Arthur's interest. "What is it?"

"It's a bar on the first level," she said. "Which means that sometimes the city folk use it when they want the thrill of being in a hive. It's . . . kind of a seedy place."

That sounded perfect. "Can you show me?"

Again, she hesitated but then nodded. "On one condition."

"What's that?"

Kenzie smiled. "You're a hive recruit now. So it's about time you meet the hatchlings."

CHAPTER 42

Instantly, Arthur was suspicious.

"Why do you want me to visit the hatchlings? Is there a Rare available or something?"

Not that it would do him a lick of good. From what he had gleaned from casual conversations with Horatio, a dragon would not link to someone who had a higher-tier card in their heart. Even if a Common hatchling found someone with a card in the same set, the presence of an Uncommon or Rare card would disrupt the bonding.

This had a dark side, Horatio had revealed. Ambitious riders could break a card link with a dragon they felt they had outgrown. He remembered two instances in his old hive of Common riders doing just that to move up to an Uncommon-quality dragon instead.

This was something that was looked down upon and was relegated to nobles who cared more about family honor than the feelings of their dragons.

Those unlinked dragons still could relink onto someone else, but the whole experience was traumatic to them.

Arthur remembered the red dragon that had given him his Master of Skills card. He had been riderless. Had something like that happened to him? Someone who had been associated with Baron Kane?

In any case, all this meant that unless there was a Legendary hatchling within the hive nest, he had little to worry about.

Kenzie snorted at his question. "What, do you think I'm hiding a Rare up my sleeve?"

This was clearly supposed to be a joke—one that Arthur didn't get. He stayed silent.

Her eyes narrowed. "How long have you lived here?"

"A little under six months."

"Oh, that explains it." She nodded once. "Well, having a Rare egg laid is a big deal. The hive throws a whole festival for it. Then another one when the dragon links up to a new rider." She grinned down at him. "It's a big hullabaloo. You'll see all sorts of snooty noble kids—not the heirs, all the spares—suddenly find a reason to transfer into the hive. Some of them practically make a career of hopping from hive to hive, chasing the next Rare egg."

"What about Legendary eggs?" Arthur asked with what he hoped was the right amount of casualness. "Or Mythic?"

She snorted. "Half of those noble kids are willing to tear out each other's throat with a smile for a Rare. Could you imagine it if a Legendary was laid? I don't even think this hive has ever produced a Mythic."

Arthur knew he shouldn't push, but he couldn't help it. "When was the last time a Legendary was laid here?"

"Oh, that's Whitaker." She waved a hand vaguely upward, indicating the high levels. "Thirty or forty years ago? He's one of the hive admins with Valentina, the other Legendary. She's ancient."

Arthur had other questions, but Kenzie grabbed his wrist and pulled him to the door, calling over her shoulder to Marteen. "I'll be back soon!"

Marteen sleepily lifted a wing in reply, more interested in dozing in the sunlight spilling in from her new window than visiting the hatchlings.

Kenzie led Arthur down a new tunnel with marble walls colored like golden sand. This one led deep into the hive, with few junctions leading off in other directions.

Unlike other tunnels, it was narrow enough for two people to pass through, but not large dragons.

When Arthur asked about this, Kenzie nodded. "It's best to keep the little unlinked dragons from the adults."

For once, she didn't explain further, which left the "why" up to the imagination.

"But how do the female dragons go in to lay their eggs?" Arthur asked.

"There's a whole different area where they do that. It's kind of an open-air arena. Once they're laid, and the dragon knows the eggs are in good hands, she leaves. The egg security teams take over the rest. Egg security is a good job if you can get it," she added as an aside. "It's mostly just waiting around since the eggs take care of themselves. But the hive pays well for the trouble. Those dragons are the future kingdom's protection, after all."

Arthur filed that away in the back of his mind. If he was hard up for card shards, he might consider it. But standing around being a guard for unhatched eggs didn't sound like a way to get more skills.

Along the way, adding skills had become just as important as gaining more cards. His skills had taken him from his borderland village all the way to the inside of a hive. He couldn't let himself forget that.

Before long, he heard the echo of distant voices down the tunnel: laughter and high-pitched calls to one another. It sounded like a daycare for small children.

The end of the tunnel opened to reveal a cavernous hollow. It held three areas fenced off from one another with basic wood planks.

Inside the fenced areas were baby dragons.

There were perhaps two dozen in total in a variety of colors. At first glance, they seemed to be separated mostly by size.

The smallest hatchlings were positioned closest to the mouth of the tunnel. Purples, blues, and one lime-green dragon tumbled, squealed, and played with one another. They were surrounded by a variety of toys from a sturdy leather ball to plush soft animal-shaped toys. Just like a child of two or three would like to play with.

Currently, the tiniest dragons were clustered around an upturned bucket. The goal of the game was to knock down whoever managed to scramble to the top first.

A tiny dark-purple dragon the size of a dinner plate glanced over at Arthur and Kenzie as they walked in. It looked away, attention grabbed just as quickly by a new king of the top of the bucket.

Arthur and Kenzie moved on to the second fenced-in area. These had larger dragons—some as large as a big dog—in other colors of fiery reds, oranges, pinks, and yellows.

One of the yellows trotted over to sniff curiously before returning to the group. They were less boisterous, and there was a certain air of intelligence that the first group lacked. This was reflected in their toys. They had balls and stuffed animals—some of which were burned at the edges—but also basic board games and one lone child's book with a broken spine.

"This second group is the Uncommons," Kenzie said. She watched the dragons closely, as if waiting for something. A reaction from the baby dragons, perhaps. To see if any of them were interested in Arthur.

She was slyly checking to see if he carried another card in his heart. None of the babies could link with him, but they might give him a curious sniff if they sensed he had another card.

Well, he was. But it certainly wasn't one of the lower-ranked cards.

Arthur pretended like he didn't notice what she was doing. "Who are they?" he asked, nodding to a few young men and women in soft white uniforms. They mingled with the baby dragons, occasionally tossing a ball for one of them and breaking up scuffles that got too intense.

They also didn't seem to be carded. It wasn't something he could put his finger on because everyone looked well-fed, but they didn't have that indefinable aura of health and vitality that clung to carded people.

With a start, he realized he had grown so used to seeing only carded adults that it now looked odd to find someone normal.

"Those are the nest attendants," Kenzie said.

"They aren't carded?"

She shook her head. "There's no rule that says you have to be to work here, but carded attendants tend to link up with a dragon eventually. Some people want to be paid well but don't want to be dragon riders." She shrugged.

Arthur was about to ask something else when there was motion from the tunnel entrance.

As one, all the Common hatchlings perked up and started squeaking like baby birds who sensed the return of a parent with a juicy worm in its beak. They crowded against the sides of the fence, looking toward the tunnel.

A moment later, a boy of fifteen years old or so walked in, flanked by two adults who must have been his parents. Judging by their sturdy but worn clothing, Arthur guessed they were from a farming community.

One of the nest attendants strode up to welcome them in. Then he led the boy to the squeaking hatchlings.

Some of the squeakers stared hard at the boy before they turned away, uninterested again.

Two blues remained, bouncing up and down and flapping stubby wings that were too small to fly.

They weren't the only ones.

A dragon in the third group looked on anxiously.

Arthur and Kenzie hadn't yet gone past the third group, but he could see they were the shimmer-quality dragons. The one that stared at the boy was tan with an overly blocky head and feet. It would have looked completely ordinary if not for the fact its scales caught the torchlight and glimmered as if flaked by chips of diamonds.

The boy hesitantly approached the squeaking blues.

The tan gave an outraged bellow. With a flap of uncoordinated wings, it leaped over the wood-plank fence . . . only to land flat on its face.

It righted itself at once and charged straight at the group to stand in front of the blues. With a gesture of its paw, an image of its card popped up in front of it.

The two blues squeaked in outrage and did the same.

From where he stood, Arthur couldn't see the faces of the cards. Blues usually had powers dealing with water and browns the element of earth. A shimmering tan would be an off version of that.

He made to move to get a closer look. Kenzie caught his arm.

"Don't. This is supposed to be private."

In fact, more of the nest attendants were circling as if trying to block the view from outsiders.

"What happens now?" Arthur asked.

"That's up to the boy."

The farmer's boy studied the three offered cards in front of him. His father opened his mouth as if to offer his opinion, but one of the nest attendants shushed him.

It was clear that this was to be the boy's choice alone.

Arthur wondered if anyone had ever rejected the dragon's cards completely.

That wasn't to be the farmer's boy's fate today. He said something to the tan and then, with a grimace, pulled down the collar of his shirt and pulled out his card from his heart.

The tan did the same, and they pressed the cards together.

There was a flash of light. A new card was born, made from the joining from the boy and dragon. For a moment all three cards flashed between them, visible as day but hard to look at. Like staring at the sun. They twisted and turned in the air, the fronts briefly facing Arthur.

Only Arthur's advanced **Reading** skills let him skim over the cards at a glance.

The boy had a Common well-seeker card, used to find fresh underground water sources.

The tan had a Common Earth-element manipulation card, with a few caveats Arthur didn't have time to read. Doubtless they were advantages brought by the tan's shimmering qualities.

The new card was a spell with the ability to use groundwater to create cutting water jets under an enemy.

The bright light was too much. Arthur blinked, and the impressions of the cards had already faded from the air.

The boy tucked his card back into his heart along with his half of the new card. Then he bent and hugged his new dragon—a friend for life and partner who had helped turn his Common card into a potentially powerful tool against the scourge.

Now Arthur understood why Kenzie had brought him here.

He wanted that, too.

Arthur was unusually quiet as Kenzie led him away from the dragon nests. He glanced behind himself before they rounded the first bend in the tunnel.

The farmer boy was still crouched next to his new dragon, petting the tan's neck and speaking softly to him. His parents stood nearby, arms around each other's waists. The nest attendants, too, looked pleased with the new dragon pair.

A couple of the unlinked dragons glanced Arthur's way, but their gazes slid over him, disinterested.

He didn't have the type of card that they craved.

For the first time, he felt truly bad for misleading Kenzie. He had to bite the tip of his tongue to keep from blurting out about the Legendary card in his heart.

Doshi had said his rider had waited five years for a Rare dragon that would link up with him. Legendaries were hatched so much less often than that. This entire giant hive had only two.

In Arthur's rare moments of free time, he had let himself wonder what kind of dragon would accept him. What card would it have, and what kind of powerful card could they create together?

Seeing the hatchling link with the boy right in front of him had made that daydream feel so far away.

The wisest thing to do, he knew, would be to focus on his skills. Those were what had carried him this far. Those were what would make him powerful and rich in the future.

Yes, being a dragon rider was one way to get enough power to help his dad and the others back home at the border. But that wasn't the only way.

Straightening, he nodded to himself and did his best to match stride with the longer-legged Kenzie. It wasn't as hard as it had been in the past. Maybe he was finally growing a little.

"Where are we going now?" he asked, belatedly realizing he'd just let her lead the way.

She smiled down at him as if she knew what he was going through. Considering she could see auras and feel emotions, she probably did.

"You wanted another kitchen to work in, right?"

"Right!" He perked up immediately, the sting of disappointment fading. How could he have forgotten? Maybe he needed to work on a memory skill.

Nah. That probably went with a body enhancement card.

Kenzie chose a tunnel that took them sharply downward, back to the ground level. It was not a lively place with half of the shops shuttered, though Arthur caught several signs stating business hours would begin in the early evening.

This was a place with nightlife.

Kenzie led Arthur to a hole-in-the-wall entrance. Literally, it was a perfectly round door cut to match a shaped hole in the stone wall. There were no windows.

She paused for a moment to look back at him, hand on the door handle. "As I said, they don't usually allow little kids in here, so you mind your P's and Q's. It shouldn't be dangerous, but men and women can get stupid when they're drunk."

"It's not even noon," he said, surprised. Even the roughest men in the caravan didn't start drinking until they'd stopped for the evening.

Kenzie snorted like he'd made a joke, then pushed the door open.

The smell of stale beer hit him like a slap in the face. Arthur almost backed out, but since Kenzie didn't flinch, pride kept him moving forward.

The inside was exactly as he imagined a real tavern to be: a bar set up in front with bench seating for people who wanted to drink together in larger groups. What got his attention were the card tables set up in the middle, dominating the room. This was also a place for people to gamble.

There might have been more, but it was currently so dark that Arthur couldn't see to the corners. He relied on Kenzie to lead the way forward.

She walked confidently up to the bar and stood next to a heavyset bearded man who sat with a half-drunken beer next to him.

The man looked at her and said, "We're not open."

Then he pulled from the drink.

"Bob," Kenzie said, "I got you a serving wench."

Arthur jerked in surprise.

Bob did, too, looking over to Arthur before he snorted a laugh. "He ain't got the tits to be a wench."

"You need someone who won't get slapped on the ass every time they serve a drink," Kenzie said. "He's only a little guy now—"

"Hey . . ." Arthur said weakly, unsure if he liked where this was going.

"But I've been watching him. He's tough and smart. He'll grow. And he's available to work." She leaned forward slightly. "For the right price."

The man looked more interested. "You can pour beer, boy?"

"Yeah," Arthur said, and on impulse offered, "I know card and dice games, too."

Bob didn't answer directly to that, but Arthur thought he caught a glimmer of interest in his eyes. His **Acting** skill whispered that Bob likely wasn't as drunk as he seemed.

Kenzie didn't seem to think so either. She haggled as if the man was entirely lucid. "He's a recruit, so you'll pay him hive rates."

At this, Bob frowned. "I ain't having a little boy serve the night crew. Not until he's old enough to knock a man in the jaw hard enough to make 'em think twice."

"I can do meal prep," Arthur said, thinking quickly. He rattled off the hours he was available to work as well as the basic duties he took care of under Barlow's watch. Then he finished with, "But I gotta get off work before second afternoon bell. I have a shift at the Salt and Spoon."

Bob's bushy eyebrows rose. "You work for Barlow?"

"I do, sir. He wants me full time, but I want a different kitchen experience."

"Ha. I bet that chaps his ass. That man's always been a snob."

Bob slapped his own knee and gestured to the back of the bar. Now that Arthur was close enough to see details, he noted the sheer wall of barrels all stacked from the floor to the very top of the ceiling. And it was a high ceiling. Each barrel had a different label and was tapped with a spigot. Two ladders on either end allowed the pourers to reach the higher kegs.

"We have the finest collections of beer in this forsaken hive, and you haven't seen our wine room yet. This place don't look it, but nobles come from all around the kingdom to sample our wines." Bob grinned proudly at Arthur.

For the first time, Arthur understood why Kenzie had brought him here. It was a rough place, but perhaps not a bad place for a boy who wanted to learn.

"Which is why you can afford to pay hive rates," Kenzie pressed.

"Yes, yes, fine." Bob drank deeply again, pausing to wipe away foam from his upper lip before he said, "Four hours a day at hive rates. That's two silver coins and a Common a week, with a bonus Uncommon bimonthly."

Arthur had to struggle not to let his eyes bug out from his head. From Bob's smirk, he didn't succeed.

"One thing," Arthur said. "You aren't calling me a serving wench."

"'Course not." Bob slapped one ham-hock hand against Arthur's shoulder. "You're a barman."

CHAPTER 43

Arthur hadn't felt this flavor of rage and despair since . . . well, now that he thought about it, he hadn't felt it since he left the borderland village. A place where everything was unfair, where he had no hope of ever getting ahead, and his greatest ambition was to live to see the end of the day.

Remembering that he practically lived in paradise compared to before gave him pause. And that was enough to cool his temper.

He put down the dirty wineglass that, a few moments before, he had been about to throw against the far wall.

The source of his aggravation still hovered in his vision.

New skill gained: Sommelier (Cooking Class)
Due to your card's bonus traits, you automatically start this skill
at level 3.

Yet another cooking skill. One that was uniquely different than the rest. And yet he *still* hadn't attained his Cooking Class.

What was he missing?

With a sigh, Arthur picked up the glass again and dunked it in the soapy sink to wash it out.

He'd been working at Bob's Fine Beer and Wines (or Bob's Tavern as everyone called it) for just over a week and had received the skill by accident.

While washing out endless wine cups and mugs that had once contained beers, ciders, and ales, he'd started playing a game to keep himself occupied: every time he washed out a new glass, he tried to identify the liquid and vintage inside it by smell.

He'd been pouring for the few morning customers for a few days whenever Bob stepped away from the counter, so he had something to compare the dirty mugs to. Honestly, he hadn't been sure he had been guessing right until he was awarded the basic skill.

"What is a sommelier anyway?" he grumbled. Something to do with wine, probably. That was the last guess he'd made.

The wine was a popular one, and he'd heard Bob talking up customers enough to learn it was grown in this valley. Wolf Moon Hive had famously bitter cold winters, and equally dry hot summers. It was those summers and the quality of the soil that gave this wine its distinctive taste.

Not that wine particularly interested Arthur. He'd tried tastes of the stuff when Bob wasn't looking. Not enough to add experience to his Thief Class. Just to see what the big deal was.

He didn't understand and chalked it up to an adult thing.

Arthur sighed again as he dunked the last of the glasses in the sink and set them up to dry. He took one look around the kitchen—all vegetables chopped in preparation for the next shift when Bob's cooks came in an hour.

Pulling off his apron, Arthur called, "Shift's done, Bob!"

Bob, who was currently visiting with one of his favorite customers—if there was one thing Bob liked better than drinking his own brew, it was having a long conversation—waved Arthur out. "See you the day after tomorrow, then. Oh, wait." He lobbed something at him in an underhand throw.

Arthur caught the object, which was a small draw bag. He looked in and saw with widened eyes that it was his week's pay, card shard and all.

He hadn't been expecting it. Normally Barlow paid his workers the day after break day. Bob had paid him a little early.

Maybe this day was looking up after all.

Arthur had to jog not to be late for his afternoon shift at Barlow's restaurant. The first few days he had arrived out of breath, legs aching.

Now . . . Well, he was still out of breath, but the muscles in his legs had toughened up. It wasn't a skill. He was just growing stronger.

"You're late," Horatio crowed, grinning at him from his baking station.

Arthur glanced at the timepiece set on the wall, saw he had two minutes to spare, and glared at his friend for making him look. "And you're still ugly."

Horatio cackled and flicked some flour his way, but Arthur had already moved out of range.

He went to his own workstation and started the usual prep for the dinner service to come. Today, Barlow had him break down the entire haunch of beef. Thanks to his **Butchering** skill, which now sat at level 9, it was a simple and much less messy process than it had been when he first started.

Arthur was just arranging the cuts of meat, deciding which were tough enough to be tossed in the stewpot and which should be kept aside as steaks, when a bottle of wine caught his eye.

It was sitting on the next station over. The cook who worked there did the entrées, but he must have been running late today.

Curious, Arthur grabbed the bottle, popped the already loosened cork, and sniffed.

He wasn't sure which skill told him, but he knew for certain that this vintage would pair wonderfully with a steak.

In fact . . .

Arthur glanced around to see if anyone was watching—they weren't. Then he moved to the wood fire usually occupied by the missing cook.

He grabbed a pan and a thin slice of steak he'd trimmed from a better piece. Once the pan was hot enough to make butter spit on it, he laid the meat on and splashed some of the wine to cook along with it.

As the pan was hot, it only took a few minutes to cook the slice of meat. Arthur ladled the combination of butter and wine over as it seared, pausing to add a dash of salt and bruised rosemary he had handy.

Finally cooked to a perfect medium rare, Arthur transferred it onto a plate, cut into it, and bit down.

Perfect.

The tang of the wine had complemented the meat just as he hoped. The fatty butter, salt, and rosemary added extra layers of flavor.

His eyes half closed in pleasure, he wondered what side dishes would be best paired with this steak. Chef Barlow had said they would soon be receiving a fall harvest and—

New skill gained: Meal Improvisation (Cooking Class)
Due to your card's bonus traits, you automatically start this skill
at level 3.

New Class!
Cooking Class – Tier 2 Crafting
It takes knowledge of fundamental skills to start down the road
of any craft. But to truly begin to master a craft, one must show a
commitment to learning and pushing the boundaries of your art.
As Cooking is a crafting class, individual skills maintain their own levels
and are not rolled into an overall average. In addition, relevant skills are
split into synergistic subcategories:
General
Baking

Mixology
Kitchen Management

Add more skills within this class to create more subcategories.
All new skills within this class start at level 5, and experience is gained
15% faster in addition to existing card's bonuses.

When equipped:
+2 to Perception (+ additional 2 to all taste and smell)
+2 to Dexterity (+ additional 3 when using kitchen specific tools)
+1 to Intelligence
+1 to Luck
Do you wish to equip Cooking Class – Tier 2 now?

Arthur stared at the message, his next bite of meat hanging out of his mouth.

He'd done it. He'd finally done it. Of course an entire class for a craft would be more complex than average. He had accidentally stumbled into Gambling and Thievery—both tier 1 classes—but he had to show commitment and a desire to improve himself to begin to master Cooking.

That was likely the same with other crafts as well. Sure, he could pick up skills in Smithing or Tannery, but he would have to put in a good deal of work to combine those skills into a class.

Based on the bonuses, it might be worth it.

"Arthur, what are you doing?" Chef Barlow asked.

Arthur whirled around to find the man staring at him, one eyebrow raised that he was not at his usual workstation.

"I was . . . uh . . . experimenting?" He gestured to the pan.

Chef stepped forward and speared the final bit of meat with his own belt knife. He bit into it, and after a moment's chewing, nodded. "That's the Sauvignon? Throw in some shallots and sliced potatoes. Make those potatoes thin as a sheet of paper, you understand?"

"Yes, Chef," Arthur said, a little stunned he wasn't being told off for experimenting when he should be on prep duty.

"You'll be cooking up five of those steaks," Barlow continued. "We have noble guests who ordered a private room tonight. If all goes well, it'll be your dinner they'll eat." With another nod and a clap to Arthur's back, he walked off.

The words didn't fully register until a moment later. Arthur snorted to himself: How times had changed. He used to be lower than the muck Baron Kane would scrape off his shoe. Now here he was, cooking multiple nobles a fine meal.

Later, those same nobles might even visit Bob's Tavern to drink fine wine out of glasses Arthur himself had washed, maybe even lose a hand of cards. Once Arthur was old enough, he could do something to arrange that too . . .

Who would have known that working in kitchens would have all sorts of side benefits? If only old Yuma back in the village could see him now . . .

A seed of an idea was planted then. Separate ideas, daydreams, and ambitions that still needed to be fully combined into one. Something that Arthur, all of twelve years old, instantly rejected.

Instead, he turned to his duties with the eagerness of someone who wanted to explore a hard-earned class.

But the seed lingered, dormant. Waiting for the right moment.

It sprouted, four years later to the day.

INTERLUDE

Cori was a good, good dragon. But Cori missed her rider very, very much.

Many, many moons ago a wicked, wicked scourgling had knocked Debrah off Cori's back while they were fighting.

Cori had flown fast, fast but hadn't been in time to catch her rider. Blood everywhere. Card in her heart torn in two.

Remembering still hurt hurt.

No one else's card smelled as good good as Debrah's. No one looked at a purple like Cori twice. They all wanted young hatchlings.

They thought Cori was old, old.

So Cori did her chores. She fought and fought scourglings during eruptions. Sometimes she showed other purples tricks like how to loop and loop in the air.

Over the last few months, her stomach had gotten big big. Cori was certain there were many many eggs in there.

No male stayed for long. They were all busy busy with their own riders.

Cori had eggs and eggs before, but this time felt strange. She felt heavier even than the time she had carried twin Uncommons. That had been when Debrah had been alive—the Uncommons had made her rider happy happy.

Cori thought if she clutched more than her usual lots and lots of Commons, someone would notice. She could be happy again.

A dawn sun rose. It was egg time.

Cori floundered into the sky. The air, which had always lifted her up and up, didn't feel right. She tried and tried but was just too heavy to fly fast.

All clutching dragons were to go to a special place—an arena.

But since Debrah died, Cori had gone to a secret secret spot. If she had lots and lots of Commons eggs, she could just leave and no one would care. But if she laid Uncommons again, she could roll them into the open and people would be happy happy with her.

She crawled into her secret cave. Cramps shivered her belly hard hard. Whining to herself, she wished Debrah were there.

Her heart beat and beat in her chest. Harder than it ever had before. Though her stomach was big big, she pushed and pushed.

One egg came out. With it, her big big stomach seemed to deflate.

The egg was tiny, even from a purple mother. It was dark and dark and dark and dark like all light had been sucked in from around it.

Not an Uncommon. Something better.

Cori touched it with the tip of her snout.

It was dark dark, like the edges of her vision, all crawling inward.

Exhausted, Cori curled around her perfect single egg.

Debrah will be so happy happy, was her last thought.

PART 4
THE SPROUT

CHAPTER 44

Four Years Later

Arthur's fingers trembled as he picked up the last corner piece. As it was a Rare, it shimmered metallic in the early sunlight. Assembled on the table in front of him was the rest of the card. Nearly four years of work represented in just under a hundred pieces.

Yes, he could have gotten it done sooner—especially with his workaholic tendencies and extra deals he ran on the side—but there had been . . . complications.

This wasn't the time to think about that. He let out a breath, tried to steady his hand, and moved to fit the final piece.

"Remember to clear your mind of extra thoughts," Horatio said. The other teen was leaning over the table, just short of being too close for comfort. "Only think about the type of card you want. Make it a simple thought. You can handle that, right?"

Arthur glared at him, and for probably the thousandth time, wondered why they were friends. Bad luck on his part, he supposed.

"That didn't work for the last two cards," he snapped. "They just did whatever they wanted."

Horatio shrugged. "Those were Uncommons. This is a Rare."

"How is that different?"

"Rares have more magic," Horatio said, as if Arthur was being a complete idiot. "They're more connected with the world."

Arthur rolled his eyes. "Give me some space, would you? Stop breathing all over my card." He pushed his friend back with a light shove.

Horatio flopped down into his chair and raised his hand as if signaling Arthur to get on with it already.

Final corner piece in hand, Arthur again looked down at his card. Bickering with Horatio had set him right. His fingers weren't trembling anymore.

And while he hadn't exactly gotten the result he wanted the last two times . . . he supposed silently wishing wouldn't hurt.

I need a combat skill, he silently chanted, picturing a sharp knife or a sword. *Or maybe the ability to throw a punch.* Anything would help. *Combat skill. Combat skill. Combat skill!*

The final piece clicked into place.

The Rare pieces flashed a brilliant white, and Arthur felt phantom heat, as if the pieces of the card were melting together. Then it was over, and he looked down at his brand-new Rare card.

Personal Space
Rare

Utility

The wielder of this card is granted an extra dimensional space, 30 x 30 x 30 sq. ft. in which to store objects. As this space exists outside of time, the stored contents will experience no aging once placed inside. Contents will resume aging normally when removed. This dimensional space is only accessible by the card wielder, and objects inside cannot be sensed by lower than a Legendary-rank seeker.

Arthur stared.

"Well? What is it?" Horatio asked when Arthur remained quiet.

"Not a combat card," Arthur said faintly.

"That bad?" Despite the fact it was incredibly rude, Horatio hopped up and leaned over the table to read the description. He let out a low whistle. "I've seen Uncommon versions of this one before, but they're not so big. Damn, Arthur, your new space is bigger than our apartment."

That was an exaggeration, but just barely. Arthur and Horatio had been out of the orphanage for over a year, but both wanted to live frugally, as their main focus was collecting card shards.

"And they usually require mana to pull objects in and out," Horatio added. "Yours is mana free."

"Yeah." That was a good thing. Really. But if he couldn't get a combat-oriented card, he had at least hoped for something to finally unlock his mana. Arthur had been fascinated by magic his entire life and had been around spell casters on a regular basis since he left his old village . . . but personal magic had, so far, been out of reach.

Skills were great and all, but he still held on to the boyhood dream of throwing fireballs around.

"So?" Horatio asked. "You going to keep it or sell it?"

Arthur shook himself. This was a great card. By all rights, he should be dancing a happy jig. His problem was that he'd set his hopes too high.

In answer, he grabbed the Personal Space card, pulled down his collar, and added it straight into his heart deck.

His new card fit nicely against his other four cards.

"Let's see how it works." Arthur snatched a bright red apple up from the table. He half expected a prompt to come up, asking if he wanted to store it. Nothing happened.

That was for the best. Life would become tedious if his card asked if he wanted to store something every time he touched it.

He focused inward. It only took a few moments to find what he was looking for. It was as if his brand-new card were a lock which opened the door to the new storage space. He sort of twisted it with his mind—a nudge that opened the card inward to reveal the cavernous space beyond.

Arthur stuck the apple in, even though his arm didn't move at all.

"If I didn't know any better," Horatio said, "I would think that you just transported that apple. It just vanished."

With a grin, Arthur repeated the process to "grab" the apple out of the storage space with his mind. It reappeared back in his palm, unchanged. His grin widened, and he took a bite. "I'm going to shove so much produce in this thing," he said between chews. "Then take it out and sell it when it's out of season."

Horatio rolled his eyes. "Of course that's where your mind goes first. Some people would consider how to use it to disappear their enemies, or transport rare and exotic items for the highest bidder. You want to sell out-of-season oranges."

Arthur didn't bother to deny it. Horatio had never been without rare, fresh fruit on demand. He had no idea what a luxury it was.

Taking another bite, Arthur gestured to the table. "So? You gonna go or what?"

"I will if you stop spitting apple juice all over the table. Don't you have a card for charm?" Horatio grumbled but stood and dumped out his own card anchor bag. A pile of Rare shards tumbled out, and he quickly arranged them into a card shape.

Arthur stood back and watched his friend work, smiling slightly. Horatio didn't work nearly as many shifts as Arthur did—he preferred getting a full night of sleep and actually relaxing every once in a while instead of hustling for shards. As a result, it had taken him this long to finally assemble one Rare card.

His father's dragon, Sams, was still without a rider. Horatio tried to hide it, but this moment meant a lot to him. If his card was in any way compatible . . . Sams would agree to link up. He'd be a dragon rider.

Arthur took Horatio's abandoned seat and watched his friend work. He didn't offer to help: Assembling your own card was a rite of passage. Besides,

Horatio was probably busy thinking about Light spells in an effort to force his card to become what he wanted.

Turning his attention inward, Arthur examined his small deck. It wasn't bad. Especially for a kid from the border.

Master of Skills (Legendary)

Return to Start (Rare)

Personal Space (Rare)

Charming Gentle-person (Uncommon)

Nullify Card (Common)

The Nullify Card had been an interesting find. Knowing that Kenzie would be on his case to put him in front of the next Rare egg that hatched, Arthur had decided to try assembling an Uncommon card first. He blamed a fit of early teenage rebellion.

Anyway, he had hoped for a combat or offensive magic skill and had received a Utility Skill to accurately predict the weather up to a week out within a fifty-mile radius.

This had some interesting applications. If Arthur was a farmer, knowing when to harvest and when to cover the crops would have been invaluable. Since Arthur wasn't a farmer—and never intended to be—he didn't want to add that card to his heart.

He took it to Kenzie, who hooked him up with a private card dealer. Arthur's gambling instincts told him to take a chance and tell the dealer about his Trap card problem.

The dealer proposed a trade. He had an unusual Common card with a very specific skill: the ability to nullify or reactivate a single card within someone's heart at will.

Since it would only work for one of the wielder's own heart cards, it had no combat value. Common cards could be like that. But it was invaluable for someone with a problematic card like Arthur's.

Arthur haggled and traded his Weather card for the Common plus some extra Uncommon shards.

Then he was able to add the Return to Start card back in his heart. The bruised ache that he had finally learned to ignore had healed at last.

His second attempt at assembling an Uncommon had given him his Charming Gentle-person card.

For up to eight hours within a twenty-four-hour period, his Charisma was increased by a full ten points.

Apparently, certain body enhancement cards were able to quantify traits, strengths, and weaknesses using numbers.

Did Arthur know his own Charisma stat? No, he did not. His card was only an Uncommon, and adding ten points was the beginning and end of its powers.

Did men seem to trust him, and women smile at him when he used it? Yes, they did.

Arthur liked to use it when he was on shift at Bob's Tavern. His tips went through the roof.

"Okay," Horatio said. "I'm ready."

Arthur stood and looked over the mostly assembled Rare card. Horatio had taken his cue from Arthur and set everything up except for a single corner piece.

He bit back the urge to rib his friend and tell him to think "light thoughts." Instead, Arthur just said, "You'll be fine."

Horatio's jaw firmed. "Of course I will." Then, almost defiantly, he clicked the last piece together.

There was a flash of light. Arthur craned his neck to look at the new card. The description was deceptively simple, but he knew it wasn't remotely what Horatio had wanted.

Second Helpings
Rare
Charm
Using mana, the wielder may create an exact material duplicate of any object. Size, rarity of material, personal stamina, and magical power are dependent on mana cost and experience level.

Horatio swore and turned away.

"By all rights," Arthur said, "that's an excellent power."

"That's what makes it worse," Horatio snarled. "I can't use this."

"You can trade it for something that will work with Sams."

But Horatio was too upset to listen. Turning, he headed for the door. "I need a drink." Then he stopped, winced, and went back to reluctantly snatch his new Rare card off the table.

He turned away before Arthur could see if Horatio put it in his heart or shoved it in his card anchor bag.

Arthur didn't offer to go along with him. He had long since become used to Horatio's moodiness. His friend wanted to be alone.

With a sigh, Arthur sat back at the table and pulled out a fresh piece of paper. Then he started drawing up a chart by memory of the months that expensive produce was in season. He hadn't been kidding about his storage space. If he did this right, he could make a killing.

Too bad it was off-season on truffles.

He was so engrossed he didn't hear the bells at first. Not until the large one down on the corner of the block started to toll again and again. Within moments, it was taken up by more down the street. Then a lighter tone as the common folk took up their own bells and started ringing for good luck.

Arthur had heard those bells twice before in his time here.

A new Rare egg had been laid.

CHAPTER 45

O ne silver?" Arthur replied with a tinge of fake outrage. "Surely you mean per case."

"Don't pull that on me. One silver per box, and there are four boxes to a case." The vegetable vendor he was haggling with crossed his arms over his chest. Arthur suspected the man ate solely off of what he didn't sell at his booth, because the man was as thin as a rail. Though Arthur had seen him lift heavy cases that would give him pause.

"Those prices are near criminal," Arthur said.

The vendor rolled his eyes. It was the end of the day, and it seemed that Arthur was coming up against the limit of his patience. "Avocados are a delicate fruit."

Aren't avocados a vegetable? Arthur thought but did not say.

The vendor continued. "They grow in the southern climates—my buyers trade down to Strawberry Moon Hive. They gotta be picked green and ripen on the way, which means we have fruit loss to pay for."

None of which was Arthur's problem, but his **Merchant** skills told him to let the man talk himself out.

The vegetable vendor was on a roll by now and lightly kicked the box with the side of his foot. "These will be ripe within the week, and they'll only stay ripe for a few days after that. Most chefs buy them now for their restaurant and make them into meals as they ripen for the next few days."

Arthur frowned. "These are all the boxes you have?"

"All the boxes worth selling."

He pretended to think about it, even though he had already made his game plan while the man had been speaking. "What about your loss boxes? Got any that are a little too ripe?"

The man stared at him. "Might be I got a few boxes of those," he said. "I know you're a cook, boy. Used to work for Barlow, yeah?"

"I did. I'm working full time in Bob's Tavern now." Barlow hadn't been happy to let him go, but he understood. Besides, the orphanage always had willing boys and girls to learn the trade—and who were willing to work for a lesser cost than Arthur was worth.

"Avocados grow brown and taste nutty when they're too ripe," the vendor warned.

"Good thing I plan to use them tonight," Arthur lied.

The vendor shrugged as if to say, *Your funeral.* Then he led Arthur to the back of the booth.

This was where the spoiled product was kept. Arthur had to wave away a small cloud of fruit flies that buzzed over a pallet of over-ripened tomatoes. Thankfully, none hovered over the avocados.

He bent to check a few by feel. The vendor was right. Most were perfectly ripe—meaning they would have to be used this very evening, which was annoying when you were buying in bulk—or just on the wrong side of overripe.

There were three boxes in total.

"I'll take them all off your hands for one silver," Arthur said. "That's a better price you'd get than tossing them out as garbage."

In the end, he arranged to have the boxes transported to Bob's storage, which was attached to the back of his kitchen.

He had a long-standing agreement with the man that he'd look the other way from Arthur's side-hustle products in exchange for a small fee.

If he understood his new card right, the items would keep fresh in his storage. Then it would be only a matter of waiting for the avocados to go off-season.

No one would care if they were slightly overripe if there were none to be had.

Lastly, Arthur went a few blocks north, across the next canal bridge to the much smellier animal yards.

It was time to experiment.

The piglet he'd purchased was criminally adorable. Only a few weeks old and small enough to be easily carried under one arm, he tried not to feel guilty over what he was about to do.

He sincerely hoped he understood the card's conditions correctly. One thing he had learned about cards was that one misunderstood word could severely alter a card's effects.

Take his Return to Start Trap card, for example. When activated, it required someone to attack him with their powers to trigger it.

But what qualified as an attack? An attempt to kill? A violation of his personal space? A scan that Arthur might consider intrusive?

There were reasons why he hadn't put it back in his heart until he had another card to nullify the effects.

So he didn't entirely trust the description of his newest Personal Space card. Time didn't pass for the objects inside, but what would it do to something living? Would the creature still need air? Would they notice any time difference at all?

Unfortunately, there was only one way to find out.

Arthur ducked in between two smelly tents and glanced around to make sure no one was looking. It was a habit to keep his abilities secret.

"Good luck," he said to the piglet as he mentally reached for the card. The piglet disappeared.

Arthur counted to thirty in his mind and reached for the piglet.

It reappeared back in his hands with a snort of surprise and then a high squeal—at least proving it was alive.

Arthur shoved it back into the storage space, waited another minute, and pulled it out.

It was in the middle of the same squeal.

Alive and well.

Shoving the very confused piglet back in, Arthur turned to the chicken vendors. Late-season chicks were cheap this time of the year. If he was smart, he could sell these same chicks at peak spring prices after winter.

A few minutes and a box of egg layers and meat chicks each later, he realized his new card came with another perk: an inventory list.

1 Suckling Piglet
21 Rockburry Chicks (F)
20 Dappled Chicks (F)
1 Dappled Chick (M)

Arthur's jaw dropped. "That son of a bitch sold me a rooster in place of a hen!" He reached and pulled it out. The little chick was a dappled peeping ball of fluff in his palm. In truth, at this age it looked no different than its sisters. Its rooster nature would only show later on, and by then the vendor would be well away.

Arthur thought about returning the thing for another hen-chick, then sighed. Well, maybe someone would want a rooster in spring. He put it back with its sisters.

Then he considered what else he should buy. The storage space was plenty large. He could fit horses in there if he wanted.

No, better to see how the chickens and piglet held out first.

With that decided, he turned back for his apartment. Unfortunately, his boots were caked in dark muck mixed with mud from tromping around in animal pens. And he had a long way to walk back home, stinking like manure.

Time for a shortcut.

He toggled the Nullify option off his Trap card and walked down the next street where he knew some buskers performed for tips.

Sure enough, one man showed off with a temporary enchantment on bits of grass that were knotted into the shape of animals. The little figures were empowered with enough magic to dance for hours on command. Cheaply made and sold, they were a delight to all children under the age of eight.

As Arthur came up, the man was finishing his sale of a grass horse to a young father and his child. The tiny horse galloped up and down the girl's outstretched arm. She watched with wide, delighted eyes.

As soon as the busker was done, he turned to Arthur. "How can I help you, good sir? A present for your son or daughter?"

Arthur slapped a half copper on the man's table. "Have one of your straw birds there fly full force at me. Ramming speed, if you please."

"I'm . . . sorry?"

"You heard me. Oh, wait a moment." He bent and unlaced his mucky boots and stepped out of them, holding them gingerly in one hand. "Okay, I'm ready now."

The man looked at Arthur like he was insane, but money was money. He took the half copper and gestured to a grass-made seagull that was flapping in circles overhead.

The two-inch creature turned and made a beeline for Arthur's forehead—right between the eyes.

Arthur didn't feel the tap of impact. There was a flash of light.

Trap Card conditions met.
Return to Start: Activated.

And in the next moment, he found himself lying on top of his own bed, boots safely in hand to keep the mud off his blanket.

Yes, he liked to keep his magic to himself, but that stunt had just saved him an hour's smelly walk. Sometimes, he let himself indulge.

"Well, I was *hoping* to run into you, but this will work too."

The voice startled him so badly that he nearly dropped the gross boots on his own chest.

Sitting up, he saw Kenzie standing in his bedroom, hip cocked and looking unimpressed.

His jaw dropped. "What are you doing here?"

She ignored the question. "Tell me you're not going to see the Rare egg tonight dressed like that."

"Of course not, but how did you get in . . ." His words trailed off as he looked past her to see a half-open window.

A moment later, the view was dominated by a silver head and one big eye, which gazed in. "Hello, Arthur," Marteen said pleasantly. She had grown into a graceful dragon. One that was tall enough to look into his second-story window. "Why do you smell like pig droppings?"

"Because I was stomping around in a pigsty to catch a piglet."

"Ah, that makes sense," the dragon said airily and dropped her head, no doubt to sniff around some passersby.

"Do I even want to know?" Kenzie asked and rolled her eyes when Arthur grinned at her. "Anyway, I came by to remind you to show up tonight *and* because neither of my recruits bothered to tell me what Rare cards they got." She leveled a look at him. "I know you two were finally putting together your shards. So, spill. Did Sourpuss get his Light card?"

Arthur winced. "No."

"Anything good enough to trade for one?"

He hesitated and shook his head. "I think it's too good to trade, so he's in a bind."

Her eyebrows rose, but Arthur refused to say more. A man's card was his own business.

Yes, he'd wanted a combat card, though he was more than happy with his new storage space, but he would have been equally happy with Horatio's new ability. The things he could double . . .

"So he's in a snit." Kenzie crossed her arms. "That boy has got to get over his moodiness. It's not like life suddenly gets fair when you're a dragon rider."

Arthur started to nod, then a bit of common sense kicked in. The corners of Kenzie's mouth were turned down. She was upset.

"Did something happen?" he asked.

"What? You get an empathy card, too?"

"No, it's just obvious you're unhappy."

Kenzie let out a sigh and sat down next to him, apparently not caring he smelled like a farm. "I haven't had a recruit link with a dragon over Common rank in over six months. And you and Mr. Dark and Gloomy are still my only Rare recruits. I need a good showing for this egg, but . . ." She bit her lip.

"But?" Arthur asked.

She sighed. "They're saying that on top of being a Rare, this egg is probably a high-grade shimmer. Every noble brat in the kingdom's going to want a crack at it."

Which meant Arthur and Horatio would be at the bottom of the totem pole. Again.

Not that Arthur cared. No Rare would pick him with a Legendary card in his heart. And Horatio had his own sights set on Sams.

"If something doesn't change soon, I'll get kicked back down to level seven," Kenzie continued. "Marteen's too large to fit in one of those apartments, which means she sleeps outside. Or I can start flying the scourge-eruptions."

"They'd make you do that?" he asked. "But you don't have combat cards."

She waved a hand. "I can buy a Common spell card on the cheap. But no, we'd probably be Lobos—on the rescue team. You know, calming people out of hysterics. I do some of that for the bad ones when they're brought in, but to be surrounded by all that emotion, all the time . . ." She winced.

A scourge-eruption would be an ugly place for a pair that dealt with emotion and auras.

Old guilt pricked at Arthur's heart. Kenzie might not be looking at a demotion if people knew she had recruited a boy with a Legendary card.

Then again, those eggs were laid so rarely . . . maybe it wouldn't be any use to her at all.

And as bad as he felt for her losing a level, it wasn't worth his life.

Kenzie must have seen or sensed his guilt and misunderstood it, because she added briskly, "Don't worry about it. We'll just have to fly out to baronies the other silvers haven't recruited from in a while."

"Are there any left?" Arthur asked.

Wolf Moon was a small hive yet had a disproportionate amount of silvers. Kenzie and Marteen were the youngest pair, which meant they had the last choice for territories.

"I might be gone for a bit," Kenzie admitted. "But not until that Rare's hatched. Which means you and Horatio have to do your best to get that hatchling's attention."

That was a mandatory waste of time in his case, but Arthur was distracted.

Deep inside his mind, the outer casing of a long-dormant seed of an idea cracked—just enough to show a hint of green within.

CHAPTER 46

That night's occasion was called the "Rare Promenade" which told Arthur a stuffy noble had been the one to think it up.

It was an event that was equal parts about the egg and political shadow boxing.

Arthur dressed his best for the night, which was a step above his normal evening work uniform: black pressed pants, a deep-green shirt with copper buttons, and a dark vest. As usual, he tied his drawstring card anchor bag to a spot inside the vest, which allowed the bag to rest over his heart. He had purchased the vest mostly for that feature.

In his bag, he kept a small handful of Rare card shards—all middle card pieces—as well as a few Uncommon shards.

The shards represented more wealth than well-off families in outer kingdom towns had access to. But in the hive, he was nothing special.

Arthur found he liked it that way. It was so much easier to be overlooked. That way he could practice his skills in peace.

The creak of a hinge from behind turned his attention to the door.

Horatio came into their apartment with a default look of discontentment carved on his face. He was dressed in his work clothing, the apron tied around his waist still spotted with flour.

Like Arthur, he had eventually moved on from Barlow's restaurant. Now he worked at an exclusive shop that made celebration cakes for the upper class. Though Horatio had a face sulky enough to spoil good milk, his cake decorations were delicate, floral, and in high demand.

Arthur thought it was mildly hilarious.

Horatio took Arthur's wardrobe in at a glance. Then he let out a long, put-upon sigh. "Rare Promenade tonight?"

"Kenzie broke into our apartment just to tell me about it," Arthur confirmed with a nod to the window. "We've got to remember to lock that."

"And she has to learn when she isn't wanted," Horatio muttered.

Arthur shrugged. He got the impression Kenzie was lonely. He'd never seen her in the company of other dragon riders and suspected Marteen's unusual level of talent for an Uncommon made them jealous. That, or if Kenzie carelessly broke into other people's living quarters, he could see how they'd get tired of it.

Horatio moved to his "room," which, like Arthur's, was some sheets tacked up in a corner around the bed.

"This egg's going to be a pain in the ass," Horatio called. "Purples and blues have been flying in noble kids all day."

"It's supposed to be a high-grade shimmer," Arthur confirmed. Rares drew enough ambitious nobles on their own, but a shimmer quality added additional power and mystique.

Arthur paused. "Are you going to try for it?"

What he was not quite asking was: Are you going to keep your Second Helping card?

Horatio didn't answer for a moment. He pushed back the sheets and strode out, looking fairly presentable in clean pants and a new cream-colored shirt. Moving to the table, he grabbed a tie and pulled his dark, lanky hair back. "Don't know yet," he grumped. "I want to take a look at that egg first."

That surprised Arthur. Horatio had only spoken about linking up with Sams. Then again, Second Helping would be a powerful card in the right hands. Maybe Horatio was holding out secret hopes.

Once the mother dragon left her clutch in the care of the hive personnel, the Rare egg was moved into a separate chamber. Then the circus truly began.

After entering the hive entrance, Arthur and Horatio were forced to show Kenzie's recruitment chip at no less than three checkpoints along the way.

They were treated to the sight of a blustering noble family getting thrown out on their ear. The nobles had managed to either intimidate or bribe their way past the first checkpoint, but the second set of guards would allow them to go no further.

Only people who were qualified and had been vetted by hive silvers were allowed to see the Rare egg.

The chamber itself was festooned with banners in Wolf Hive colors of silver, tan, and white. It was lit with so many torches and candles that it was nearly bright as day. However, hive workers with wind-based or air-purifying utility cards were placed here and there to obliquely funnel the smoke out of the way.

The egg was located in the back of the room, placed up on a molded rock stage so all could gaze upon it. It was bracketed by two guards in hive colors, always on alert.

A line of people was allowed to slowly walk past it, and more guards ensured no one stopped or lingered for long. The line would circle the outer perimeter of the room and come again for another pass.

On entering, Arthur dutifully took his place in line. He'd been through this twice so far. Though other Rare eggs had brought in nobles, this one was on a whole other level. The promenade had barely begun, and the line already stretched around the room.

Though Arthur's clothing was a fine standard for a non-noble, he looked drab next to the fine silks and tailored suits the other boys wore. Those in turn were outshone by the dresses the noble girls pulled out, complete with exquisite hairdos that must have taken hours.

They looked like they were going to a fine gala at the king's palace. Not just walking past an egg.

Arthur exchanged glances with Horatio, who rolled his eyes.

Well, it was nice his friend wasn't intimidated.

I have noble blood, too, Arthur reminded himself—though quietly.

It was enough for him to straighten his shoulders and keep his eyes focused ahead, as if he was truly interested in the prize.

Despite the guards' efforts, the line moved slower the closer they were to the egg. Soon, Arthur had a good view. It was clear why it had gained so much attention.

Unusually large, the top of the shell would have come up to his waist. Every inch of it glittered with the reflective light cast from the torches and candles. It was as if it had been encrusted with glittering diamonds, though here and there were spots of other gemstones, blue-eyed sapphires, red rubies, and pink opals.

All of this was an illusion. The real dragon's shell was much like a chicken egg's. But Arthur couldn't help thinking that it glittered with the hatchling's reflective power.

What kind of a card would that hatchling hold? he wondered. *Something to do with earth? Was it a Rare-quality Treasure Seeker?*

How could its power help fight the scourglings?

Looking around, Arthur doubted any of these fancy nobles had ambitions to link with a dragon to fight. No, this Rare egg represented power and prestige.

All chatter within the line stopped as they stepped close to the egg. Now people had looks of intense concentration on their faces. Some looked outright constipated with the effort.

Dragon eggs were different from birds in that they hatched when they hatched, without a strict timeline. More than once, a hatchling had surprised everyone by breaking its shell and springing at someone with a perfectly matched card.

Most figured it couldn't hurt to concentrate on their own card to nudge the hatchling inside one way or another. There was much mystique around dragons.

Maybe the baby dragon's card was still forming. Maybe the decision could be influenced.

Arthur knew he didn't have a chance with the baby dragon. Instead, he took the opportunity to glance around, memorizing faces and categorizing reactions.

Some nobles looked bored, as if they didn't care one way or another. One of the girls behind him looked about ready to cry for longing of the hatchling. Horatio looked like he was trying to glare a hole through the shell.

Was that Horatio being Horatio, or was he trying to reach out to the egg?

The motion of the line took them past the stage, and most lost their intense expressions.

The promenade would continue nightly. Thankfully, Arthur wouldn't be expected to show up *every* evening. The ambitious nobles would, but he had to work.

This was only the first stage. If the egg didn't hatch within thirty days, prospective dragon riders would be allowed to ascend the stage and touch and spend time with the egg to encourage the hatchling inside to come out and greet them.

Then, if the egg hatched out naturally on its own, the nobles would be allowed to greet the newborn one by one.

Position to be the first to touch the egg or greet the new Rare hatchling was fierce. The hive would announce an official rank list at the end of this week, with the prospectives listed by noble rank, then would work its way down.

These ranks would move up and down as card duels were offered and bribes to drop out were accepted.

The fact was, it would be a minor miracle for a nobody like Arthur to get in. Even Horatio was usually listed well above him due to his father's former rank.

The only way Arthur would ever get in to see the hatchling was if the egg failed to hatch and then the hatchling failed to link up to any of the nobles and any of the well-off merchant and craft guild scions who bought their way in *and* the children of the hive elite, not to mention any ambitious card duelists.

Then Arthur would get his turn to meet the unlinked hatchling.

It made him glad to have his Legendary card. With it in his heart, he didn't have a snowball's chance in a firestorm of linking with the Rare.

But all the drama was a lot of fun to watch.

More importantly, all the new noble visitors to the hive were profitable.

Do you wish to equip Performer Class?

With practiced ease, Arthur switched out his Scholar Class with his Performer Class.

The world felt a little dimmer, as if he couldn't make connections that he had before. That was three points of his intelligence draining away.

Conversely, he felt the casual gazes of others sharpen on him. Even nobles automatically made way when Arthur brushed past, and smiles were easily given.

That was his three points of Charisma, thanks to the Performer Class. The two additional points to his Dexterity didn't hurt either.

Achieving his Performer Class last year made him realize the same skill could be used in different classes. His **Acting** skill had been long since added to his Thief Class. But it was also the foundation of his Performer Class.

He supposed that made sense. A carpenter could build a house, a business, a wooden stage, and many other things. Why shouldn't a skill be multi-disciplinary?

He needed his extra Charisma and Dexterity to thread his way through the hive tunnels while avoiding stepping on noble toes. It was packed. When he got to Bob's Tavern, it was even more so, with a line waiting out the door for tables.

Arthur ducked into the shadowy side entrance that led back into the kitchen. There, he was met with the boxes of produce he'd purchased from the market. Whoops. He'd forgotten about those.

Bob, who was walking past, noticed his arrival. He nodded to the boxes. "These yours?"

"Yes, sir."

"Get them out of the way. We're going to be busy tonight, and we don't want anyone tripping and breaking their neck. Then I'll need you up front for the rest of the night. You're to provide the *full* experience to these rich idiots."

Arthur nodded, glad he'd already switched the cards.

He picked up the boxes one by one and walked them to the back. When he was certain no one was looking, he shoved the boxes into his Personal Space instead. From the outside, it looked like the full boxes popped out of his hands into nothingness.

That done, he took a moment to retrieve his rooster chick to check its health.

The baby chick peeped and struggled to jump out of his hand but looked healthy and well for being in storage for hours.

Satisfied, Arthur put it back and walked to the bar. Time for a show.

He'd achieved his Performer Class while copying the antics of some of the more flamboyant bartenders. Technically, Arthur was too young to serve alcohol, but Bob paid the guards to look the other way. It helped that Arthur's vest and clothing gave him a mature air.

He'd finally hit that growth spurt, and while he hadn't bulked up, he had become tall.

The bar was packed with nobles demanding outlandish drinks, the finest wines, and the best-brewed beer. Bob's two other bartenders were hard-pressed to keep up.

Arthur stepped in and started his show.

He didn't just grab a wine bottle. He flipped it over his back, caught it as it came down in the front, and poured. Multiple glasses were poured with him holding the bottle high above and somehow filling them equally without spilling a drop. For larger orders, he stacked the delicate glasses in a pyramid and did the same.

Soon, half-drunk customers noticed and started calling out requests. Arthur grabbed three wine bottles—dummies he'd placed ahead of time, filled with colored water—and started juggling them in the air.

Hoots and laughter accompanied his show.

Normally, Arthur would catch the dummy bottles by the neck and bow to the customers while subtly switching a fake bottle for a real one, which he'd use to pour.

This time, a male voice drawled over the laughter, "Look, Father, we've got a jester for our entertainment! Let's see if he can handle this!"

Movement flashed in the corner of Arthur's eye. He caught an empty wine bottle on pure instinct and flung it up with the three dummies to the oohs of the crowd.

But the weight of the empty bottle threw his rhythm off. The empty bottle went too high and took too long to come down. Arthur's juggling rhythm bobbled before he caught the empty again and threw it to join the others.

"Another!" the same man called.

Arthur felt like accidentally tossing one of the bottles at the man's head. He might not have a choice. Keeping five items in the air was possible with his **Juggling** 9 skill, but not for very long.

This time he was ready and caught the new bottle as it came in. The new bottle was smaller and slimmer than the others, which added even more difficulty.

Arthur was managing—barely—and had decided to catch the rest of the bottles and bow out after the next couple of throws.

Then a voice boomed out, "That's low entertainment, Penn. I wonder if he can juggle a broken bottle?"

It wasn't what the man said. It was the voice. His father's voice.

Arthur fumbled his next grab, and the dummy wine bottle slipped past his fingers and hit the floor. It didn't break, but the next one did, sloshing colored water behind the bar. Arthur barely heard the mingled laughs, cheers, and boos. He managed to catch the last dummy and the two empties and turned to stare.

The heckler had his father's voice, and a version of his father's face. Tall and broad with a neatly trimmed beard his father never had, streaked with gray.

He stared at Arthur with laughing, arrogant blue eyes.

A foggy, half-forgotten memory in Arthur's distant childhood swam up in his mind.

This was his father's brother, Arthur's uncle.

CHAPTER 47

Arthur's uncle laughed uproariously.

All Arthur could do was stare. His mind was scrambled in shock. He wasn't sure if the man was laughing out of casual cruelty because Arthur had bungled his juggling, or if he recognized Arthur and had decided this played a fine trick.

Then Arthur's mind snapped into action again. He realized the man was red-faced under his bearded cheeks. He was drunk.

One thick arm was slung around the shoulders of a boy who looked very much like his father. Perhaps eighteen years old, the boy was burly and broad with the same square chin and dark hair.

That boy must be his cousin.

All these impressions came and went in a flash. Bob stomped over and glared down at the mess of spilled colored water and broken glass. "What is this?"

"Nobles thought they'd have some fun."

Bob's lips turned down into a frown, then he nodded. "Get a mop and bucket. Hurry up."

Not getting yelled at was likely the best Arthur could hope for. Knowing Bob, he had seen the situation brewing but had not been fast enough to stop it.

By the time Arthur returned, Bob had taken over his spot in the back of the bar, selling drinks to those who had been waiting.

The nobles who'd caused the problem had new mugs of beer in hand. The last thing Bob would want to do was insult them. Of course it was Arthur's fault he had screwed up while juggling, not theirs.

Burning resentment toward the nobles was not new, but Arthur wasn't used to feeling it so strongly since he had started living at the hive.

The rest of the night went by uneventfully. Arthur kept an eye on his uncle and cousin, but they only returned to the bar for new drinks. Neither paid special

attention to him. It seemed once they had their fun upsetting his juggling routine, they'd put him completely out of mind.

Or it was some kind of a ruse. But try as he might, he couldn't figure out why
they would bother.

Little by little, Arthur relaxed. The shock wore off, and he reminded himself
that he didn't take after his father in coloring or build, being tall and thin. He
figured he would bulk out eventually, though that day hadn't yet come.

Was it possible for his uncle to link him to his brother's child? A boy he
hadn't seen in a decade, and who's looks didn't take after the male side of the
family? A boy he probably thought was dead?

Maybe. But likely not while as drunk as the man looked to be.

By the end of the night, the noble was boneless and leaning against his own
son as they walked out of the tavern. Neither one glanced back.

No, they didn't act like they recognized Arthur.

But Arthur knew them, and he was determined to find out more.

The second night of the promenade had markedly fewer people.

Arthur figured most knew with so many nobles in attendance, they would
not get so much as a sniff at the Rare egg.

Arthur was not there for the egg.

Tonight, Arthur had dressed differently for the occasion, in a white shirt
and dull gray pants. On top of that, he wore a long dark cloak that would help
obscure his shape.

His cousin hadn't been as drunk as his father had been, so Arthur had washed
his hair in fresh lemon juice to lighten it a few degrees. Then he brushed it back,
away from his face, with oil to keep it in place. It gave his face a severe, pointy
look.

Looking in the mirror, he imagined he could have fit in with the nobles, had
his life turned out differently.

Lastly, Arthur switched out his Performer Class card for his Scholar Card
again, which effectively traded a boost in Charisma for a boost in Intelligence.
Then he changed the focus of the Nullify Card to dampen his Charming Gentle-
person card, further reducing his Charisma.

The last thing he wanted was to stand out tonight.

Upon entering the chamber with the egg, Arthur stood against one of the
walls. He wasn't alone. Many nobles saw this opportunity less as a chance at
a Rare egg and more to mingle with their peers on neutral ground. There was
much laughter, flirting, and fine wine poured out by hive staff.

Arthur drifted to a forgotten corner, licked his fingers, and snuffed out some
of the candles nearby. Then he stealthed into the shadows, drawing up his cloak
to further conceal himself. From there, he watched.

His cousin was in the circling line for the egg. Like many others, he used this opportunity to make connections with other young, ambitious nobles—and to talk to a few ladies who batted their eyes in his direction, but he went quiet every time he came close to the egg.

His eyes were half closed as he concentrated on the developing hatchling.

Arthur's eyes narrowed. He'd wracked his brain all day, and the only memory he had of his cousin was during play—running after a bounding puppy on a green field. But it was so old and forgotten that he might be imagining the entire scene, or it might have been a different boy. Arthur caught the name Penn in the bar, but that might not even be his full name.

Some two-thirds forgotten memory told him Penn was his uncle's oldest son. If that were the case, why lose him to the hive?

Had his uncle fallen out of favor thanks to Arthur's father?

It seemed reasonable. Except . . .

The fine-cut clothing Penn wore was simple in design. It was a deep-green tunic with brown edging. Emblazoned on the shoulder was a pin of silver: a broad-leafed oak tree stretched above with the bare roots sinking into the ground below.

Arthur knew that crest. It had been painted on his mother's plates.

Was that the crest of his house?

Beneath Arthur's cloak, his hands curled into fists.

When his cousin left for the night, Arthur followed.

He had long since become used to the twisty hive tunnel system. It was all new to the visiting nobles, and they were much too important to waste time wandering around lost. So the higher class paid for and received attendants to escort them to the egg chamber, their quarters, and to important locations in the hive.

Hives in general were infamous as a place to collect new cards. So when an influx of nobles came in, the commissaries hiked up their prices accordingly. Arthur had checked in yesterday and found the prices for cards to be the same as in city shops.

He hoped his cousin stopped by one now and was fleeced out his noble nose.

Instead, the attendant directed them up and up, all the way to level five. This was quite high for a non-dragon rider.

It meant his uncle and cousin had wealth, rank, or both.

Arthur followed at a distance, staying a few tunnel bends back and only getting glimpses of his quarry. He tracked them mostly by sound.

He sped up only when they reached the level area for hive guest apartments. All of these were on the outer wall of the hive with windows looking out to the magnificent sight of the city below.

Arthur walked past the group as the attendant stopped to open the door for his cousin. He glanced to note the number over the door.

His cousin didn't look his way at all.

* * *

That night, Arthur found he couldn't sleep. He lay in bed, listening to Horatio snore on the other side of the room. His right hand rubbed over his heart.

It felt like there was a lump of coal, long banked, lodged in his chest. It had darkened over his years in the hive.

Now a blast of cold wind had stoked that dormant fire. The coal was glowing.

His noble cousin had come to his hive, finely dressed, wearing the insignia of his family. In all probability, he lived the life Arthur should have had.

Arthur had experienced more injustices in his life than he could count.

Now, he found he couldn't let this one go.

One benefit of working in a tavern was that Arthur's off hours were in the late morning and early afternoon. Times that enabled him to get chores done.

Or sneak into places he should not be, counting on others to be out and about.

It had taken two days of discreet watching. When Arthur saw his uncle and cousin leave the hive entrance to explore the city, Arthur made his way in.

He weaved his way through the tunnels, doing his best to look purposeful and as if he belonged. No one stopped him.

No one was in the stretch of tunnels that led to the level-five guest apartments, either. That could change at any moment. He had to be quick.

Arthur put his **Lock-Picking** skill, now at level 15, to the test.

It took him less than a minute to gain access to his uncle's apartment.

CHAPTER 48

Arthur opened the door a crack and saw darkness beyond. No candles were lit. He swiftly stepped in and shut the door behind him, heart beating fast as he listened for any sign he had been noticed from outside, or from within.

All was quiet.

The only light came in through the windows, and the curtains were currently drawn. He stepped across the room, barking his shin once on a low piece of furniture.

Pushing the curtains back to let in the light, he looked around and was shocked at the state of the room. Dirty clothes were strewn about everywhere, as well as dishes left over from earlier meals—most still containing crusts of bread and glasses stained with the dregs of wine.

His **Tidying** skill, which had gotten quite advanced over the last few years while working in the kitchens and cleaning up after himself, itched at his mind.

Ignoring it, he looked around. This apartment was meant for important guests and had two individual bedrooms as well as a private privy.

Arthur stepped to the first bedroom. Unsurprisingly, the bed was unmade. Half of the pillows were still scattered on the floor.

Didn't these people know how to clean up after themselves? Why hadn't any hive attendants checked on this apartment or done any cleaning for them?

Arthur didn't have much experience tending to the needs of visiting nobles, but he knew most brought an entourage of footmen, maids, and other couriers. Arthur had concocted a story in his head of needing someone to sign off for a bill left over from the bar, in case he ran into any of them.

But not only was the apartment deserted, it seemed no one was attending his uncle or cousin.

The first bedroom belonged to his cousin, judging by the style of clothing strewn everywhere. Arthur hunted around but didn't find anything of note. Not even a coin to take.

He moved on to the second, larger bedroom. This also had an undone bed, but most importantly the writing table was strewn with paperwork.

With eagerness, Arthur started reading.

Most of it was correspondence to other nobles. Talking about the state of the fields they shared along a mutual border. It seemed the harvest wasn't as good as his uncle had hoped.

His uncle's signature was Duke Lional Rowantree, with a wax seal impressed with what he suspected was the top of a signet ring.

It wasn't a surprise, but it still hit like a punch to the gut. Arthur leaned over, breathing in deep.

His father had told him that the king had given the duchy to one of his friends.

Did Arthur's father not know? Did he just not want to go into the whole, sad story? Or had something happened in the last few years?

Had his uncle betrayed his father?

Gritting his teeth, he shuffled through the remaining paperwork, scanning over it as fast as his **Reading** skill would allow.

More incomprehensible correspondence, but a few choice letters with the same simple letterhead, had the first few sentences inquiring about the state of the family before moving directly to the heart of the matter: the duke planned to sell a part of the family's card library.

Arthur's lip lifted from his teeth in an involuntary sneer.

"That's *my* library!" he hissed, and continued to dig through the letters. It seemed that the duke was writing to all the noble families, minor and major, who had come to the hive.

Setting the parchment down, Arthur went through the desk for more. There were only supplies.

Finally, he searched through the duke's bags, letting his **Thieving** skill guide him. He found no card shards or coins—not a surprise, as the duke likely had a card anchor bag and would carry any personal wealth on himself.

However, he did find a list written out in different handwriting from the duke's writing, neat as a line of printed text from a book. At first, none of it made sense. He almost put it back, thinking it to be about crop yields until the acronyms caught his attention.

MoB (L)

LR (R)

UL (R)

EB (R)

MH (U)

And so on, with ten more U's followed by twenty C's.

Legendary, Rare, Uncommon, Common.

This was a list of cards. He had no idea what the acronyms meant, but he assumed they were the names of the cards. There had to be a key somewhere. Arthur searched through the luggage but found nothing.

Perhaps the duke kept the key with him. The cards, too, might be kept in an anchor bag.

These were the cards he was trying to sell off. One of them was a Legendary.

The last pieces came together in his mind.

The lack of additional hired help. The fact that the duke's eldest son was vying for a dragon when that was a position for lesser sons. Parceling out powerful cards like they were common goods.

They were in financial difficulties.

Good, Arthur thought viciously. Better that the king take back the land than to see a family traitor on it.

Of course, he had no idea of the depth of his uncle's betrayal . . . but he was certain it was there.

In any case, he had lingered long enough. Every minute he spent in this apartment was a risk.

Arthur replaced the luggage and papers back where he found them. The general disarray helped cover his tracks.

Arthur cracked open the front door and looked out to the corridor beyond. No one was within sight.

He stepped out and straightened his shoulders as if he belonged there and had nothing to hide . . . and quickly made his way out.

He was about to round the corner before he almost, quite literally, ran into his cousin.

Both boys were brought up short, eye to eye.

Quickly ducking his head, Arthur mumbled an apology and made a move to step around him.

A hand landed on his shoulder. "Hold on a second. I know you, don't I?"

Almost involuntarily, Arthur looked back up to his cousin's face. It was . . . not a bad face, he admitted grudgingly. Compared to any boy in the border village, Penn would have been downright handsome. Clear skin, a broadly muscled frame, wide mouth and light-blue eyes. His tousled, curly hair was dark, and he wore clothing of a fine cut.

The look in his eyes wasn't of anger, just puzzlement. He clearly knew Arthur's face but couldn't say from where. The alcohol the other night hadn't helped.

He had to act quickly before he connected him to the juggling bartender. "I was at the promenade for the Rare egg," Arthur said with a quick dip of his head. "Trying my luck, you know."

Penn's face cleared. "Oh, that's right." Then to Arthur's shock, he stuck out a hand. "Pennrow Rowantree. Call me Penn."

Arthur's **Acting** skill gave him enough improvisational ability that he didn't hesitate. He simply blurted out the first name that came to mind. "Ernest Kane."

"Kane?" Penn asked.

Two entire seconds into this lie, and Arthur already deeply regretted it. "I'm not surprised you haven't heard of the name. We're a small barony out near the borderlands. We're nothing like your family's lands, I'm sure. You're the duke's son, if I'm not mistaken?"

As he spoke, he let his words become more clipped and precise in the fashion of some of the nobles he had heard.

"That's right, my father is the duke," Penn said, happy to talk about himself, like most nobles. "Well, Ernest, based on your outfit, I bet you're going to try your hand at the duels today."

Arthur's mind briefly stalled out. Duels? Then he remembered that nobles challenged each other for the first to see the egg. "Ah, yes," he invented, happy to take up the excuse for why he was dressed simply by noble standards. "I was hoping to get a lay of the land before the duels began." He gestured down the corridor.

"Well, speaking of the lay of the land . . ." Penn cast a chagrined look over his shoulder. "I seem to have left my hive guide behind. Would you mind waiting here a moment while I change? Then you and I can go to the dueling grounds together. You know the way?"

"I do," Arthur confirmed, just to encourage his cousin to go away.

"Good man." Penn clapped him on the shoulder. Then he made his way back down the tunnel to the apartments. "I won't be gone long!" he called again.

The moment the man's door closed, Arthur turned and sprinted down the tunnel.

He only got a few steps before he pulled himself up short.

He had questions about the dutchy, about his cousin and uncle . . . and about their cards.

Plus, Penn had made a point of recognizing him. If he ran now, he would have to stay out of his cousin's way for the foreseeable future.

If he walked away, he would waste a prime opportunity and put himself under suspicion.

Arthur turned and walked back.

When Penn walked out of his apartment a few minutes later, he found "Ernest Kane" still waiting for him.

CHAPTER 49

Are you certain we take the right-hand tunnel?" Penn asked with a tone in his voice that implied he wasn't asking at all. "I'm fairly certain the dueling grounds are to the left."

Arthur knew for a fact they needed to go the right. The left was a shortcut to the hatchling nests.

But it didn't take a genius to know that acting too knowledgeable about the layout of the hive would lead to suspicion. As much as he wanted to tell Penn off on principle alone, Arthur knew he had to be smart.

He was trying to ingratiate himself with the other noble and gain his trust. The best way to do that with the upper class was to give them their way.

He hesitated for a moment. "I think you may be correct."

"I've always been blessed with an excellent sense of direction," Penn said as he confidently led Arthur down the wrong tunnel.

Soon enough, they stumbled right onto the nesting grounds.

It had been a while since Arthur had last seen this place. He didn't often like to visit, as hatchlings looked at each new arrival with hope in their eyes. That hope dimmed when they felt the incompatible card in Arthur's chest. Not to mention he was always in danger of running into a sensitive baby silver who might start asking uncomfortable questions about the high-powered magic it sensed in him.

So Arthur was shocked at the changes he saw. There were three pens more than before, and every one of them was full of Common and Uncommon hatchlings. Some were almost as big as a donkey. They'd been there awhile.

He flashed to Kenzie telling him the hive admin was pressuring her and Marteen to have active recruits.

What was going on with all of the Commons and Uncommons?

Penn stopped short upon seeing the cavern. "What—Oh. This where the young beasts are kept?" He paused awkwardly. "They are . . . rather cute."

Arthur nodded, watching a few purples tumbling over each other in a wrestling match.

One red dragon spotted them and dropped a torn blanket it had been using to play tug-of-war with a green. "Over here! Over here!" it called in a high, childish voice.

Almost all play stopped as dozens of heads shot up to look around at them.

A dirt brown dragon standing nearby sagged so dramatically its wings spread on the floor. "Don't bother. They don't smell right."

A chorus of "awws" followed its pronouncement.

Penn shifted uncomfortably. "What do you think they mean by that?"

"Because of our Rare cards," Arthur said.

A harried-looking nest attendant came up to them, bowing awkwardly. Luckily, it wasn't someone Arthur recognized.

Arthur nodded to her. "Do you know the way to the dueling grounds?"

"Ah, yes, milord. You want to go down that tunnel. Three right turns at the junctions should do it." She dipped in a little curtsey before rushing off.

Huh. She'd seen him as a noble. That had never happened before. Then again, Penn looked every inch a noble, so it must be the company he kept.

"You are a strange sort of noble," Penn commented as they made their way back.

"Why?" Arthur couldn't help a small jab. "Because my sense of direction is better than yours?"

"You asked the help for directions, not demanded."

Arthur rolled his eyes. "She isn't the help, seeing as she doesn't work for me."

"Still." Penn went quiet, and Arthur had to work not to show any nervousness and act like he didn't care about Penn's opinion one way or another. "Still," Penn continued, "it's not a bad thing. Some of our peers are insufferable, don't you think?"

Arthur chuckled nervously, not wanting to fall into a trap of agreeing or not.

Thankfully, Penn let it drop.

Arthur hadn't visited the hive's private dueling grounds often, either. He and Horatio went to the main city arena as often as they could during festivals and occasional competitions. The only ones to use the much smaller hive dueling grounds were riders who had conflicts that couldn't be resolved, or more commonly, bored noble brats.

Most of tonight was to be blustering and shadowboxing. Arthur preferred the official matches.

When he and Penn walked in, to his relief, no one was currently dueling. All the young nobles stood around in plain dueling clothing. However, the cut and fabric were still of exquisite quality. Much better than his own.

He felt eyes pass over him and land on Penn, who was much more richly dressed.

Quickly, Arthur deactivated the Nullify on his Charming Gentle-person card and activated it on his Trap card instead.

Some of those gazes returned to touch on him briefly before moving away.

I am a noble, he reminded himself. It was meant to be a lie. *I need to ingratiate myself with Penn today. Earn his trust.*

"Come on. Let's see what trouble we can stir up," Penn said and led Arthur to a knot of other boys who were talking with glasses of wine in hand.

One of the boys raised a glass to their arrival. "Penn! Just who I wanted to see." He turned to a side table behind him and poured out glasses for Penn and Arthur, though he was careful to shield the wine bottle with his body. Turning back, he gave them their drinks, eyes on Penn. "Go on. Give it a go."

Penn raised the glass to his nose and gave the wine a performative sniff. Then he sipped and made a face. "Well, I can tell you that this is definitely not to my taste."

"He's stalling," another boy said with a grin.

"I know I would be shamed if this swill came from my vineyards," Penn said, and the three other boys chuffed a laugh.

Curious, Arthur took a taste. His **Sommelier** skill kicked in. Penn was right. This wasn't very good at all. Practically cooking wine.

More than that, he had tasted this vintage before.

"This is that crap they sell from around here, isn't it?"

Instantly, all attention was on him. Arthur pretended not to notice, swirling the deep red wine in his glass and taking another sip.

"Yeah? Which vineyard," the boy who had poured asked.

Arthur smiled. "I'd hate to jump ahead. I believe Penn still had to make his guess?"

Penn had a glint of amusement in his eye. It was obvious to Arthur he didn't know where the wine had come from, but Arthur had provided him a valuable hint.

Due to the Wolf Moon's northern climate, local vineyards only grew the hardiest of varieties. The taste reflected that. These wines were better for cooking than drinking.

But those who knew that much already had a good guess. There were a few major vineyards near the hive.

"This is a Half Moon vintage. Those quaint fields on the slopes of the northern mountains," Penn said. Then he lobbed the metaphorical ball back to Arthur. "What do you think?"

Arthur took another sip. "Yes, I do believe I catch notes of pine needle."

That earned another derisive laugh from the nobles. They were too easy.

The boy who had thrown down the challenge sighed dramatically and brought out the bottle. Sure enough, it was a local Half Moon vintage.

"Who's your friend?" he asked Penn.

Penn grinned back. "May I introduce young Ernest Kane, son of Baron Kane."

"Kane?" one of the other boys asked.

"It's a small barony on the outer edges," Arthur said. "We don't have much to do there other than sit around and drink."

"I hear that," said a friendly-looking boy. "I'm Mattew, Baron Rockhound's fourth son."

Arthur shook hands and got names from the rest. None meant a thing to him.

Abruptly, Penn placed his glass aside. "Well, are we going to duel, or are we going to sit around here and talk?"

"I can sit around here and *look*," Mattew pointed with his chin to a flock of noble girls who were clustered together.

Penn rolled his eyes. "I've got enough girls in my dutchy to keep me entertained. Who wants to fight?" He pitched his words loud enough to be heard throughout the room.

Instantly, conversations went quiet, and all attention turned their way.

With a slanted grin, Penn moved to the middle of the room. There was a sunken ring, clear of furniture with deep edges meant to mark boundaries. This was the arena.

"Well?" He extended his arms out and turned, issuing a challenge to them all. "Who will go first?"

A boy stepped up. "I will!"

As the challenger jumped into the ring, one of the noble girls peeled off from the rest. She put her hands on her hips and looked around. "All right, let's keep this clean, gentlemen. All fights end at first blood—"

"What if you got a blood card?" someone called out, to general laughter.

She glared at the interrupter. "Then you fight to yield. Anyone may bow out at any time without strike against their honor. We all know why we're here."

Those rules seemed toothless to Arthur, but then again, these were the children of noble houses. Whether they got the Rare hatchling or not, all had lives of privilege and leisure in front of them. No one wanted to risk that.

Murmurs of agreement echoed around the room.

Penn and his challenger bowed to one another, and Arthur settled in for a good show.

He expected the duelists to immediately reach for their card anchors—arm tattoos or bags they held.

Instead, the challenger ran straight at Penn as if he planned to tackle him to the ground.

Two steps in and he disappeared, only to reappear a moment later five steps away and to the right, still running full force at Penn.

Penn turned to meet him, but the boy flashed away yet again, this time appearing on Penn's other side, a stride closer but still running at him.

Just as Penn turned, the boy once more vanished.

He had a teleport power.

Teleport powers were . . . contentious throughout the card-wielding community. Common and Uncommon teleport cards were restricted by huge mana costs, long cooldowns, and restrictions on distance.

Though Arthur's own Trap card, Return to Start, was at Rare rank, it also had cooldown restrictions as well as an inconvenient trigger to get it to work. The benefit was it didn't require mana and there were no boundaries on location. Arthur could teleport across the kingdom if he could manage to key in the right point.

This noble's teleport card was likely a Rare, as he was aiming for the egg. However, Arthur would bet cold money the teleportation was restricted to within a few feet of its starting location.

Though the boy blinked around Penn, sometimes closer, sometimes farther away, he never teleported more than twenty feet or so from where he started. He was trying to throw Penn off his game with the ability to instantly pop in everywhere.

Judging by the way Penn was a moment too late to turn to face the boy, it was working.

Finally, after a full turn to try to face him, the challenger blinked right behind Penn with a knife in hand.

Before Arthur had time to do more than suck in a breath and think *I hope that blade's dull*, Penn reached behind himself and caught the challenger's wrist as it came down.

Then with a twist of the body, Penn brought the other boy up over his shoulder and threw him flat on his back on the ground.

The boy's wheeze was loud enough to be heard through the silent room.

Still holding his wrist, Penn plucked the knife from the boy's limp hand.

"Do you yield?"

"I yield," the boy croaked.

Penn looked up to the watching crowd. "Who's next?"

The second challenger was a noblewoman who wielded a sword covered in magical purple fire. Echoes of that same purple fire danced to the right and left in daggerlike shapes, making it look like she was surrounded by a storm of fiery blades.

Penn must have been somewhat familiar with her ability already. Seeing her enter the ring, he excused himself for a moment and pried a wooden leg off of a nearby table.

The leg still had wooden dowels sticking out of the end, giving it a savage appearance. Arthur expected him to use it like a club.

Instead, when the challenge began, Penn moved like the bulky table leg was a short, perfectly balanced bow staff. He turned aside every slash from the fiery sword, earning only char marks on one end of the leg. With the other, he drove the girl back, so she was the one giving ground. She struck out with the fiery daggers, but he ducked and weaved around them as if they were standing still.

He backed her against the edge of the ring. Her heel caught the upraised lip that marked the barrier, and she fell on her back.

Victory to Penn.

"Anyone else?" Penn called to the cheering crowd.

"That was amazing," Arthur muttered.

"Oh, he's always like that," Mattew said, sipping his wine. Unlike most of the boys, he looked distinctly annoyed, like he was waiting for this to be over so the real fun could begin.

"What do you mean?"

Mattew gave him a look. "No offense meant, but your barony's a little out of favor, yes?"

Arthur stiffened. Not because he was insulted but because he worried he'd made a mistake. "Yes. There was . . . an incident with a card some years back."

Mattew smirked. Then he took pity on Arthur. "As I thought. Well, whenever we young nobles get together, inevitably the challenges begin. And I'll tell you one thing." He raised his hand to point at Penn. "He wipes the floor with us every time. It gets downright exhausting."

Arthur stared at Penn, who was preparing for his next duel, walking around the arena and shaking out his arms. "Every time?"

He suddenly was more grateful that he had not been caught snooping in Penn's rooms.

Mattew nodded. "With weapons, without weapons, it doesn't matter." He took another sip and mumbled his next words behind his glass. "I would pay a lot to know exactly what kind of card he has."

Arthur took a chance asking his next question, as Mattew had already given him the excuse of being an outsider. "Every duel I've seen, the participants pull from card anchors. No one has done that yet."

Mattew snorted his wine so bad that he choked for a few moments. Then he looked at Arthur in unconcealed amazement. "You really are from the back-end, aren't you? No, don't take the insult," he said with a wave of his hand. "I get it. I am, too. The only reason I'm here at all is that my father recently became rich off a mine on his land. No, only commoners and exhibitionists use card anchors. Officially, noblemen fight only with the cards in their hearts. We fight heart-to-heart, you see?" He tapped his chest meaningfully. "And you know there's a limit to what any sane person will put in their heart. Technically, it's a poor showing to use more than one card in a duel, but of course, nobody would ever be able to prove it."

Arthur nodded and turned his attention back to the ring. The next duel was set to begin.

This, he thought, *might be Penn's match*. His opponent had manifested a glittering silver bow out of thin air, a matching quiver of ghostly arrows on his back.

Seeing this, Penn barked out a laugh and held up a finger in the universal "wait a moment" gesture. Before the opponent could argue, he leaped out of the ring to one of the tables with appetizers set out. Delicate pastries went flying as Penn stole one of the plates and came rushing back into the ring.

"Okay," he said. "Now I will begin."

"That's not legal," called out one of the onlookers, echoing Arthur's thoughts.

"We allowed him that table leg before," another called.

"Because it was a damn table leg. Not a weapon."

"He made it a weapon. Maybe that's his card's power."

"Gentlemen, please. Allow me to explain." Penn held up the plate. It had a pretty floral design on it and looked as fragile as spun sugar. "It's only a piece of porcelain. Not even reinforced. You have my word."

The girl who had been playing referee up until now looked to the challenger. "Do you have any objections?"

This put the young noble in an awkward spot. He had the right to object, of course, but Penn had just staked his honor on it being a regular plate. And who would be frightened of that?

After a moment's hesitation, he shook his head.

"Very well, then," the noble lady said. "Make it clean, gentlemen."

That last phrase seemed aimed directly at Penn, who just grinned impishly back at her.

The fight began, predictably, with the challenger firing one of his ghostly arrows at Penn. Not only did he seem to have an unlimited supply in his manifested quiver, but the arrows also could curve in the air and come at Penn from different angles. He fired one after another, and within seconds, five gleaming arrows rushed across the ring.

Penn used his plate like a shield, intercepting them so fast it was as if he had foreknowledge of where they were going to arrive. In one smooth, liquid motion, he had stopped every single arrow. As they hit, each dissipated into steam. Chips flew off the porcelain plate, proving that it wasn't reinforced.

Then, before the challenger could fire more, Penn threw his plate with a deceptively easy flick.

The plate spun through the air like a decapitating blade.

The challenger yelped and tried to hunch away in an instinctive reaction. As he did, he lost control of his manifested weapon. The ghostly bow and arrows evaporated as the plate struck him on the side of the shoulder.

The plate cracked into dozens of pieces, leaving the challenger unhurt, but a little stunned.

Penn grinned at him with teeth. "Do you want to continue? There are plenty more plates in this room."

"I . . . I yield," the noble squeaked.

"I bet he is using multiple Rare cards," Mattew muttered.

It seemed since he had found a sympathetic ear from Arthur, he was more than happy to continue. Compared to most nobles, he was downright friendly.

Arthur nodded to keep him happy, but inside he doubted it.

A suspicion had risen within him.

The sheer variety of Penn's abilities, from defense to offense, plus the easy competency in many different forms, told Arthur that he was using skills.

Worse, as the son of a duke, Penn should have access to Legendary-rank cards. They had enough to actually sell one.

It would make sense to give one to his heir.

That would explain why the duke was willing to put his son up for a Rare-ranked egg. Arthur had proven it was easy to fool a silver dragon who didn't know any better into believing he had a Rare card. Or the admin simply trusted a nobleman not to lie.

With a Legendary in his heart, Penn was not at risk of accidentally linking with a Rare hatchling. He was here for personal connections. To sell cards.

He had a Legendary skills card. Very much like Arthur's.

Maybe almost *exactly* like Arthur's own.

Could he be seeing someone using a card from the same set as his Master of Skills?

It took five duels to see Penn defeated. It wasn't through any particular effort, but because it seemed his stamina had finally worn out.

The girl who had been acting as a referee finally stepped in, conjured a bear made of pure fire, and ran Penn around the arena until he was exhausted.

Penn did not give up without a fight. He tried to go after the caster, who seemed to be completely unprotected. But the flame beast simply puffed into smoke and reappeared right in front of her before Penn could strike with a fist.

Penn might have combat skills, but he could still burn.

Panting heavily from exertion—and likely a little smoke inhalation—Penn aimed a wide grin at the girl.

"I yield."

This received a round of applause that was tinged with relief.

However, when Penn jumped up to the main level, everybody around him immediately offered drinks and praise.

Following nudges from his **Acting** skill, Arthur made to do the same.

He was stopped by a tap on his shoulder.

He turned to see Mattew smiling at him crookedly.

"What do you say? One son of a minor barony fighting another?"

"I hadn't planned to duel," Arthur admitted truthfully.

"Just here to see the show?" Mattew asked.

Arthur nodded, glad that the other boy understood.

Mattew clapped Arthur on the shoulder. "Take it from me, the best way to keep the sharks away is to dive right in."

With that, he turned and jumped into the middle of the pit.

"I, Mattew Rockhound, fourth son of Baron Rockhound, challenge Ernest Kane to a duel. What say you, Ernest?"

Turned out he was wrong about Mattew being friendly.

They were all sharks here.

Arthur felt the eyes of the nobles turn his way.

Those who didn't know "Ernest Kane"—and most of them shouldn't, considering he didn't exist—figured out who he was through context clues.

Declining now would mark him as a coward. Not that he cared what nobles thought of him, but he assumed Penn would not want to associate with the cowardly.

Not only did Arthur have to accept the duel, but he also had to put on a good show.

Unfortunately, all of his skills were utility based.

He'd learned a couple of defense moves over the years from Kenzie. From what hints she dropped, her life before linking with Marteen had been difficult. She was a born scrapper.

So Arthur knew a few holds and throws—nothing spectacular, or anything that his card took notice of.

Luckily, he had figured out a couple of tricks to work around his card's foibles.

"I hadn't planned on dueling," he repeated, louder for the watching audience. "Do you mind if I grab something?"

He nodded to the table of appetizers.

"I recommend the dishware," Penn called, lifting a fresh wine glass in salute.

People laughed around him, and Mattew graciously nodded.

Arthur went over and plucked a bread knife and a serving knife. One had a serrated edge to cut through crusty bread, and the other was broad and flat with an edge that was of questionable sharpness.

They would have to do.

As Arthur jumped into the ring, he double-checked his classes to see what he had equipped.

He needed the Dexterity and Perception of his Thief Class card, the luck of his Gambler Class, and every skill of showmanship in his Performer Class.

But what he needed the most right now was his Cooking Class.

Luckily, since that was a tier 2 class, he always had it equipped.

Arthur and Mattew faced each other. Though Mattew had put him here, his smile didn't have any malice to it. He looked like a man who knew the rules of the game and wanted to get it over with and play as soon as possible.

The noblewoman who'd acted as a referee before stood to lay out the rules one more time for everybody's benefit.

Then she yelled, "Fight!"

A knife in each hand, Arthur braced himself.

He knew this was likely a hopeless battle. He could lose in too many ways to count. The best he could hope for was to put up a good fight and not embarrass himself too badly.

The two boys stared at each other for a moment, as if daring the other to make the first move.

Suddenly, Mattew brought his hand down in a short chopping gesture. At the end of his chop, a bobcat sprung into being. It leaped from a small split in the air and then sat obediently at his feet.

Another chop, and a gray wolf did the same at Mattew's other side. This got a few appreciative claps and whistles. Not a surprise, seeing as this was the Wolf Moon Hive.

The animals were indistinct and washed out, almost as if Arthur were looking at paintings of the creatures instead of the real thing.

They weren't real. Mattew had a summoning card.

He had just gotten very, very lucky.

Focusing on his **Butchering** skill, Arthur's gaze landed on the bobcat. His mouth stretched into a grin.

"Here, kitty, kitty . . ."

He lost.

But the duel was closer than it had any right to be. His **Butchering** skill gave him the wisdom of how to use the knives to cut, and exactly where. He even had some knowledge of how to skin the creatures, should they have stayed still.

The problem was there were two of them and they did not stay still.

Arthur got a few cuts in on the bobcat as it leaped for his throat. Cuts that would have filleted muscle from bone quite nicely, had the creature been flesh and blood.

Instead, after his knife hit, the bobcat poofed away into mist and returned to Mattew's side, whole again. Within moments it was running back to leap at Arthur.

It seemed Rare-ranked summoned beasts could return to the world several times in a row. That was . . . inconvenient.

The bobcat didn't get the chance to reach him a second time. The wolf had already circled to get at Arthur while he had been distracted.

Arthur turned to see the animal—which was much, much larger than a dog—in mid-charge.

For a lost moment in time, he was no longer in the dueling ring. He was twelve years old and in the wilderness, facing down scourge-wolves with mouths full of teeth.

His tenuous hold on his **Butchering** skill broke. He stabbed down with the bread knife out of panic and without any finesse.

A bread knife was rounded at the end, with the most "dangerous" part being the serrated bottom.

It did nothing to the summoned wolf.

Jaws clamped down on his forearm—tight, but not crushing. Mattew was holding his beasts back.

"I yield!" Arthur yelled.

Just like that, the wolf and the bobcat poofed away.

"Winner! Mattew Rockhound!" the referee called, to cheers.

Losing wasn't as humiliating as he feared it would be. The audience clapped for a job well done, and when Arthur stepped up to the main level, Penn offered another glass of wine.

"That was a tough matchup," Penn said in commiseration.

Arthur shrugged. "Not really. Mine's a utility card, and that was about as good as it'll ever get."

"A lover not a fighter, eh?" a nearby girl asked. She batted her eyes.

Arthur felt his cheeks go burning hot.

"More of a worker than a lover," he squeaked out, and then abruptly wanted to crawl under the nearest rock. Why had he said that?!

The girl took pity on him, tittering a laugh and then reaching out to pinch his cheek before turning away.

Penn gave him a sympathetic look. "It's not hard to talk to pretty girls, but it does take practice."

Arthur gulped his wine.

Behind them, the crowd started to clap as another pair of duelists took the ring. Penn used the cover of noise to lean in.

"Say, if you're ever interested in a card good for fighting, I might have a line on something."

Shoving a flash of exhilaration down, Arthur put on a polite but curious expression. "I already looked at the card shop prices around here. They're good, but . . ." He trailed off.

Penn grimaced. "Yes, I know what you mean. Even the hive card shops only have cards fit for peasants. No, what I have is more specialized. Something . . ." He looked around. "From a personal library."

"Now that is interesting," Arthur said. "Tell me more."

"Not here." Again, Penn glanced around. "If you're still interested, meet me at the promenade tomorrow."

Arthur returned to his apartment so late that it might as well be called early, riding on the high of his success.

True, he hadn't gotten his hands on the cards yet, but he had pried some very valuable information out of the noble brat.

He stopped short when he opened the door and realized most of the candles in the room were lit. And . . . since when did they have so many candles?

Actually . . .

He blinked and looked around again, realizing his head was foggier from the wine than he wanted to admit. The sparely furnished apartment he shared with Horatio was now cluttered. Extra plates, cups, and blankets littered the floor. All arranged in pairs.

"Finally decide you still live here?" Horatio grumped on seeing him.

Arthur stepped in and shut the door. He had to walk carefully to avoid stepping on anything. "Why are you still awake? Don't you got work at your bakery early in the morning? And what's all this?"

He stopped as his mind finally caught up to what he saw.

There were *doubles* of objects everywhere.

His gaze snapped to Horatio. "You're keeping the card?"

"Yeah," Horatio said with the air of someone who had just announced his own execution. "Put it in my heart this morning."

This was big news.

"Then why are you acting so moody about it?" Arthur asked. "That's a valuable card, even for a Rare."

"I know!" Horatio snapped. "And it works perfectly!" He angrily gestured to the double pair of candlesticks in front of them, like they had insulted his mother.

Arthur rubbed at his forehead. He wasn't sure he had the patience for this tonight.

Seeing this, Horatio sagged.

"I know it has incredible potential. It's just . . . I found out Sams is coming."

"Your dragon?" Arthur asked, shocked.

"He's not my dragon. That's the problem. But yeah, word must have got to him that I got a Rare card—probably Marteen running her mouth. Dragons like to talk—and Sams sent word through a purple messenger. So now I have to tell him . . ." Horatio took in a sharp breath as if he were bracing himself. "That I picked a great card over him."

Arthur looked at his friend. His best friend, who had been with him through thick and thin. Yes, Horatio could be a pain in the ass. But though he grumbled and had a constant pessimistic attitude at life that made Arthur want to scream sometimes . . . he had never betrayed Arthur's trust.

And how had Arthur rewarded him for this? By being absent for the last few days while Horatio had made a wrenching decision.

"Why don't you show me what you can do with the card," Arthur offered.

Horatio brightened a touch. "I'm just getting started. It's one of those cards where the more you practice it, the more it levels the magic. It's a little like those class cards you read about, sometimes."

Arthur nodded his understanding.

Horatio continued. "Right now, I can only double small, simple things. And nothing alive." He shook his head. "I tried doubling a cooking apple while making pies this morning, and damn near fainted. But I think if I keep practicing, I'll get there."

"It uses mana?" Arthur asked.

"Yeah, which is another limitation. But then mana costs reduce with the more experience I gain with the card. I can double one of these candlesticks about every other hour or so."

He grabbed up an unlit candlestick and tossed it in a light underhand throw. Arthur easily caught it.

He weighed it in his hand and examined it closely. There was no indication that the thing had been created by magic. There was even a small dollop of extra wax near the wick, a tiny imperfection that the original likely had.

"And . . . it will last?" he asked. Sometimes objects made by low-level cards would exist for a short time before evaporating back into a magical state. Sometimes they were no better than illusions.

"So far," Horatio said with a nod. Then he let out a long-suffering sigh—one he was practically infamous for—and looked at Arthur sideways. "I was thinking if I could get good enough at this, you could let me in on the scheme you're planning."

Arthur jerked as if he had stuck his hand into an Uncommon lightning charm. "What scheme?" His voice was a touch too high.

Horatio rolled his eyes. "Whatever scheme has kept you away for the past few days. Plus, you're always up to something, Arthur. You're either angling for a new side job or working some weird, convoluted deal between merchants where you get a cut. Like that time you crashed a busker contest by out-juggling them, and still damn near won even though I hadn't seen you juggle anything in your life—"

"I'm not that bad—"

Horatio continued. "Now you've gotten your hands on a Rare storage card. Tell me that you're not planning to do something profitable with it. Go on. I'll wait."

His friend looked smug, and for good reason.

Arthur looked away. "I have . . . a couple of ideas."

"Yeah?" Horatio perked up. At least, as much as he normally did.

Arthur hesitated. There was so much he should tell Horatio, but keeping secrets had long become a habit.

Plus, his half-baked idea carried far more risk than any of his schemes had before.

He shook his head. "I'm still working out the details, but as soon as I have something solid, you'll know. Tell me about Sams," he said, quickly changing the subject.

Horatio looked surprised. "What do you mean?"

"You said he's coming? When?"

The corners of his friend's mouth pulled down into a frown. "Tomorrow. Why? Do you want to meet him?"

"Yes," Arthur said simply.

Having a dragon on his side would prove invaluable for his scheme.

No. Not a scheme. A heist.

That long-dormant seed cracked, and a sprout took root.

CHAPTER 50

The next day, he and Horatio waited on a bare, rocky outcropping on the north slopes of the hive. Due to a constant, chilly wind from the northern snowy mountains, this side of the hive wasn't well populated. The bits of vegetation that dotted the slopes were stunted and twisted by the wind. But being here gave Horatio and Sams privacy to speak.

Arthur wasn't entirely sure how dragons visited between hives—or why Sams wasn't allowed to stay. The more he learned about dragons, the more glimpses he got into a society hidden among themselves. One with their own ranks and rules.

Some dragons, like Doshi, were allowed to travel far and wide between hives in search of recruits for future hatchlings. Others—mostly the combat-oriented dragons—lived an almost militaristic lifestyle with inner ranks. They spent their days drilling and practicing fighting scourglings, with the main excitement occurring during new eruptions.

Then there were the dragons who lost their riders. Or the few who never linked to someone as a hatchling.

They seemed to be outsiders. Some performed fetch and carry chores to keep the hive running. Some assisted directly with scourge-eruptions without the magical aid of a rider's card. Some, Arthur heard, disappeared into the wilds, never to be seen again.

He suspected the red dragon who had given him his Master of Skills card was like the last.

From what he understood, Sams lived in minor disgrace within his own hive. He was a Rare-ranked dragon. As such, he was expected to link with another rider as soon as possible. He didn't have the luxury of waiting, like Commons and Uncommons.

But he had chosen to wait for Horatio anyway. His rider's son.

Horatio was rightly worried that Sams would not wish to wait much longer.

Horatio had been told, approximately, when and where Sams was due to arrive. But it was a surprise when a small portal opened in midair. Usually, spatial-manipulation dragons, which were the high-grade shimmery greens, reserved their mana portal techniques for hive eruptions. But again, Sams was a Rare and could pull strings.

A large shape flew out of the portal. Its long tail barely exited before the rip in the air snapped shut again.

Sams looped around once to get his bearings. He was a magnificent dragon, long and delicate looking with a pointed head like the tip of a spear. His color was a burst of sunshine yellow, with a hint of luminescence shining out from within.

While Sams was a Rare, he held no particular shimmer quality to his hide. That was likely why he had been allowed to stay unlinked from a rider all this time.

Sams spotted them before long—dragon eyesight supposedly rivaled a human's—and he glided down on great wings to meet them.

His claws barely touched the stony ground before Horatio bowed to him, which was more courtesy than Arthur had seen him show . . . ever.

Sams ducked his head, peering narrow-eyed at Horatio as if he were nearsighted. "Little one, is that you? You have grown large."

Horatio choked out a laugh. "And you are as big as ever, Sams."

The dragon ruffled his wings at the praise. But as he did, the wind shifted, and Arthur got a whiff of him. He smelled acrid and rotten, just like the dragon soil fields. It wasn't a pleasant smell.

"And you have the feel of Rare magic," Sams replied, still gazing at Horatio. His wings drooped slightly before his next pronouncement. "But I sense your card will not fit with mine."

"I—I tried," Horatio said. "I'm sorry, Sams. I ended up with a good card . . . but not something that would fit you."

Arthur held his breath, waiting for the dragon's reaction. He fully expected anger, even insult. After all, Sams had waited all this time for nothing.

Instead, the dragon dipped his head and touched the point of his sharp muzzle to the top of Horatio's hair. "You created a Rare card out of mere shards. Your father would be proud."

"No, he wouldn't," Horatio said bitterly.

"He never expected perfection from anybody else," Sams replied. "Only from himself." Then he heaved a giant, dragon-sized sigh. "But I must find a rider soon."

Horatio closed his eyes as if bracing himself. "I understand."

"Why?" Arthur asked.

The dragon's head swung around to look at him. He didn't answer, so Horatio spoke up. "Sams, this is Arthur. He's my best friend out here."

Sams regarded Arthur silently, and Arthur was reminded that adult dragons didn't always speak to other people. He was used to Marteen and the simpler but gregarious purple dragons.

Finally, Sams spoke. "I must find a rider because to be without one means a loss of privileges. I am lucky that I'm not required to attend the scourge-eruptions. Instead, I'm relegated to using my powers to dry out the dragon soil fields."

"Damn," Horatio said softly. "I didn't know that, Sams."

"It's not a bad job," Sams replied, and Arthur noted that he was much less formal when speaking directly to Horatio. "It is not as if I stand in the fields. I can fly above and work my magic. It is . . . bearable."

"Can you add another card to your heart deck?" Arthur asked. "Something compatible with Horatio's new card?"

"He's still a little new to hive life," Horatio said to Sams. Apparently, that had been a stupid question.

"We may add new cards to our heart deck, as well as secondary and tertiary decks," Sams replied patiently. "But there may be only one card in the core of our being. It is the magic that we dragons are built around. The new card we release into the world upon our deaths. I cannot simply exchange it for another."

"I'm sorry," Horatio said again, sounding wretched. "If I knew that they'd put you in the damn dragon soil fields, I would have sold this card. I don't care how good it is—"

"I . . . might have another option," Arthur said.

Both Horatio and Sams turned to look at him.

Arthur hesitated. "But it's not, um, exactly legal."

"Your scheme?" Horatio guessed. He glanced back at Sams. "He always has some card-shard-making venture in mind."

"No. This one is more of a heist." Arthur took a breath and threw the metaphorical dice. "My noble uncle is selling cards from his private library. I want to get my hands on them first."

There was a long, long pause. Sams looked politely interested, Horatio gobsmacked.

"Wait," Horatio said. "Since when do you have an uncle? And since when was he a noble relative? Or *any* relatives?! We met in an orphanage."

Arthur winced. "You know I don't like to talk about my family."

"Yeah, and I figured that was because they were eaten by scourglings," Horatio's voice grew sharp. "Why don't you start talking."

So, Arthur did. On the bare slopes of the hive, where the wind whipped by strong enough to cover his words from outside listeners, Arthur told Horatio and Sams his story.

Well, most of it.

Horatio listened with one hand resting on the side of Sams head as if he needed an anchor. His eyes narrowed in several spots, but he didn't interrupt. Sams listened quietly, too.

"I didn't know my uncle inherited the duchy," Arthur said. "I didn't think that I had any link back to it at all."

"I don't think that you do have a link to him, legally." It was the first thing Horatio had said in nearly fifteen minutes. "People who go to the border villages . . . they are supposed to be dead men walking."

"That is not technically true," Sams said.

"What you mean?" Horatio asked.

But the dragon kept silent.

After a moment, Horatio turned to Arthur. He stared at him, and Arthur found he couldn't read the expression on Horatio's face. He couldn't even tell how upset his friend was with him.

"I can't believe you didn't tell me," Horatio said. "No wait, I can. No one comes from those border villages."

"Children are allowed to leave once they turn eighteen," Arthur replied, but he couldn't keep the heat out of his voice. "They're sent off without any education or a clue of how the real world works. But they can go if they want to leave their entire family behind to die without them."

Horatio shook his head but didn't look like he was arguing. More out of disbelief.

"I guess . . . I get why you didn't tell me all that," he said. "But I have two questions."

Mentally, Arthur braced himself. "Go ahead."

"Does the fact that you are a former duke's son have anything to do with that high-powered card in your chest? Not the Rare. The other one."

Arthur stared. The one thing he had kept back was the story of the red dragon giving him his Master of Skills card. He implied his father pulled strings to sneak him out with Red's caravan.

Horatio's lips quirked up, which was his equivalent of a wide grin. "I've been your friend for how long? You pick up things fast, Arthur. Too fast. And you're not that smart."

"Hey . . ."

Horatio shook his head. "I mean, okay, you're smart, but you're no genius. Yet I've seen you replicate things in the kitchen that takes other cooks years to figure out. And you always have some scheme running, but you're not hungry for cards like it's a matter of survival. You don't want that Rare egg, even though it's your ticket to a good life in the hive. I think it's because you know you will never link up with a Rare one at all. You have something better, don't you?"

Arthur stared at Horatio, knowing he was putting his life in Horatio's hands. He nodded.

His friend let out a breath. "Damn nobles . . ."

Well, if he was going to believe that Arthur's father somehow wrangled him a Legendary-rank card, Arthur would let him believe it.

"What's the second question?" Arthur asked.

"What else?" Horatio said with a mirthless chuckle. "Does your noble uncle have any Rare-rank cards that would fit me and Sams?"

Arthur grinned. Horatio was on board.

"I don't know. But if he doesn't, we could always fence what we find."

Abruptly, Sams spoke up, surprising Arthur. "You could not sell stolen cards locally. The moment the theft is discovered, your noble uncle will hire discreet high-level treasure seekers to sniff out the cards."

"How high level?" Arthur asked.

Sams took his time answering. He reached up with his hind leg and scratched the side of his head. "Why?"

Horatio snapped his fingers. "You want to stick them in the storage space? That's a Rare-ranked card power. So if the duke hires an Uncommon seeker, they might not find them."

Arthur shook his head. "I have something better in mind. Something . . . I'd rather keep to myself for now."

Horatio frowned at his friend and then rolled his eyes. He didn't seem too upset about Arthur's secrets. Perhaps because at the end of the day there was little difference between being from the back end of a nowhere farm or being from a border town no one had heard of.

More likely, though, Horatio was excited about the idea of getting another Rare card for himself.

"I haven't heard of a seeker above Rare rank within the hives," Sams said at last. "I have no doubt the king has a card for it in the palace libraries—if it hasn't degraded from disuse. Would your uncle have access or be able to afford the services of such a person . . .?" He trailed off and shrugged one massive wing. "Who knows. But I believe it's an acceptable risk for the reward."

Arthur stared up at the dragon, a little surprised at his sound logic. He was also a touch ashamed of his surprise. Sams was a Rare-ranked dragon. He just hadn't expected him to reason like a person. Even Marteen wasn't that deep of a thinker.

That red dragon who'd given him his card had also thought like a person. Motivations of spite and revenge and all.

"I'm . . . a little surprised you two are taking this so well," Arthur admitted. "I thought I would have to talk you into it."

"Stealing cards is a fine dragon rider tradition," Sams said, puffing out his chest. "Though the hive administrators have tamped down on it over the last few generations."

Arthur hesitated. "When I was younger, I was caught near a scourge-eruption. I saw a pink dragon being attacked by other dragons. I think they were after its cards."

That deflated Sams a tad. "That is not supposed to happen during an eruption, though . . . if the dragon and rider are far enough out of favor." He shrugged his wings again.

Arthur decided to set that topic aside. He looked to Horatio. "For this to work, I'll need to test something." Without waiting for Horatio's reply, he reached into his storage space and pulled out a box of peeping chicks.

Then he pulled out the piglet, which took a look up at Sams and started to squeal in panic.

"Are you laying out a lunch?" Sams asked.

"Nothing like that." He looked at the animals, who seemed perfectly fine after their extended stay in storage. But he had to be absolutely sure. Arthur lifted his gaze to Horatio. "Do you trust me?"

"That depends on what you're about to ask me."

Arthur stared at him, steady. "I need to see if I can store a person inside my storage."

Horatio jerked back in surprise. "Why?"

"I can't say." Arthur held up a hand before his friend could speak. "The less you know about this, the better. But yes, it's part of my plan to steal the cards. So far, I've stored chicks and this piglet in there, and they're all fine. But I need to know what it's like inside. If it's . . . tolerable for a person. And it's not like I can put myself in. I'll pull you out after ten seconds," he added.

"No," Horatio said after a moment. "Give me thirty seconds. That'll give me enough time to look around, but it won't be long enough for me to suffocate. Probably."

Arthur knew he was asking a lot of his friend. Hopefully, he would be able to repay his trust. With a nod, he put his hand on Horatio's shoulder and mentally reached for his storage card.

Nothing happened.

"Uh . . ."

Sams lowered his head to look at the two of them. "I've heard of similar powers before. Is there a restriction on sapient creatures in your card's description?"

"No," Arthur said.

"Spatial magic can be finicky," Sams continued. "A lack of acceptance or trust from the other party may be enough to block the card. Because he is self-aware, Horatio may have to give express permission to store him."

Horatio blew out a breath. "Fine. Arthur," he began grandly, "I give you my permission—"

Arthur felt the sensation of a tug, and a moment later Horatio disappeared into his storage. His hand dropped.

He was so shocked he forgot to count for a moment. Quickly, he started.

"Twenty-nine, twenty-eight, twenty-seven . . ."

"You had better be correct about this being safe," Sams said as he stared at the spot Horatio had been.

Arthur nodded and did not stop counting.

At one, he pulled Horatio out again. Thankfully, he did not need to ask his friend's permission first.

Horatio returned exactly where he had been standing.

"—to throw me in your over-powered storage space," Horatio continued. Then he looked around, seeing the two staring at him. "What?"

"I just pulled you out of it."

"No, you didn't." He stared around, reading their expressions. Then he looked down at his hands as if searching for a change. "Wait, really?"

"You didn't feel anything?" Arthur pressed.

Horatio shook his head, doubt on his face like he wasn't sure if Arthur was playing a trick on him or not.

"I guess the card description's accurate about not experiencing time." He nodded. "Thank you, Horatio. That helps. Though it's a shame I can't toss anyone who gets in my way in there." Specifically, whoever was guarding the cards.

Horatio shuddered dramatically. "That card is scary enough."

"Sometimes," Arthur said, "I wonder about utility cards. People overlook them, but they're often more powerful than they appear."

CHAPTER 51

The next day, Arthur went to visit Kenzie.

He, Horatio, and Sams had stayed up until the night's last bell discussing logistics for the plan. Sams could only be at Wolf Moon for a few days, which put a hard time limit on their schedule.

All agreed they would need Kenzie's help to pull it off.

Thankfully, Kenzie had always been morally flexible.

Kenzie gave him a searching look as she let him into her and Marteen's apartment. "I've heard you've been at the egg promenade several nights in a row. Think you got a chance with the Rare?" She couldn't hide the hope in her voice, which made Arthur feel bad.

Kenzie had long hinted she knew Arthur was more than what he seemed, but she had never pried. He hoped he wasn't taking too much advantage of that, and, like with Horatio, he would be able to repay her trust soon.

He shook his head. "It's something else. But first, Kenzie, what's going on with all the new hatchlings? I went by the nesting grounds the other day, and there are more than I've ever seen before."

Her face fell. "Truthfully? A combination of things. There have been some nasty scourge-eruptions near some of the bigger farming communities. That's resulted in a lot of deaths, so families . . . just don't have the kids to spare."

"What? Why haven't I heard of this?"

She raised an eyebrow. "Do you often help out with the eruptions?"

Arthur flushed. Many people in and around the hives whose jobs didn't directly involve fighting scourglings volunteered instead. Over the last few years, Arthur's main drive had been to work on his skills and gain more card shards. Plus, helping during eruptions carried the risk of running into more silvers or even one of the mind-reading white dragons.

There was almost zero chance of that happening while in the lower levels of the hive. So that's where he spent most of his waking hours.

Kenzie let him stew for a moment before she added, "To be fair, the worst of the eruptions haven't been in our territory. Wolf Moon helps out as always, but we weren't the primary hive. So news hasn't spread far."

"Oh." That helped, but he still felt guilty.

"On top of that, all the females seem to be on a clutching spree. I think Marteen's even due for her first clutch soon. That's why she's out tonight—she's spending time with her admirers."

"Oh." Now Arthur blushed even harder. "Uh, congratulations?"

Kenzie grinned at him. "Yeah, I'm looking forward to recruiting for her future eggs. Anyway, that can't be the only reason why you're here."

He shook his head. "It isn't." Reaching into his pocket, he pulled out a small wrapped package. "I need to send this."

"Then . . . give it to the correspondence desk?"

This was it. "It needs to go to a border village. And it needs to be quick. And . . ." He swallowed. "That dragon will need to pick up something on the return. The details are inside."

For a long moment, she stared at him. He stared levelly back.

She was the one who finally blinked.

"Arthur, you know I'm always willing to stick my neck out for you, but—"

"What if I told you I have a solution to get the hive admin off your back over new recruits?"

That stopped Kenzie short. Her eyes narrowed. "What do you mean?"

"I can't tell you specifics—right now," he added. "Kenzie, once I pull this off, you'll understand. But until then, I need you to trust me." He hesitated. "Can you do that?"

She made a show of sucking her teeth and shook her head. Then she said, "What I was *going* to say was I'm willing to stick my neck out for you, but what you're asking will cost you. Even if it does magically help me in the long run."

He grinned. Then he pulled out his card anchor bag and shook out every single card shard, Common, Uncommon, and Rare, out into his cupped palm.

"We got a deal?"

"Damn." Kenzie snatched up the shards so fast it would have been easy to mistake her for a starving farmer rather than a dragon rider. "I hope you know what you're doing."

So did Arthur.

"I can't sell the cards directly, mind you," Penn had told Arthur and a few other interested nobles later that night. Behind them, the line to see the Rare egg circled the room. Penn used the murmurs of conversation and gossip as a shield to conduct his own business. "We're going to be running a friendly little auction. These things must be kept discreet."

Which was a way of saying that it needed to be kept out of view of anyone closely connected to the king. His Majesty's agents kept an eye on the sale of cards—especially the higher-powered cards, in case someone got the idea to form a powerful set.

Or in case they stumbled across a card that could rival the power of the throne.

Arthur noticed those boys and girls around Penn who introduced themselves were all lower to minor nobility. Barons, baronets, esquires, and even a few off-spring of magistrates in charge of a single small town. People who could use a little extra power.

"When is the auction to occur?" one boy asked eagerly.

Penn's smile was pure indulgence, like a man who was giving away presents of candied fruit to his poor neighbors. "Three days from now. We must wait for the cards to arrive."

"Wait, you don't have them with you?" Arthur blurted.

A girl laughed. "You expect him to pull them out of his heart or something?"

Arthur knew he had mis-stepped somewhere. He looked to Penn. "Well . . . I assumed they'd be in a high-level card anchor bag . . ."

Penn's indulgent smile broadened. "You must forgive Ernest *Kane*," he said with emphasis on Arthur's supposed last name. "No doubt transporting cards in safe carts has . . . gone out of fashion around his family."

There were chuffs of laughter all around. Apparently, word of Baron Kane's misfortune of losing a high-level card was well-known.

Arthur looked down as if embarrassed.

Inside, he smiled.

"The cards are coming by cart?" Horatio threw his hands up in the air in frustration. "That's just great. It's not like there are dozens of carts coming and going to this huge hive all hours of the day . . ."

Sams, however, didn't seem bothered. "The noble whelp said by 'safe cart'?"

"Yes," Arthur told him. He paced over the flat spur of rock where they'd agreed to meet, still in his itchy fine clothing. "We don't have to monitor every cart that comes into the hive's city. Just the ones that Duke Rowantree and his son visit. Between Horatio and me, we should be able to follow them. We know the city better than visiting nobles."

"What?" Horatio grumped. "You want to follow them all day and all night? You think they won't notice?"

"Well, you might be able to pose as a servant. I'm sure they'll need to hire someone—"

"No need," Sams said.

Both boys looked at him.

"You must never have seen a safe cart from the air," the dragon continued. "They are distinctive from merchant carts. What direction does Rowantree's duchy lay?"

"To the south, toward the center of the kingdom."

Sams bobbed his head. "If you fetch me a map, I will determine their most likely route. We will watch that."

Arthur grinned. He had firsthand knowledge that guarded carts were still susceptible to a dragon's attack.

Horatio looked more disturbed than he had before. "Won't they get a clue if a big Rare yellow dragon attacks a duke's cart?"

"How would they pin it on Sams?" Arthur asked. "He's not officially a part of this hive. Plus," he added when Horatio looked like he was about to argue, "how deeply can the duke investigate when he's selling cards illegally?"

Horatio shut his mouth, thought for a moment, and then reopened it again. "Someone will notice if you disappear for a few days."

"Penn Rowantree thinks I'm someone who doesn't exist," Arthur said. "And I have a plan for myself . . ."

"One more thing," Arthur had told Kenzie after she had counted out all his extra shards and declared "it would do."

Judging by the way she was holding back a smile, she planned to take a large cut from whomever she roped into this. "As my silver recruiter, I need you to sign off on a leave of absence form."

"You're taking time off from Bob's place?" she asked, eyebrows raised.

He shrugged, unwilling to say more.

As a recruit for a Rare dragon, it was his option to take days off work whenever there was an egg available to spend time around it and increase his chances. The hive would compensate his employer.

Arthur needed a paper trail.

"Fine," she said with a sigh. "Anything else?"

He thought about it and shook his head. "Wish me luck?"

Kenzie did more than that, swooping over to plant a sisterly kiss on the side of his cheek.

Stunned, Arthur stiffly stood in place until she drew back.

"Good luck," she said, his card shards in her hands and a wide smile on her face.

* * *

New skill level: Dragon Riding (Animal Husbandry/
Dragon Rider Class)
Level 5

It had been a while since he had leveled that skill up.

It was also easier to focus on that rather than the fact that Arthur was currently so high up that the land was nearly unrecognizable. The flashes he saw through the scant breaks in cloud cover looked like multicolored squares.

The only exception was the top of the hive cone, which broke through the bottom layer of clouds. It made it look like a tiny mountain peak of its own.

"This is amazing!" Horatio cried. Sitting in front, he stretched his arms out as he whooped.

It was by far the most exuberant Arthur had ever seen his friend. He was happy for him. He really was.

Mostly, though, he was trying not to think about falling.

He clutched Sams's warm hide. At least the dragon flew at a steady pace—none of the uneven bobbling in the air like that time he'd flown on Marteen, or none of Tess's crazy acrobatic buzzing in different directions. Sams's wingbeats were even and measured, and he didn't seem to be bothered at all by air pressure changes.

The dragon had been on patrol for most of the last day before he said he found something they should see.

"Do you see it yet?" Arthur called.

"You just asked five minutes ago," Horatio called back. "Give him some time. Enjoy yourself."

"Who are you?" Arthur demanded.

His friend laughed and spread his arms wide again as if he wanted to embrace the clouds.

A bypassing red dragon swooped near enough for its rider to wave to them. Horatio waved back, grinning.

"Will you knock it off?" Arthur demanded. "Don't bring attention to us!"

"It would be weird if we didn't wave," was Horatio's easy response.

Once again, Arthur felt like they had switched personalities. But he was tense. They'd only get one shot, and although Sams would help . . . this had to go right.

Sure enough, the red dragon and its rider flew off. Sams continued scanning the pass leading up to the hive.

"I see it," Sams announced.

Arthur looked down, saw the tops of the clouds, which seemed like unforgiving snowy rocks, and swallowed hard. "Where?"

Sams pumped his wings and brought them to a tiny break in the clouds where the land could be seen . . . far, far below.

It all looked the same to Arthur. Multicolored fields cut by rivers, streams, and dark bands of green that must be forests. He couldn't identify a road, much less any carts on it.

"You're sure?" he called.

Horatio scoffed. "Sams is a Light-based dragon. He can see better than us during the day. If he says he found them, then he found them."

Arthur nodded. At least he would soon be on the ground again. "Then it's time to drop me off, Sams."

CHAPTER 52

A half hour later, Arthur lay crouched under thick brush on the side of a road while he waited for a cart to arrive.

This felt familiar.

Only now he was a well-grown sixteen years old, not a scrawny, underfed little boy. He had the tools, skills, and allies to help him out.

This time, he wouldn't be at the mercy of a dragon to give him a card. He would take the prizes himself.

Traffic on the forested road was sparse. A light merchant cart pulled by a donkey and a single rider passed by. Though Arthur was shielded by the underbrush, he concentrated on his **Stealth** skill to keep him hidden.

No one so much as glanced his way.

When the duke's safe cart rolled up, Arthur again felt a surge of déjà vu.

It was an ostentatious thing painted blue with silver filigree, pulled by four black horses, and accompanied by uniformed guards on foot. One leaned an oversized hammer against his shoulder like Arthur might carry a stick.

Arthur took a bracing breath, then pulled his dark hood over his head and an obscuring strip of cloth over the lower half of his face. He didn't know how many people had powers of seeing through time like Doshi and his rider, but it was best to conceal his identity as much as possible. Lastly, he checked to make sure his Nullify Card was set to stop his Return to Start trap card from activating.

There came a shattering roar from above.

Sams had dived down, using the sun's angle to keep the guards from spotting him. When he reached the height of the treetops, he snapped open his wings and roared out his entrance.

He blazed like the sun itself. Sams had a Mirror Light card and could take in and reflect out the sun's dazzling light. All shadows beneath him evaporated.

Without a rider to link cards with, Sams wasn't a full-on threat. He reflected only the light and not the heat. But he could provide an effective distraction.

No one expected an unfriendly dragon so close to the hives. Especially not one with a rider on its back.

The guards shouted and either staggered to the front of the cart to face the dragon or calm the plunging horses. But they were all working three-quarters blind. Sams at full power was eye-wateringly bright.

Horatio was wearing similar coverings to obscure his face and had been directed to pull on a sleeping mask to save his eyes from the light. He was only there for show, to throw off the trail so the guards would not report a riderless dragon later on.

Keeping his eyes firmly on the ground, Arthur scrambled out of his hiding spot and tried to **Stealth** his way to the cart. The land all around was still painfully bright. He stumbled through watering eyes, and his only saving grace was that the guards were doing the same.

"What is the meaning of this?!" one guard bellowed up at Sams. "Rider! Call your beast off and explain yourself!"

Horatio called, "We have received reports of contraband being brought onto our land. By order of the Wolf Moon Hive, you are to stand down and show your paperwork and proof of entrance fees."

"How dare you! We will do no such thing. This is a legal transport, vouchsafed by my employer, the honorable Duke Rowantree—"

And so on.

Arthur hardly listened. He needed to move fast.

Half shielding his eyes, Arthur made out the form of a guard standing a few feet from the carriage's side door. The man had his back turned, paying more attention to the argument than what he was supposed to be guarding.

On silent feet, Arthur crept up and pulled out his lock-picking tools.

Every spare minute he had spent not buddying up to Penn or working on the logistics of this plan, he had been practicing his **Lock-Picking** skill. He picked his way into his apartment, solved toy puzzle boxes, and purchased cheap locks from secondhand general stores with the very last of his coppers. Then he worked until he sprung those, too.

As a result, his **Lock-Picking** now stood at a very respectable Apprentice 24. He only hoped it would be enough to get him past the door.

So he was utterly shocked—and a little affronted—when the door sprung open at a pull. It wasn't locked at all.

The inside of the carriage was a dark, incomprehensible mass to his bright-blind eyes. Arthur crawled in and closed the door behind himself. The silent hinges didn't make a sound.

Unfortunately, he was all too obvious to the guard riding in the carriage.

A card-strength-enhanced hand grabbed him by the base of the throat and shoved him up against the closed door.

"Laramie!" the guard called. "We've got a break-in!"

"I knew it! It's a trap! Fire on the dragon!" the guard outside bellowed.

Arthur heard the twang of a bow, Sams's roar, and rapidly beating wings as the dragon retreated.

Gasping, Arthur scrabbled behind him to find the lock on the door and pull it. The lock engaged with a click.

"Clever," the guard commented, unconcerned. His grip tightened on Arthur's neck, nearly cutting off all his air. "How'd you rope a dragon rider into your scheme, kid? I thought they were supposed to be above all that."

Arthur pounded a fist against the man's wrist, but it was like striking a wooden beam.

If he was arrested, he had to protect Sams and Horatio. "Nothing to do with it," he croaked. "Saw the carriage stopped . . . tried my luck."

With an easy, deliberate effort, the man slammed him against the door for his obvious lie.

"Want to try that again?"

Someone tried the door on the outside, found it locked, and started pounding against the wood.

"Otto! What's going on in there?"

"Just having a chat with my new friend," Otto called. "Be out in a moment. Now." Again his fingers tightened on Arthur's neck.

Arthur gagged, trying to pry the fingers loose. It was no use at all.

"Who are your accomplices?" Otto asked.

"Don't . . . have . . . any . . ." Arthur choked. His eyes had cleared of Sams's brightness, and he could make out the form of Otto. He was a massive bear of a man who seemed to take up the entire interior of the already-large cart. There was no chance of defeating him by force.

A gilded box sat on Otto's other side. The box Arthur needed but couldn't reach.

"One last time," Otto said. "Name. Your. Accomplices." Each word was accompanied by a squeeze that made Arthur's windpipe feel like it was about to collapse.

Wheezing for air, Arthur shook his head.

His sight had returned with enough detail to see Otto roll his eyes.

"Fine. We'll see what the captain has to say. He's not as nice as me. Hope you're not too attached to your fingers and toes."

With his free hand, Otto reached to his own forearm—the one currently choking Arthur. The man's sleeve was rolled up, showing a visible card anchor tattoo.

Arthur's next move was one of pure desperation.

He slapped his hand over the tattoo a moment before Otto did and reached for his **Card Shuffling** skill.

The ghostly edge of cards flicked across the pads of his fingers. He drew out the top one straight from Otto's card anchor deck.

A card appeared, pinched between Arthur's fingers.

Otto jerked and let out a strangled sound of pure surprise.

Arthur had no air to say the words, so he mouthed them, instead.

Full-Body Bind.

Arthur felt something pull from his heart. He had never cast a spell before, but the mere act of it took effort.

Otto went stiff from head to foot. Though his fingers were locked around Arthur's neck, the tension was gone. Arthur pulled away and to the side, sucking down fresh air.

The guard, meanwhile, fell flat to the floor of the carriage. Only his darting, wide eyes moved.

"Otto! Otto, what's going on in there?" Whoever was outside pounded his fists so hard the door shook. "Stand back, we're coming in!"

No time to think. Arthur threw himself across the bench seat, grabbed the box, and shoved it in his Personal Space along with the card.

He had time to reach for his Nullify Card and toggle it off the Return to Start card before the carriage's side door was ripped away.

Arthur wasn't sure what kind of card power they used on him—some sort of magic-effect eraser was his guess, because a cool light washed inside the carriage. Otto immediately jerked back into motion and reached for Arthur again.

Conditions for Trap Card met.
Return to Start: Activated.

The next moment, Arthur found himself lying on his back on something flat, wooden, and unforgiving. A kitchen table.

Adrenaline pumping, Arthur sat up and looked around wildly. He was in a simple two-room cabin, the walls patched and dirty, with a weak fire burning in the woodstove.

"Thief!" bellowed a voice. "Get out of my house!"

Arthur whipped around to see an old man stagger out of the secondary room. There was more gray in his hair than Arthur remembered, with thin clothing and sunken skin. He held a knife, but Arthur didn't fear him.

His voice came out rusty from emotion and the trauma of nearly being strangled. "Dad?"

Calvan stopped short. He took Arthur in like a stranger, like he didn't want to believe his eyes. "Arthur?"

CHAPTER 53

But I thought you were . . ." Calvan didn't finish the sentence, dropping the knife and running forward to grab his son in a tight hug.

Arthur hugged him back and was shocked at how thin he felt. While Arthur had grown, it seemed Calvan had shrunk.

Calvan pulled back to look at him, eyes wide. "You shouldn't be here. How are you here?!"

In answer, Arthur shifted aside. The remains of a thin package lay under his butt. In it sat a tiny pebble. One on which he had keyed his Return to Start card.

He held up the pebble.

"A dragon rider dropped this off?"

"Just last night," Calvan confirmed, sounding faint. "Talking nonsense about me placing it somewhere out in the open. I had no idea what she meant, but when a dragon rider asks you to do something . . ." He trailed off, hand still on Arthur's shoulder as if he wasn't sure his son was real. "You've grown, boy." Then he embraced his son again. This time, Calvan's shoulders shook in suppressed sobs. "I thought you were dead."

Pain lanced through him. He could very well guess why, but he had to hear it. "Red?"

"That sonofabitch." Calvan leaned back and swiped at his eyes. "I told him to take care of you, and he lost you in a scourge-eruption. There was no body, but . . . no word, either."

Arthur shook his head, self-directed anger making his heart ache. "I was saved by a dragon and taken to a hive. I've been at Wolf Moon for years—I should have sent word, but . . ." He trailed off, looking down.

He could have sent a letter, but it was both risky and expensive. Instead, he had unintentionally let his father think he was dead.

"I'm sorry," Arthur whispered.

"No . . . no, you couldn't have reached out. It wouldn't have been safe. You shouldn't be here!" Calvan insisted. "Why are you here, son? You got to a hive. You *made* it. This village is the last place you should be."

"I needed a place to lay low for a bit. And I wanted to help."

"Help?" he repeated.

In answer, Arthur pushed off the table and stood. He reached into his storage space and removed a box of slightly wilted lettuce. The vegetables were too far gone to make for proper eating in the hive's city, which was why the entire box had been set out by the trash of a popular restaurant.

Then Arthur plucked out a crate of tomatoes, again, slightly off with fruit flies buzzing over it. But still eatable. More importantly, the seeds were good for planting.

Next came two full crates of plump potatoes. Nothing wrong with them. He'd purchased them himself.

Then he pulled out more and more slightly off vegetables, until boxes and crates covered the floor.

Then came the late-season chicks. Three baskets in total, including one of ducklings. Finally, Arthur removed one squealing piglet.

"The rest I have isn't fit for eating," Arthur admitted with a grimace, knowing it likely would be eaten anyway. What was a little spoilage to someone who was starving? "I got it from the trash around the city, but the seeds should be good for storage and would make decent deer bait."

His father, who had been quiet all this time, only stared. Finally, he blinked as if coming back to himself.

"Of course. You managed to get another card. You were at a hive. That . . . that makes sense."

He looked like he wanted to sit down.

"I've got more than one card," Arthur admitted. "Dad . . . we need to talk."

First, Arthur took a ladle full of water from a nearby bucket. The bracing yet bit-terly iron-tasting water was both nostalgic and helped soothe his throat.

Then he returned to sit across from his still-stunned father and started talking.

He gave a brief outline of his life: his stay with Red's caravan, how he made it to the hive, and some of his minor exploits there.

Then he told his father all about meeting his uncle.

Calvan jerked in place as if he had just been stung by a bee. After that moment's shock, he slowly nodded with acceptance. "I'm glad to hear Lional has taken the duchy."

Now it was Arthur's turn to be shocked. "How can you say that? The duchy should be yours—it ought to be my mom and sister's home. Mine too!" he added in indignation.

He hadn't let himself dwell much on it, but seeing those carefree noble kids, all well-kept and dressed like they had never known anything but the best . . . Well, it had stung.

His father gave a defeated sort of smile. "The duchy hasn't been my own in a long time, but it has been in our family for centuries. So yes, I'm glad that the bloodline still has some control—however long the king allows Lional's leash to be." Finally, a little bitterness entered his tone. "I wish Lional luck. It can't be easy."

Arthur couldn't let it go. "What if taking over the duchy was Lional's plan? If he cared anything for the bloodline, couldn't he have gotten us out of this village? Arranged something? You got Red to take me in."

"And you saw how that turned out. Red had the care of you for how many weeks before he almost lost you to the scourge?" Calvan shook his head. "Besides, Lional could never remove me or your mother from this place. We swore an oath to stay on one of the king's own cards."

He stared at his father. "You swore an oath?"

"Most of the convicted adults do," Calvan said. "It's why we stay."

"And . . . the kids?"

"They're allowed to leave when they turn eighteen, or before, if it can be managed," his father said with the ghost of a smile.

Arthur exhaled in relief, even as his mind chewed over this new complication. Well, there was only so much good he could do in one night.

"Lional could have gotten my sister out, if he really cared," Arthur muttered. "Or me."

His father shook his head in answer and then leaned over to place a hand on his shoulder. "You've done well for yourself, son. But . . . I'd be lying if I wasn't worried about what all this cost you." He looked around at the boxes of fruits, vegetables, and the young meat animals meaningfully.

"Well . . . there's something else you should see," Arthur admitted.

Then he reached into his storage space and withdrew the card box he'd taken from the carriage.

About the size of a breadbox, it seemed to glitter with ornamentation in the dim candlelight. Now that Arthur had a chance to look at it while not being half strangled, he realized that the raised gilded edges and fanciful arrangements of glittering stones had a purpose.

The box was covered in runes. These went well beyond his current **Lock-Picking** skill, as they used mana. Also, he had no key.

His father stared at the box as well. "This is a card box. Arthur . . . what have you done?"

"You told me to steal a card if I had to," Arthur said. "I might have gone a little overboard."

"Don't tell me . . ."

"Lional and his son were selling off parts of their private card library."

Calvan stood so abruptly that the bench seat behind him tipped over. He stared at the box with a flood of emotions crossing his face. Foremost was horror.

"If it helps," Arthur said as the silence stretched on, "I like to think of it as my inheritance."

"I . . . don't know what to say." His father pulled one hand down his face. "I know your early years had you growing up wild out here, but Arthur . . . to steal from your own duchy . . ."

Arthur shot to his feet. "It's not my duchy! My uncle left me to die—Mom and my sister *did* die. Now they're selling off pieces of land and what should be all of ours to other nobles." Only respect for his former home kept him from turning his head and spitting on the ground. Instead, Arthur growled, "Lional's lost my loyalty. I hope losing these cards hurts him."

His father seemed to deflate. Silently righting the bench, he sat back down. "It will."

Arthur stared at him, expecting something more. Growing up, his father seemed to be a never-ending fountain of wisdom. He always knew what to do and what to say.

Now he looked old. And tired.

Eventually, Arthur sat back down as well. "I don't know how to open it," he admitted. "I wasn't able to grab a key from the guards."

His father heaved a sigh and then looked at his son ruefully. "Well, it's not as if you can return the thing now you've brought it out here. Leave opening it to me."

An hour later, Arthur was alone in his childhood cabin.

After his pronouncement that he knew how to get the card box open, his father had gone for the door and told Arthur to stay put.

"The baron is paranoid about his people collaborating with bandits," he had said. "He has more guard patrols here than he used to, and they wouldn't react well to a new face. Stay here."

Then he left.

Arthur spent the first few minutes organizing the boxes of produce. He stacked most in the secondary room, which seemed empty except for bits of firewood.

Then, for lack of anything else to do, he organized the contents into new boxes so each held a measure of different fruits and vegetables. All were ready to be distributed to the rest of the village.

After that, Arthur paced.

Now that he had nearly reached his full height, the two-room cabin seemed tiny. It was even smaller than the apartment he shared with Horatio.

How in the world had his father managed to fit an entire family in here? He remembered the eastern wall being where he had kept his own sleeping cot. How small had that bed frame been?

Mostly, though, he tried—and failed—not to worry about his father.

It was as if something vital was missing from the man. The spark he'd always had, even when he faced challenges and tragedy. It had given him an air of dignity and resolve.

Now that spark was snuffed out.

Arthur wasn't sure if it had simply worn down over the years, or if something specific had happened. And he didn't know him well enough anymore to know how to ask.

It bothered him that his father didn't approve of him stealing from the new Duke Rowantree. It made Arthur question himself.

Back when Arthur had been new to cards, he'd been worried that taking the Thief Class would change him. It was a part of his Master of Skills card, which lived in his heart.

But Arthur had never stolen from other people, robbed, or extorted them.

Not until today.

Now that the deed was done, he was a little alarmed with how easy it had been to plan. How he never stopped to ask himself if what he was doing was right.

Stealing these cards would strike a blow against his own family by blood.

And still . . . Arthur couldn't find it in himself to feel regret or shame.

If his plan worked as he hoped, these cards would do real good. They wouldn't just be sold to other nobles who wanted a little more power to give them an edge over their peers.

That was worth any risk or pain to his former duchy.

A scrape at the door alerted Arthur that his father had returned. The front door swung wide, and his father stepped in. At his heels came a sickly thin woman with an unfortunate, weasel-like face.

The woman's watery blue eyes went wide as she saw Arthur. She dropped into a clumsy curtsey. "Milord."

Arthur glanced at his father in confusion. Then it hit him. He had the vitality and health of a carded man. To anyone used to seeing the state of others in the borderland village, Arthur would look like a high noble.

"Please stand. I'm no noble," Arthur said awkwardly.

His father stepped forward to introduce them. "Arthur, this is Lena. She was sent here because she possesses a certain . . . skill set."

"For the right price," Lena muttered, eyes still warily on Arthur.

Arthur knew exactly how to deal with that. He strode to the attached room where he had stacked the extra foodstuffs. Bringing out a full box, he set it on the table.

"Will this do?"

Lena's eyes widened, and she nodded quickly. "What do you need me to do, milor—" She stopped and glanced hesitantly at Calvan.

Calvan didn't look happy, but he gestured for Arthur to explain.

Again, Arthur went to the secondary room. This time he came out with the card box. "I need you to unlock this."

"I see." Lena's gaze sharpened, the look of wonder replaced with professional interest. "Could I trouble either of you for a piece of paper?"

A moment later, Calvan provided her with the back of an invoice and a piece of charcoal to serve as a writing instrument.

Lena set the paper on the table and started to scribble.

"Do you mind telling me how your process works?" Arthur asked. "I have an interest."

An interest in gaining a new skill . . .

Lena's hand didn't stop her scribbling for a moment as she spoke. "Well, you see, these runes are usually arranged in patterned chains. Unlocking them is usually a matter of finding which pattern doesn't match. But it's not as easy as spotting a break in the chain. The differences can be subtle, especially with well-made locks like this."

Arthur peered carefully, realizing Lena was copying the vague swirls and dots that made up the filigree and gemstone coating.

Next, he glanced at the box but had a tough time finding the exact part of the pattern Lena was looking at. It completely covered the box, like staring into the depth of a mosaic.

Only after about ten minutes, and when Lena turned the box to the other side, did he finally spot the exact place from where she was copying down.

Borrowing another blank page from his father, Arthur tried working the problem on his own.

Lena was clearly an expert. Perhaps even to Master level. Arthur's efforts were basic at best, whereas Lena saw more patterns than he knew to look for.

Finally, something clicked.

New skill gained: Rune Lock-Picking (Thief Class)
Due to your card's bonus traits, you automatically start this skill
at level 3.

And just like that, Arthur saw more patterns in the ornamentation.

Still, he only had an inkling of how it worked—enough to help him open a very simple rune lock. This box was well beyond him.

It took Lena the better part of an hour, all the while copying all six sides of the box before she finally identified the one she needed.

She pointed to a pattern at the corner. "This is what we're looking for."

Arthur squinted but couldn't quite identify the change in the pattern. He had to trust that Lena knew what she was doing. "So, we can unlock it now?"

"Sure, if we had a key. That's what fits at the top of the box. The best I can do is break it without blowing us up along with the entire cabin."

Both Arthur and Calvan took a step back from the box.

Lena chuckled.

"You're joking," Calvan said.

"I'm not." Lena slapped a hand on the top of the box, making father and son jump. "There's a lot of magical energy contained in these beauties."

"Will you harm the contents inside by breaking the box?" Arthur asked.

"It depends on how delicate those contents are. Fine dishware may not survive."

She didn't know this was a card box?

The fact that she was so confident about breaking it open but wasn't aware of what it actually was made Arthur nervous.

Magic cards were supposedly durable, but he'd never heard of one being caught in the middle of an explosion.

Calvin looked at his son. "It's up to you."

He shrugged. "Well, they aren't doing any good sitting in that box."

"That's what I like to hear." Lena's grin was skeletal. She picked up the box. "Best we do this outside. Just in case."

Lena's solution to the problem was to write down what she said was the missing part of the pattern, impale that slip of paper on the end of a pointy stick, and poke at the correct spot on the box.

Also, she used a long stick.

Arthur braced himself. The moment the missing part of the pattern touched the runes, the wooden box shattered like struck glass. Which was odd, because it was made of wood.

"Told you!" Lena crowed, walking to it. She kicked the splinters aside. Within the mess sat a smaller, metal box.

Arthur wasn't sure why he was surprised. His Master of Skills card had been doubly protected as well.

Lena spent a moment inspecting the smaller box for traps. After declaring it all clear, she brought it back into the cabin.

"This is a real pickle," she said.

"How so?" Calvan asked. Arthur was relieved to see a little interest in his eyes. He might disapprove of stealing from the duchy, but this was a fascinating problem to solve.

In answer, Lena pointed to the top of the box. It was completely smooth and without any seams or decorations except for a single wide circle on the top. Inside the circle was a flat depiction of a single red droplet.

"This is a blood lock," Lena said. "Whoever set this one did it with a blood inheritance card. That requires a member of the family to open it."

Arthur and Calvin looked at each other. Chances were the duke had set this up before transferring custody to the guards.

"I'll do it," the two said at the same time.

Calvan turned to his son. "I won't allow you to risk yourself. There might be a backlash if it wasn't Lional."

"There may be backlash for you even if it was him," Arthur shot back. "Didn't you just tell me you were under a king's oath? Would that interfere with unlocking something made by a king's servant?" He directed this last question to Lena.

She hesitated. "It might."

"See? Besides, I'm the one who brought the box here. It's my risk." Plus, he had the health and vitality of a card wielder. His father didn't, not anymore.

Calvan looked like he wanted to argue, but Arthur had already withdrawn his belt knife and pricked his finger.

Holding his hand over the lock, he allowed a single drop to fall into the circle.

The blood hit and started to sizzle. Then the metal began to melt away as if it were hot wax.

In its place, bundled up in parchment paper, was a stack of magical cards.

Lena inhaled a sharp breath. Her hand went out as if to touch them. She retracted it just as quickly. Likely, she was under an oath as well.

Arthur carefully lifted the stack and unwrapped the parchment.

The top card was, of course, the Legendary.

Master of Body Enhancement
Legendary

Utility

This card grants the wielder the ability to gain proficiency in any body enhancement technique or muscle-memory-based skill.

In addition, the wielder will be able to view their base attributes translated into a numerical value, with twenty being the base-point human average. Newly learned skills and techniques start at a base level three and are learned at a base 25% accelerated rate. Previous experience and/or the learning of a skill or technique taught by a master may increase the starting level and further accelerate proficiency.

This is a body-enhancement-only card. Seek additional cards in this set to include combative, skill-based, magical, and other special abilities.

This was it. A card that was a brother to his own. Part of the same set.

CHAPTER 54

It took every ounce of Arthur's hard-forged determination and self-control not to shove the card in his heart right then and there.

Instead, feeling every mote of him protest the action, he held it out to his father.

Calvan, however, had turned his head away.

"I can't."

"Why not?" Arthur demanded, all but pushing the card at him. "Do you know what this is?"

"Of course I do," he said sharply. "Arthur, I made a promise to my king not to take any cards, and a binding oath not to leave. I did this in exchange for my family's life."

"Mom and my sister are dead!"

"And you're not." The fire that had been missing in his father's eyes had returned—banked, but not completely dead. "My word means something. This place has cost me everything except for you, and my pride. I refuse to exchange it for power."

If it were possible, Arthur would have tried to shove the card into his father's heart. But he knew that was the sort of thing that had to be voluntarily accepted. It was one thing to rip a card out of an anchor tattoo, but the heart was another matter.

"If that's the case, why did the baron's men bother searching you for cards?" he asked, frustrated. "It's not that you can't, you won't!"

His father remained pinch-lipped and stubborn. "Not everyone is required to swear an oath, and even less to their king. To some, breaking their word and taking a card is worth it. Not to me."

"Dad—"

A thump to the side interrupted Arthur.

Lena had fallen to her knees, hands clasped in front of her. "Milord, I beg for you to share your generosity. Not to me. I know, thanks to my crimes, I'm not worthy. But I have two girls. They're barely thirteen, milord. They've done nothing wrong, and it's only luck that they've lived this long . . ."

"Please stand." Arthur reached to help her to her feet, feeling sick. While he had been arguing with his father, he let himself forget others would welcome a card—any card. "Of course I'm sharing these around." He glanced at his father, frustrated. "Why do you think I came here?"

Lena blinked. So did Calvan.

"I can give your girls a card." Arthur held up the thick stack. "There's more than enough to go to the children who can have them—and anyone else who is willing to leave."

The next second, he was holding a sobbing woman. Lena clutched at him, almost hysterical with joy. "Thank you! Thank you!"

Unsure what to do, Arthur looked at his father for support. Calvan shook his head.

"It's not that easy, son. The baron's men won't allow that to stand here. If any child takes a card, they must leave for their own safety."

"I'm counting on it." Gently, Arthur disengaged himself from Lena. Thankfully the woman was visibly trying to pull herself together again. "The hive needs dragon riders. Or, if any prefer not to fight, they can live better lives than here in the hive city. Carded lives."

"How . . . how will you take them all the way to the hive?" Lena asked, wiping at her eyes. She shot a worried look at Calvan. "We don't have horses to carry them all, and the roads aren't safe."

In answer, Arthur placed the stack of cards in his storage space. To an outsider, it looked like they flashed away in his hand. "They'll be tucked away in my storage. It's completely safe. Time doesn't pass in there. To them, one moment they'll be here. The next . . . over there." He hesitated because he was speaking to a parent, and he had to be honest. "It might be awhile until I can remove them from storage again. The people I took these cards from will be looking for anyone with similar powers. So I'll have to wait until suspicion dies down."

Lena looked to Calvan as if for confirmation.

With a frown, Calvan nodded.

Lena looked back to Arthur. "But they'll have new lives away from here. Can we do it, Cal?" she asked, turning back to him. She seemed afraid to hope.

Calvan nodded. "I think we can get most of the children out without much suspicion. I can add them to the latest casualty reports."

"What casualty reports?" Arthur demanded.

The muscles in Calvan's face shifted. His frown was so deep it looked engraved in his skin. "It's been a hard season. A new scourge-sickness swept through. I'd say half the village is gone, including those who picked up and fled from fear—oath or no oath."

"They can do that?" Arthur asked, sensing hope, despite the horror.

Lena answered for him. "It depends on the exact wording of the oath, and to whom. I have to stay, but my children . . . they carry my hope."

Arthur took the hint. "The food will help those who stay. But we'll need to work fast to get the children out." He looked outside. His internal clock had it as late afternoon, but true night had fallen here. He looked back to the adults. "Gather who you can, and do it quickly."

Lena, of course, went for her twins at once.

They were pretty girls, with strawberry-red hair identical to the freckles on their faces. And they were so thin that it looked like a stiff breeze would snap them in half.

Arthur let them choose from the Common and Uncommon cards. It would be easier for the girls to blend into their new lives if they had a lower-rank card.

Though the girls were in awe of Arthur, who was a stranger since Lena's family had arrived after he left, they were smart enough to look through the cards and weigh their options—even if they had trouble reading the descriptions.

One settled on an Uncommon Minor Health Restore card.

It was an all-purpose card that would allow her to heal minor ailments with the use of mana. The main drawback was inefficiency, as she couldn't target a specific illness. Her power cast a blanket of healing energy over the patient. Minor sicknesses and discomforts would be healed. Major wounds and illnesses would become marginally better. Birth deformities, tumors, and scars would remain untouched.

While having such a card made her unlikely to ever link with a dragon, she could always find good work in the city.

The second twin, who carried a young kitten in the crook of her arm, gravitated toward a Common Animal Empathy card.

She might have a future as a dragon rider but could also work in the stables or kennels for any noble house.

After they had accepted their cards into their hearts, Arthur explained he would be transporting them to the hive. But he needed their permission first.

The second twin only agreed to go if Arthur stored the kitten, too.

The girls hugged their mother goodbye, though it was obvious to Arthur that they didn't quite understand the full scope of what was happening to them. Like Arthur, neither could imagine what life would be like outside the border village.

However, their acceptance was all Arthur needed. He placed his hands on their shoulders. A moment later, they disappeared.

Lena stared at the place where they had been. She looked at Arthur. "Do you think I will ever see them again?"

"Count on it," Arthur said. "I don't know how or why, but I'm coming back. And I intend to get people out."

There was a soft knock at the door. Calvan opened it to find a haggard couple standing outside with three sickly children in tow.

Not every child received a card. Arthur had no stone to determine when someone was mature enough, so he only risked handing out the cards to the teenagers.

Some parents flatly refused to be separated from their young children, though they happily accepted the boxes of food. Others practically pushed babies into Arthur's arms—sometimes with tears, sometimes with grim determination.

It was a lucky thing he was able to place the babies into his storage with their parent's permission. The line seemed to be drawn around three or four when the children had limited capability to reason.

Twelve children came in all. Five of them were able to accept cards.

There were no adults. Likely because those who could leave had already done so during the scourge-sickness.

When the last family was gone, Arthur was left in the cabin with his father. Arthur removed his card stack, reserved the Legendary and one of the Rares, added the Full-Body Bind card he took from Otto the guard, and pushed the stack to his father.

His father stared at the cards on the table. "What do you want me to do with these?"

"Spread them to other children of the nearby border towns—whoever's about to be eighteen and wants to leave. Or give them to the bandits nearby. Don't pretend like you don't have contact with them," Arthur said with a smile.

His father didn't smile back. "Won't you need them?"

"I can't afford to be caught with them. My storage is supposed to keep most seekers at bay, but I can't guarantee how hard the duke will search. And I can't fence these cards locally." Arthur shook his head. "Best case, I can sell them for coins. But here . . . these cards will change lives."

Arthur took a breath. "All I ask is that you keep one of the Rares for yourself. Hide it far in the woods—past beyond what any seeker could sense. That way if I ever find a solution to unbind your oath . . ." He trailed off.

Calvan didn't answer. He only stared at his son, his eyes wet.

"Can you do this for me?" Arthur asked.

"Yes." Then his father held out a hand for him to shake.

Bemused, Arthur did so.

Their hands clasped, then Calvan jerked him into a hug.

Though his father's arms weren't as strong as he remembered, they were more than good enough.

CHAPTER 55

As dawn broke, Arthur went out to the woods. At his insistence, his father didn't follow. Arthur didn't want to risk anyone seeing him with a stranger.

He was determined to someday learn the full truth of how Calvan had come to be sentenced here. However, tonight wasn't the right time for that story. Not with his father's loyalty to the duchy. One thing was for certain: Arthur was far from done with his old home.

Pausing, Arthur turned back to look at his cabin one last time. It was smaller than he remembered. As small as a prison cell.

One day, Arthur would find a way to break his father out of it.

His father had described a common meeting place for outsiders who wanted to conduct clandestine business with the village. Arthur hadn't known about it as a child, of course. But his father had drawn a simple map that led him to a clearing surrounded by large boulders. Easy to see from the sky.

On arriving, Arthur looked up to see a descending purple dragon. They had been ready for him.

He also recognized the dragon and rider.

"Tess flew fast!" the purple chirped.

Her rider, Johanna, grinned at Arthur. "I'm here to pick up a package? Hey, wait." She squinted at him. "Do I know you?"

He smiled. "You and Tess once saved my life during a scourge-eruption."

"The tree!" Tess broke in, hopping from foot to foot. "Tess catch boy in the tree!"

"That's right," he said, surprised she remembered. "You were a good girl."

"Tess is a very, very, very good girl!" she agreed.

"Huh," Johanna said. "I would say you've done well for yourself, but considering you're here . . ."

"I'm not one of the residents," Arthur said. "And there's no oath that keeps me here."

Her face squinted up. "Let me guess. You're the package we're to pick up?"

"You had to be wondering why you were paid so well." Despite Arthur's self-assurance, he was holding his breath. If Johanna denied him, he had no way to get back to the hive within any reasonable length of time. His absence would be noted by the nobles soon.

And he still didn't know if Horatio and Sams had made a clean getaway.

Johanna let him dangle a moment longer. "These high-paying jobs are always a pain," she said, and then extended a hand down to help him up. "I hope you know how to ride."

They flew through the rest of the day, and well into the afternoon, passing into evening. Sitting behind Johanna, the wind screamed past Arthur's ears and dried out his eyes to the point where he only occasionally looked down. Tess's wings were a blur, and her stamina seemed boundless. Arthur would have paid good shards to know what cards she was hopped up on.

There was no chance for conversation. Johanna didn't once suggest they stop to rest, either. It was an endless marathon.

But Arthur did add five additional levels to his **Dragon Riding** skill.

He wished he could discover what this sort of endurance run would do to his body enhancement card, but he didn't dare add it to his heart deck until he knew it was safe.

The presence of the card itched at him from where it was tucked away in his storage. It was as if his Master of Skills and Master of Body Enhancement cards longed to be reunited.

Finally, after what felt like an endless time, Johanna called, "Look sharp. We're close!"

Arthur cracked open eyes that had gone crusty with wind tears. Sure enough, the hive's cone was visible in the distance.

He was nearly home.

Tess slowed from her breakneck dash into a relatively quick pace that matched other purple dragons in the sky. The other dragons on courier duty were endlessly ferrying people and goods to and from the hive, so they didn't stand out.

"Where do I drop ya?" Johanna asked.

Arthur directed her to his apartment block. Tess touched down neatly on the street in front of the door. She drew a few looks, but his neighbors knew Arthur was a recruit for a Rare.

Helping him down, Johanna's hand lingered on Arthur's wrist, squeezing it.

"I had a feeling you were slated for interesting things the day we rescued you. Don't be a stranger."

Before Arthur could figure how out to reply—or do more than find the nearest strong wall to lean against; his legs were killing him—Tess jumped into the sky.

The door to the apartment house opened.

"Those bowlegs of yours can't be healthy. Should I send for a card healer?" Horatio's voice asked.

Arthur turned, every muscle protesting. "You made it back."

Horatio raised an eyebrow. "Back from *what*?" he said pointedly.

Arthur shook his head, relief sweeping through him and threatening to unsteady his already wobbly legs. Horatio rolled his eyes and came over to offer a strong shoulder.

Somehow, Horatio was able to drag Arthur's sorry butt the two flights of stairs to their shared apartment.

"How's Sams?" Arthur asked the moment the door was shut.

"He needs to leave tonight," Horatio said as he helped lead Arthur to his cot.

Arthur fell on it with a groan.

Now that he was no longer sitting with legs locked around the ribs of a small dragon, every muscle in his thighs, ass, and stomach were cramping.

"I meant . . ." he started to say.

"We're fine," Horatio said. "The guards fired some arrows and threw an enchanted spear, but Sams isn't a spring chicken. He got us away without a scratch. We were worried about you." Horatio peered down at him. "Are you okay? Did it work?"

Arthur chuckled and reached for his storage space. He pulled out the single Rare card that he had reserved for his friend. "You tell me."

Horatio stared. Then with trembling fingers, he reached and took it.

Ultraviolet Light Manipulation
Rare
Elemental Manipulation
The wielder of this card is granted the ability to see and manipulate ultraviolet light, which is not normally perceived by the human eye. When combined with mana, ultraviolet light may be strengthened to a form suitable for combat.

It was a short card description, but elemental manipulation cards were usually strong enough to speak for themselves.

"This is . . . Are you sure?" Horatio sounded unexpectedly vulnerable.

Arthur struggled to sit up, pressing his back against the wall. "This is the whole reason you helped me out, right?"

"No, damn it! I helped you out because you're my friend."

Horatio must have been truly stunned to be so sentimental.

"Take the card and use it well," Arthur said.

With a suspiciously watery nod, Horatio pulled down the front of his shirt and slipped the card into his heart.

His eyes flashed a whitish purple before returning to normalcy. He blinked and then blinked again, looking around. The expression of amazement faded, and his top lip curled in disgust.

"What's wrong?" Arthur asked.

"I don't think the landlords cleaned this apartment as well as they said they did before we moved in."

Arthur raised an eyebrow, but Horatio shook his head and refused to elaborate.

His friend went serious again. "I have to leave. Sams is supposed to return to his hive, and I need to get moving now if I want to let Kenzie know."

His friend was going to be living in the Buck Moon Hive. His former home.

Arthur knew that this was going to happen. In fact, it was for the best right now, as it would put Horatio far out of reach of the duke, who was no doubt searching for his cards.

But it was still hard to say goodbye to his friend.

"We'll meet again," Arthur promised.

"We'd better. I want to show you a *real* hive one day."

Arthur rolled his eyes but grinned. He was happy for him.

Horatio wasn't the hugging type. He was mostly silent and a little contemplative as he quickly packed his things. Like Arthur, he didn't have much to pack. His wealth was in his cards.

Meanwhile, Arthur stretched out on his bed and tried to relax his screaming muscles. The knowledge he could likely ease his suffering by adding his Master of Body Enhancement card was all the worse.

He would be a fool to put it in his heart right now.

Finally, Horatio was as packed as he was going to be. He stopped at the door. "Will you be okay?"

"I'd better be. Ernest Kane needs to show up at the promenade tonight."

"What, why?"

"So I can have my heart scanned by the hidden seekers who are sure to be there," Arthur said. "Which is more reason for you to go. Tell Sams I'm sorry I couldn't see him off."

Horatio hesitated for a moment and then dropped his bag at the door.

He was wrong. His friend could be a hugger . . . under the right circumstances.

EPILOGUE

Four Weeks Later

"Leader Whitaker says he's seen cracks in the Rare's shell," Kenzie reported in between puffs of breath. She and Arthur were hiking the more remote northern slopes, exploring the dips and valleys. "Says it'll be hatching any day now."

"It took its time." Arthur stopped at the edge of a rocky spur and looked out. It was a clear, cold day. The land seemed to stretch out forever, broken by winding rivers edged with early frost.

Kenzie stopped as well to take in the view. "Rares hatch out in their own time. I'll just be glad when the little guy either picks or rejects the snooty nobles face-to-face so they can go home."

Arthur nodded, though he was no longer as annoyed as Kenzie.

Duke Rowantree and his son had quietly packed up and left three days ago.

Losing the cards had been a scandal, though a minor one. The investigation was kept discreet, as they weren't supposed to be selling cards in the first place.

Subtle seekers were brought into several noble gatherings over the last few weeks. None had physically touched Arthur, but he had felt odd brushes against his heart.

Likely, these seekers had been searching for specific cards from a list the duke had provided. And none had pierced the veil of his Personal Space.

No one had brought up the fact that "Ernest Kane" had a Legendary in his heart. Arthur doubted he was the only one.

He'd given it a few more days to make sure. However, it seemed if Lional and Penn were still searching for their cards, they were no longer focusing on the hive nobles.

Arthur was finally free to add the Master of Body Enhancement to his heart deck.

And what better place to start his enhancement training than with an invigorating hike?

Kenzie had come along because he needed a lift to the northern slopes. Marteen had flown off to flirt with the male dragons, but Kenzie, it seemed, wanted an update.

"When do you think it'll be safe to bring those kids out?" she asked, staring flatly at his chest.

"I'll start once the Rare's linked up, but I don't want to do it all at once. Most will be taken in by the orphanages. I dropped a hint to Freyja and made sure they'll have good places." He looked at her and added for what felt like the twentieth time, "I'm not going to promise they'll all be dragon riders."

Kenzie smiled wickedly. "I just want to have a chat with a few who had those good cards you told me about. Speaking of cards . . ."

"Yeah." Arthur was almost vibrating with excitement. He had waited long enough. He took out his Master of Body Enhancement card, pulled down his collar, and pushed it in.

Master of Body Enhancement (Legendary) has been added to your heart deck.
Master of Body Enhancement is a body-utility card, it has automatically been slotted into your body slot.

Card synergy found. You have added a second card from the same set (Master of Skills + Master of Body Enhancement) to create a pairing. Due to this pairing, you are able to create new classes that require both utility and body-based skills. These new classes may add to your attributes. You have unlocked your personal base-point attributes. Card effects and classes may add or subtract from your base attribute score on a temporary basis. See additional card and class description for more information. See Heart Deck for additional display options.

Base Attribute Points:
(20 = average)
Strength: 18
Stamina: 16
Dexterity: 16
Perception: 14
Charisma: 17
Intelligence: 22
Wisdom: 25
Luck: 20

Heart Deck
Total cards: 6
Total completed sets: 0
Paired cards: 2
Linked cards: 0
Mind: 3
Body: 1
Spirit: 2

"Good card?" Kenzie didn't know all the details, of course. But she had already been let in on most of the story and was sharp enough to guess the rest.

Arthur let out a shaky breath. "I want to run. I want to climb. I want to do everything."

With a chuckle, she extended an arm to the rocky slope. "Go for it."

There was a crack on the opposite wall. Arthur grabbed it and pulled himself up. He grunted with the effort.

New skill gained: Rock Climbing (Mountaineering Class)
Due to your card's bonus traits, you automatically start this skill
at level 3.

Twenty feet up or so was a ledge. He pulled himself up to it, gulping air and grinning.

Then he turned, seeing a small cave beyond.

"How are you going to get down from there, smart guy?" Kenzie called.

"Don't know. Hey, did you know there's a cave here?"

"It's a hive. There are caves everywhere."

He couldn't say why, but this felt different. Still breathing hard, he peered within the gloomy cave and let his eyes adjust.

New skill gained: Night Vision (General Body Class)
Due to your card's bonus traits, you automatically start this skill
at level 3.

He grinned, already loving this card.

His grin faded as what he thought was a dark rock resolved into a wall of scales.

"Kenzie! There's a dragon up here! I . . . I think it's dead."

"What?"

Say something for Kenzie. She didn't have a skill to help her out, but she immediately started climbing the wall too. Arthur leaned over the lip and grabbed her hand to help her up the last few feet.

Nodding her thanks, the dragon rider brushed off her dirty clothing and walked past him, straight to the corpse.

It was a purple dragon, positioned so that her hind end nearly blocked the narrow portion of the cave. The front half lay in the light where the rocky ceiling broke above to reveal the sky. It was an oddly peaceful scene.

"What happened to it?" Arthur asked.

Kenzie shook her head, looking upset. Inching past the corpse, she stopped.

Arthur looked over her shoulder and froze as well.

The dragon was lovingly curled around a single black egg.

The egg was tiny for a dragon's egg—perhaps as big as two fists pushed together, with such a dark shell that it seemed to suck in everything around it. Arthur found himself leaning forward as if drawn in.

Kenzie took in a sharp breath. "Back up! Back up! Get away!" She pushed him viciously back, nails digging into his shirt when he didn't immediately give way.

Shocked, Arthur did. Kenzie didn't stop shoving until they reached the edge of the cave lip.

"What's wrong?" he demanded. "Why did you do that?"

She stared around, eyes wild. "I've never felt magic like that before. I think it came from that egg . . . Oh no . . ." she groaned, hands coming to her cheeks.

"What's wrong?"

"I've heard Legendary eggs can be like that. The magic in them is completely wild. It's dangerous."

"A . . . Legendary?" Arthur started forward again, but Kenzie gripped his arm.

"Don't go in there. Didn't you feel that pull? What do you think happened to that purple? Oh, wow." She blinked. "A Legendary laid by a Common purple. I wonder what that'll be like."

Arthur barely thought about his answer. He was still looking back toward the egg. "The most extraordinary things can come from the simplest magics."

ABOUT THE AUTHOR

Having selected banker as her profession and purchased sturdy oxen as well as all the ammunition she could afford, Honour Rae loaded her family into a wagon and set out to establish a homestead. Unfortunately, she could only keep two hundred pounds of the deer, elk, bears, bison, squirrels, and rabbits she massacred along the way. Soon, dysentery set in and attempting to ford the river proved to be a huge mistake. Somehow, Rae and her family pulled through—albeit with the loss of any extra wagon parts. The Oregon Trail conquered, and having made it to the Willamette Valley, she sat down to write this book.

THANK YOU
FOR SUPPORTING HONOUR RAE

CONNECT WITH THE AUTHOR
BY VISITING THE FOLLOWING:

 @HONOURRAE

 PATREON.COM/HONOUR_RAE

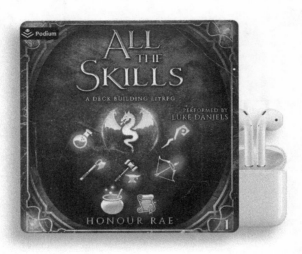

Continue building your deck with the *All the Skills* audiobook.

Experience Arthur's journey as performed by master of narration Luke Daniels.

DISCOVER
STORIES UNBOUND

PodiumAudio.com

Printed in the USA
CPSIA information can be obtained
at www.ICGtesting.com
JSHW021056050824
67522JS00001B/1

9 781039 470217